Debbie's Gift

Debbie's Gift

An Erotic Story of Female Dominance

By Amity Harris

Daedalus Publishing

This trade paperback is published by

Daedalus Publishing
2140 Hyperion Avenue,
Los Angeles, CA 90027

daedaluspublishing.com

Debbie's Gift is a work of fiction, and all resemblance to actual persons, living or dead, is purely coincidental.

Distribution in the United Kingdom by Turnaround Publisher Services Ltd.

First Edition: December 2004
ISBN: 1-881943-21-6

Cover Art by Brian Tarsis

Printed in the United States of America

Dedication

The red thread of my life – the best friend who showed me who I was and accepted me for who I am – was taken too soon from my world. Without her, there would be no novel because I would have had no experiences. Had our lives not walked together for those dozen years, I would not have felt free to write what I knew. If we had not shared a common path for so long, I would never have known the delight of living that created this novel. CA, for you, with joy.

Amity Harris
September, 2004

Foreword

When I began writing *Debbie's Gift*, it was a four-page short story. It was another time and I was another person. I knew something inside made me different from other women and rampant fantasies flew through my brain instead of sleep at night. Living in the South, I didn't meet women like myself until one day, at a casual meeting over two café mochas, I met the first woman who was, simply, just like me. The only difference was that she had a name for it and had learned to be comfortable with the dominant side of herself. She showed me who I was.

Debbie's Gift is the result of that meeting.

That was then. Since its first online publication, *Debbie's Gift* has become an underground classic and occasional chapters have been housed on an assortment of obscure Web sites dotted across the Internet for years after I had taken the work offline. Now, only the "Old Net Folk" may remember it was ever online.

So what happened? How did this story grow from four pages to a long novel? It wasn't a straight shot. Finding myself overeducated and under challenged, I spent a lot of time watching pay-per-view and mail-ordered videos. It didn't take long for boredom to set in. Without interesting characters and a gripping storyline, even full-frontal nudity quickly became dull. There had to be other women like me, who wanted something more titillating. I wanted something written for me; that touched me; that told my story.

Not being the shy type, I vented my frustration to my best friend. After a moment's shocked silence, she began to describe – in great detail – what, for her, made erotica erotic. We talked about what interested us, what excited us, what was sensual and what was sexual, and whether there was any difference between the two. We traded stories about furtive trips to big-city sex toy/ lingerie boutiques and laughed over teenaged attempts to hide copies of *Fanny Hill* and *The Story of O* from our parents. We shared our realities. We outted ourselves to each other. Finally, as the instigator of the discussion, she challenged me to do something about the dearth of literate, engrossing, hard-core erotic fiction. *"Do you think you could write something that speaks to US? Can you write OUR story?"*

I sure could.

It was easier than I'd anticipated. It took barely three days to transfer all the dreams, fantasies, real-life experiences and wild imaginings that had for so long filled by brain – and other parts of my body – onto four single-spaced pages. Reading them over, I had second thoughts about showing what I'd written to my friend: my very short story was very graphic. Masking my uncertainty with bravado, I gave the first copy to her and watched her read. I managed to sit quietly for the several minutes it took her to read it, all the while trying vainly to see if she raised her eyebrows, if her breathing changed, if her fingers tightened their grip on her coffee cup. Nothing – no sign. After taking what I felt was enough time to read it twice (which she later told me is exactly what she had done), she folded the papers precisely and tucked them carefully into her handbag. Only then did she turn to me.

"When are you going to write the REST of it?" she demanded.

I was a writer! With the encouragement of my other friends, who invariably showed up in my kitchen every morning eager for the latest chapter, the first draft of the novel was completed within a month. When *Debbie's Gift* first hit the Internet fifteen years ago, there was a rush to download all 31 chapters, even though, at the time, it took hours to access the file. E-mail, for which people then paid for by the hour, stacked up in my inbox. Not only was I a writer, I was a writer with readers!

I am often asked if Debbie is Amity. My flip response has always been: I should be so lucky.

Come to think of it, I am.

Amity Harris 2004

Chapter One

"Here, let me put this on you," and with a gentle yet firm and determined push, she managed his penis and testicles fully through a silver ring. With an unexpected twist of her soft white hand, she tightened the ring and the shiny metal glimmered through his dark hair. She knelt back, her white legs in sharp contrast to her red silk chemise, and smiled. "Now that wasn't too bad, was it?"

He bent down to inspect the new gadget that his wife had just secured onto him and was surprised that the cold and uncomfortable metal he expected to feel was really a warm and snug addition to his cleansed body. The shower left his skin damp, but Debbie had dried him herself, carefully and coolly with a plush aqua towel, kissing and massaging his most private areas before slipping the pink ring onto its nesting place. At the height of one of their frequent passionate sessions last week, Ron had agreed (and he would have agreed to just about anything then) to become her slave, her sex slave specifically, and this ring was her gift and reminder of his promise.

"You are really mine now," Debbie said as she slipped carefully and noiselessly up to a standing position and brought a bright pink net out of the folds of her silk robe. "Watch what this does. The ring is magnetic and this net's filament is attracted to it. This is your new outfit. Are you ready?"

Ron gave a silent nod and watched intently as her long red nails worked the netting onto the ring. He stood naked except for the bright net bag guarding his penis and testicles and wondered about its purpose. It was a bright, hot pink! Debbie held out her arms to him and he stepped forward to embrace her.

"No!" she sharply, "not until I give you permission. You cannot do anything until I give you permission. Do you remember your promise?"

Ron giggled. This was getting pretty funny. A sharp swift pain in his testicles and penis silenced him and brought him to his knees. "What the hell. . ?"

"You made a promise and I intend to have you fulfill it." She spoke with a low sultry voice that was new to his ears. "Perhaps you need more training. Expert training. Let me explain what this ring can do and what you are going to learn to become a sex slave who pleases me every day."

Ron struggled to look up at her from his kneeling position as he continued to grab at his pained and maligned genitals with both hands in an unsuccessful effort to comfort them. His tingling penis told him in no uncertain terms that this ring was significantly different from the other "toys" they shared in their rather enjoyable love- making. He finally looked up and saw her in her flowing red robe standing over him, her black stiletto heels ominously close to his still-tingling crotch. Her raven hair flowed around her diamond- studded earlobes and onto those milky shoulders he loved to nuzzle. Her blue eyes pierced his now- fading smile.

Holding out her left arm, she showed him a bracelet--at least he thought it was a bracelet--with multicolored stones on a leather backing. She held a perfectly manicured finger above a stone. "This is a trainer," she continued, "and it will convince you that obeying me at all times is the best course of action for you. Any disobedience on your part will be punished with a squeeze as you just experienced that will help convince you I mean business. The netting is retractable, and it has other interesting capabilities. The only thing you need to know is that I control its total operation and if you attempt to remove it without the proper sequence of buttons on my wrist, you will experience a rather," she paused for a second as if looking for the right word, "uncomfortable shock. A painful uncomfortable shock. I want you to understand that you will be trained to be the slave you promised to be. Do you understand what I'm saying?"

Ron did not move from his totally submissive position on the floor directly at her feet. Gazing up at her, his mind wanted to be outraged; his body wanted to yell, flail, kick, and hit at her. But he knew he could not either experience or tolerate a second or possibly higher dose of that pain. Was she kidding? "I said, Do you understand?" And in a flash, Ron was writhing on the floor, grabbing at his crushing testicles with both hands. "Answer me!" she spoke firmly and flatly. There was no compassion in that sultry voice, only authority and expectation of an answer.

"Yes," he whimpered, "yes, yes, yes! Make it stop!" He was screaming now and rolling his six foot frame into a ball at her feet as he tried to loosen the death grip of the pink net on his genitals. She watched him coolly, counted to five, and pushed a single button. He fell limp, his face at her feet, his mind uncomprehending anything except the experience and memory of the pain.

"Good. You are now ready to begin the training."

Ron gazed up at her through the involuntary tears that filled and then spilled forth from his eyes and onto his clean-shaven face, and his prone body was greeted with the crashing sound of their bedroom door flying open. Three men rushed in, scooped him up, and wrapped a black cape around his head and body. Naked and screaming inside the black shroud, Ron was hauled down the stairs, out the back door, and into a waiting limousine that began moving as soon as the three men flung him inside, entered themselves, and shut the door. In the black of the night, he was whisked away. Debbie casually walked down the same stairs, locked the back door, and stared out into the dark night. She poured herself a drink, Amaretto and cream--her favorite-- and went to the master suite to relax on the king size bed.

Chapter Two

The limousine ride was merciless for Ron and his assaulted genitals as the three brightly dressed figures silently forced Ron into a kneeling position on the floor of the back seat of the elongated limousine and pushed his head down into the plush carpet. His hands flung out for balance and his wrists were immediately locked into position in buckled leather straps. His ankles were also tightly bound, and a cold metal clasp was fastened around his waist. Although he was outraged, the locked metal grips prevented his moving even the slightest from his doggie-style position. His three kidnappers, apparently finished with their initial work, sat back on the leather seats behind their prisoner.

Unceremoniously, they whisked the cape off his naked body and tossed it aside. Although the night was warm, Ron shivered in fright. The three stared at the naked attorney who was securely assigned to an "all-fours" indignity in front of them. One of them flicked on a small light and the three checked Ron up and down, top and bottom, front to back.

"He's a specimen, isn't he?" the one in the green shirt queried. "A real beauty! Let's see if he understands what's going on." Ron felt the white-shirted partner look him over carefully. He felt the satiny white shirt touch his chest, neck, and ears. He felt the caress on his back, and he tensed as the hand moved down toward his backside.

Slowly and mercilessly, the hand traveled toward his buttocks and tenderly smoothed over each side.

A second hand invaded Ron's tightened gluteal muscles and without warning, spread his cheeks uncomfortably apart.

With the indignity of his behind spread wide, Ron heard the white shirt comment, "He seems cold. Are you cold?"

Ron could barely shake his head no in answer to the ludicrous question. His body was rigidly tense and he fought against responding verbally.

"Speak!" the white-shirt ordered.

"No." Ron's voice was almost inaudible as he remained immobile on all fours, his mouth muffled against the carpet.

"Speak clearly!" he heard in a somewhat louder voice. Without warning, pain shot through his genitals from the constricting net bag attached securely to his silver testicle ring.

He writhed and pulled at his restraints in vain in a useless effort to grab his pained private parts, but his manacled hands remained flat against the floor. "Speak!" he heard the white-shirt order once more. The genital pain continued unbroken and the voice Ron's lips uttered and he heard was not his own.

"No! I am NOT COLD!" Ron screamed, his face pressed into the limo's plushy carpeted floor. Miraculously, the pain ceased. Tears of relief flooded his eyes and his nose ran unwiped onto the thick carpet pressed against his face.

"Good. Your name is Ron," the green-shirt spoke clearly. "Well, for now, we'll forget that. You just assume everything that is said is for you, and we won't use your name at all. Got that?"

"Yes," he responded immediately to avoid another dose of that awful pain. Anything to avoid the pain! It was a voice Ron didn't recognize, but it was his own. Ron struggled to concentrate and hear what he was asked by the three in the limo. He could not take another dose of squeezing.

"Well done! You seem to understand, but we'll see just how quickly you learn as your time with us progresses. You are being taken at your wife's request to participate in a special kind of schooling. You will learn how to be obedient; how to serve and service her well; how to be that special sort of slave you promised to be. And you won't be the only one. We are collecting the last of the new trainees tonight, and we will arrive at the facility before daylight. This will be a very interesting experience for you and I am sure you will like it." The voice silenced and Ron knelt naked and alone within his horror.

Although Ron couldn't move, he heard the other two men sifting through a container and sorting metallic-sounding materials. He could see only parts of the three men and noticed that the third wore a blue shirt and that all three shirts glistened and sparkled in the eerie glow of the limo's muffled rear lighting. The windows in the back seat were pitch black. No outside lights were visible through their opaque glaze. As he tried to view his surroundings, the floor beneath his hands suddenly began to shift silently downward and his hands and face were pulled within their locked manacles along with it. As the floor lowered, his head sank deeper and deeper and his hands held more of his weight. He still could not move any part of his body and his neck began to ache. His new position was unmistakable: his head was dropping and his behind was pointing almost directly upward toward his captors. For the first time, Ron clenched his teeth in fear.

"Now just try to relax," he heard, "and this will go much easier for you. If you struggle, it will be hard." Incomprehensibly, Ron felt a warm finger lubricate his rectum. It reached far inside, up and around, and outside. Breathe, he commanded himself, breathe! It will be all right if you just breathe. He concentrated on that and nothing else. Involuntarily, he held his breath. The warm finger made a squishy sound that fogged Ron's brain before it was finally removed from his helpless rectum as silently as it had been inserted. With nothing left emotionally to fight back with, Ron cried tears of anger as a warm rod was inserted into his most private entry point.

Slowly, carefully, and surprisingly without pain, his rectum was filled with a pliant object that had both a will and eyes of its own. It gathered its forward force from his captor's outside pushing, but once inside, it expanded, bent, twisted, and filled up every space inside of him. Warmth filled the apparently hollow tubing and his rectal muscles fought against its entry as he tried in vain to force the intruder out.

"Look, Green," one of them called, "he's trying to push it back at me! No sir, it's going in. We told you it would be easier if you would just collect yourself. Now relax! We are not trying to hurt you. The more you resist, the more intense the pain will become."

The man pushing the unknown object into his rectum was stronger than Ron's muscles could manage to push back against the intrusion. The object was reinserted more forcefully this time, and came to rest completely inside his body. His legs felt long strings from the offending tubing waft against them as the limo turned a corner. One of the men tenderly massaged his stomach, while another rubbed his neck in an effort to calm the lawyer who was approaching a mental breaking point.

"We're not here to hurt you," one said in an effort to reassure him. "We want you to learn to be obedient, and sometimes that causes pain. Try to take this as it comes, and whatever you do, don't fight against us. We have trained many, from the weak-willed to the strong, and we have never failed to create a total, complete slave. Don't fight us, you'll only cause yourself pain." With that, Ron felt the insert grow warmer. He was sickened for allowing himself to momentarily enjoy the fullness and the warmth.

"You should be feeling some heat. If I want, I can make it cold. In fact, I can make it vibrate, thrust, grow larger or smaller, or just about anything. This is your goal for your training. You will come to love this insert and it will be a sign that you have become obedient. If you are offered insertion, it tells you that you have done well. If we withhold it, you have done badly. We all wear these inserts when we have done especially well, and we get them from the Mistress when we are good and we please her. When the time comes that you are fully trained and she inserts you herself, you will know that you have done your best."

Ron gritted his teeth. The floor beneath him began to rise slowly and he was thankful that the weight was lifted off his hands as the floor finally leveled off. The three men reached out and swiftly unbuckled his hands and feet. The metal waist lock was removed and retracted into its casing under the carpet. Together the three brought Ron to a kneeling position as the limo pulled to a stop. For the first time, he could see their faces. Two were dark-haired, and one was a shaggy blond. All three could have represented any product on a billboard ad campaign. They were unmistakably handsome, well built, and frighteningly strong.

"We're here. Now that you know the purpose of the insert, it will be removed. Carry the memory of this with you and learn that your goal is to be inserted every night. We will train you and the others to be the best slaves you can be. And we take this very seriously. Let's go. Take a deep breath. You won't like this." The White shirt seemed to be in charge as he nodded to the Green shirt to proceed.

Ron felt his rectum explode when the Green-shirt grasped the dangling leather strings of the intruder, pulled quickly, and the insert was forcibly removed. He caught his breath and tensed every muscle he could locate to prevent his defecating into the back seat area of the limo. He was totally exhausted and couldn't stand or move at all. The three yanked open the doors of the limo and dragged him out as unceremoniously as they had dumped him inside. Deposited gingerly on his feet on the pavement of the darkened garage, Ron struggled to maintain his balance, and caught a glimpse of five other men wearing pink net bags on their genitals, their faces streaked with tears and sweat, standing naked on the pavement of the black garage. And Ron made the sixth.

Chapter Three

The haggard group of sweating and tear-stained naked men limply climbed aboard the specially designed grand touring bus and were directed each to a compartment. The remodeled cruiser housed about ten compartments, each of which was separated from the main area by a private, locked door. Ron was ushered into his cubicle and told to sit on the comfortable and inviting leather seat. The window had been replaced by a television monitor and the air inside Ron's compartment was fresh and clean. Everything from the leather to the video screen had a new smell. Ron sat upright and tense, but the man in the green shirt who accompanied him into his compartment urged him to relax.

"This will be a really exciting experience for you," he said, "and my job as your personal trainer is to make it as worthwhile as humanly possible for you and your wife. She wants you to be her perfect slave, and she has spent a lot of money to register you with our program. She loves you a lot."

Ron snorted. Debbie's love was a rather questionable issue for him right now.

"Yes, truly," he continued in his tender manner, "we are very careful with those we select. She cares deeply and wants your relationship to move onward and upward. A stale sex life is bad for a marriage. I know."

Ron looked quizzically at him with an unasked but apparent question.

As if in answer to his gaze, the green shirt added, "Yes, a stale sex life is nothing to look forward to; it's no life. When you're young, you can jump into bed with almost anyone and have an orgasm. But that's not really a sex life. A good sex life is one in which one partner looks forward everyday to new and exciting ideas that the lover brings to the relationship. One day, we are all forty. Then we can't just get it up when we want to, and some of us can't enjoy sex every day anymore. Once a week becomes once a month, and the routine is predictable. Some change is good. Your partner recognizes that and she was selective in choosing this avenue for your lives to grow and get better. You will learn things you never imagined were possible and enjoyable and that skill will change your lives completely."

In spite of his anger and chagrin, Ron was beginning to like the green shirt. He had to find out some answers to his questions and this seemed an appropriate, private time to ask. This nightmare had to end soon, and Ron wanted all the information he could get.

"What's your name?" It came out hoarsely, and Ron hated himself for making meaningless small talk with his perceived enemy. But he wanted to find out everything he could. It was the only logical course of action for him to take, given the situation.

The green shirt smiled. "No, we don't use names. Names get in the way. I'm "Green"' because my protector is green. You'll meet other Greens, as well as Blues and Whites. Just call a man by his color. If you train well, you may even meet a Gold. Golds are the top, you know. Greens are the trainers. Blues are the programmers who come up with the training you will receive. Whites are the leaders who are in charge of daily activities.

The Golds are the special ones who create the ideas around which we change and grow. You'll see for yourself soon. Just sit back and relax because we're in for a long ride tonight. I'll come back and check on you shortly."

Green left and Ron heard him lock the door behind him. Trainers? Programmers? Golds, Whites, Greens? Ron was confounded by the new vocabulary and foreign concepts that Green had just so casually introduced. Naked and frustrated but annoyingly comfortable, Ron sat back in the plush leather seat and noticed as the television monitor came to life. A handsome, tanned man's face filled the screen and his authoritative voice began to fill the compartment. He was naked from the waist up Ron decided to name him, "Gold," for the sparkling gold armband he wore across his broad bicep .

"Welcome to training," Gold began. "Your lover has entered you into our program because she urgently wants you to add a new dimension to your sex lives. Your cooperation is essential and we are confident that we will be successful. Your program will begin in earnest when we reach the facility, but we would like to take this opportunity to show you what is in store for you. This particular program is designed to instruct men to become pleasing love slaves to their spouses. You have been enrolled to learn the art and technique of total submission and obedience. Please continue to watch the monitor."

Ron leaned forward in rapt concentration as he watched in fascination what must be the "training facility" that was their destination. He saw net-bagged men moving in groups around a magnificent facility and engaging in various sexually provocative activities. The first scene showed five naked, pink-netted men jogging around a track. Their faces showed no pain or discomfort. Hell, they seemed to be enjoying their exercise! They were monitored and encouraged each by a Green ("trainer," Ron recalled). Another group was similarly naked and in a great pool, and each was being washed tenderly and carefully by a Green. This was a bath, Ron guessed, and was amazed and just a little excited at the sight of the naked maleness that permeated the pool. A third group was sitting around a carefully decorated and dimly lit room in plush armchairs with box-like devices over their heads and others that were attached to their magnetic rings. With their faces as well as their genitals completely covered up by these magnetically attached boxes, the men lay limply and then began to thrust their hips in apparent sexual ecstasy. Some gyrated slowly in their chairs and others evidenced the height of sexual pleasure and passion. Ron watched intently as one after another experienced the ultimate ecstasy of orgasm.

Yet another group stood at attention while a White barked directions. The smiling men then jumped, spun, knelt, and performed oral sex on each in horrifying but rhythmic unison. Finally, Ron saw a group of pink-netted men choosing garish leather and chain clothing, entering dressing rooms, and emerging as costumed sadomasochistic wonders. They carried riding crops and cat-o-nine- tails and the group performed a rhythmic dance of whip cracking and prodding before engaging in a provocative strip show. He stared open-mouthed at the screen and its pornographic movie, and was amazed to discover his penis' rapt attention and excitement. Until now, Ron realized, every man he had seen on the video, trainees and trainers alike, was absolute naked, except for the colored net bags they wore on their testicles and penises. The Greens and Whites on the monitor sported matching armbands. But not one had on any clothing.

Gold's face returned to the screen as the movie ceased and interrupted Ron's growing excitement. Gold's warning was clear. "This is a small sample of the training that is ahead. You will enter a realm of sexual excitement you could never have imagined before this training. Sit back, now, and relax. It's late and you have a full day ahead."

Ron sat back in the warm compartment as a pleasant aroma of vanilla spice filled his tiny cubicle. Within a few seconds, he was sound asleep.

During this drug-induced slumber, Ron neither saw the three men enter his cubicle nor did he feel them attach leather bracelets onto his ankles and wrists. He never saw them lock the cuffs into place, nor did he witness their careful and tender application of depilatory that removed all of his thick black pubic hair. He could not feel the warmth of the soothing lotion they applied and massaged gently into his bare skin. He did not see the green, blue, and white net bags attached similarly to their genital rings. He slept like a baby and awoke the next morning when he sensed that the bus had stopped directly next to the entrance of the training facility.

Chapter Four

Ron's head jerked up and around as he viewed his tiny surroundings. He had to remind himself forcibly that last night's activities had not been a dream and that he was truly in a little room on a bus heading for a sex slave training facility, still absolutely naked, except for the net bag he remembered and the leather wrist and ankle bands he now noticed. His damp and aching crotch told him to find a bathroom urgently, and his complaining rectum recalled the previous evening's violation. He first bolted upright when he saw his hairless crotch and stiffened again as Green entered noisily, carrying two cups of hot coffee. Ron's had extra milk just the way he liked it. He was furious and embarrassed that his bald pubic area was so fully exposed to Green's invasion of his compartment, but the smell of the coffee muted his growing hatred. It was getting very hard to dislike this guy.

"Good morning," Green cheerfully intoned. "We're finally here. First have some coffee and we'll tend to your obvious needs." Ron tried to stand, but his legs would not obey.

"No, sit! I'll tell you when to get up," Green ordered in a voice harsher than Ron had expected to hear. Ron glumly sipped the offered coffee and was grateful for the steaming warmth. "When it's your turn to enter the facility, you'll be instructed. Enjoy the coffee." There was an edgy finality to Green's voice that Ron did not like. He was torn between liking this guy and distrusting him to his core. He sipped the coffee. Damn, it was good.

The video screen came alive with the face and voice of a golden-shirted narrator and both Ron and Green listened attentively. Green, Ron noticed, sat stiffly at attention. "Shortly you will be told to walk to the front and enter the facility. This will be done silently. You will not talk once inside the facility unless you are directly spoken to. There is strict obedience and no discussion. Do as you're told and this will be a rewarding experience. Disobedience is punished severely and immediately. Good morning." With that, the picture faded to black.

"We wait," Green answered Ron's unasked question.

His bladder ached and his rectum complained. Ron sat silently as long as he could, then, when the discomfort rose to an unbearable level, he blurted, "I need to go to the bathroom!"

Green looked him over, up and down, and shook his head side-to-side and frowned. He reached out with a muscled arm and grabbed Ron's netted package of genitals completely and roughly in one of his massive hands, pulled and squeezed the sensitive and bursting organs and rebuked him as if he were a child caught masturbating in his bedroom. "You don't get it, do you? You go to the bathroom when you are told. You eat when you are told. You will have an erection when you are told. You will experience orgasm only when we want you to have one. You have no rights here, no privileges, and especially, no control. We know what is best for you and you will obey every order, command, direction, and request. Drink your coffee." With that, Green sat back in his leather chair.

Startled by Green's directness and blunt discourse, Ron also sat back. Ron saw no recourse but to position himself likewise. His full bladder's need to empty itself was forgotten for the moment, and he considered this new information silently, although he could hardly bring himself to relax.

The cubicle lights flashed on and off twice. Green stood up quietly with an aura of dignity and motioned for Ron to follow. In silence, he led the shackled and naked lawyer who was reduced to degradation in his nudity into the bus's main section, deserted now except for the White and the Blue Ron had "met" the night before. They looked him over, checked the locks on his leather restraints and tugged at his pink net to make sure it was in place. Where were the others who had gotten on the bus with him? And just where was he going?

"You're next," they unemotionally offered. Oh, Ron guessed, the others must already be inside. Ron relaxed and thought that he might as well follow the leader and he silently worried that there was nowhere to flee. That was the worst of it, he concluded. There was no escape from these three captors. Where would a naked, shackled lawyer run, his almost-crazed brain demanded?

The bus doors creaked open with the swish of hydraulics that reminded Ron of his first day of school. But now he could see only blackness as the bus had pulled up and connected to an elongated entranceway. Several pairs of hands emerged seemingly from nowhere and reached in, grabbed his own hands and feet by their leather cuffs' steel rings, and proceeded to secure the loops on Ron's wrist and ankle restraints to heavy metal hooks. He felt the tethers attached to the hooks first tense, then tighten, as he was yanked from his standing position at the bus's door on a journey into an endless void of blackness.

His journey dangling into nothingness began with a quick upward lift as Ron hung freely in the air from hooks. He was too scared even to be humiliated as he felt the warmth of his bladder emptying itself all over his legs and onto whatever lay beneath him. Crying tears of humiliation, anger and fright, Ron realized the trainer had been right. He had no control. He was a child who wasn't even potty trained, and the White, Green, and Blue were his "parents" who held the key to all his wants and needs. Utterly helpless, Ron cried as he hung from the tethers, urinated over his legs, and continued on his journey into the training facility.

The odyssey persisted unabated through the air of blackness and silence. Ron felt earphones placed on his head and strapped securely under his chin. He heard the voice of the Gold from the television screen speak inside his brain. His body still dangled from tethers attached to his wrist cuffs and the conveyor moved him further along in emptiness and solitude. The blackness encompassed him and the calm voice of the handsome Gold urged him valiantly on. He felt himself sweeping upward, across, and occasionally down as the conveyor carried him incalculable distances inward. The voice continued to urge him calm. Relax. Hang limply. We will take care of you. Ron clenched every muscle from jaw to toes in absolute terror. He would not be calmed by an invisible, faceless, and nameless voice in this insane black void.

Hands reached in from the blackness to lather a warm soapy mixture all over his sweaty and soiled body. The legs he had worked so many hours on in the gym were pulled easily apart and his now-smooth, hairless genitals and rectum were scrubbed with a soft but intently directed brush. His straining armpits did not escape the soaping and the aroma of lavender soap assaulted his nostrils. Farther along, he felt a fine, warm, misting spray reach him from beneath and from above. His toned legs were pulled away from his body by the constricting tethers, and they were drawn sharply away from his arms in their nooses. The pull of the tethers caused him to lie flat on his back yet suspended in the middle of the air. With arm and leg muscles screaming from their strain and their discomfort, his hair was hosed, soaped, lathered, and rinsed.

His body was returned upright and his now-numb legs thanked the invisible stars for the end of their torture as the blood rushed back into them and gave him feeling. For a moment, the blackness was replaced by intermittent flashing strobe lights, and he could had only partial glimpses of the other trainees being similarly hanged from hooks and cleansed. He had sympathy for them and strained and struggled to recognize a face, a body, a friend. He also felt an awkward sense of excitement at the sight of their highly muscular and toned shapes. Ashamed of that ludicrous notion of sexual arousal, Ron closed his eyes rather than admit to his prurient interest in the other men's bodies.

The voice in his earphones returned and told him to reach down with his feet and rest on the floor that was temporarily beneath him. As his toes barely touched the flexible flooring, the tethers on his arms gave way, and Ron was terrified as he fell freely for a moment before the ropes tightened again. Now his position was apparent and he regarded his vulnerable situation with fright: he was bent in half with his arms and feet touching and his backside hung straight down toward nothingness.

The voice continued to urge calm. Ron tensed and tried to concentrate on breathing. It didn't work. He gasped audibly when a small plastic tube entered his unlubricated rectum and the terrifying experience of last night's anal insertion came flashing quickly to his mind. But this insertion's aim was very different. Without warning, a hard rush of cool liquid was forced into his rectum, and just as quickly as the offending hose was removed, another device quickly was inserted. Ron swung his hindquarters violently from side to side as he struggled to free his backside from the torture, but his position allowed him no control. His behind hanging low beneath his tethered hands and feet, he wanted desperately to evacuate the hated intrusion into his bowels, but the plug that had been inserted firmly into the orifice held fast. He felt a guttural noise begin to rise from his throat. He tried to stifle his rising phlegm, but could not. Both uncontrollable vomit and a scream of terror shot forth from his lips.

He heard the voice again. "You will empty your bowels when we tell you that you may. Your job simply is to hold it tightly inside until you are told to release." Then there was only silence.

The conveyor belt of naked human men suddenly stopped. Their screaming and whimpering filled the great black void with a chorus of pain.

How many busses had arrived? How many men's rectums were filled with this hated liquid? Ron's only alternative to witnessing and bearing the others' pain was to scream louder and drown out the others' tortured voices to relieve his ears and his mind from the awful vision he had glimpsed in the momentary flashing light. He wanted to push the liquid out of his bowels violently, but the plug prevented his emptying efforts. He decided that he could take no more of the liquid, the pain, the humiliation. He screamed and yelled a cry of the tortured and hopeless. But the screaming inside his own head and throat could not overshadow the pain emanating from his bursting rectum.

"Now," uttered the calm voice on the earphones inside his head.

With that single word, the plug was removed roughly from his anal orifice and Ron's forced squatting position afforded him no control over his own muscles as his rectum emptied itself all over whatever lay beneath him. The others must have been similarly unplugged and reacted in a like manner because emptying rectums filled the room with an intolerable stench. Without warning or wiping, the conveyor belt started up again, and the washing routine was repeated. This time special intense attention was given to his anus and legs. His tethers moved him up and down, side to side, and Ron was hauled like beef on a hook toward yet another unknown destination. This time, his visual and physical perspective was shifted violently.

Ron and the others were now forced into hanging upside down, their arms flailing wildly for an anchor and finding none. His ankles were forced apart and a metal rod was inserted and locked into place in hooks attached to his ankle straps. His weakened legs were forcibly spread violently apart as the rectal hose was deeply reinserted into his aching dry hole. Again his rectum was filled with cold liquid and the damned plug was again administered. Ron gave in to his horror and screamed wildly now. He cared nothing about the others; he cared nothing about anything except his violated rectum and bowels. The rod attached to his ankles was jerked up and down repeatedly; shaking Ron as if he were a cocktail shaker and his rectum contained a disgusting martini. His insides strained and wanted to burst from the pressure, yet the voice in his ears urged calm. His unseeing eyes were open wildly and he desperately searched for an object on which to fix his blurring vision. The black void faced him squarely and as suddenly as it began the shaking ceased.

His stomach churned and his backside ached inside from its violations. This was all the anal intrusion he could take. Incomprehensibly, he felt the net pouch tighten as his penis and testicles were squeezed. Slowly, carefully, with growing intensity, the net constricted and his testicles and penis were crushed within its unrelenting fist. Forgetting for the moment about his anal discomfort, he cried out again in both pain and fear of pain, and lights flashed. His manacled hands could not grab his aching organs and he moaned and cried in his agony. He tried but could not locate the other men hanging upside down, and did not witness or hear their screaming mouths open and their faces streaked with tears and sweat. Ron realized with horror and a sick sense of pride that the body could take even more pain and humiliation than he had imagined possible.

Hands from nowhere again reached out to steady him and Ron was returned upright once more.

The plug in his rectum wanted to explode outward and his rectal muscles tried in vain to push it out, but the voice calmly commanded him to prevent such unordered expulsion. "Hold on," it said. Screaming was the only thing available to him and Ron screamed for a long time with all his might. But he managed with pride to hold his bowels until he heard the soft voice's permission.

The voice said simply, "Now."

The plugs were pulled and the rectums emptied again according to their own volition. Mentally and physically exhausted and finally silent, Ron concentrated on nothing but evacuating his rectum, his bladder and his tears. Hanging limply in exhaustion and humiliation from the tethers attached to his wrists, Ron and the others were washed, brushed, scrubbed, and rinsed as the conveyor belt of men moved uncaringly and unceasingly onward.

This time he was lifted upward and toward a light. When he felt firm ground below, he tried to rest his weight on his feet, but the tethers kept him from planting himself solidly on the floor. On tiptoe, Ron heard the authoritative Gold voice again.

"Congratulations. You have arrived. Greens, remove the tethers."

Exhausted bodies fell with thumps onto the cushioned floor. Men looked around wildly and surveyed each other, horrified at the faces and bodies they saw. Naked men tried to stand, and were assisted by Greens, one assisting each exhausted man. Their red, raw nakedness and their common bald pubes shamed them and Ron and the others sought to cover their genitals with their manacled hands. The Greens urged their hands downward with silent, disapproving gazes and the men obeyed, recognizing they were in no position to resist such orders. The men were herded unceremoniously toward a narrow hallway and were instructed by a Green to jog along the path. When one tall, muscular man objected to this forced run, he was reduced to a writing pile of muscular flesh on the floor as he grabbed at his constricting genitals. His pink net pouch twitched and the other men learned that disobedience was going to be punished immediately and swiftly. Ron gazed in horror and empathy, and began jogging down the hallway in earnest behind the others. The writing man was jerked to his feet, and he jogged unsteadily behind the line of trainees toward their official introduction and welcome.

Chapter Five

Thumping feet along the carpeted hallway was the only sound that filled his ears. Ron concentrated solely on the floor beneath him, rather than on what horrors might lay ahead. His penis tossed up and down with each step and he felt the burning in his rectum, complaining from the intrusions it had so recently suffered. Grimly, the group of men jogged forward. They glimpsed more Whites, Blues, and Greens along the way, their shirts now removed and their colors from their net bags unmistakable. The jogging newcomers were greeted with silent glances from amused Whites, Blues, and Greens as the group jogged steadily and silently onward.

Sweating and exhausted from their run along the twisting narrow hallway, the men were slowed then stopped by a single voice intoning, "Halt." Their Greens quickly lined the new trainees up and strapped them into waistbands, curved metal hooks that locked around their midsections and prevented their moving from their assigned spots. Their leather wrist cuffs were locked together behind their heads and every man, standing fully exposed and naked, could see only the one man lined up in front of each of him. Each Green stood before his trainee, naked man facing naked man, and checked out his charge. When the Green was confident that his trainee was ready, he stepped to the front of the room, folded his hands behind his back, until all the Greens were standing in a row, waiting silently and at attention.

Five Whites silently strode in. They took their places at the front and pointed at the Greens and then pointed at the floor.

The Greens fell immediately onto their knees, leaned back, and parted their legs. Whites checked the Greens' net pouches, pulling at one and then another, careful to ensure their security and when satisfied that all were in place, stood at hushed attention. As the Greens' backsides hugged the floor and their quadriceps begged for mercy, their mouths were silent as a solitary woman walked into the chamber.

Her flowing multi-colored robe stood in sharp contrast to the naked men who could be distinguished only by the colors of their net bags. She moved with a lightness and a grace that Ron found insanely appealing. He wanted to run in fear of her, but his torso was locked firmly in cold metal and his hands were trussed behind his head. He could neither move nor bend, and running away was out of the question. Besides, where would he go?

She motioned toward the ceiling and four rows of naked pink-netted men struggled to look upwards, but their bound hands locked behind their necks prevented their heads from moving. The Greens arose and each walked to a manacled man, reached up, and brought a mask down. The headpiece covered Ron's head and ears completely, and he imagined that each of the others was similarly geared. When the mask snapped shut, Ron smelled the sweet, mild vanilla, uncomprehendingly began to calm down, and heard the clear female voice in the earphones of his mask.

"This mask is a specially designed device that will make your introduction to training more personal and individual. Note that you can choose according to your personal needs and preferences. You have a choice of music, of pictures, that is, a total personal experience. Please view the choices." The woman's clear voice was haunting within Ron's mask. "When you hear the type of music you enjoy, squeeze your muscles and wag your tail for me. When your Green sees this motion, he will know that you have made a selection. The music choices begin now." Then there was a moment of silence.

The brief respite was shattered when Ron heard strains of violins invade his mask and knew that classical music was the first choice he could make. What was that she said? Make my tail wag? He tried to pull himself together and twitch his penis, but the poor thing had just had a terrible series of experiences and wasn't listening to Ron's brain. Slowly, the violins faded and guitar and folksong took its place. Ron gritted his teeth and concentrated. His penis would not move and his body was locked into place. As the guitar drifted, the heavy metal that invaded his head made him want to reel from the noise, but it too was quickly gone. Ron decided that whatever music came next would be his choice and he took a deep breath and tried to make his penis jump for her. As the welcome 60s rock came over his speakers, he heard the eerie female voice again inside his head.

"Good. I see you like rock."

Ron's penis had moved! He was exhausted but proud from the successful effort, an exhaustion that vaguely reminded him of post-orgasm happiness. He shuddered at the thought of comparison and concentrated on her voice once again.

Another demand was forthcoming from the merciless woman. "Now for the scenery. Use the same signal technique and you will complete your personal selections. Begin." Again there was the brief silence and Ron's exhaustion overcame his ability to obey her incomprehensible command.

Ron's throat responded to his personal distress and he groaned audibly. Not again. He wasn't sure he could do it one more time. He needed rest, but he was convinced that it would not come soon.

A sharp, sudden slap violated his genitals. Each of his organs felt personally and individually attacked. He screamed within his mask although in silence to his invisible audience, because he was unable to caress himself or give himself any comfort. That wretched but alluring voice again filled the silence of his mask.

"There is no talking. This is a warning." Then a brief quiet assuaged him in his torture.

The pictures flashed and Ron could only see through the tears that fell unashamed from his eyes. Skiing scenes, underwater photos, mountains, trees, landscapes appeared and Ron fought to control and force his aching penis to dance for her one more time. He squeezed, he tensed, he tried to make the damned thing jump.

Had the band not been fastened securely around his waist, Ron would have fallen to the floor, exhausted from his effort.

"Good. You have chosen." Then the awful silence penetrated his mask again and Ron felt utterly and horribly alone.

She allowed him an intermission, and for a short time, Ron heard rock music and saw sights of open fields. So that was what he had chosen! He barely cared. But the sweet vanilla odor and the beautiful pictures helped him relax. In his frustration, this moment of calm was heavenly. His body swayed slightly within its confines, and Ron vowed to simply enjoy the moment. The future looked bleak and the past was now a jumble of mixed emotions. The moment was the only important thing now, and Ron hung limply within his manacles and tried to make the most of this situation.

The voice cut in as the pictures faded and the music was silenced. The unrelenting voice filled his ears. "Welcome. Here you will learn how to please your partner in every possible sexual way. You have been assigned a personal trainer, a Green, and he will become the closest thing you will have for a friend. Perform well for him and he will treat you well. When you have completed Stage One training, we will meet again for further instruction. You must complete all five stages of training before you are inserted with my seal that certifies you as a fully trained slave."

The woman's introduction filled the shackled man's head with uncontrollable fear as she continued. "Let me make a comment about resisting. Your partner wants and has agreed to your training. I have never failed to return a fully trained slave to the sending party. There is no will too strong or constitution too great that I cannot complete your training. Your resistance is ill- advised because the punishment routines are strict, swift, and severe. On your way to your private quarters, you will stop and visit the punishment room. There are three levels of punishment and two will be demonstrated to you for your personal edification. We want to punish no one, but I will punish every infraction. Perhaps if you witness punishment and its very lasting effects, you will decide that compliance is preferable to resistance. Disobedience is not allowed. Greens, take your man." The voice he heard this time was as new as it was severe. Ron flinched involuntarily as would a scolded child.

The voice went silent and the mask was lifted off Ron's head by his Green. His eyes squinted involuntarily in the stark light, and he could see the backsides of those lined up in front of him, naked and sweating in the cold light. He could only imagine the faces of the men lined up behind him. What music had each chosen? Which scenes to enjoy? Green saw to it that his hands were released and his waist lock removed. Ron flexed his arms in an attempt to return feeling to his limbs and noticed that the woman was gone, and the Whites were exiting. His Green pointed toward another door and then toward Ron. Ron turned and walked through it without question. To the punishment room. To a sight he could never have imagined and a vision that would haunt his every decision for the duration of his training.

Chapter Six

Ron's military experience had been limited to reserve duty in the central command offices where his legal background helped Uncle Sam's recruits with mundane and minor legal problems encountered before and while on duty. He rarely had an opportunity to pursue the arrest of a soldier, and the one or two times he had participated in the serving of a warrant, he was required to accompany the arresting officer and prisoner to the section of the armory used as a makeshift stockade. Punishment for minor infractions, the only sort of offenses Ron dealt with, meant sitting at another end of the same building until a more permanent group of professional soldiers came to take their man away.

The humiliation of being surrounded and escorted by such a convoy was anxiety-provoking enough to convince Ron that he would take all steps possible to avoid a similar occurrence in his own life. The "Punishment Room" at this training facility made that armory situation seem like kindergarten.

The room was really a suite of three rooms, separated from each other by what appeared to be one-way glass from its burnished shine and poor transparency. Each of the rooms was sunk behind and beneath a walkway for outsiders that afforded such observers a clear view of all three rooms, their occupants and activities. The lighting outside on the walkway was soft, dim and comforting, Ron noticed, but it shined glaringly fluorescent within the sterile accommodations on the other side of the one-way glass. Ron and the other trainees were ordered to line up single file along the walkway, facing toward the mirrored wall, and were ordered to press their noses up against the glass. There would be no talking, as there would be no turning of heads to view one's fellow trainees. Six pair of eyes from Ron's group fixed straight ahead and shifted as one to the first punishment room as the fluorescent lights were turned up and the other two rooms were dimmed.

For the first time, Ron noticed the decor. Sterile white walls and black and white checked cold tile flooring decorated the glaringly bright room. In its austerity, the room emitted a physical warmth that caused Ron's feet to begin sweating in a sympathetic gesture. The view was unrestricted and there was no problem seeing the Green, arms behind his back and head lowered, being led into the room. Walking unsteadily, he stopped in the center and faced the walkway of staring trainees, who were invisible to the Green within the room. That same female voice began.

"Green, you are assigned punishment level one. Do you know why you are here?" Ron and the other trainees heard the voice clearly. There was no mistaking that was the voice of the woman he had "met" in the Welcome Area. He wanted to pee in fear. He held his bulging bladder tightly with both tense and sore muscles as well as with the last remnants of his willpower.

"Yes," the Green mumbled, in a voice barely above a whisper. After a while of uncomfortable silence, he added, "I should be punished for disobedience."

"How did you disobey?" That voice again. Cold and dispassionate. Ron's bladder ached from his depriving it of now-needed elimination.

"I. . ." the Green started but hesitated before completing his confession, ". . . did not respond quickly."

"Yes, that is disobedience. You will receive level-one punishment for a prescribed period. You may choose the time."

The Green hesitated again. The trainees on the walkway overlooking this poor man's torture stared open-mouthed in wonder. Choose his own time of punishment? Ron couldn't believe it! Why, this man was going to punish himself!

"One minute," the Green replied, as he looked directly toward the floor.

"Blue, White, prepare him." The voice was again stilled as the scene of fright unfolded.

A Blue and a White entered the room and without looking at the dejected and frightened Green, began harnessing him into wrist restraints attached by slim metal chains to opposite walls. His arms now tightly stretched straight out directly from his sides, they attached his feet into clamps bolted securely to the floor. With the Green vertically spread-eagled and naked now, the White pressed a wall button and the green net bag loosened its magnetic grip on Green's genital ring and fell silently to the floor in a pitiful lump of shining color. The Green began to whimper, almost silently, and his body trembled. Ron and the others held their breath in anticipation of an unknown looming horror they all felt inside their bones. The shock of the next scene filled them with dread and wonder. Ron's bladder screamed, but his mouth was silent. His penis throbbed and jumped of its own accord. Ron pressed his entire body closely to the warm glass and tried to will sympathy and encouragement to the man who was chained completely naked before the eyes of the newest class of trainees.

The Blue attached the mask that fell from the ceiling to surround the Green's head, and the room and walkway became even more eerily silent as the trainees neither breathed nor spoke in their mutual uneasiness. A floor panel opened between the Green's outstretched legs and a spoke-like device rose directly below his crotch. The Blue adjusted it until the round, polished wooden head of the spoke rested squarely against the Green's totally exposed genitals. He motioned one finger to the White, and they exited the cubicle. The Green was alone with his fear and humiliation. And Ron and five other trainees constituted his audience.

Suddenly, the spoke lowered, shot up, and planted itself directly into Green's organs at a great speed and with shocking severity. Inside the room was silence as the Green's screams fell soundlessly into his mask that was playing the calming music and scenery he had chosen at a time earlier in his own training. His body quivered and jerked, but the restraints held him fast, spread-eagled and vulnerable. The spoke dipped ominously down toward the floor. Again it shot up, and the Green winced in obvious but silent pain. The trainees grimaced, reached for their own genitals in empathy, and watched the punishment continue in silent horror. For an eternity of just one self-selected minute, the Green was disciplined as trainees watched. Ron's penis jerked of its own free will. He could neither stop its motion, nor, surprisingly, did he wish to.

Suddenly, the session appeared done. White and Blue re-entered and removed carefully the restraints from the Green's arms and feet. One put an arm tenderly around his waist as the mask was removed and prevented the now punished trainer from falling to the floor in his agony. The handsome face of the muscular trainer had been reduced to a crying, shrieking face of anguish and the trainees peered silently as Green was steadied upright in the center of the room. The dreaded voice came over the speaker once again.

"It is done. Would you like to speak?" Her silence indicated that an answer was expected.

The observers on the walkway gazed aghast as the Green struggled to utter five incomprehensible words to his silent and unseen torturer. "Thank you for my punishment." The words were a jumble of pain, humility and strange appreciation.

The White and Blue led him out of the room. The men on the walkway, in utter shock and amazement, were ushered onward toward the second cubicle to witness an example of what must be level two punishment, Ron imagined. He felt his body shake and his penis quiver, as he wondered what disobedience would result in "level two." His question was quickly and horrifyingly answered.

Two Whites led a Blue into the punishment room. The offender was a good-looking, muscular and tanned body-builder who walked confidently to his position. Gently pushing his shoulders, the Whites lowered him to a bent-over kneeling position. A leather collar was buckled firmly around his neck and a chain was attached to a hook on the collar at one end, and to the loops of his blue net bag at the other. His head down and his glistening metal chain in place, the Blue stared dispassionately at the floor. The Whites stood at attention and the unmistakable female voice again spoke over the speaker.

"Blue, you are assigned punishment level two. Do you know why you are here?" Again the silence filled the room as the disobedient man was required to answer.

"Yes," he replied in a clear, deep voice. "I was disobedient."

"How did you disobey?" the incessant voice inquired.

Blue did not answer until he formed the words he wanted in his mind. "I resisted a direct order."

"You may choose your time period now. How long should you be punished?" The awful silence frightened Ron almost as much as did the impending penalty.

"The order was given by a White. I deserve severe punishment. Please punish me for two minutes." Silently, the big man knelt with his head pointed toward the sterile floor and waited for the severe anguish to begin.

"You may have your two minutes. Whites, position him."

The Whites placed a metal clamp around his waist at one end and attached it to a hook on the wall at the other. Slowly, the clamp was raised up by a silent, unseen motor. The upward direction lifted the Blue completely off the floor. His legs dangled freely but the sheer force of the man's well-developed muscular legs kept his knees bent so his feet could not touch the tile. Ron watched in amazement as his sheer strength, evidenced by bulging and straining leg muscles, kept him in a kneeling position at least two feet off the floor.

"Whites, attach." The voice again. Ron began to sweat in sympathy and admiration for the Blue, and Ron's own penis again began to fill. He pressed his entire body up against the glass.

The Whites each gently pulled one of Blue's feet to the floor, and as they attached the feet to restraints, the Blue began a cacophony of anguished shrieking. Level two punishment was clearly meant to be heard as well as witnessed as the chain, long enough for comfort when Blue was kneeling with his head down, was shortened naturally as his body became erect. The tightening of the chain caused constricting of Blue's net bag. Incredibly, the man was punishing himself by torturing his own genitals simply by standing up. Ron and the others sucked in warm air in a single collective gasp, but they were careful not to utter a single sound. Such punishment was hardly conceivable, but the trainees were witnessing personal horrors that caused each man to experience the other's pain directly and deeply within his own organs. The shrieking Blue cried sounds of pain and agony, but never broke down or called for the cessation of the torture. He bore it as well as any man could, Ron thought, certainly better than Ron could foresee himself doing. No, he thought, this will not happen to me. I will obey every time. And quickly. With a slight turn of his eyes to his left, Ron noticed several trainees were pressed similarly hard against the glass, their eyes wide in wonder, pain and sympathy.

The scene captured their attention for the full eternity of two minutes of level two punishment. Ron and the others, their noses pressed to the glass, could only observe in terror. Mercifully, the punishment ended, and when the Blue was dropped back to his knees, his feet unfastened, and his chain and collar were removed, the trainees witnessed a face of pain they would recall in dreams and nightmares to come. He was hoisted to his feet by the attendant Whites and was left standing unsteadily and alone in the center of the room. The voice returned.

"Do you wish to speak?" So calm. So clear.

In horrific amazement, the trainees heard the five ominous words again, "Thank you for my punishment."

The Whites led him from the room and the trainees were silent in wonder. The Green at the head of their line spoke to the men.

"Do not move your noses from this glass. Remember what you have seen. Every one of you will receive some sort of punishment in the course of your training. You will decide on your own sentence, and Greens, Blues, and Whites will carry it out. Look at these rooms and remember well. It will happen to you. We will not witness level three punishment today because the Mistress is concerned that you might be unable to grasp its importance just yet. We will share level three punishment with you shortly. Every trainee is punished at one time or another. It happens to you all." Green was silent as the men stared into the empty chamber of horror. No it won't, Ron vowed, not to me.

With a realization of sudden abject horror, Ron felt his penis begin to harden again and more fully of its own volition. He willed it go down, to soften, to simply hang limply between his legs.

Afraid to move his hands in fear of punishment, Ron stared at the punishment room, his nose and body pressed tightly against the glass, his mind unsuccessfully willing his organ to deflate. It would not. He considered pressing up against the glass harder to press it downward, but he was in fear of moving against the orders of the Green. He was terrified of all the possibilities of his body's own mind and will. Ron was near tears.

"I have one!" a voice behind him cried.

"He's hard! I see it!" another added.

"Let's all see it," the head Green ordered. "Turn and face us."

The hand on his shoulder allowed Ron no room to doubt who the Greens were discussing. He turned and looked at his feet, his hard penis standing erect in its glory directly in his line of sight toward the floor. There was no place to hide, to run, or to cover his shame.

"Face me," the lead Green ordered in his no-nonsense voice.

Ron obeyed and was greeted with six amazed faces of Greens watching his penis enjoy its fullness. Ron was humiliated and afraid, but he stood still as his mind went blank from fear.

"Here's one who gets off on others' pain," a Green opined, "a real credit to his fellow trainees. That must set a new hard-on record for trainees. Let's all have a look."

The six Greens gathered around his erect penis as the other trainees stared into the punishment room, their noses pressed against the glass. Ron was alone in his terror and degradation, and the Greens were merciless. They touched his member to ascertain its degree of hardness and rolled their eyes in admiration and wonder. Ron could not look even one of them in the eye and he bore the men's touching his private parts in shame and degradation. Finally, one spoke and mercifully ended his ordeal of male touching.

"You will have no erection until you are ordered to," he stated, and pressed a button on his leather bracelet. Ron fell to the floor, writhed in pain from his constricting pink net bag, and entertained no thoughts except uncontrollable desire for relief from his pain. He grabbed his crotch, moaned and cried, and tapped his last ounce of strength to will his penis down. The trainees listened and imagined in silence. Finally, mercifully, the independent penis obeyed, relaxed, and hung limply within his grasp. The pain administered by the Green was stopped.

"Put him up against the glass," the Green again ordered, "and all the trainees should remember this little incident. The punishment I gave is lower than that which you witnessed in the rooms. I advise you to remember that."

Ron leaned against the glass for strength to stand. Sweating and crying, he gave in to the wall, his feet no longer willing or able to support his exhausted body, at least one Green arm held tightly but tenderly around his waist. Breathing in short, sharp breaths, Ron tried to calm down. Another Green from behind him put an arm around his behind and advised, "You're mine. We will begin training shortly. Let's get you settled."

The men were ordered to turn left and march in step to the sleeping quarters assigned to them for the duration of their stay. Ron struggled to keep his position at the end of the line and saw only the bare, tight and tanned backside of the trainee in front of him moving up and down with each step. Afraid to look up or down, he followed the trainee's backside in line until he was stopped and ordered to enter a room on his left. Once inside, he continued to stare down at the carpeted floor until a Green's voice ordered him to sit on the bed. Only then did he notice the room, a comfortable area with a bed, a chair, and cushioned metal stand. A door led out the back. With a silent sigh, Ron dropped onto the bed, without noticing how comfortable and appealing it was.

"Sleep now," his Green ordered in a soothing, calming voice. "I'll be back soon and we'll begin."

Ron's head fell against the downy pillows and the Green covered him with a soft, warm comforter, caressed his shoulders, and kissed him on the cheek. Pulling the mask from its clamp on the wall above the exhausted trainee's head, Green secured it around Ron's face and ears. The soothing music and pleasant scenery he had chosen calmed him and the sweet vanilla aroma lulled him toward unconsciousness. Too exhausted to be either afraid or disgusted, Ron immediately fell fast and sound asleep.

Chapter Seven

When he awoke, Ron felt too cozy and comfortable in his luxurious bed to panic when he realized he was imprisoned within the mask that played the soft music and the comforting scenery within this macabre training facility that promised to turn him into a fully trained sex slave for Debbie's delight. The horrors of the previous day--or night--were only vaguely recalled as he felt his aching bladder call him fully awake. Lost in reverie, Ron did not hear the soft whoosh of the door sliding open. Without introduction or warning, the Green who had befriended him during his ordeal at the punishment rooms entered, looked him over, removed the mask, and urged him out of bed.

Planting his bare feet on the warm plush carpet, Ron struggled to fix his vision on his surroundings. He could not focus and recognize the rather spartan, but comfortable room. The bed was huge, a California King, he conjectured, and it was replete with silken sheets and multiple pillows. The easy chair was just that: an inviting, upholstered furnishing that was enticing to his eye as well as to his sore and aching body. The aqua and peach decor was not unlike the master bedroom he and Debbie shared at home. Debbie! For the first time in what seemed like ages in his truncated experience, Ron thought of Debbie with a mixture of great warmth and frigid antipathy.

"Your training begins," the stoic Green said as he led Ron by the hand through the rear exit of his room. Ron felt reduced emotionally to the status of a child as he grasped his penis in one hand to prevent its relieving itself all over the carpet and held Green's hand tightly in his other, as if to gain strength from the big man to allay his fear of what lay beyond the door. Green grasped his hand back even tighter, as if to reassure the reluctant newcomer. He noticed Ron's pained expression, his gripping hand, and his dripping penis.

"When I give you permission, you may relieve yourself," Green casually mentioned, "but not before. You must first learn self-control as well as your personal morning procedures."

The other side of the door revealed a massive chamber that housed what Green called "personal morning procedures." Hand-in-hand, the trainer and the neophyte entered an enormous well-lighted, warm pool area that Ron recognized immediately from the video on the bus. The pool was not too shallow, about chest high, the water incredibly sparking blue, clean, and inviting. The sight of the warm mist rising from the water made the poor man's bladder ache even more. Gritting his teeth to hold back his bladder's urgency, Ron's eyes took in his surroundings, an old military training technique for basic survival and escape tactics, and he noticed that from each of the doors surrounding the pool emerged similar duos of Greens holding trainees' hands who were leading the novices to their morning bathing. Each Green looked confident, assured, and rested even in his nakedness, save for the green net bags and sequin head bands, while the trainees, a totally bedraggled lot, gripped their Greens' hands with one outstretched arm and held tightly to their own penis with the other.

A quick count revealed more than twenty-five trainees, each of whom walked with a Green trainer.

There were no bathrooms in sight. Ron gnashed his teeth in anger and frustration, but vowed to hold his bladder at all costs rather than repeat the humiliation and punishment he recalled of the previous gathering. The trainees were a sorry-looking lot, Ron thought, then grimaced when he realized that he was possibly the sorriest looking and feeling of the group. A double door on the side of the great room opened electronically. Five of the best-looking, muscular, and tanned Whites he had ever seen entered, and the woman in the brightly colored flowing robe emerged from the White gathering. Ron's nakedness no longer embarrassed him because his urgency to pee overcame his personal shame.

She spoke quietly to the group in a clear voice that Ron recalled with both horror and admiration from their first meeting, "Trainees," she began, "this is Morning Routine. You will be cleansed, both inside and out." She stared at their huddled, shivering bodies and smiled.

Ron shuddered at her look and her pronouncement. Washing was fine, he thought, but just who--and where--would be washed?

She continued with only the slightest pause, "Your Green will see to each of you. When you are ready, I will return." She exited without looking back, and the Whites accompanied her through the double doors. They seemed to vie for the privilege of opening the door for her, and what must have been the Head White led the procession. Ron's thoughts darted quickly back to his own immediate needs. His penis close to bursting, Ron implored his Green with pitiful eyes. Green shook his head from side to side.

"Soon," was all he responded, but pointed to the steps leading into the shallow pool that lay next to the great pool and then to Ron. Ron, who was as eager to avoid punishment as he was reluctant to immerse himself in the pool and the unknown future that awaited him inside the warm water, started and stopped toward the stairs. The other trainees, he noticed, looked toward him for a lead or clue.

The Green grew impatient and urged him, "I am here to train you. Do not become a hero to these men. They will suffer if they cannot learn to think for themselves. Make your decision and be ready to suffer the consequences of your actions." As his finger hovered over the jeweled bracelet on his right wrist, the Green waited for Ron's decision.

Ron stepped toward the small pool, reluctantly released his Green's hand, and climbed slowly and with trepidation into the warm water. Careful to keep his bursting penis from the water's warmth, he stood thigh-deep in the comfortable bath.

"Squat. Hands out," his Green ordered.

Although he knew the consequences of this action, Ron's need to obey and escape imminent punishment caused him to bend his knees agonizingly slowly with his hands outstretched for balance. He felt his penis give in to the comforting warmth of the water. His own inability to prevent elimination both angered him for his lack of restraint, but comforted him in his relief. Mortified yet happy, he did not move, but chose to enjoy the comfort of his emptying bladder. He appreciated his Green's command to squat for he realized this was his opportunity to urinate, even if it had to be done in such a public place. He would pee, he vowed silently, exactly and only when they told him to do so, even if he did not realize what the order meant at the time. This was a clever plan, he acknowledged, and he peed and peed until there was no more to come from his appreciative bladder. By now, he noticed, the other trainees had entered the pool and urinated their full bladders dry. Each face had a look of contentment and gratitude for the permission given by their Greens. A small blessing, Ron admitted, but a blessing nonetheless.

The pools' pumps quietly started and a wash of chemicals was churned throughout the shallow pool. The color of the water soon returned to its brilliant blue, and the Greens led the trainees from their joint elimination and into the great pool for bathing. They entered the pool as a single-file group; then each trainer walked directly and silently to a position in front of his man. Without warning, Ron's Green grasped his now-empty penis and pulled it toward himself. Ron could only sputter and struggle to keep up with his retreating trainer. Green pulled, tugged, and yanked on Ron's "handle" until he had his man standing exactly in front of a low cutout in the pool's pristine wall. The silence demanded of the group of trainees being shockingly and gruesomely pulled by their most private and sensitive organs was overpowering, yet it gave the group a strange bond of camaraderie.

His Green pointed at the cushioned cutout and then at Ron's neck. Reluctantly, Ron realized his order was to place his neck in the cushioned area and to do so meant having to lie on his back in the deep warm water. Struggling to keep his head in its cushion, Ron's feet disobediently floated toward the surface. Green waded over to the cushion and closed down a thick curved padded bar that blocked Ron's view of anything except for the ceiling of the great room. Green secured the bar and waded back to

Ron's dangling feet, lifted them in two powerful arms, and spread his legs uncomfortably wide. Securing his ankles into two unseen restraints, Ron was again spread-eagled and helpless, his body bobbing inches below the surface of the pool water. He tensed as Green reached for a floating basket of supplies and the "morning routine" began without mercy.

Each trainee's body was lathered and scrubbed all over by his trainer. The pleasant lavender aroma of the soap wafted above the water's surface and entered invitingly into Ron's nostrils. His mind, concentrating first on his fear and then simply on taking even breaths, fought the urge to give in to the conflicted feelings he was now experiencing. The washing was welcome and aromatic, although the intensity of the brushing was unbearable at times. Every orifice of Ron's body was scrubbed: his skin, his rectum, his neck, between his fingers and toes, his legs, groin, and belly. Green's pushing on his stomach caused Ron to sink briefly and rinse, although his head, secure in its cushions, was always above water.

Finally, Green began his work on Ron's totally exposed-but-netted genitals. Carefully but firmly, a soft but directed brush cleansed every fold and layer of his penis and testicles. Cream was applied to the bristling baldness of his pubic area that Ron did not recall receiving during his unconscious bus ride, and while the cream did its work, Green moved his attention to Ron's face. Peering into his visage, Green began applying the cream to his new whiskers. The expected malodorous depilatory was surprisingly agreeable, and Ron closed his eyes and gave into the comforts of the duration of the bath. Carefully and with technique honed from experience, Green removed the cream and the whiskers with a cloth and without warning, flipped Ron, head restraint and all, completely over into a facedown position in the water. His head still enmeshed in its collar, Ron was in no danger of inhaling water, but his mind rejected the calm and even breathing he had so carefully strived to maintain.

Gasping in fear, Ron's eyes could only direct themselves forward as Green waded to his lower body and insert a lubricated finger into his aching rectum. Horrified at the prospect of a repeat of the conveyor belt "cleansing," Ron unconsciously tensed every rectal muscle with all the strength he could muster. Green slapped his buttocks with a resounding crack and ordered, "Relax." Ron heard similar slaps, and trembled at what was happening to himself and to the other trainees in the bath.

Breathe, Ron demanded of himself, breathe and it will be over soon. Willing himself to calm down with a silent strength he could not identify as his own, Ron relaxed his buttocks, thighs, and stomach and waited for the newest violation of his humanity. Green rubbed his backside with caring and tender strokes until the muscles obeyed to his satisfaction, and Ron, still spread-eagled and helpless, gave in to the inevitable thorough cleansing.

Green lubricated Ron both inside and out, reaching farther into his anal area than any doctor would have found necessary for a complete exam. His feelings were a mixture of humiliation, lack of control, and a strange feeling of fullness and comfort that confused Ron in its contradictory nature. Suddenly, an almost-unbearable thought struck him. He was enjoying this! He wanted his anus cleaned, and he wanted it cleaned by this Green. This ultimate luxury of cleanliness was a comfort to Ron in his otherwise hellish nightmare of training. Although Ron could not see his face, Green allowed a slight smile, and after checking silently with the other similarly occupied Greens bathing the rectal areas of their charges, he noticed that they too had reached the first level of rapport with their trainees. Stage one training had been successful.

Tubes of warm cleansing liquids were discharged into the trainees' now-willing rectums and plugs inserted to prevent leakage as the Whites again ushered the flowing robed woman into the bathing area. She stood in front of the group of restrained but now-calm trainees, whose positions afforded them no view except of her and her attendant Whites. Ron stood bent over and nude in the group bath as his shackled head was forced to stare directly at the woman's feet. Degraded beyond comprehension, Ron faced the hem of her flowing robes and felt his churning bowels scream for relief. He was not alone. Naked and rectums full, the trainees bore her words silently in their urgency and degradation.

"This is morning routine," she intoned, "and at every wake-up during your training you will enter willingly and cooperatively for bathing. After your plugs are removed, you will line up in the training room. Greens, finish up. I await you there." Her ominous voice indicated that their plug removal better commence and be completed with alacrity. Ron felt his agitated bowels tense.

She exited as she had entered – in silence – and the hushed trainees were led out of the pool, hand in hand, each with his Green, and back to their bedrooms for unplugging and readying. Ron was grateful to return to his bedroom but was reluctant to engage in what she had referred to ominously as "unplugging." He knew what that meant, but he had no idea where that deed was to be accomplished. Since his arrival, Ron had not seen a toilet, and he was confused as to how this unplugging would unfold. He had to trust Green for this as well as for every intensely personal activity for he had no answers or suggestions to solve his ever-increasing urgency to evacuate his inflamed rectum. Green led Ron toward the door of his room and entered behind him, caressing the horrified trainee's rear cheeks now straining to relive what was behind them as the novice urged his muscles to respond and hold their charge. Ron stood naked and full of liquid in the center of the room and waited for Green's instructions. Green eyed him up and down, nodded approvingly, and commented as he ran his massive hand up and down Ron's glistening, soft, and very clean body. Ron felt his body quiver at the compliments and the man's touch and felt the uncontrollable rising of his glistening penis in its pink net bag. Against his will, his manhood asserted itself in appreciation of Green's kindness, stroking, and thoroughness, yet Ron was aghast at the prospect of impending punishment for his unordered erection. His flesh tingled in a mixture of pride and horror at his situation. His penis now fully erect, his rectum burning with urgency, his body warm and clean, Ron gave in to his stupefaction and degradation and wept quietly as Green watched the metamorphosis complete itself. Smiling inwardly, Green realized that Ron was now fully his.

"Unplugging," he broke the silence with the single word, "requires your cooperation. Kneel."

Without a second urging, Ron knelt on the carpeted floor. Spread your knees," Green ordered and Ron unquestioningly obeyed. Anything, he pleaded silently, I'll do anything. Make this go away. Help me. Green continued, "Drop your backside onto the red square in the center of the floor." Ron's wild eyes located the spot on the carpet and he struggled on his knees to obey this latest command.

His quadriceps screaming in agony, Ron lowered his backside until it touched the red carpet and he wriggled and squirmed until he was firmly planted on the red area. Without warning, the red square dropped away and disappeared. Ron's rectum was suddenly drawn by the force of gravity through the open hole. He was able to maintain his balance, but hardly his dignity, as his elbows smacked into the carpet and his unmoving thighs were stretched almost completely flat.

Without warning, Green reached between his legs, uncomfortably close to Ron's crotch, and as he bent over his supine trainee, pulled the rectal plug and withdrew his hand as Ron's bowels began to spasm. Hot liquid burst forth from its unwelcome home toward the unknown beneath Ron's backside. With a retractable hose pulled from its socket in the wall, Green washed Ron's aching rectum with warm and caressing water. The scented wash continued until Green's intruding finger came up clean and odor-free, and Ron was encouraged to stand up by Green pulling Ron's semi-erect penis straight up. Struggling and sputtering from his ordeal, Ron managed to straighten up and await Green's next order.

With a smile, Green informed him, "Let's go. She's waiting. Now you will learn what it is like to be a successful slave. You're partway there already. But remember this: I am completely in charge of you. Your successful training will be a reflection of my ability. I am up for promotion to Blue, and the speed and depth of your accomplishment will weigh heavily upon the decision. I am counting on you. Come." He turned and began jogging away with the sputtering trainee's limp penis planted firmly in his muscular hand.

Ron was forced to jog quickly to keep up with Green who led him by his roughly grasped limp member through the door, down the hallway, and toward the imposing red doors of the training room in which Ron and the other trainees would learn the true meaning of obedience in every imaginable, and often unimaginable, way.

Chapter Eight

Debbie awoke in her plush and satin-sheeted king-sized bed that wonderful spring morning to the aroma of brewing coffee and the unmistakable scent of freshly baked bread emanating from her kitchen.

Too comfortable to arise quickly, she gazed momentarily at the bedside clock and relished the thought of her lazy vacation day that loomed before her. The training center had sent her a carefully designed schedule to which she was required to adhere, and this day off was the first requirement that had been presented to her since they had taken and entered Ron into the program. Carefully following the directions, she freshened herself in the newly designed aqua bathroom and unwrapped the red-papered box the training center had provided her. Enrobing her not-too-bad-for-forty body in the red silk gown within the package, she arranged her still-firm breasts through the openings in the underwire bra-top and smirked at the frontal slit that opened all the way from her manicured toes to just below the bra enclosure. Silky and sheer, the red gown was appealing to her both in its satiny luxury as well as in its daring presentation. Following the enclosed instructions exactly, Debbie slinked between the satin sheets and arranged the multiple pillows comfortably in the center of the wide bed as she waited for the presentation of her breakfast and the important video promised by the facility's instructions.

She was not kept waiting very long. Entering her bedroom in a silent yet austere manner, a muscular, tanned, and well-built deliveryman brought a gleaming silver bed tray to her and arranged it carefully across her lap. The steaming coffee with its hint of vanilla was aromatic and enticing. Her servant's careful manner bespoke exquisite training and experience and Debbie vowed to enjoy every moment of this rare pleasure of breakfast in bed. She also enjoyed the sight of his toned muscles as he poured the cream from the silver pitcher into her porcelain cup and stirred it gently with a matching silver spoon. Placing the spoon silently on the saucer, he stood at attention at her side. He had yet to utter a single word.

Debbie sipped the hot and welcome brew and noticed the attractive array of breakfast choices laid out before her. Scones (her favorite) and croissants decorated the china platter and jams and jellies in matching porcelain pots dotted the overwhelmingly beautiful tray. She smiled at her bearer and alternately drank the coffee and munched the treats in quiet silence. Finally she spoke.

"When does the show begin?" she casually asked from her enthroned position.

Silently, the server walked to the large-screen television and tuned in channel zero, a pay-per-view station Ron and Debbie had rarely used in the bedroom. Tuning in exactly the right combination of equipment that Ron had set up for his own viewing and listening pleasure, Debbie was amazed to recognize the training facility she had seen in the video from which she had chosen this program for Ron. This time the trainees contained a recognizable face--Ron! In the immense room, Debbie noticed that Ron was encased in a cubicle on the lowest of several levels. His was one cubicle of what must have been at least forty, and was absolutely naked except for the pink net covering his penis and testicles she had so recently placed there herself. In this regard, he looked exactly like the other thirty-nine men, each of whom was standing erect in his own identical cubicle. Standing next to Ron, as well as next to each of the other thirty-nine, was another nude man, only this one sported a green net bag and a green armband.

On the second, higher tier of the training room, Debbie saw a network of similarly clad blue-netted men facing the semi-circle of forty. The Blues sat on perches from a vantage point overlooking the entire semi-circle, although it appeared that each of the eight Blues was concentrating only on five trainees and trainers. At yet another higher level were five Whites, each in a moveable chair with a desktop computer in front of him. Apparently each White was responsible for eight trainees and trainers. At the final lofty height was a single chair on a revolving arm that afforded the single occupant ample view of every position below. The engineering was top-rate, Debbie thought, and she marveled at the room's simplicity and functionality. She was truly impressed.

The Gold-netted visitor to Debbie's bedroom finally spoke. "This is Ron's first day of full training. You must watch the process and learn the techniques. You must become fully acquainted with every aspect of his training to make this event successful. As a Gold, I am an expert trainer and advisor and I will assist you in making the transition when Ron's course of study is completed and he returns to you. The most difficult aspect of this process is yours: you must become as one with the trainer and increase and change your expectations for your partner accordingly. I will facilitate this process for you both."

With that short but authoritative introduction, Debbie lounged backward into a comfortable and elongated position on her bed and sipped the aromatic vanilla coffee while she viewed the proceedings on the screen in front of her dreamy eyes. Her eyes darted occasionally from the massive man's golden netting to her husband's perch on the television screen. Wondering briefly what he would be like without his gold protection, Debbie's thoughts strayed from the stranger to the screen. Strangely relaxed, Debbie was eager to witness Ron's first training.

Each trainee was ordered into his booth. The walls extended forward just far enough that no one trainee could view another and afforded each captive a strange sense of privacy and intimacy. Yet all were equally accessible to the Blues and the overseeing Whites on their perches as well as to the intrusive eyes of eager spouses and trained Golds. Soundlessly on the screen, Greens began coating their charges bodies with gleaming oil until each trainee glimmered in the glare of the spotlight focused upon him. Each trainer carefully oiled every part of his man's body, front and back, inside and outside, under and over, until every man was a shimmering vision of muscle tone and sweat.

Using hand gestures only, Ron's Green showed him how to position his body in the style similar to that which all other Greens were attempting with their individual trainees. Soon, all forty men were standing erect, shoulders straight, heads high, hips straight, knees only slightly bent, and feet about shoulder-width apart. Apparently satisfied, each Green retreated to a corner of the cubicle behind his man. Debbie's attention was drawn quickly to a resounding slap she heard on the speakers that emanated from a booth to Ron's left.

A trainee had flexed his back and arched his neck without instruction, and his Green swatted his behind with unrelenting force. No other trainee shifted his glance or his body. My, Debbie thought, such good training in such a short time. The offending trainee was re-positioned and stood firmly at attention. Debbie thought she saw a tear fall from his eye, but her view was panoramic, and she could not be sure. Confident only of her own heightening passion, Debbie continued to leer at the spectacular show.

The camera shifted and focused on the highest perch, the moveable armchair that could swivel and angle to view any part of the proceedings in the enormous room. Led in on the arms of two Golds, a flowingly-robed woman emerged and took the seat. Two Golds stood at fixed attention, each on one side of her. As she smoothed her robes beneath her, Debbie focused on the woman's calm face, a visage of authority, knowledge, and yet laden with compassion for those she would now begin to train.

She tenderly fondled the testicles of the Golds on both sides of her chair, apparently in approval and thanks for their assistance in her entry. The woman quietly ordered, "Begin." It was the only voice heard in the room.

A churning wave of movement accompanied that single order. Whites began whispering instructions into microphones at their stations and electronically positioned their chairs to view one trainee, then another, and yet another. They hovered over the Blues and added instructions that the Blues, in turn, relayed to their Greens. The flurry of movement was well orchestrated and meticulously timed.

Debbie turned her attention to Ron and asked the Gold standing at attention next to her bedside, "Can I zoom in on mine?"

He bowed slightly in absolute obedience to her request and in a single motion took the remote control in his hand and turned dials until Ron's singular image filled the screen. Debbie was overwhelmed with the vision of her ordinary husband transformed into a sweating, gleaming, naked vision on the screen. Her nipples stood out from the confines of her unencumbered silk gown and she felt moisture begin to form in her deepest regions. The Gold, noticing her obvious physical pleasure, added, "I am glad this excites you. This shows that you have chosen your program wisely. You must try to maintain this level of excitement for the duration of the training. It is my job to help you accomplish this."

In her increasing excitement from the show on her television screen, Debbie barely heard his message but she clearly felt his hand pull back her sheets and comforter. The open slit on her red gown was lying apart, exposing her completely from bosom to toes while her breasts also stood naked and on their own from the open-cups in the bra top of her gown. She shifted her gaze violently from the screen to the man intruding on her pleasure.

"What the hell?. . ." she started.

The Gold pointed to her leather bracelet and advised, "You control me totally as you do your husband. Because I am netted, I cannot perform sexual acts with you without your consent. I am here to arouse you and keep you aroused. There will be no sexual act between us unless you desire it. You must initiate all encounters. Often, there are no encounters between Golds and female partners. However, I am expertly trained in arousal and I can keep you excited throughout Ron's session. Please feel free to exercise pain or punishment on me. I am your servant." He backed off and stood at attention at her bedside.

The idea of having total control over this hulk of a man excited Debbie even more than the faraway images on her television screen. She tested him by pointing one finger toward his head and then toward her breasts to see if he would silently accede to her demand. His response was immediate. Using only his lips, teeth, and tongue, the Gold exerted a passion on Debbie's nipples that she had never before experienced. He was careful to contain her excitement and bring her to the brink of ultimate pleasure without allowing her to lose total composure lest she ignore the video screen in front of her. He tickled her with his tongue as he circled the dark nipples of her exposed breasts. His teeth firmly yet gently tugged at her gown, causing her breasts to sway ever so slightly to and fro. His hands never left his sides as his mouth moved casually but intently down her midsection and approached her tightening belly. Kneeling now, Gold used his smoothly shaven cheek to nudge her tensed thighs slightly apart and his tongue flicked and darted around her femininity without either entering her or bringing her to extreme arousal. Debbie had trouble concentrating on the screen, but Gold was an expert and instinctively knew when to back off, to lessen her excitement, and to allow her to recover her concentration to keep a keen eye on her husband's progress.

Ron's simultaneous experience was of a totally different nature. After the Mistress's initial visual inspection of the forty new trainees, each man was commanded to his knees for the first lesson in total submissiveness and obedience. After Ron knelt, his Green stepped directly in front of him, bent his legs slightly and positioned his green net bag directly at the level of Ron's mouth. The aroma of Green's maleness was foreign to Ron's senses and he instinctively pulled his head back from the offending sight and smell. Green grabbed the trainee's hair with two hands and pushed his face directly into the trainer's limp penis and genital area. Ron tried not to gag, moan, or utter even a sound in fear of ultimate punishment in front of the others, but a noise of disgust began deep within his throat and emerged slowly from his mouth with a will of its own. Green pushed Ron's face closer and closer to his own body; ignoring the instinctive bellowing of degradation

Ron could not submerge. Grabbing a huge clump of Ron's dark hair, Green forced his head backward and stared into his trainee's horrified eyes.

"Bring me to erection," was his simple command.

Eight Blues simultaneously released forty Greens' net bags causing forty bare and exposed genital areas to face forty kneeling and naked trainees. Ron's mind went blank and he feared he might disgrace himself and faint in front of this entire array of onlookers. Worse, he thought, was the idea of taking Green into his mouth. There was no escape and he had to make a decision. The worst part, Ron thought, was that he had no idea what the others were doing. Some, he assumed, were already engaged in arousing their Greens. Others, he feared, were already on their way to punishment, and neither of the punishment rooms constituted an end Ron envisioned for himself. Debbie gasped in delight when she watched Ron's next moves.

He took a very deep cleansing breath and closed his eyes tightly. Trying to imagine soft music and Debbie's sweetness in place of Green's limp member, Ron parted his dry lips and extended his parched tongue. He took one lick of Green's penis. Green smiled above Ron's bowed head and the Blue in his jurisdiction noted the time on his terminal. The White above him whispered into his microphone and Blue relayed the message to Green's earpiece.

Green spread his own legs farther apart and said, "Good." Then he reiterated his demand, "Now bring me to erection."

Ron took a deep breath as he relaxed momentarily from his tonguing the slightly bulging penis that dangled before his tightly shut eyes and he tried to breathe evenly in an attempt to maintain his lucidity and gather his strength. Green was tired of waiting for the errant neophyte and had been informed by his Blue that two trainees down the line had already taken penises fully in their mouths. Ron's Green was not to be outdone, especially on this, his trial training for promotion to Blue. "Now!" he commanded mercilessly to the suddenly frightened trainee, "Make me hard!"

Grabbing yet another handful of the man's hair, Green pushed Ron's gasping mouth forward and thrust his head back and forth for the unwilling trainee. "Hands!" he shouted, "Use your hands! You know how you like it!" He gathered up Ron's hands and placed them one on each of his cheeks and guided them to a pulling and pushing motion so that Green was forced in and out of Ron's now salivating lips. He thrust by forcing Ron to pull and push his trainer's hips and buttocks and he relished in the feeling of his hardening member. He looked up at his Blue and smiled again as Ron continued forcing Green to thrust within his mouth. Blue again checked off the time and signaled his White. On the chart in front of him, the White simply checked off the second box and turned his attention to the other trainees in his charge who were not yet acceptably underway.

Debbie noticed Ron's fingers most of all. His hands were first limply holding Green's backside, then they gathered more force and intent of their own. Finally Ron was firmly pushing and pulling Green into his mouth by positioning his thumbs into Green's pubic bones and wrapping his fingers under Green's gleaming cheeks. He moved his Green forcibly forward and backward with a slight but distinct up-and-down motion that Debbie knew Ron enjoyed so well. If Debbie didn't know better, she would have assumed that Ron had prior practice in men's enjoyment.

Noticing her glum stare at that realization, Gold interrupted her thoughts.

"Men know how to make it feel good for other men because they know how it feels good on themselves. The hard part is to force them to try it on another man. Only then can a man know what it takes to make it feel good. Now Ron has learned he can and will perform sexual acts that before had not occurred to him. He has learned a valuable lesson in submission because he will now perform any act with any one you require of him." Gold hesitated so the excited woman could catch her breath.

"The next portion of the training is obedience. I think you will enjoy the lesson," Gold added as he re-positioned himself between Debbie's long legs. He knelt in supplication as he began kissing her red-polished toenails. She continued staring at the screen. The thought of obedience caused her long legs to twitch. Gold noticed the slight spasm of her toes in his mouth.

As Green's organ stood firm and tall in Ron's thrusting, licking, and drooling mouth, Green placed his hands firmly on Ron's shoulders and pushed the kneeling man backward, causing him to lose his balance and fall on his backside onto the floor. Stunned, Ron looked up at his trainer in wonder. What had he done wrong? Had he failed training? Was he going to be punished?

The trainer eyed his charge up and down as Ron sat silently on the cushioned training cubicle's floor, in fear of the man's wrath. Green stood at complete attention, his legs slightly bent, his feet apart, and reached out with his right hand in an upwardly cupped motion. He said nothing. Ron looked quizzically at his trainer and shook his head from side to side in wonderment, hoping for a clue. The Blue stared intently on this sprawled trainee and noted the time on his terminal. Green continued to stand immobile with his cupped hand out. Ron stood up slowly and, fearing punishment, resumed his "at-attention" pose.

Green was a resolute statue holding out a cupped hand, an increasing look of disgust and displeasure furrowing his handsome face and brow. Ron would have done anything at all to remove that glare of displeasure and bring back the kinder face of his trainer. Ron sidestepped to his left and then to his right, hoping to attain some sort of change of facial expression in his now-angered Green. He tried backwards, also in vain, and his fearful steps forward were rewarded with only a modest change in Green's very serious frown. Ron slowly took another step forward. Green frowned slightly less now. Ron took another step forward, this time with serious intention, and Blue again noted the time.

Ron was now almost face-to-face with his trainer; their only separator was Green's cupped and outstretched hand. Something must go in his hand, Ron conjectured, but what? Ron had nothing to give him save for himself. Himself! Ron wondered at his apparent stupidity and immediately raised himself up on his toes and placed his entire pink-netted bag of genitals into Green's hand. Green smiled and squeezed Ron's pink bag gently and with approval. Blue noted the time. White checked off a third box. Debbie's thighs tingled while she watched her husband smile as Green fondled his testicles and penis in his tan and muscular hand.

Debbie stared in amazement as Green darted from corner to corner of the cubicle and stretched out his cupped hand. Ron dashed from side to side and jumped, tiptoed, and knelt to place his genitals into the trainer's rapidly shifting hand. Green made it very difficult for the trainee to accomplish the prescribed mission. Often he would raise his hand high and force Ron to jump; other times he would lay his hand practically on the floor and Ron was forced to spread his buttocks' cheeks apart to lower himself flat on the floor. Debbie was amazed at his agility and willingness to please the trainer.

By now, Gold had kissed and licked each of Debbie's toes and was moving his warmth up her calves. He stroked each calf separately with a touch that bespoke hours of training in giving pleasure. She smiled at the pleasure while she ignored the man in her bed and watched her husband jumping, dancing, falling, and prancing to place his genitals into the ever-appearing hand of his trainer. She watched Ron whirl and spin as Green turned his hand this way and that; she delighted in his strict obedience and anticipation of Green's every move. It was a game between the two men, and both seemed very much to enjoy playing.

Gold bent Debbie's knees aside and parted her long legs. The split center of her gown opened and the satin fell totally away from her body as she lay fully exposed to the nude man in the center of the satin sheets. Readying himself to give her still more pleasure, he knelt tall and fully erect on the red satin sheets on the bed between her legs but his shoulder partially blocked her view of the screen for a brief moment. Casually, she touched a series of buttons on her bracelet and as Gold writhed in pain, tossing and grabbing at his testicles and penis in the space on the bed between her legs, she motioned, "Shhh. . ." with her finger to her lips, continued to watch Ron's training, and silently reaffirmed her decision to enter him into the program.

Chapter Nine

After the morning's training, the exhausted trainees were hooked together by chains at their penile rings and jogged to breakfast. By this time, day and night had intermingled, and their only measure of time would be that clock to which the facility training adhered. Ron was beyond the point of caring; he wanted only to eat and relax for a few moments. The second round of training, something Green had called Level Two, was to begin immediately after this food break. He desperately wanted to eat, but equally as much Ron wanted to talk to other trainees and find out how their sessions compared to his.

Ron was intrigued by the speed of his own "progress" and was anxious to learn how he fared in comparison to the others. He bore the jogging single file as he endeavored to keep up with the man ahead, staring ahead at the backside of the trainee in front of him, and concentrated on his wonderment rather than on his aching legs. The aroma of coffee and breakfast filled his nostrils, and his mouth, already salivating, was eager to be filled with a more palatable dish than what he had tasted in training.

The dining room tables were neatly set with appropriately colored cloths: white, blue, green, and pink. There was no question which tables belonged to the chained and jogging group of trainees. Their oiled skin and aching legs set them apart from those of the upper echelons. Afraid to claim a seat in fear of rebuke or punishment, the sweating and oiled trainees stood awkwardly in the entrance to the formally set room. The other tables were filled with Greens, Blues, and Whites, and a smaller gold-clothed table sat empty in the center of the room. The trainees were milling about waiting for instructions when the already quiet room hushed totally silent as the Whites, Blues, and Greens rose in unison and the Mistress entered, attended by two Golds. Leading them in a dignified procession to the center table, she sat gracefully on the center chair, gently squeezed the genitals of her escorts, and nodded. All then sat quietly in their chairs as the trainees still congregated at the entrance.

She gazed at Ron's group briefly before whispering to the Gold on her right. He stood at his place and announced, "You are hereby referred to as Pinks. You may sit at a pink table. Please sit." With that, his private parts were patted lovingly by the Mistress, and he sat again at her side.

Ron could not be sure, but he thought he detected a grimace on the part of the other Gold who attended the Mistress. Was it jealousy? Shaking the ridiculous thought from his consciousness, he looked around for an available seat and chose one at the middle pink table. On his right he noticed an attractive Pink comrade and glanced at him, hoping for a return glance. Not one Pink uttered a word for fear of punishment, but all were eager to talk and relate their shared training experiences. Ron wanted to know who these men were; where they came from; who sent them here; and most of all, where was here?

Food was brought to the tables by gold-netted servers, and Ron, as well as his table mates, was shocked by their servile behavior. How could a Gold be assigned a job as lowly as cafeteria work?

His incredulity was overwhelmed by his voracious appetite, and Ron devoured all the offerings before him. Cereals, fruits, grains, breads, jams, and coffee--lots of good, hot, vanilla flavored coffee--appeared and were downed by the hungry trainees. The Golds brought more food to each pink table, much to the amusement of the Greens, Whites, Blues, and most of all, the head table, and the men, unashamed of their hunger, devoured it all. Their bodies oiled and reeking of sweat, the men's appetites were undiminished by their nudity or perspiring appearances. Ron thought of the refrigerator magnet Debbie had purchased on their trip to Cape Cod: "Life is uncertain, eat dessert first." In this confused time of his mid-life, that adage rang uncannily true.

The head table soon emptied of its sated occupants and the remaining staff and trainees ate in silence. When his stomach could hold no more, Ron sat back on the comfortable padded dining chair and he turned to his neighbor. The man's wavy brown hair and green eyes danced in greeting, and for the moment, no words were exchanged. In fear of punishment and rebuke in front of his fellow trainees, Ron sat silently and awaited instructions.

At the table on his left, a Pink coughed and all eyes turned to the offending noise. "Excuse me," the Pink offered, and at the sound of his words, a table of Greens arose and surrounded the trembling offender. The poor transgressor began shaking with the result that his bladder, rich with vanilla-flavored coffee, emptied itself of its own free will and fear.

His neighboring Pinks were immobilized, afraid to move from the scene of his inflammatory action and receive the possible wrath of their own angered trainers. A frightening silence permeated the dining hall as the sated Blues and Whites exited in one jogging, smirking line. Alone with the entire staff of trainers and thirty nine horrified trainees, the Pink arose, offering himself to the trainers for punishment. Hands clasped behind his back and his pink net bright against his oiled skin, the shaking man was led from the room as thirty nine pairs of eyes followed the procession with sympathy and compassion as well as with a little exultation that the offender was not himself. One of the two remaining Greens spoke to the group.

"You will witness his punishment and you will partake in its infliction. This is the best way to learn that obedience is strict and punishment is swift and complete. Follow." His silent turn demanded that the Pinks rise and jog single file behind his exiting form. The thirty-nine trainees rose and allowed the Green to lock their penile rings in a jogging and chained processional toward the now-familiar punishment room.

"Who will volunteer to administer his punishment?" the Green inquired and was greeted with a chorus of silence and horror. Ron's mind was a jumble of mixed emotions. If he volunteered, would his fellow trainees shun him? If he did not, would the Greens inflict punishment on him? Given the two reprehensible choices, Ron remained silent until the Green repeated his question with a new twist.

"If no one volunteers, all will receive punishment."

Now there was no choice because a decision had to be made. Ron stepped forward in awkward silence as the remaining trainees looked at him with an odd mixture of both respect and horror. How could he volunteer for such a thing, he asked himself silently. How could he not volunteer, he countered, playing devil's advocate with his own stirring emotions.

Green answered his audacious stepping forward with, "At least there is one man among you. Come with me." He motioned with a curled finger toward Ron. From the corner of his eye, Ron noticed the remaining Green forcibly press the remainder of the group flat against the wall, genitals pressed tightly against the glass, and spread each man's cheeks as wide as possible to flatten each pink netting indecorously to view the punishment.

Ron was led down a side corridor and through a door marked "Level One." The disobedient trainee was already in the room, a solitary occupant in an inoffensively tiled chamber. His fear reeked from his pores and was readily apparent to the Green and his chastening Pink. The man's wobbling body shook from head to toe, and his poor bladder drained itself repeatedly in tiny puddles on the gleaming white tile. Although his skin glistened from the oil of the morning session, his eyes were wet with tears. His face was stained with the crying of the condemned and Ron's heart ached for his colleague.

The man was quickly and expertly manacled by the Green on both his hands and feet and he stood spread-eagled in the center of the room. The mask hung above his head and Ron was ordered to pull it over the poor man's suffering face. Trying to be comforting as well as obedient, Ron pulled it down and clamped it shut, finally ending the whimpering noises the trainee did not have the self-control to stifle. Ron was glad for the sudden silence and he fought the urge to gaze at the onlookers he knew were on the other clear side of the one-way glass. What must they think of him now? What did he think of himself? Ron fought that question to the back of his mind somewhat successfully and waited for Green to give him new instructions.

The voice on the intercom interrupted his thoughts. "The offender was not asked the duration he wanted for his punishment. Therefore, Pink, you must decide for him."

Ron gasped. His error would cost the man his chance for reprieve or control over this intensely personal aspect of his training. There could be no pleading by him or no momentary mask removal. The point was clearly made by the Mistress and the decision would have to be Ron's. One minute? Two minutes? How long was long enough but not too long? Ron considered the offense: the man excused himself for coughing. But there was a second offense, the emptying of his bladder in fear in the dining room. Which was the worse offense? How in the hell could they expect Ron to judge this man?

As he fought with the question and his own values, Ron felt the unstoppable and unwanted rising of his own pink-netted member. Oh no, he cried silently as he struggled to cease its rise and gained only a furthering of its engorgement. The Green was not amused with Ron's delay and the voice on the intercom noted, "Decide."

Ron offered weakly, "One minute."

The intercom intruded once again, "The punishment is set for one minute. Secure the pole." Then there was silence.

Ron bent low and lifted the wooden spoke from its home retracted in the floor, slid back the shackled trainee's pink netting, and rested the pole against the offender's naked penis. He could only imagine what that slight feeling was doing to the trainee who was reduced to crying and gasping in his mask while he was forced to listen to his chosen music and view peaceful scenery. "Exit," the Green's voice ordered, and Ron followed his trainer from the punishment room. Closing the door tightly behind them, Ron leaned against its solid coolness for support as his exhausted body sagged from the mental turmoil he had just experienced. He wasn't sure which was worse: the spoke itself or Ron's required administration of it to another. In the anteroom occupied solely by Ron and the Green, the punished trainee's anguished screams could be heard clearly on the recessed speaker. The suffering man cried in his pain and in the fear of impending pain. The spoke did not strike in an ordered fashion or with a regulated rhythm. It came and went at the whim of the incessant voice on the intercom. Ron was aghast as the man begged for cessation, mercy, and ending of his agony. The tears that fell from Ron's eyes were for the punished man as well as for himself. But in spite of his anguish, Ron's penis continued its dreaded and frightening ascent.

"You really get off on others' pain, don't you?" the Green asked as he grabbed Ron's offending engorging penis in his tight grasp. "You will be a finely trained slave, you know. I've met others like you. They do very well here." Ron's heart sank as he recognized the finality of the Green's words.

The agony of the faceless voice finally ceased and Green prodded the reluctant Ron to re-enter the punishment room. At Green's command, Ron released the mask, unshackled the manacles, and lowered the dreaded spoke. Finally he removed the clasp on the waist hook and barely caught the hulk of the shattered man as he nearly crumpled onto the cold tile floor. Ron tenderly dragged him to the corner of the room, as far away as possible from the intruding eyes of the onlookers and stroked the man's face until some color reappeared.

The voice on the intercom interrupted Ron's assisting the bedraggled trainee who was still sprawled in his arms. "It is appropriate that the punished speak. He must thank you for administering his punishment in recognition of his disobedience." The awful silence filled the sterile chamber.

Smiling the false smile of encouragement, Ron tried to help the depleted man once again to rise.

Something within the punished trainee would not respond to Ron's efforts. Anger, pent up from the humiliation and degradation of the training, emerged in violent fury from the core of this humiliated and violated man. The crazed trainee jumped up in pain, doubled over in his agony, grasped his own genitals as if to protect them from further abuse, and began with an effort that bespoke raw energy and deep personal suffering, to shout violently at the mirrored glass behind which the amazed trainees had their faces and bodies closely pressed. They all heard every word he uttered.

"No! NO MORE! I will not tolerate this any more! Do you hear me? You cannot treat me like this! I will not be treated like a slave! You cannot make me do this! I refuse!" The man's agony and anguish permeated every word, every phrase, and every syllable of his diatribe. Green smirked and winked at Ron. The voice on the intercom calmly interrupted his ranting.

"Disobedience is not tolerated. You will be corrected and you will beg for the renewal of your training. Your outrage is inconsistent with our goals and is not tolerated. Blues, devise his renewal program." The voice again was silent as the dread within Ron's heart grew.

Suddenly, the screaming trainee was surrounded by invading Blues and whisked away from the punishment room. Ron's penis was standing hard, as were many other unseen genitals pressed firmly against the one-way glass above. The group could only imagine the "program" that the poor man would be forced to endure. And they wondered how long it would take to break him, as they readily imagined that they had probably broken so many others in the past.

Green winked at Ron and murmured, "I give him two hours."

With that pronouncement, the Green and his horrified trainee rejoined the jogging, chained procession of thirty eight remaining slaves-in- training toward the afternoon training session and their attempt at mastering Level Two.

Chapter Ten

Their introduction to Level Two training was as swift as it was unlike the individual efforts of the morning's schedule. Returned to the immense tiered training room, Ron was assigned a cubicle with another trainee. A single Green, Ron's Green, was put in charge of the novice duo. Re-oiled tenderly yet fastidiously inside and out by the trainer, Ron and his partner were set face-to-face in the cubicle and for the first time since his arrival, Ron was close enough to study the facial features and body style of his counterpart. He couldn't help but notice the man's shockingly black hair, his amply muscled arms and legs, and the awe-inspiring rug of dark hair on his broad chest. This man was a body-builder, Ron assumed, or at least he was in training. Probably about forty years old, the man was a specimen of masculinity and had Ron ever entertained thoughts of a liaison with another male, this example of humanity would have been made to his order.

The only feature that was out of character on this trainee's body was his bald genital area, similar to Ron's, and it struck him that the man's missing genital hair only enhanced Ron's view of this particular trainee's generous endowment. Embarrassed at his inspection of the size of the man he squarely faced, Ron shifted his eyes to meet the other's stare, and wondered as to his assessment of Ron's size and ability. Ron's workouts in the health club were always concluded with a shower, but there was an unwritten rule in the men's locker room that all conversations were held at eye-level. No man ever allowed his gaze to drop lower than his companion's chin. Although nudity abounded in the locker room, visual inspection of another's size or endowment was strictly prohibited.

The other, a corporate accountant in his civilian life, returned Ron's stare with a cool, dispassionate, and unwavering look familiar to those who experienced routine health club workouts. Eye contact was established and maintained between the two and the Green was slightly taken aback by the pair's failure to visually inspect each other. Oh well, he thought, this will soon change. Unbeknown to Ron and his counterpart, the two men would soon become intimate friends. Level Two training assured an unusually close physical relationship between partners.

When the robed woman resumed her perch on the overhanging swivel chair, a ghastly silence of ominous expectation befell the enormous room. With a single nod to her Gold, an announcement was delivered to the group in crisp, clear tones.

"Level Two begins. Partners on the left, kneel. Partners on the right, about face." The Gold stood silent as the Whites, Blues, and Greens scurried to enforce his command.

With his trainer's demand for swift compliance, Ron found himself forced into kneeling on the cushioned floor and staring directly into the backside of his partner. With a mild wash of amusement leveled with admiration, Ron recognized the carefully toned gluteus muscles as well as the lack of a tan line from an offending bathing suit.

The voice overhead continued, "Kneelers, spread his cheeks with both your hands." Again there was silence and enforced obedience.

Ron paused momentarily, a fact that did not go unnoticed by his Green. He gingerly placed Ron's two well-oiled hands on the man's similarly oiled buttocks but they slipped helplessly off his slick cheeks. Obviously, similar results were experienced in the adjoining cubicles.

The voice interrupted their futile efforts, "Standers, grab the handrails in front of you." The silence that followed his directive was greeted with the trainer's action.

Ron watched the big man help the trainee bend at the waist to grab the low bars on the wall. With this new position, his slippery cheeks were already well spread and needed little of Ron's cumbersome efforts.

"Again," they were directed.

Ron reached for the flesh somewhat less tenderly this time and with the tips of his fingers inserted well into the crack of the man's buttocks, he pulled softly to spread the tightly-tensed muscles. Green pushed Ron's hands away with a swift and authoritative slap and with his own free hand smacked the backside of the bent-over trainee with a crack that resounded throughout the cubicle, if not the entire hall. Several mobile chairs swiveled to face Ron's location, and the embarrassed kneeling lawyer pleaded with his eyes to ascertain what had gone wrong. The Blue noted something onto his screen and spoke into the White's personal microphone.

"Relax your muscles," Green hissed to the bent-over man, "and allow him to spread you wide."

He nodded at Ron who re-attempted his required duty. Obviously, others had experienced similar difficulties.

The voice overhead spoke again, "Grab the lower handrails. Kneelers, spread him wider." Ron sensed the urgency rise in Green's face.

Ron tried to steady the already bent-over man with his slick and oiled hands but was not able to assist him in any meaningful way. As the man struggled downward to grasp an even lower set of handgrips, Ron empathized with the man's apparently aching hamstrings that were now stretched beyond their limit. The lower handrails were almost at floor level, and the poor man body formed an inverted "U" shape, an uncomfortable position anyway, but the spreading of his buttocks could only add to his agony. With fierce determination not to let down his Green or risk personal or dual punishment, Ron dug his hands into the man's loins and pulled with all his strength. The man gasped as Green reached into the space Ron provided and forced his unlubricated index finger deep into the man's anus, pushed it deeply into his rectum, and rotated it in several directions until the man's moaning from humiliation, discomfort, and pain filled the cubicle with the horrifying sounds of agony. Ron did not move from his frozen position, kneeling behind his man, spreading his cheeks wide, and allowing Green to enter his body in a most peculiar fashion.

The intercom interrupted as the intrusion continued, "You are witnessing the initial procedure for the Insertion Ritual. Each trainee is assigned a partner to ready him for Insertion. When he is readied for insertion, the process will be reversed and he will ready the other. This is a sacred culmination of our training procedure."Ron heard the voice intone the words, but his mind reeled at the prospect of having his own anus violated so forcefully. He felt his backside twitch at the thought.

The voice persisted. "When you are inserted, you are marked as a fully trained sexual slave. You will come to enjoy the insertion; you will look forward to it. When it is denied you, you will be overcome with shame because it signifies that you did not please your trainer in performance of your activities. Every member of the facility is inserted daily if he gives ultimate pleasure to his Mistress. Blues insert Greens and Whites insert Blues. The Golds insert the Whites. Only the Mistress inserts the Golds."

His silence washed over Ron's supplicant position with a frightful wave of anal quivering mixed incomprehensibly with desire.

The Gold completed his announcement. "The ritual is an evening's finale, and when you are an accomplished performer, you will be allowed to witness an insertion ritual. When you are fully trained, you will be inserted by the Mistress at your completion ceremony. Until then, you and your partner will practice the rituals and habits of insertion until you both come to experience the joy it brings and will long for its entering."

All eyes were riveted on the Gold speaker who intoned this message as he stood next to his Mistress's right hand. Each trainee stared as she tenderly fondled his gold bag while he spoke and all the trainees and trainers in the chamber watched the Gold's penis harden and climb until the net bag strained with its engorged contents. The Mistress viewed the gold net bag and shook her head from side to side with obvious displeasure and the Gold could do little but stand perfectly at attention as Ron could almost feel him trying to will his penis down. No one, he guessed, not even a Gold, was allowed erection until he was ordered.

Green, Blue, White, and trainee eyes focused on the man's plight. The Mistress sternly gazed at the offending organ and announced simply to the Gold who stood mortified yet erect at her side, "You will not be inserted tonight."

The massive hulk of a man remained at attention while the stares of all the men darted from his bulging penis to his tearful eyes. Ron almost felt sorry for him as the tears coursed down the big man's face.

"Please," the hushed room heard him beg, "please. . ."

Without turning her glance toward the pleading man, she slapped his penis hard with an open hand and the man fell immediately to his knees. He hung his head in despair, pain, and humiliation as she ignored his plight and turned to the Gold on her left. "Continue," she remarked, ignoring the whimpering man who knelt sobbing by her right hand. The group was amazed at her lack of attention to his weeping and whimpering. Almost without pause, the new Gold spoke.

"Denial of the Insertion Ritual is a specific part of Level Three Punishment," he remarked as the Mistress stroked his gold net. "You will come to know this ritual as the culmination of your sexual pleasure. Even orgasm will become an exciting, but nevertheless secondary, event of gratification in your sexual life."

She massaged him carelessly but tenderly as he spoke and Ron could feel the love and intimacy that existed between the Mistress and her Golds. The punished Gold's public humiliation did not diminish the intense look of caring and pleading the chastised Gold directed toward his Mistress, even though she did not readily return his stare. The well-trained Gold awaited the reply he knew she would eventually bestow on his supplicant form. Her lack of response was a part of his punishment and Ron conjectured that this man was suffering untold emotional as well as physical pain.

With a nod from the Mistress, the training began anew as the Greens re-directed their charges' efforts to the insertion ritual practice and training. Ron's partner's rectum was fully exposed and the Green was satisfied he was empty and clean within his rectum. Now Ron understood the reason for the daily cleansings he and the others were forced to endure and that he had come to appreciate. Still on his knees, and his partner still bent in half with his anal area fully opened, the two remained silent in their trepidation as the Green opened a large jar of brilliant pink lubricant.

"Use of this cream allows insertion to be completed with ease and comfort," Green advised, "and you will learn to apply it to your partner with great care and tenderness. Listen carefully, because if you misapply the cream, he will suffer and you will receive punishment in two forms--the pain of incompetent insertion as well as Level Two Punishment."

Ron and his partner faced the trainer from their awkward positions and listened attentively to Green's discourse as the two continued to kneel, bend, and spread themselves in front of the vast audience.

His instructions were precise. "First, dip two fingers fully into the cream. Then reach deep inside the man's entry to lubricate as far as the width of your hand will allow. Simply, the deeper the cream is applied, the more competent the insertion will become. Then, remove your hand and apply the cream to all areas leading up to the deepest point."

He paused as the two took in his advisory cautions. Green continued, "Finally, lubricate the entry point so that when he is exposed to his inserter, a carefully painted circle of pink is clearly visible. This circle is the signal that the man is ready for insertion. The greatest failure of insertion and the single most frequent cause of punishment is carelessly applied cream. Insertion cream must be accomplished with care and style. You will learn both during this afternoon's session." He handed Ron the jar of bright pink cream and Ron dug his fingers as far as they would reach into the contents.

The cream was warm and comfortable to his touch without feeling greasy or oily. Its brilliant pink hue was shockingly bright. As Green instructed Ron how to hold the man's cheeks apart with one hand while inserting the cream with the other, the kneeling trainee dutifully reached deep inside the fully exposed anus and was surprised at its tightness and the muscles' involuntary fighting back at the intrusion. Depositing his contents, Ron quickly removed his fingers. Without warning, Green shoved three of his own unlubricated fingers into the man's anus, causing a sudden gasp from the trainee. His knees buckled, but valiantly, the man hung onto the handrails.

"Do not resist," Green spoke angrily to the suffering trainee, "and relax your muscles. Do not fight the insertion ritual or you will be punished without warning or compassion." The irate face worn by the trainer filled Ron's soul with terror.

Ron thought he heard the offended man's sobbing but with his own punishment on the line, Ron re-applied the cream deep inside the man's anal region. Again he felt the tight muscles and was unable to move his fingers in the side-to-side and up-and-down motions he had been instructed to perform. Green became infuriated quickly with the man's lack of compliance and jerked him upright by grabbing his pink net bag and its sensitive organs with brute force. With a yelp of surprise and pain, the black-haired trainee stood half-bent and gingerly before his trainer and Ron felt sympathy for him as he watched helplessly the tears that coursed from his eyes and onto his cheeks. "Punishment!" Green called loudly, and a Blue emerged to lead the sobbing man out of the immense room.

"Another!" Green called, and Ron was immediately assigned a new partner. To his utter astonishment, Ron was given as a new partner the very man he had administered punishment to after the morning meal. This was the same man who, earlier in the morning, had cried out in defiance after his punishment was administered and had been led away for his "program." Green had estimated he would be fully conditioned in two hours. As the man was positioned, his hands nestled without resistance onto the lower handgrip and his buttocks spread wide as he eagerly awaited Ron's intrusive efforts, Green muttered to Ron, "You see, forty-five minutes. He didn't last very long."

This trainee was a markedly different man from the one who had resisted and cried out at his punishment barely an hour before. When Green slapped his backside and ordered him not to resist, the man's buttocks loosened immediately and he tried to spread his own cheeks without Ron's help. He eagerly accepted the lubricant and Ron was able to fully administer the cream with no resistance, either voluntary or involuntary, from the now-accepting trainee. With his task accomplished, Ron removed his hand to complete the careful pink circle he was required to make to signify the man's readiness for insertion. To Ron's surprise, Green soundly smacked the raised hot-pink cheeks of the decorated trainee and the echo of the spanking reverberated throughout the hall. The Blues noted the time and the White entered another check on the form spread out on his elevated desk.

Green nodded a gesture of approval toward Ron and his partner and drew a circle in the air with his finger to indicate a change of position for the two men. Ron was able to throw a glance over his shoulder at his new partner and saw a face empty of hatred or anger, a man fully accepting the role to which he was now totally resigned and one which he seemed eager to accomplish. What Ron could not determine from the single quick and furtive glance was the extent of transformation the former resister had made. All Ron recognized was the need to bend over, spread his legs, grip the handrails, and have his anus violated by a man who seemed as eager to enter Ron's rectum as far as his arm would allow.

The Blues' program for compliance for first-time resisters was a carefully designed routine that guaranteed the breaking of almost any man's will. But critical to the program was the replacement of animosity with a feeling of desire for training. The Mistress's directions were clear to all her workers: do not break a man without replacing his hatred with desire. Failure to promote desire for the training did not constitute the real and total breaking of anyone's will. Blues had worked daily for weeks with various stubborn recruits to perfect a program that would accomplish both of her ordered actions and their ideas. The program had been tried on many, techniques honed to perfection, and administered to the most hardened resisters the training facility had recently enrolled. And in every case, the dual-edged sword of the program that returned compliant and eager trainees, all of whom became fully trained graduates of the program. Long-term reports supported the program, and although some modifications were made for individuals, the successful program remained basically intact.

Earlier, when the screaming resister was brought to the program room, he was greeted by a host of Blues and Whites who massaged him tenderly with oils and placed his personal relaxation mask on his head. With just the right amount of vanilla-scented aroma for his height and weight, the man calmed down dramatically and was ready for the program's administration. While still in his slight daze and relaxed by the massage, scenery, and music, his knees were placed each on a padded, raised surface, and his hands were buckled behind his back. Slowly and carefully, his head, still encompassed by the mask, was lowered forward until his chin rested outstretched upon a detached padded bar. Mounted upon this tripod, the resister was fully opened to intrusion: his cheeks were spread wide by the distance between his knee mounts, and his pink net bag dangled freely beneath him. As the music ceased and the scenery darkened, the comforting mask was removed.

The resister, now helpless to either move or utter a word, was left in this submissive position until a parade of Golds entered the program room and stood facing his upturned eyes.

The Mistress entered silently and stood in front of the line of muscular and tanned Golds. She viewed the resister up and down, touched, fondled, and stroked him from below and from behind, and finally she returned to her forward position.

"You will be trained," she spoke calmly and with the assurance of experience, "and you will desire it with a burning passion." She turned toward the Golds and ordered quietly, "Begin."

The pink net bag dropped from its magnetic berth and a three-sided box whose fourth side contained a circular opening was attached to cover his penis and testicles and adhere magnetically to the ring. Without warning, the insides of the box contracted and formed snugly around his organs and began dispensing gentle pressure in an up and down motion that astonished the organ's owner. He felt an intense erection starting and he was gripped with fear of punishment for unordered engorgement. The Golds smiled at his dilemma.

"Pleasure and pain," the Mistress offered. "This is the program. You may have pleasure when I allow it; and pain when you resist me. It's very simple." Then she added, "And it's entirely up to you."

She looked at the Gold behind her and she grabbed and pulled him by his surprisingly large male organs to a front-line position. He stumbled awkwardly at her unpredictable urging and followed her to a point where he stood dramatically in front of and slightly above the man's face.

"Do you want pleasure or pain?" he asked the manacled trainee.

"Pleasure," the man barked with an audacity that resulted in the rest of the Golds, as a group, rolling their eyes upward with silent assurance of the eventual outcome.

"Then pleasure it is," the Gold remarked casually, and nodded toward the Blue standing at a wall panel of switches and dials. The stroking and massaging of his maleness increased until the resister joined in his delight and soon was unable to control his hip thrusting and eagerness for completion.

"Pain," spoke the Mistress simply to the overseeing Gold.

Suddenly the trainee's organs were gripped in an intense crushing administered by the strange box that was accompanied by the sound of a wooden crop stroked several times very briskly across his exposed buttocks. The combination of crushing and whipping was executed before the man could react with a crazed bellowing that filled the otherwise silent room. His engorgement necessitating orgasm was immediately replaced by a suddenly flaccid and abused member and a stinging, reddened, and welting backside. Tears flowed uncontrollably from his eyes as his voice screamed for cessation of the torture.

"Pleasure or pain?" queried the Gold without mercy.

Unable to form a coherent answer, the screaming man attempted to voice the single word that would end his flagellation. The Gold waited in absolute stillness and the Mistress glanced at the line of Golds who witnessed the program's administration.

"Pl. . . pleas. . . ." he attempted a single word but could not withstand the agony being inflicted on his most private and personal organs.

The whipping continued mercilessly as the crushing of his testicles and penis proceeded without pause. The Golds remained immobile as the man's tripod position afforded him no opportunity for movement or escape from the agony inflicted by the device magnetically attached to his most intimate personhood or the whip that cracked incessantly across his reddening buttocks.

With a gasp and a concomitant moan, he whined a grotesque and tearful, "Pleasurrrr. . ." and the persecution was replaced with the soothing caress of an unseen Gold applying scented oils to his welted buttocks and the immediate re-administration of the provocative massaging of his manly organs. Breathing deeply and trying to maintain lucidity, the man tried to relax in his confusion to enjoy the moment of sexual pleasure he was now allowed.

As soon as she was assured he was relaxed and enjoying the magnetic device, the Mistress stepped forward. Before she could ask the dreaded question another time, the man pleaded, "No! No! I only want pleasure! Please stop the pain! Don't allow the pain!" Shrieking, the trainee continued to plead with his Mistress.

She smiled and looked at the Blue who dutifully marked down the time. "That was simple, wasn't it?" she asked politely, as if addressing a recalcitrant child. "Pleasure is better than pain. Comply with the training and you will receive pleasure. Resist and I offer you immediate pain. The choice is and always will be yours." She was right, he realized, the choice would be his and he would exercise his option continuously to receive the pleasure even if it meant a prior experience of pain.

The man breathed deeply and calmly now and his entire body gave in to the experience of impending orgasm he was approaching. The box-like device seemed to have a mind of its own and it knowingly caressed him in a unique manner that he had rarely experienced with any human partner. The unending manipulation of his sexual organs drove him to greater and greater heights, and he could barely contain his glee at the novelty of the mechanical masturbation activity he was enjoying. He thrust his hips as far as his precarious position allowed. The uncertainty of his balance only served to add to his heightening sexual pleasure. He closed his eyes and gave in to the totality of the experience and as the box completed its work, he emptied himself with a force unknown in his recent sexual history. Completed and exhausted, the trainee managed a small smile that drew smirks of recognition from the assembled onlookers who were intimately familiar with the experience. The Mistress exited the room of pleasure and pain, the smirking Golds followed, and the again-successful Blues began wrapping up the remains of this now-broken trainee.

"Not bad," one whispered, "he was easy."

As he was led from the program room and returned to the training room, he noticed Ron's first partner being led to the same door from which he just exited. He smiled at the man and wondered how long he would take to realize how to conduct himself in the training process.

Not realizing either the extent or results of the man's ordeal in the program room, Ron gingerly planted his feet and reached for the handgrips to begin his receipt of the insertion ritual practice with his new partner. With extreme effort, physical concentration, and a sigh of resignation, Ron tried to relax his own buttocks and internal muscles to allow the man easier entry to his deepest region to practice lubrication and achieve avoidance of punishment for them both. Unbeknownst to Ron, the newly programmed trainee was more than eager to please his Green and all the Blues and Whites in attendance than he was to give Ron any semblance of delight. Reaching deep inside the new jar of pink cream, the man pulled two fingers full out and inserted them without hesitation or embarrassment into Ron's darkest and most personal region with a force and intensity that caused the standing man's knees to sag and a sudden gasp emerge from his lips.

Working furiously in an effort to please his superiors with

his new-found willingness, talent, and speed, and to receive more pleasure from the box-like gadget with which he was now both familiar and eager to repeat with assistance and approval from the overlooking trainers, the man circled every millimeter of Ron's insides with a force and severity that astonished the recipient. Fighting the urge as his bowels strived to relieve themselves of the offense, Ron involuntarily tightened his buttocks, a reflex that drew a severe stinging open-handed slap on his behind from Green; a sound Ron knew that echoed resoundingly throughout the tiered training chamber. Fingers roughly withdrawn from the maligned orifice, the kneeling trainee reapplied more pink cream to the canal leading to Ron's depths, and drew a circle between his stretched out cheeks signifying completion of this first part of the insertion routine. Kneeling back on his haunches, his most private organs fully exposed to Green as well as to all who watched the procedure, the trainee looked up for approval and received a tender patting by Green on his reattached pink net bag. Ron received a firm spank on his lubricated cheeks from the forcefully driven hand of his trainer.

Gazing up at the Mistress surrounded by her Golds, the trainee sought confirmation of his improved attitude and momentarily empathized with the plight of the earlier-rebuked Gold. He vowed silently that this training could give him ultimate pleasure such as he had never experienced and he intended to receive every positive sexual favor he could gather during his stay. To that end, he swore, he would become the best, most inventive, and most eager trainee they had ever trained.

At the conclusion of the session, each trainee was inspected by his Green, then by a Blue, and finally by a White. When all were pleased with the internal lubrication and satisfied that the visible circle was well-drawn, each man was moved to a central viewing station and placed under a spotlight. The overlooking superiors gazed intently at the handiwork before raising the platform on which each stood to a height at which the Mistress could first inspect and then either approve or disapprove each training team's effort. The first trainee to be raised was a man Ron had seen at his breakfast table, a golden-haired swimmer who ate only fruit and drank coffee and what seemed like gallons of juice. The lack of wisdom of that choice would soon become apparent.

When the platform reached its full height and the Mistress leaned forward to perform inspection, she prodded his rectum with an elongated wide spoke, moved it in circles as well as in and out, and withdrew it suddenly to test his reaction. Then the unimaginable happened. The poor man's rectum, swollen with fruit, juice, and coffee, emptied itself onto his legs and his platform, splashed his Green, and mortified the regal swimmer in the spotlight.

The Mistress sat back in sudden horror and admonished the Green as well as the trainee with full constriction of their net bags. Their quick depositing to floor level was greeted with many-colored workers who cleansed the entire area with disinfectant and deodorizer and ushered the writhing, screaming trainer and his trainee directly out of the auditorium.

When Ron was raised on the platform with his Green, the latter first bent Ron completely in half, exposed his backside to the Mistress' full view, ungraciously spread the bent-over trainee's buttocks, and adjusted the spotlight to concentrate on his anal region for the Mistress' observation. With a wide and surprisingly cold metal stick that Ron could fully feel but not see from his exposed position, the Mistress plunged the tool deep into his rectum, spun the rod, moved it up and down, and withdrew it with a force that sent shivers down his trembling legs. He tried to breathe and was intent on controlling his sphincter to avoid embarrassment at all costs. His Green tensed, waiting for the horrible to happen. The two were physically and mentally relieved when she waved her hand, an indication of approval, and their net bags began slow contractions and gave undulations of pure pleasure to the two men's testicles and members. The ride down was pleasurable.

Ron remembered the pleasure and vowed to receive it whenever he could.

As Ron stepped from the platform and was released from his half-bent position, he looked at the next to be brought up, his partner, the man who had just maligned his rectum with such zeal and glee, and he noticed for the first time since the transgressor's program was administered, that this formerly reluctant trainee was more cooperative and eager than ever. There was an identifiable zeal he exuded, and Ron wasn't sure if having him assigned as his partner was a positive or negative omen for the duration of the training. Glaring up at the rising platform, Ron vacillated between enjoying the sexual pleasure of his undulating net bag and watching incredulously as the man bent completely over before he was positioned by his Green and then grabbed his own cheeks in well-oiled hands and spread them farther apart than Ron thought humanly possible.

He could not help but notice the smile on the Mistress' face and the smirks from the Whites and Blues on the upper levels. Most bewildering of all, Ron thought, was the look of pure jealously on the otherwise handsome face of the previously punished Gold who stood silent in his castigation next to his Mistress on the uppermost level.

Chapter Eleven

It was very difficult for Debbie to concentrate at work that Thursday. The thrill of the scenes she had watched of Ron's training, coupled with the Gold in absolute attendance of her every need, coursed through her brain and interrupted her concentration several times during her presentation to the Board. She struggled to remember to make frequent eye contact, but instead of seeing their eyes, Debbie could only imagine each man sitting at the great conference table totally naked except for a brightly colored net bag securing his genitals. She also fondled the leather bracelet absentmindedly once or twice during the lecture, even though it was hidden beneath the long sleeve of her red jacket. Although she was distracted by her enthusiasm, her presentation was distinguished by a new eagerness and confidence that bespoke her excitement regarding the closed-circuit show she had seen earlier during Ron's training. Her next appointment to view his training was set for tomorrow, and Debbie wished the remainder of the work-day away in her newly discovered arousal over Ron.

When the meeting broke up and the attendees congratulated Debbie on her optimistic forecast for the next fiscal period, she returned to her office to find the quiet she required to visualize the training Ron was receiving at the facility while she was busy making financial forecasts for the Board of Directors. Sinking slowly into her leather swivel chair, she leaned back, spread her legs, and savored the daydreams she was reliving of the show brought to her by the Gold. He was scheduled to be returned to her this evening for discussion and review of procedures to be used when Ron returned and her rising excitement, invisible to those who worked around her, was clear to herself as her nipples stood erect by themselves from the open-cupped bra under the black silk blouse she was wearing, a bright blue one sent by the facility to match the other lingerie they supplied for her sampling during the length of Ron's stay.

Her ample bosom filled the cups adequately, and shiny satin fabric tingled against her clear white skin. The blue garter belt and black silk hose were a new addition to her usual wardrobe of confining light-support panty hose, but the crowning touch was the pair of matching open crotch panties included in the Thursday package. Opening one package per morning was a delight for Debbie; a moment truly worth waking up for.

When she put her key into the lock of her front door, Debbie was apprehensive about the Gold's activities in her home in her absence. Tonight, she realized, was the "discussion" he mentioned that would enable her to recognize and deal with her newly trained husband in a novel and unique fashion. The testimonies of satisfied customers with whom she had talked prior to enrolling Ron convinced her that this experience would cause a gigantic change in their lives, a change that each woman spoke of in glowing, if not almost sacred terms. Both frightened and eager, Debbie entered her own home, a place that felt slightly foreign but comfortable, and bolted the door shut behind her.

Gold was not in her immediate sight, but Debbie could both smell and feel his presence. The man who carried her and Ron's sexual future in his muscular hands had made his mark upon their home, and she anticipated locating him waiting attentively for her, waiting for her timing, her convenience, her pleasure. And the thought of that--her own power of timing and control--greatly excited her. Setting down her purse and briefcase with a small thud by the coat tree in the foyer, Debbie noticed the bedroom light on, a small illumination, probably from the bedside lamp.

Her heels made an echoing clicking sound on the hardwood as the confident executive strode directly toward the master suite. The extra-wide bed was sumptuously decorated with satin sheets, a down comforter, and too many extra shams and pillows, as Ron always complained. The small glow from the reading lamp was quickly extinguished and revealed a candlelit wonderment of dancing, sparkling lights that gleamed on the shiny satin. Gold knelt silently next to her bed and awaited her entry.

He stood upon her arrival and helped her off with her jacket then moved to help her with her skirt zipper and button. Her blouse was next to be removed in this silent strip tease, and she finally stood revealed in the blue satin lingerie and black silk stockings supplied to her for that day's activities. Her pale skin reflected a creamy color from the glow of the dancing candlelight as she remained immobile in the center of the spacious room, her eyes shut, her mind waiting to proceed with the discussion. The Gold knelt at her feet, silent and bronze, the oil from his skin glistening in the dancing candlelight.

She opened her eyes slowly from her reverie to digest the scene one flavor at a time. She noticed a gorgeous man at her feet, she in her blue satin lingerie, and a long, thin package offered to her from his outstretched hands. Taking the gift-wrapped box in her red-manicured fingers, she flipped off the top, unwrapped the tissue, and discovered a gleaming leather crop with one end feathered with loose straps of dark leather and a firm, wide handle decorating the other. Holding it tightly by the bulbous handle, Debbie swished the crop through the air, took in the hissing noise with her avid ears, and allowed her skin to raise its goose flesh in her excitement and arousal. Her exhilaration was barely containable.

Gold gazed up at the woman in blue satin as she slashed her new whip through the air and beheld its noise while her body became physically aroused.

Good, he thought, the discussion can begin. Standing up slowly and with great respect for her continuing practice with the crop, Gold approached his superior and offered, "You will be expected to use this. Let me help you learn its many possibilities."

Debbie emerged from her trance, silenced the whip, and

looked up and down at her Gold instructor's rippling body. "Show me," she breathed heavily.

Gold bent over, his backside revealed to the satin-clad woman, and used his long, muscular arm to illustrate the most sensitive points of his own buttocks, thighs, and genitals that would reap pain or excitement from receiving the whip's strokes. He carefully instructed Debbie as to which areas, when whipped, Ron would perceive as punishment, and which would be felt more as pleasure. Guiding her hand that was wrapped tightly around the whip's handle, he encouraged her to whip alternately hard and soft; he showed her how to tease his genitals with the leather strips of fringe; and he illustrated just how authoritatively to stand when administering this device to her husband-in-training.

Debbie took the instruction very well, asked a few insightful questions, and showed expertise in her handling of the new toy. Gold was pleased with her progress. Every time she struck him with authority and preciseness and raised welts on his buttocks, thighs, and back, he rewarded her with kisses on the hand that held the whip. The lesson continued for a very long time, until Debbie no longer needed the guiding hand for strength or accuracy and until the Gold pronounced her, "capable."

"If you would like to become more comfortable, we can watch his training continue," Gold offered as his charge nodded up and down forcefully in her titillation.

Debbie strode immediately to the bedside where Gold rushed to pull back the covers for her.

She sank deliciously into the cool satin that soothed the excitement of her burning skin and positioned herself to gain a clear view of the television on the bookshelves across the room. Gold adjusted the picture and the speakers and retreated to her bedside where he knelt on the carpet as he narrated the training process they were witnessing.

"Ron has been assigned to a group in which the skills to be learned include a significant portion of the training. Up until now, he has learned two very important traits: submission and obedience. Ron will submit to any activity asked of him and he will accomplish it quickly and without question." Gold watched

Debbie's reaction to his pronouncement. When she imagined her husband as a totally obedient slave, Debbie's inner self trembled with delight. Witnessing her slight shudder, Gold inwardly smiled.

"However, the training insists that this is not enough," he continued. "All trained graduates must desire the sexual experience and initiate it for their partners. It is not enough that they simply obey your whims; rather, the critical issue is their invention of sexual scenarios and the bringing of excitement to your relationship. The portion we are viewing now may be considered the innovative experience. Please watch." She drank in his words.

Debbie leaned farther back into her pillows and did just as Gold requested. She watched Ron's group being ushered into a furnished room that could have passed as a den or family room in many homes. The group's leaders consisted of a White, a Blue, as well as a Green, all of whom had specific tasks in this training segment. White spoke to the men about bringing excitement to their own as well as to their partners' lives, and Blue discussed the fine art of planning novelty and titillation. The group viewed videos of successful trainees' performances and finally the voice on the intercom announced, "Time. Please begin."

The assembled men were led out of the room and into a large closet equipped with costumes of every imaginable design. Multiple sizes of different outfits filled the racks in the center of the room and the walls were adorned with all possible accoutrements. Pink frill was abundant next to gold taffeta; white and ivory lace bedecked one rack while every imaginable color of sequins filled yet another. The maze of costumed clothing continued the entire length of the huge closet. The group was given its task: each member was to dress up in a provocative outfit that would excite his partner at home, and devise a scenario that would be suitable for greeting his partner when she arrived home in the evening from work.

The men were further instructed that arriving home before one's partner was an essential aspect of a novel relationship and care must be taken to ensure the process's success. Their lesson stressed that careful planning and arranging were critical to their innovative talents regarding this endeavor. Each scenario proposed and acted out by each trainee would be evaluated. The best scenarios would be approved and disallowed ideas would be rejected, modified, recreated, and perfected. Every man had to devise a fitting, approved program of an evening's entertainment for his partner. The increasingly well-trained men did not question the task nor did they wonder who their judges would be. There were no questions about the consequence of disapproval, either.

Gold interrupted Debbie's viewing the video program as the men milled about the room, inspecting costumes. "Each man must devise at least five "welcomes" for his partner in order to graduate from the program. He is free to choose any costume and supplies to enhance his plan. Tonight we will watch Ron's group's first attempts. Favorable attempts will be rewarded with pleasure. Disallowed or boring scenarios are rewarded with pain." Debbie stared at his face with a questioning look. Gold continued.

"You will watch Ron's progress and determine his success with your bracelet. Please use the green button for approval and his receiving pleasure. The purple button is for disapproval and pain. Use great care because if you approve a design that does not please you, you will not reap the full benefits of the program. Only approve a design that you imagine will fulfill your desires." His directions were clear and sparing. Debbie massaged the colored stones that decorated her wrist.

The Gold added more cautionary information. "If he chooses a costume that you do not believe will excite you, press the purple stone once. He will know immediately that he has made a poor choice. When he has chosen the outfit you prefer, push the green stone once. He will receive acknowledgement of your approval. Use your imagination. The program must be tailored perfectly for the two of you." Debbie absorbed his directions like a sponge. Green buttons. . . purple buttons. . . her mind was ablaze with the thrill of her power.

Gold quietly raised Debbie's arm from underneath the covers and exposed her fingers massaging her bracelet. He reminded her about its functions and added a further inducement for her edification, "The purple button is for pain. If Ron chooses unwisely, he and I both will be punished."

He placed Debbie's braceleted wrist on her midsection and offered, "I am trained to maintain your excitement throughout this process. When I fail to please you, please punish me." Her warm lower lips tingled with the thrill of her strength.

As if in reaction to her sudden realization, Debbie's nipples stood hard and on edge under the satin sheets while Ron and the others walked through the closet and touched, lifted, and inspected first one costume and then another. Her husband picked up one slinky black dress off the rack, looked it over, silently rejected and replaced it. He moved slowly and with careful attention from the lacy and frilly section to the leather, from the glitter and sequined outfits toward the display of skin-tight leotards. He was totally absorbed in the process of decision as, in his own home and on his own bed, Gold gently massaged Debbie's toes and feet. As Gold rubbed moisturizing cream on her legs and continued toward her thighs, Ron held out a set of leather straps aloft as in victory and looked at his Green.

The trainer took the straps from the hanger and fitted them on Ron. Grasping his limp member roughly and moving him toward the mirror and a complete view for the video camera, Green afforded the unseen Debbie a better view of her husband's selection. She gazed in wonder at the screen. Her husband was gleamingly oiled and clothed in a leather harness around his broad shoulders and chest. The straps continued down his torso and ended in buckled ankle restraints, with a short chain connecting his legs. The entire costume left his genital area as well as his backside totally uncovered and available. Finally, a collar of studded leather was buckled around his neck. Sleek as a stallion, he was a fully harnessed wonder, gleaming in the spotlights, but seemed uncomfortable, confined, and too covered up in the get-up. Debbie frowned, a frown that sent a small shiver of fear through Gold at his stolen glimpse of the satin-clad lady watching television as he aroused her for her husband. Her finger hovered over the bracelet but paused.

"How do I tell him that leather is O. K. , but I don't like that one?" she asked her masseuse.

"The purple stone indicates that you do not approve," Gold responded in a matter-of-fact tone. She pressed the purple stone once.

Both Ron and the Gold suddenly grabbed their genitals and doubled over in pain. Simultaneous shrieking emerged from the television and from her bed as the button Debbie pressed dispatched official disapproval to her two well-trained men. She delighted in the quickness of the message and she gently rubbed the purple stone against her now-erect nipple.

As quickly as the moment happened, the pain subsided and the men righted themselves again. Gold recovered, thanked Debbie for signaling her displeasure, and his trembling arms continued massaging Debbie's legs, this time concentrating on her right thigh. With her gaze carefully intent on the large screen, she silently urged Ron toward the frilly, lacy costumes. Things she could never tell him in words she urged at him silently and telepathically, hoping he would guess her secret desires. Gold moved toward her left leg, careful not to interrupt her view, as Ron positioned himself in front of the rack of sequins and shining outfits. Oh well, Debbie thought, he'll have five of them. Might as well have one that glitters.

Ron touched the fabric of several vibrantly hued costumes before finally settling on a deep purple outfit that he held approvingly aloft for his Green. Again Green grabbed the trainee by his most sensitive organs and walked him back to the fitting station. Green adjusted Ron's choice on his tanned body: a sequin-covered leather collar, glittery crisscrossing chest straps, and a shining leather belt with hooks and rings. Standing with his feet at shoulder width and his hands on his hips in the bath of the spotlight as he had been instructed, Ron appeared to Debbie as an image of a sexual circus fantasy and she was eager to approve. She pushed the green stone once and waited for his reaction.

Both Ron and Gold paused instantly in awe of the newly discovered function of the net bag he and the Gold wore. The tensile wires of the bags constricted mildly and formed perfectly fitted pouches encircling the men's sensitive organs. Slowly squeezing up and down, in and out, a perfect massaging of their maleness was the reward Debbie had given them for his pleasing choice. Ron closed his eyes to enjoy the fantastic and unexpected pleasure of the moment while Gold knelt back on the bed between her legs where he had just exhibited the contortions of his pain and exposed himself to Debbie so she could view him enjoy his pleasure. She watched them both with careful scrutiny and learned to value the power of her bracelet.

The men remained immobile in their passive acceptance of the reward she had given them. After several moments the sensual activity ceased and they both returned to the physical world and moved along in the training of her husband in the perfection of his first "welcome" scenario.

Ron's group had chosen an intriguing assortment of possible costumes. Debbie's pleasure in imagining her husband's scenario was heightened by watching the choices made by the other men. Some of the ideas they came up with were absolutely incredible to Debbie and she never would have approved them for herself and Ron. They deserved instant pain, she pondered, and wondered about their partners. Who would have approved that short flaxen-haired one's choice of a long, slinky black dress with slits up to the tush? And those spiked heels? They must have been at least five inches high--how was he going to perform anything for her while wearing those things on his feet? The boa was a nice touch, she conceded, but the wig? And that sandy-haired tall one's choice of a French maid's costume! Debbie looked him over carefully. There was a vacant look about his face and he was concentrating very hard on something, someone, or somewhere else. He was truly remarkably attired in his little flounced black skirt, garter belt and silk stockings; tall black high-heeled shoes that still enabled him to walk; and somehow he had chosen a false, but perfect replica of a bosom that fit nicely inside the ruffled elastic top. He was chic enough to pull the shoulders down so a little fake cleavage was exposed and the sweet little hat on his head was a nice touch. His partner could have some interesting options for their pleasure and a French maid seemed a possible choice for another of Ron's "welcomes." She would have to think about that.

The men were then lined up in front of the trainers who supervised this activity. The instructions were brief and clear. Each man would be given an individual chance to perform his "welcome" on a woman who would enter the empty room. The man could use any prop, accoutrement, or article from the storeroom to entice the woman.

The trainers carefully explained the evaluation procedure. Each man would be successful only when the female trainer was sufficiently aroused by his performance that she agreed to use the whip similar to the one that Debbie had just mastered and to strike the trainee with force enough on his backside to raise welts. The woman, the trainers further explained, never knew from episode to episode just what the mark of success was. That way, she could never be influenced by prior encounters and each performance would be judged solely on its merits.

The trainees were led out of the room into a holding area in which they would later receive either the pleasure or pain their trainers could inflict after witnessing the performance on the video. They sat down to watch their comrades performances. The Green neglected to mention Debbie's control over Ron at this point in his training. Perhaps it was just as well, she thought, to have him think she didn't know what he was doing. She watched the process with an intensity that Gold had rarely witnessed in a spouse so early in the training.

Debbie readjusted herself to witness each performance. As she tried to push herself upward, Gold's hold on her upper thigh touched a sensitive spot and her leg jerked reflexively upward. Gold was appalled that he had hurt her or caused her displeasure.

"Punish me," he pleaded, "please, I deserve to be punished."

Debbie shook her head negatively and mentioned in an offhand manner, "No, not this time. It wasn't really your fault."

Gold was beside himself with remorse and shame. He whimpered, "Please, please punish me," as he lifted his six-foot body from her bed and stood at her bedside, waiting for the worst.

She gazed at him, shook her head again, and continued to watch the screen. The man could take no more.

Standing humbled at her side he cried in shame. "You must punish me!" he fairly screamed at her. "No one has ever refused to give me the gift of punishment! Please, please, I must be punished or I can never again wear the colors of the Gold. Don't let this happen to me. . . I worked so hard to get to this level." His whimpering bothered her ears.

Debbie watched the quivering man carefully, moving her gaze up and down his naked body, and reached out with her braceleted arm, grasped his penis firmly, and pulled his entire body closer to her bedside. She sat up, still holding his rapidly engorging member, and yanked adamantly straight down. With a gasp, the Gold was forced into kneeling on the floor with his face positioned directly in front of hers.

She said to him quietly but intently, "When I am ready I will punish you."

And with those words she again yanked his stiffening shaft directly upwards, standing up as she pulled him up with every intention of raising him to a height beyond the limit of the length of his fully erect member, and in his surprise and distraction, she took up the whip in whose use he had so recently given her instruction.

Still hanging on with great force to his fully erect organ, she pulled him down violently at an angle toward the floor, bent the muscular man almost in half, and kicked once between his straining legs. He immediately parted his feet to a wider berth and she sarcastically remarked, "Now, punish yourself. Pull hard on your own organs until I tell you to stop. If you do not obey, I will whip you until your organs either bleed or bloody well fall off! Now shut up while I watch this."

And Debbie positioned herself again on the satin sheets to watch television as the totally obedient doubled-over Gold tugged on his own penis, grunted with pain, and pulled again, repeating the performance for the duration of the first scenario presented by the short man costumed in the black evening gown and stiletto heels. The rather unimaginative performance on the television was interrupted only by grunts and whimpering from the Gold who continually pulled his member to a point of pain, cried out from that very pulling, and then composed himself enough to pull it again. Debbie kept one eye on the contorting Gold and again relished in the thought of her power.

When the short man in the long black dress was given tips and hints to make a very sensual performance for his partner, he was dutifully whipped by his female companion and was summarily removed to the holding area for pleasure administered by that same unseen partner. During a pause in the screen's activities, Debbie sat up and with her crop swatted Gold once casually on his backside. He never stopped the pulling and paining of himself she had ordered. She struck harder and a single welt began to rise on his sweating buttocks. "Turn toward me," she said, and the great groaning and bent-over man turned toward her to afford her a better view of his self-punishing routine until she ordered, "Stop." He ceased his pulling and fell panting to his knees on the carpet by her bedside.

"Thank you for my punishment," he said to the startled blue-clad woman lying on the satin sheets in the middle of the large bed.

She sat up and turned toward him, whispering into his sweating head that she cradled in her milky white braceleted arm and into his ear, "Bring me almost to arousal." And she laid back, kicked the covers off, and spread-eagled herself in the center of the bed. He stood up quickly, climbed between her legs, rested on all fours, and began licking, biting, caressing, and sucking on every part of her body to bring her almost to the point of orgasm, all the while being very careful never to allow his shoulder to block her view of the screen.

She closed her eyes and imagined Ron on top of her, and when she felt ready to explode with pleasure brought by his well-trained lips, tongue, and fingers, she pressed the purple button one short time. Readjusting herself in the plush bedcovers, she watched the great man writhe between her legs, scream at the intensity of the pain she inflicted on him, and moan incomprehensibly between her legs on the satin sheets. When the episode ended, she pointed for him to kneel beside her on the floor, his head resting near her bracelet on the arm lying casually on the satin sheets by her side. He kissed the purple stone and breathed heavily for control as she continued to watch the scenes playing out before her on the television.

Chapter Twelve

Ron's odyssey that evening into the production of a satisfying "welcome" for his wife's return from work was a mixture of hard work, creative ideas, and raw animal sexuality that startled him with its intensity and drama. Having witnessed the work of all five of his comrades and having been sufficiently aroused to feel the stirrings of throbbing in his deepest sexuality, he hungered for his turn at creating a perfect scenario for him and Debbie to share. He had seen men greet partners at the door and perform incomprehensible positions with them, and he witnessed teasing games of lust that dragged on and on in their cat-and-mouse routines. Ron wanted to surpass those efforts in his creation of a program of total submission and obedience to another's will; after all, he mused, that was the purpose of the program and that must be what Debbie wanted. The only shock he experienced was the imaginative invention of his partner from earlier in the day, the man whose manner and attitude had undergone so great a revolution after his disobedience had been punished that afternoon.

That man's acted-out experience proved startling and revealing to Ron. In his eagerness to create a scene that would please his partner and bring the promised pleasure to his most sensitive organ, the man's greediness for pleasure overcame his common sense and especially his timing. In his French maid's costume, he urged the woman trainer to order him to actions of absolute cleanliness about the comfortable setting in which the two were paired. He encouraged her through his actions to force him to bend and clean corners and bottoms of furniture, activities that were designed to expose his backside to her waiting whip.

When she withheld the desired whip from his buttocks, he prompted her with machinations designed to provide her ample opportunity to grace his cheeks with the leather rod. Occasionally he dropped his cleaning tools, actions that forced him to bend completely down or even kneel to gather them in again. He exposed his behind so much that Ron almost forgot what his face looked like. During the course of the routine, he consistently spread his legs farther and farther apart until his testicles and penis hung down in their sack like a great dog's and the entire group wanted to reach out in unison and grab the offending organs until the man screamed for mercy.

Insistent on obtaining the pleasure for himself, he allowed himself too much exertion into sexual role-playing and caused his penis to fill beyond its limit. Before they could punish him for having an unordered erection, he exploded beyond the confines of his net bag and came all over his partner and himself. Grousing Greens huddled him into the holding area and administered the punishment themselves to the near-hysterical man. Then they insisted that the humiliated trainee whip himself repeatedly to raise the welts needed for administration of the pleasure.

The most shocking part of the whole scene was that even in his punishment, the trainee was eager to punish himself by flagellating himself directly on his most sensitive organs when he had difficulty reaching his own backside with the whip. Watching him perform contortions that almost created a sort of dance in a macabre ritual with the whip in one hand and his other reaching out to pull his buttocks closer, Ron shuddered inwardly at the man's horrifying persistence. Finally in exhaustion and pity, the Greens refined the French maid routine for him and had him act it out. Only then was he eligible for the pleasure, a joy he barely experienced from having spent himself only a few minutes earlier. The pleasure, in fact, was a further frustration for the depleted man, because he knew its potential but could not experience it in his dismal condition. Instead of enjoying the administration of the massaging, the hulk of man sat slumped in his chair and sobbed.

The Greens then finally pointed at Ron. For his turn, the lawyer-turned-trainee took his mental outline and turned it into staged drama. First, he figured, the woman trainer assigned to him needed to recognize the importance of the whip and the place it must be used for approval of the plot and action to be made. When the unsuspecting woman in her role emerged in her business suit through the front door, she discovered Ron kneeling on all fours, his head penitently down between his hands, and his hind quarters raised, open, and pointed directly at her entrance. Facing her straightaway upon entry was the sight of the well-lubricated whip jammed as high up into Ron's lubricated rectum as he could manage.

The Greens nodded unseen approval in the holding room at Ron's unique beginning. In her great satin bed, Debbie placed a milky hand between her thighs and began rubbing herself deep within her femininity at the sight of her husband's prone body with the great whip protruding from his bare backside. Her Gold, recovered enough to recognize the beginning of one of those special "welcome" scenes, tenderly cupped his great hand over hers to help show the woman how to stimulate herself and to bring her full enjoyment to the presentation.

The woman entered farther into the room and placed her purse and briefcase on the floor close to Ron's head. He felt the thud of the planted objects and smelled the leather of the case and purse. The aroma urged him on. Spreading his legs as far as he could without pain, he lifted up from his knees to his feet while maintaining his submissive head-down position on the floor. She stood behind him, grabbed the thin end of the extended whip and pulled slowly out, then pushed in, and out again without dislodging the sacred crop. She turned it half a rotation left, then she revolved it to the right.

Debbie's hand and fingers were flying now in the darkest region of sensation. She felt the hardened clitoris engorge and her thighs rippled with the ascending pleasure. The Gold kissed and nipped at her breasts through the open-cupped silk bra. He kept his large tanned hand over her small white fingers and guided her fervid motions. She could barely keep her hips from lifting off the bed.

Ron swung his hips round and round in slow rhythm with the woman's turning of the whip. He lunged forward and backward with her thrusts and parries. He jerked his lower body up and down as she manipulated the whip that jutted from his rectum. It was as if the rod linked the two partners and the sexual dance would culminate in a unified orgasm. Ron fought to maintain control over his newly excited member. He became fearful of orgasm and vowed never to receive the self-punishment he had seen inflicted on his former partner. Pushing his knees together, he pounded his poor penis between them, resulting in a shock to his system that drove him to his knees with a gasp as it relaxed his stiffened hardness.

Again, the Greens nodded silent admiration. The diligent trainee worked his way up again to standing position and met the woman face-to-face, the whip still sticking out of his anal area. He turned quickly and the whip graced her right side. Spinning quickly the other way, he forced it to graze her left hand. With his deep purple sequined straps shining garish reflections from the spotlights the trainer had carefully positioned, Ron's glow was an eerie profile of a muscular man sporting a strange bull-like tail.

As the woman removed her jacket, Ron bit the buttons from her blouse with animal-like grunting and tugging. Without using his hands at all, his mouth pulled the shirt away from her open-bra and its silkiness fell slowly from her shoulders to the carpet beneath their feet. He sucked her nipples eagerly like a calf at its mother's teat. The elastic waistband on her skirt was no match for his impatient teeth, and the garment fell noiselessly to the carpet at her feet, revealing a woman dressed in revealing lingerie identical to what Debbie wore.

As the Gold pushed Debbie's tingling legs apart and kissed her thighs in an upward motion toward her mound, the woman on the television felt Ron's drooling lips licking up her leg toward the red garter belt she sported. As Ron moved his hungry lips and mouth toward the secrets of her desire with the whip still jutting out from his backside, the woman bent over his kneeling form to reach for the holy rod. In her bedroom, Debbie suddenly grabbed the whip on her bedside and forced the Gold into an upright kneeling position between her legs.

"Stand," she ordered, and when he leapt to an erect position on the bed between her legs, she sent the unlubricated fat handle of her leather whip directly up and into his rectum. He shrieked with surprise as the dry intruder defiled the confines of his inner sanctuary. Unflinching in respect for his total training, the Gold knelt between her legs when she again ordered him into position, kissed her all the way up to her quivering sanctum as she reached over his balled-up body and grabbed the whip's narrow end. She maneuvered him up and down, side to side, and in circles. His entire lower body moved with her pulling, but his mouth never left its business in her readying temple of delight. The lust on the screen approached the eagerness in the bedroom, and both sets of partners brought each other to astonishing climaxes.

Debbie achieved climax in a wash of emotion, still hanging onto the whip protruding from Gold's rectum. In her delight, she barely noticed the woman on the screen tug the bull's tail from its home until it nestled snugly in her grip, and then flail away at her husband's backside, raising envied welts on his gleaming well-oiled buttocks.

When the two women recovered from their delights, Ron was ushered into the holding area and Gold, his penis also hard and ready, reminded Debbie to offer them both the pleasure they deserved. When the Green pulled down the mask of delight and secured it onto Ron's sweating head, Debbie complied by compressing a green colored jewel on her bracelet, and succumbed to the softness of her pillows and satin sheets as she watched Ron enjoy the ultimate luxury of tensile masturbation.

She concentrated on her husband's rising and excited form. His face was hidden by the mask, but his body revealed every moment of pleasure he received from the treatment the pink net offered and as he approached fulfillment, the jealous eyes of his five comrades and those of the observing Greens, White, and Blue had to be satisfied with vicarious enjoyment of his prolonged and deserved orgasm. But, his Green noted with pride, he had earned it.

Debbie's Gold silently allowed himself to experience a similar pleasure, an act that was barely witnessed by the woman at his side. He kissed her sweaty breasts tenderly and covered the consumed and spent woman with the satin sheets and down comforter. Then, with no immediate orders to the contrary, he relaxed on the floor by her braceleted arm and silently experienced the pleasure simultaneously with the creative and innovative attorney.

Chapter Thirteen

Opening Friday's package filled Debbie with lustful delight. Whereas blue had been the color for Thursday, Friday's tone was a lustrous teal fringed with black lace. Carefully bathing and outfitting herself in the greenish costume, Debbie chose her day's wardrobe to conceal the dark tones of her newest lingerie. Finally choosing a dark float dress, Debbie confidently proceeded to her office to complete two appointments before lunch. The day could end early, she hoped, and she would have to speak to her secretary about not arranging late afternoon appointments.

Once she was ensconced within the security of her private office, Debbie sat luxuriously on her leather swivel chair and pressed an intercom button that called her secretary immediately to her side. Having a male secretary had not been Debbie's idea, but the man truly worked out well. He was an excellent typist and took well to the word processors ordered by the Board. Although he and Debbie were both willing to make the morning coffee, he was simply the better brewer of the two, and he willingly and graciously took up this routine chore. Consequently, Debbie always remembered his birthday, his anniversary, his children's and wife's birthdays, and she had been careful to send flowers to his mother when she was admitted to the hospital earlier that year. The two got along well, and his most endearing characteristic was the uncanny ability he had to anticipate her needs. He knew when she would need her printer adjusted and he was on good terms with the important maitre d's in town for expediting lunch and dinner reservations. She never had to correct a thing he did, nor did she ever recall a single time he was unavailable to her demanding schedule.

His entry into her office that fateful Friday marked a new stage in the further development of the close relationship between the two. He handed her the pink message slips and as she reached for them, the long sleeve on her right arm fell back, revealing the leather-jeweled bracelet she wore with pride. His eyes enlarged when he recognized the device, and for the first time since she had met him two years ago, he stammered when he spoke.

"You. . . you. . . have an app. . . appointment at nn. . . nn. . noon," he barely got out.

"Tony," she remarked, "what's the matter? Is something wrong?"

"No," he barely muttered, his eyes unyielding in their gaze at her uncovered wrist, "but is that a new. . . bracelet?" His tone was revealing in his guardedness.

Debbie stared first at her jewelry and then looked directly into the man's wide black eyes. Her mind was flooded with avalanches of explanations and her brain could barely contain the overwhelming realization she just entertained.

She focused on his increased breathing rate, his tense grip on the pink messages, and the small beads of sweat breaking out on his smooth upper lip. She considered her answer carefully.

"Do you like it?" she asked without answering the awestruck younger man. "I recently got this from my husband. What is your favorite color?" She waited patiently and playfully for the almost-hyperventilating man to gather up the courage to answer.

"Black--then green. I like black--then green." He stood nervously but expectantly beside her right arm.

Debbie considered his answer with great care.

If she pressed the combination he mentioned, she was unsure if the results would bring him great pleasure or great pain.

"Lock the door," she advised, and the man fairly jogged across the room to perform the ordered task. "Stand by me," she commanded.

He rushed to comply with her order and she attempted to size up his attitude as her red-manicured finger paused above the jewels on the leather gracing her wrist. As the urgency of his expectation increased, his pace of breathing became more rapid and the sound of his inhaling and exhaling filled the room.

Closing his eyes, he threw his head back, and urged in a throaty voice, "Please."

Debbie pressed the sequence he requested and watched the young man fall to his knees, grasp his crotch with intensity, and moan silently with the pain she had just administered to her obedient secretary. He sobbed and whimpered as he rolled on the floor at her feet, all the while grabbing, holding, and massaging his most private parts through the fabric of his well-tailored suit. When the moment passed, he raised his head slightly, leaned up and kissed her bracelet with eager lips.

"Thank you for my punishment," he offered through his tortured gasps.

Debbie sat back and contemplated the kneeling man's words and the new dimension to their working relationship. Now she had experienced the delight of controlling the pain and pleasure of Ron, her Gold, and most recently, Tony. How many others could she affect? Was she able to send jolts of pain and pleasure by randomly selecting sequences as she walked around her office? As for Tony, was this training he had undergone responsible for his willing attitude and almost perfect skills on the job as her subordinate? The immensity of the situation stunned and excited Debbie as she evaluated the bracelet's ability.

She stared straight into the black eyes of her kneeling secretary and asked, "What is your pleasure?"

"Black--then purple. That gives me pleasure." His lips were dry but his eyes were moist from his tears and sweat.

"Do you want the pleasure?" she innocently inquired. "I would be happy for you to experience pleasure after the pain." She paused for an answer. When none came, she continued as she played with the jeweled bracelet carelessly, "Tony, how long have you been trained?"

Her question seemed to shake him from the intensity of the ordeal he had just experienced. His passionate eyes looked up at his superior and he muttered, "Two years. The best two years. It's made all the difference."

Two years, Debbie mused silently as the young secretary gave her his head to comfort in her willing lap as a child would seek petting from his mother. As she stroked the thick black hair and massaged the tears from his cheeks, her hand reached down toward his neck. Proceeding intensely and slowly, she loosened his tie and opened the top button on his starched white shirt.

He moaned softly when she crept her red nails through his thick chest hair and guided her long white arm toward his heaving stomach.

Rubbing in a rotating motion, he swayed with her soft hand, rolling his hips in a gentle arc with her steering his trembling body. Gently inserting her long nails into the waistband of his tailored suit pants, he gasped audibly as she manipulated the hook above the zipper. Reaching as far as she could, she forced the zipper downward at an excruciatingly slow pace. Her fingers told her what her brain already had guessed; the handsome young man wore no underwear and she was free to roam his most secret places without restriction. At long last her search ended as she discovered the net bag attached to the metal ring securing this special area from prying fingers. She teased him by gently stroking then pulling at his netting attached to his astonishingly hairless pubic region. He tried to rise to a full kneeling position to accommodate her reach, but her caressing arm held his head firmly in her lap. She had him now just where she wanted him, but she wasn't sure just what she wanted to do with him there.

The disheveled recipient of this exploration gave in completely to her wanderings over his body. After discovering his net and ring secrets, she bade him rise and the handsome young secretary moved slowly and carefully to comply with her request. She watched his legs flex apparently well-toned muscles under the straining trouser legs and she marveled at his strong arms through the clear, crisp whiteness of his shirt.

He stood before her, his arms locked behind his back, head down, his posture submissive and at her ready, and Debbie finally concluded that he would wait forever until she gave him further orders. As she watched his tailored trousers slip dangerously low, she relished in the idea of her control over this aspect of his life. Her thoughts about his wife and family jumped quickly to her consciousness and brought her back to the office building in which the two were now enclosed. And she inspected his bald pubis, its shining silver metal ring, and almost transparent net bag surrounding his just-tortured genitals.

"Your wife. . . . Patti?" Debbie asked expectantly.

"Patti enjoys my experiences," he cautiously admitted, "and the more exciting my experiences, the more pleasure she gives me." He stood silent, waiting.

"Then, Tony, you will have many stories to tell and much pleasure to receive from her now that you have shared your secret with me." Tony smiled as he considered the potential of her promise.

"I want to give you pleasure, and I am well-trained," he said distinctly, looking first at her loose fitting dress and then at her dancing eyes. "Please tell me in what ways I can please you most. I am very good," he added.

"I have an appointment," she said, moving her eyes from the muscular body to the calendar on her desk, "and you are in no shape to greet my next client. Look at you!" she chastised mockingly. He hastened to button, tie, and zip himself into an appropriate state of dress. She chuckled at his intensity in re-dressing himself and wondered about how many times and for whom he had done this before. And she wondered about Ron; with whom he would eventually experience mornings like this and how she would feel when he related the stories to her?

Debbie added, "Mr. Fried will arrive shortly.

Show him in. I expect our meeting to last until ten-thirty. Then Grace Lashley will come in for about forty-five minutes. That will take me until lunch. Cancel my noon appointment and bring me lunch in here." Her terse orders were clipped out in a practiced fashion.

Tony scribbled notes on his steno pad, his dark eyes concentrating on her words.

"And Tony, let's not make any appointments after lunch. Be here at one. And be ready." Debbie's eyes went back to the papers on her desk.

She dismissed the startled young man with a flick of her flaming green eyes. Fairly stumbling over his eager feet, Tony ran for the outer office, plopped in the swivel chair at his L-shaped desk, and sobbed silent tears of happiness and gratitude for the gift Patti had given him for his thirtieth birthday two years ago as he heard Debbie call to him from inside her lair, "I'll have you for dessert."

Chapter Fourteen

By the time noon arrived and overtook Debbie's concentration that sunny downtown day, her appetite, a lust she had to purposefully override in its own willfulness, was beginning to get the better of her. Even Grace had commented on her stomach rumblings during their appointment and Debbie had managed to laugh off her cravings with a smile. But when noon finally struck, Debbie was very, very hungry and was in no mood for Tony's delay in obtaining her simple request for in-office lunch.

She knew he was never intentionally late, but the crowd from the busy office often overwhelmed the few satisfactory restaurants in the area. Tony loved to eat as much as he loved to do almost anything else and bringing Debbie lunch meant, of course, that Tony would bring something for himself, too. The two of them often ate together in Debbie's office, usually at the huge conference table. Tony always very mysteriously provided diet sodas and something chocolate and wicked for "dessert." Once he startled his boss with elegantly spread out china on cloth, linen napkins, and crystal goblets for their diet drinks and her "salad in Styrofoam." He was as innovative as he was a pleasure as a dining companion.

A leisurely lunch, however, was not on Debbie's Friday agenda. She anticipated having to work through the noon hour and nibble while reading, an act Tony often sarcastically termed "grazing." As he watched her eat and work, he would often shake his head in mild disapproval and caution that she was not taking the time to enjoy the break from the routine that would serve mainly to energize her spirit as well as feed her body.

She understood more now about Tony and realized that his protectiveness and attentiveness were carefully developed talents that he and his wife had gone to great lengths to secure. His nurturing of her mental and emotional health was the result of a particular training and an attitude that should be cherished, especially in a subordinate. When he finally arrived, panting and sweating from his jog back to the office from the restaurant around the corner, she could hardly maintain her dismay at the time it took for the tall and olive-skinned young man to satisfy her lunch request. But her agitated mind knew that this lunch hour was certain to provide her with more than a simple meal.

Tony bustled in with his packages, one for her and the other apparently for himself. With an upraised eyebrow he asked her a silent question, "Where?" and she replied in equal silence with a flick of her eyes toward the enormous table. He placed the packages on its highly polished surface and unpacked their contents. The aroma of Chinese cooking filled the sunny room and Debbie's hunger increased as her expectations for the afternoon began to crystallize simultaneously with her secretary's arrival. His white shirt clung to his sweating back and clearly outlined his muscular form.

She could hardly help but notice the ripples in his shoulders caused by his reaching across the wide table to set out their food. He smelled right, too. Tony had a unique way of wearing cologne and it suited him perfectly. He never smelled like a bottle of fragrance; rather, it mingled with his hormones and perspiration in a marvelous mixture of elegant aroma. His tiny waist and hips fit his image of a runner and lifter and the beltless pants outlined his lower body with an elegance that only the young and physically fit can manage with ease. Great buns, she thought one more time, tight little ass. Today she had plans for them both.

Tony turned from his culinary duties and waited expectantly for his supervisor to pause from her work and join him at the table. After signing yet another contract approval, she finally put down her pen and looked over toward the still-panting runner.

She rose from the great leather swivel chair with elegance and felt her nipples begin to raise from their unrestricted home to rub pointedly against her flowing dress. Turning her look toward the conference table, Debbie watched the dark hair descend as Tony fell to his knees on the plain brown-carpeted floor.

"Lunch!" she exclaimed. She added with mock disdain, "What took you so long?"

He bent his head in horror and disgrace as he asked, "Did I displease you? The line was very long." Still he knelt silently in deference to his superior.

She laughed, patted his head, and offered him a chair next to hers at the table. Still on his knees, he replied, "May I sit on the floor at your feet?"

Debbie was slightly taken aback. She had thought the two would first eat lunch, and then participate in "dessert" afterward. But Tony apparently had another idea. She thought quickly, then decided to allow him to offer the direction for their afternoon's activities and realize for herself how careful and complete his training had been.

"If you wish," she responded simply and added, "Make yourself comfortable."

With a wide smile of delight, Tony crept to her side and nestled snugly by her ankles. Removing her shoes carefully, he massaged her feet with a delicacy and intensity that both astonished and relaxed the seated woman. He crept under the table and became completely invisible to her eyes but was readily available to her other senses. His strong hands kneaded her calf muscles and her thighs tensed with excitement as his touch climbed upward. Nibbling at her meal with a hunger that suddenly abated, Debbie rested back in her chair and inspected the long, polished conference table that stretched out in front of her.

"Tony, get up and look at this," she ordered as the young man climbed from his hiding place and knelt again at her side. "This table--look at it. It's huge. And it shines like the sun."

From his submissive position, Tony's face lodged several inches higher than the tabletop and he was afforded an amazingly clear picture of the image of the tabletop that appeared to his lowered eyes strangely as a stage or dais of delight. His thoughts raced as he re-imagined and re-worked the drama he had set out to perform with her. She interrupted his deliberations as she rose, walked slowly to the office door, locked it with great care, and made sure they both heard the final click of the cylinder. Turning down the rheostat on her overhead light fixture, she dimmed the glare of fluorescent bulbs and brushed the room in a dim glow. Closing the blinds with a turn of the plastic rod, the office now resembled a darkened studio, a room for both work and play.

Still standing in front of the door, she turned and commanded in a voice that surprised even herself with its authority, "I believe you can do something interesting with the table. Let's see how inventive you are. Just how good is that training?" She sauntered to her desk and sat on its glass-topped corner waiting for the young man to begin.

Rising with both self-assurance and a flush of excitement, Tony stood slowly and with great deliberation, loosened and removed his tie, unbuttoned each button on his crisp white shirt, unhooked the latch on his pants, and pulled the zipper slowly toward its lowest point. Debbie turned only to initiate the radio and provide some background music to break the incredible silence she felt washing over the room and its dreamlike occupants. The clear net bag covering the secretary's most private parts cast a shiny glimmer from deep against his shadowed skin. The metal ring gleamed. Debbie felt a hot flush begin under her dress and rise upward, encompassing her neck in an eerie red blush and resulting in a glow of perspiration rising on her face.

She nodded at the disheveled young secretary and flicked her head back with a "Let's get on with it," message.

Tony rushed to strip the clothes from his body and stood naked and victorious, as if in triumph of his liberation from the confinement of his clothing. As his chest heaved with excited breathing, she ambled toward the pile that had recently been his wardrobe and tenderly and carefully deposited them across a chair, lest they leave telltale wrinkles or creases. Now poised only inches from his aromatic and naked body, she scanned the man up and down, touched the parts that gained her interest, and finally spun her finger in a circle. Tony snapped to position and about-faced with an authority and spark that only served to increase her excitement.

Closing her eyes, she cupped his two firm cheeks each in a soft hand and rubbed, patted, and squeezed the contents until she her massaging hands cried out for relief. In her reverie she stepped back and instructed him, "Pose," and the secretary performed a well-executed series of positions that offered her clear inspection of all his recommending attributes. She marveled at his prowess in both showing himself off to her while provoking her at the same time. Barely concealing her eagerness for his body to perform more for her, she raised her sleeve, bared her arm, and exposed her black-jeweled bracelet. His eyes fixated on the band encircling her wrist and he writhed slowly in expectation.

She reminded him of her earlier consideration. "Can you think of a better use for this huge table than simply having a business meeting?" she asked in a throaty whisper of expectation.

Tony spun and faced the table. Without warning, he jumped on top of its gleaming surface and rendered a unique and exciting dance that was designed for her eyes alone. The music in the background provided him a rhythm that he used and abused for her pleasure. With each extension of his arms and legs, each shift of his torso, every step and flex of his beautiful body, Debbie was astonished at the supple and lithe lines mixed with passion he evoked with his interpretation of the music. Her gaze never shifted from his naked performance upon her conference table; the stage for her lunching offered a new drama of cuisine for the hungry executive.

Tony's arms moved wildly up and down in perfect rhythm with his bouncing invisibly netted genitals. His revolutions atop the table in tempo with the music threatened to spin him completely off the huge surface and Debbie was not sure if Tony would even notice his dislocation if it occurred. His rapture was heavenly and she savored every moment.

Only her tuned ears heard the knock at the door. Tony, in his daze and passion, was overcome with performing to the music and pleasing his superior so he never heard the ominous sound.

Debbie moved with swift motions to shut off the radio and with a brisk gesture, grabbed the driven man's netted genitals in a firm clutch and pulled his undulating body literally back to reality.

Slow to recognize his familiar surroundings, Tony finally realized the potentially dangerous situation. With mounting fear, he jumped from the table, gathered his pile of clothing, and looked helplessly with pleading eyes at his boss. She motioned him silently to a concealed position well under her great desk and, when satisfied he was hidden, she turned toward the door. The only sounds penetrating the room were Tony's panting breaths.

"Just a second," she called absently to the locked portal. "Wait, I was eating."

Debbie unlocked the door with a twist and stood facing two co-workers, men with whom she vaguely recalled a meeting scheduled for the middle of next week. "Bob, Terrance! It's lunchtime. Doesn't a girl get break anymore?"

The two men offered a pair of good-natured laughs and followed Debbie as she returned to her desk chair. Noticing the remnants of lunch on her conference table, Terrance asked, "Do you want to finish that while we talk? It'll get cold if you don't eat it."

Debbie shook her head and pushed herself in the leather swivel chair closer to her desk. Her feet reached out to reassure her that Tony was safely secreted in his place. Her legs finally secured themselves around his sweating and silently panting form and he took hold of her right leg and foot, and placed it squarely on his netted member in an effort to calm her worries about their plight.

Terrance continued, "The contract with Jones Metal is due by Friday next week, and I'd like to go over the two recent clauses the supplier asked for. Look, it's here in my updated copy." He rose, moved toward Debbie, and offered her the papers.

In eagerness to prevent his approaching the closeted secretary's secret lair too closely, Debbie reached out to take the sheets from his outstretched hand and in doing so, revealed the jeweled bracelet that graced her right wrist. Terrance, oblivious to the secrets of the mysterious device, continued his discussion of the added clauses and Debbie made two serious objections and one casual reference to a previous situation that Terrance agreed to research further.

He called over to Bob who was leaning against the front wall of her office and not contributing to the discussion, "Whaddya think? You want to look up Tomlin for the Jones account or should I?"

Two pairs of eyes fixed on the suddenly immobile co-worker. Debbie saw his reaction and at once recognized its importance. The contract became almost meaningless for him as he first saw then recognized the device adorning her arm. In the silence of ignorance, Terrance waited patiently for his colleague to respond.

His eyes bulging, Bob muttered a simple, "You do it." He then stood silent and with profound respect and a new air of submission, his vacant eyes surveyed his female superior.

Terrance, laughing at his friend's awkward brevity replied, "O. K. , you're too busy. But if I find what I think Debbie means, it'll mean that the two of us will be very busy next week. Listen, you two, I'll go try to find it in the data bank, but it could take me an hour or two. Can you two keep busy till I get back?"

Bob deferred silently to Debbie and the woman replied suggestively, "I think I can keep Bob occupied. You go find the Tomlin deal and Bob and I will stay busy here. And I'm going to finish my lunch."

"Bob," she added, turning toward the immobile man, "do you want to stay and have some?" She left the question dangle with its dual edges fully exposed. He nodded in silence as the bustling Terrance left the room.

"Lock it," she said tersely. "Sit."

The stolid man jumped to fulfill her commands. He rested on the edge of the chair as ordered and faced her directly as she stared at his gray suit pants and striped shirt, the leather belt, the highly polished shoes, and the conservatively knotted paisley tie. Wondering what secrets lay beneath this business outfit, Debbie posed only one direct question. "What is your favorite color?" she inquired while her nimble fingers played teasingly with the jewels on her bracelet.

Bob fell into a chair and sat upright, spread his legs apart as his hands gripped firmly on the armrests either for position, or as Debbie conjectured, for support.

"Black," he uttered tersely, "then purple."

Debbie knew what the result would be. He wanted pain from her first before he would allow himself to experience her gift of pleasure. Pain must be considered the well-trained slave's first wish, she quickly surmised and she realized with delight that the "something-then-purple" sequence was the universal pain administrator. It was identical to Tony's pattern and she guessed it might be Ron's potential pattern, too. How many others were out there was the question that filled the endless series of potentialities that flooded her mind.

As she sat comfortably amid the contractor's uneasiness, she chose her words carefully as she pushed her foot harder and more pointedly into Tony's silently receptive organs, and finally said, "Find a comfortable place that will afford me a clear view."

He fairly jumped from the chair and stood in the middle of the brown-carpeted area at the side of her desk.

"Lose the tie. In fact, lose it all." She sat back, played with Tony, and stared at the man silently disrobing.

Bob was an amazingly quick stripper. His clothes soon lay in a pile on the floor near her desk as the now-naked contractor exposed his glistening net bag with pride to his project coordinator. She looked for his specialties: well-toned muscles, tight legs, a somewhat hairy chest that was offset by a strikingly bald pubic area. She motioned with a spinning finger and the male executive revolved slowly for her continued inspection. Great tush, she thought, and fought the urge to rise and grip it as she had experienced Tony's tightness so short a time ago.

Tony! The thought struck her as remarkable and problematic. What would she do with Tony now that Bob was here? Having two of them similarly unattired was an exciting thought, but she was unsure how the one might react to the other. All she needed was jealousy between them, she contemplated. She pushed even more firmly with her bare foot into Tony's penis, signaling him to stay silent and hidden for the duration of Bob's ordeal.

Her finger poised above the black jewel and she teased him as his eye noticed her actions and he tensed every muscle in his still revolving body. She knew that he would continue his slow turning until she ordered him to cease and she watched his lingering spin with admiration and pride. He was very well-trained and she appreciated his efforts to please her.

Finally, when he looked as if he would explode with desire, she called, "Face me," and he stopped, assumed a submissive position of spread feet, slightly bent knees, and head lowered.

"Please, please give me pain," he begged. She obliged him.

By now, Debbie knew what to expect, but the sight of the man falling and writhing slowly and deliberately on carpeted floor still excited her. She watched him grab at his hairless organs, attempt uselessly to massage the pain away, and moan by her feet. His noises were familiar to her ears, yet they brought about an ever-increasing level of anticipation within her deepest regions.

With the pain fading but its memory fully intact, Bob rose to his knees, looked up at her seated form and amazed her with, "Thank you for my punishment."

Her black stockinged foot felt Tony's penis well into its unmistakable ascent. To her amazement, she realized that witnessing Bob's pain, even from his hidden vantage, brought Tony to sexual arousal. Too soon, she thought, it was simply too soon for her plans for the afternoon.

"Stand," she commanded, and the naked man arose and stood before her. The aroma of his masculinity mixed with his after shave provided an infectious fragrance that filled her nostrils with sexual appetite. "Come here," she said quietly as she grabbed the glistening bag in a firm grasp and pulled the sputtering man to within inches of her face.

"Does your wife enjoy your experiences?" she asked. He nodded in quick assent. "Does she give you pleasure when you tell her your stories?" she continued and he responded again in the silent affirmative. "Good," she summarized, "because tonight you will have a good story to tell."

"Tony," she called to the man under her foot, "join us." Bob's mouth dropped open as his self- control wavered momentarily in his shock at her words. She slid her chair backwards as the naked and chagrined secretary emerged from his hidden position.

"Let's see you both," she ordered, and the two stood in identical submissive positions in front of her but surveyed their counterparts with keen gazes. She swiveled to get an optimal look at the naked duo and she relished in her increasing sexual desire. "Who's bigger?" she asked playfully.

The two men hesitated momentarily before turning to face each other squarely. Bob, the shorter of the two, rose to his tiptoes to match his maleness with Tony's and the men attempted to push their organs together so Debbie could compare their relative size. Her excitement grew and grew as the two men struggled to place their sensitive members in direct contact.

"No," she uttered, barely suppressing a giggle, "I mean when you are full. I want to see you both hard and tall, and then I will decide who is bigger. The larger man will receive pleasure." She was quiet as the pair drank in her challenge.

Leaping into action, Tony and Bob began masturbating to increase their male handles to their maximum. Tony worked his palms along his already sweating chest and stomach to gain moisture and then moved down toward his organ. Slapping and pulling on it with alternating hands, Tony's member rose and threatened to strain the netting that housed it.

Bob, having just returned to physical comfort from his odyssey into pain, closed his eyes and tapped his testicles from beneath. Incredibly, his maleness responded to his urging until finally both men stood firmly with hardened members rising upward from the hairless patches of their bodies. Proud and tall, the men remained immobile while Debbie reached for her ruler in the top desk drawer.

Slowly, she turned and wagged with a finger for Tony to step forward. She pulled his testicles from beneath and extended his penis as far as she could onto her flat plastic ruler. She admired his length, then sent him silently back to his position. Motioning toward Bob, she pulled his balls firmly and planted his maleness onto the plastic. She noticed the wetness remaining on the measuring instrument when she silently recorded his size.

Looking up at the two expectant men, she smiled and informed them that one was truly longer than the other and she would eventually reward the better-endowed one.

The men beamed, each confident that his size was the larger. They were not concerned with the absurdity of their situation of standing naked in the office, stripped to masturbate their way to success in the business place; their only thoughts were to please the woman who sat in front of them with the ruler gripped tightly in her hand. She hesitated for a moment, perceived by the expectant men as lasting an eternity. Then she ordered them to kneel at her feet. Raising her bracelet above their heads, she tapped out a series of codes on the colored jewels and watched in rising sexual excitement as the two men fell down and thrashed wildly about the floor, grabbed their aching testicles and organs, massaged themselves and moaned. She exulted in their helplessness and willingness. She delighted in her control. As the pain subsided, she ordered them to their knees.

Looking directly into their sweating and tearful faces, her command was simple. "I do not reward you simply for a moment's pleasure. I prefer a more enlightened and extensive experience."

Her tone was careful yet clear. The kneeling men looked to her for elucidation.

She continued without hesitation, "The game is on, gentlemen. I want to see you each bring the other to complete fulfillment. The one who reaches orgasm first is the. . . loser." Filled with her rising sexual throbbing between her now-aching thighs, Debbie relaxed back in her leather chair and allowed her command to settle into the men's torrid brains.

Closing their eyes in expectation, the two counterparts understood that their mission was clear. Each man was required to bring the other to full orgasm and only then would she be able to determine the greater of the two. They waited patiently for her command to begin and Debbie sat further back in comfort in the great leather chair. Unmoving, they devised mental plans of action. Debbie interrupted their reverie. "Tools. Accoutrements. You may use anything in the room."

She paused for the full effect to sink in. "Begin," she ordered.

Bob dived for Tony's penis. His mouth eager with saliva, he took the hesitating man's member fully in his mouth and pushed the olive-skinned secretary's hands apart with his strong arms. Tony, recovering from the initial attack, pushed his naked behind onto the carpet and reached in with powerful legs to take Bob's glistening net bag between his educated and trained feet. Using his head as a battering ram, Bob drove into Tony, upset the younger man's precarious sitting position and forced him supine onto the carpet. Spinning his torso above the naked secretary, Bob's mouth never left its target as he stood atop Tony's outstretched hands.

Bob's backside, now fully exposed to Debbie's delighted view, was spread wide apart. Exposing his glistening netted members to her full delight, he jeopardized a rear attack, but Tony was helpless beneath the shorter, but stockier man. Sucking wildly and with passion, Bob continued his assault on Tony's most private region. Tony's feet and legs thrashed wildly in an unsuccessful effort to dislodge the contractor's oral grip on his engorging member. Fearing the ultimate embarrassment, Tony bent and yanked one arm loose from the man's well-placed foot and extended a fist upward toward the man's netted private parts. With a thud, he landed an expert blow and the stronger contractor yelped in surprise and pain. Rolling off his prey, Bob rolled his body into a ball in a vain attempt to protect his violated organs.

Tony's retaliation was swift as he grabbed the suffering man's ankles and spread his legs wide. Sinking to cover the man's torso with his own, Tony flattened himself on Bob's chest, his face above the lower man's groin, and fixed his elbows between his knees, forcing his cheeks wide apart. Using two unlubricated fingers, Tony entered Bob's rectum with vigor and Debbie recognized his success when she heard Bob's muffled and anguished cry. Arm muscles flexed and straining, Tony pushed straight up into the agonized contractor's deepest recesses with one well-placed hand, and stroked his rising member with the other. Elbows still firmly planted and forcing his knees to drop to the side, Tony circled his sweating palm around Bob's rising organ and stroked it up and down until it fully engorged with excitement and fluid.

He continued his assault until Bob ceased struggling, dropped his knees apart willingly, and savored the excitement he knew that he was unable to terminate. Moaning softly, Bob laid back, closed his eyes, and thrust his hips slightly in expectation and unrealized assistance to Tony's goal and his own forfeiture. His hands still pursuing their individual targets, Tony became like a wild man in his delirium. The two men rose and fell in a unified rhythm and Debbie savored the drama unfolding on the carpet at her feet. With little warning, Bob shrieked, "Aaahhh. . . . ." and completed his indescribable journey, coming all over himself through the netting of his confinement. Having won the game, Tony rolled off the spent man and shed tears of exhaustion.

Debbie quietly observed the two totally consumed players. Tony lay on his back, his knees raised and apart, and cried tears of joy. Bob, also lying supine, had spread his legs wide and cried in contentment mixed with tears of humiliation and fear. She delighted in their plight and enjoyed the rising tension that she felt in her upper thighs as it moved violently upward and threatened her serene sitting position. She moved her hand to her open-crotched panties and tenderly stroked the moist outer hairs of her deepest femininity. She allowed the men some time and space to collect themselves before she pronounced their sentence.

"That was very nice," she complimented them. "Now get up."

The men rose and stood shaking before her gaze. Reeking of male pleasure, Bob's messy pubic area contrasted sharply with Tony's dry, naked, and erect member.

"Comfort yourself," she advised Tony, "and I will deliver your pleasure."

The exuberant secretary turned and walked over to sit on the placid easy chair in the corner of the room. Bob stared at his better and threw jealous glances in the direction of the younger man's impending deliverance of delight.

Debbie noticed the man's anger but continued, "Your punishment, Bob, is to watch him have his well-deserved pleasure."

Bob looked stricken at her order. Moving her line of sight from the chagrined contractor to the excited young secretary, she uttered the single word, "Enjoy," and pressed Tony's pleasure sequence on her bracelet. He sank back in delight as his net bag constricted to fondle his maleness in tender and expert motions of rapture. Tony began thrusting his hips slightly to increase the sensation as Bob, Debbie noticed, looked on in envy. Too bad, she thought, he should be happy for the man's success.

"Bob," she called to the glaring contractor, "I want you to assist Tony so he can gain a fuller experience. What can you do to help him?" She waited patiently for the angered man to respond to her implied order.

Tensing, the stocky man marched to the open legs of the joyous secretary and put two fingers in his own mouth for lubrication. Placing the now-wet fingers at the entry point of Tony's darkest insides, he pushed gently, almost lovingly, into the man's anal canal. Thrusting the fingers in and out, he repeatedly pulled the electrified secretary almost out of the chair and returned him again with care. Bob saw the culmination begin and added a third finger to his efforts. Tony reached greater heights in his delirium and finally spent himself all over the determined and envious contractor's belly and chest. Dripping from both his own and now Tony's juices, the contractor removed his fingers and turned to face his superior. She motioned him forward and saw the tears of envy and anger spill from his eyes. Truly gushing with a variety of liquids, Bob stood naked and mortified before his controller. She relished in his embarrassment and ordered him to dress himself, then to dress the spent and delighted secretary.

When both men stood clothed and awaiting further orders, she rose from the leather chair and muttered, "I would like to finish, too. Now get out of here so I can get some work done."

The two obediently marched from her office and to their respective stations in the outer office and down the long hall. Closing, then locking the door as they exited, Debbie removed her floating dress, stood transfixed in her teal and black lace, and brought herself to euphoric completion. Only Tony heard the noise that signaled her culmination and he smiled in delight, as if in effort to share her joy. The only thing that could make him happier would have been to bring her to that point himself. Maybe Monday, he thought, but won't Patti be thrilled tonight!

Debbie redressed herself, and alone in her office, nibbled on the cold Chinese lunch still featured at the end of the long conference table. Chewing slowly and deliberately, she thought of Gold, his reaction to her experience, and contemplated the evening's entertainment.

Chapter Fifteen

Friday's schedule within the training facility paralleled Debbie's afternoon as both were filled with incongruity. Expecting finally to see the light at the end of the tunnel of training, Ron instead was offered an unforgettable lesson in the perplexity of the absurd. Green's wakeup call, his removal of the pleasure mask, and his brutal conductance of Ron's morning routine served to roust Ron from his dreamy contemplation and submerge him in the warm waters for what would become a diabolical ritual. After their community bladder relief in the shallow pool, Ron and his comrades were ushered into the great joint bath for their regular external as well as internal cleansing.

Today's routine differed markedly from prior morning's events. Ron could not seem to do anything right, or what was more likely to be the problem, he conjectured, was that the Green was upset about something and was taking out his distress on Ron's own poor rectum and vital organs. First, Green yanked Ron by his newly netted "handle" and virtually flung him into his neck brace for the bath, instead of somewhat gently guiding the flustered attorney to his place. Second, while washing his delicate organs, Green abused the poor straining man with his intense scrubbing instead of his somewhat gentler probing and washing. Finally, when his formerly lubricated anus was rubbed raw from Green's thoroughness, the insertion of the tube that engorged its purifying contents into Ron's well-exercised backside was done without care or concern; rather, Green simply propelled the instrument into the gasping man's behind and launched its contents with violence and urgency. Plugging the orifice with a thumbing that sent Ron's already-gritting jaw into a howl of agony; Green unlocked his neck brace and "handled" the beleaguered trainee into his cubicle for expulsion and final inspection.

Today's rectal inspection was also brutally irregular. After Ron's bursting backside was allowed to dispel its contents, Green virtually lifted the man by his limp netted member and flung him onto the cushioned bars in the tiny cubicle for the trainer's probing and scrutiny. He positioned Ron with his belly on the cushioned bar but this time twisted a heretofore unseen handle. When the bar was released and Green pulled up and away, the trainee's feet dangled precariously from their perch. After inserting the blocks that would be his footrests and making sure his legs were spread wide, Green raised the blocks so Ron's backside was elevated and his cheeks were violently forced apart so his inner sanctum was garishly displayed. His head now lower than the rest of his body'\, Ron felt a rush of blood to his brain that threatened him with fainting. Concentrating once again on the simple act of breathing deeply and evenly to gain some control over his growing anxiety, Ron was forced into combating both the degrading position and his growing fear of Green's harsh attitude.

"Today you will beg me for pain," Green threatened in a harsh voice that sent the younger attorney into shaking uncontrollably in fear. "You will ask for it, demand it, do anything for it. You will want it so much that you will even thank me for it." His threats rammed another dose of fear into the quaking trainee's straining heart. He continued unabated.

"The damned Blues have really come up with a program for you this time."

Ron gasped in his sudden realization of the cause of the trainer's mood shift. Apparently, his Green had been turned down, and very recently, Ron suspected, in his application for promotion to the Blue level. And the angered man was taking out his displeasure on the handiest object of the moment, that is, Ron's backside. The dangling man quivered and trembled, his backside involuntarily flexed, and Green slapped him across his vulnerable cheeks in punishment for his disobedience with a forceful open palm. The jolt of pain brought tears to Ron's eyes and Green seemed to take pleasure in his charge's affliction.

He slapped him again, harder this time. The trainee wailed in agony yet his voice was unheard in the silence of his soundproofed cubicle. He persistently shrieked with misery when the torment continued unabated as at least ten strokes were unleashed on his reddening buttocks in powerful succession. With each wail emitted by the suffering trainee, Green stroked harder. With each of Ron's ensuing cries, Green seemed to take delight and intensified his windup. As a finale, Green brought his personal leather whip from its secreted station and unleashed its fury on the welted cheeks that were poised for the trainer's view. In utter despair, pain, and exhaustion, Ron hung his head limply between his dangling arms, too exhausted even to cry out or moan. With bitter incongruity, his sphincter muscles also flexed and an embarrassing gush of the hated cleansing liquid propelled from the tortured man's rectum. It drooled down his leg and onto the block supporting his right leg. The odor was unmistakable and inhaling it seemed to urge Green onto a greater height in his cruel morning's greeting to the trainee.

Enraged at both Ron's carelessness and his own denial of promotion, Green forced Ron bodily from the cushioned rack and stood him, naked and soiled, directly under the taller man's glare. Horrified and humiliated, Ron was unable to control his fear and he whimpered tears of utter dread.

As a final degradation, the stunned man's bladder discharged its final drops that landed only a few inches from Green's feet. The abusive trainer's reaction was swift and thorough. He dragged Ron from the cubicle by his limp, damp member and wrestled him directly toward the corridor that housed the punishment rooms. Ron's horrified view caught a glimpse of the confines of Level Two punishment and as they loomed before his stricken eyes, he struggled for any means of escape. Feeling his trainee struggle within his iron grip, Green pressed a button on his bracelet by smashing the leather against a wall and assistance of all Colors leapt into the corridor to assist the trainer in securing Ron in his harness. Blues, Whites, and other Greens emerged from the corridor's recesses and wrestled the struggling trainee into position.

The collar was buckled and secured firmly around Ron's neck and the short chain was likewise hooked to the loops of his netting that were designed for its connection. A wire running through his net bag was tightened and attached to the chain's other end while the helpless man's hands were manacled and restrained. The waist hook was applied, locked, and lifted, taking the screaming man's struggling body on a nightmarish upward rise. Drawing his knees upward toward his chest in both supplication and self-preservation, Ron hung from the punishing device until he looked down and saw Green take over the final preparations for infliction.

In one horrific motion, he jerked Ron's ankles downward and locked them into floor bolts, thereby introducing the excruciating chain-tightening Ron recalled with spastic trepidation from his recent introduction to the punishment wing and thereby initiated Ron's torture. There was neither sense, vision, nor hope, and Ron realized without knowing that the body could react without the mind's instructions. With his thought process completely interrupted, Ron bellowed and screamed with all his might, hoping against hope that the physical effort of making such noises would cause the pain to end. His voice rising well beyond the limits of comfort or control, Ron pierced the soundproofed room with intense agonized screams that fell unheard on the secreted Green's ears. The punishment lasted an eternity.

Green had programmed the device for one minute.

When he was finally lowered from his perch of pain and the suffering began to subside, Ron attempted to open his eyes and readjust himself to this nightmare reality. Green entered the cubicle that now contained the remains of Ron's final involuntary bladder and rectal discharges and looked over his man.

"Well?" he questioned, and waited patiently for an answer.

"Whhhhaattt?" Ron's raspy voice barely managed to utter the syllable.

"You must thank me," Green offered in a voice that dared the dangling trainee to decline. "Every trained slave always thanks his superior for his punishment." He waited patiently as Ron tried to collect his confused thoughts.

"Thh. . ." Ron began but could not continue. The legacy of his screaming left his voice gone and his mind aflutter.

"Further pain will be inflicted if you do not thank me," Green warned, "and promptly. I will wait only thirty seconds." With that, he stood at attention, hands folded behind his back, his chest displayed, and his green net bag menacing the bedraggled trainee.

Ron fought for control in an arena in which he knew he could have none. "Thhhaannkk. . . . yyy. . . . ," he attempted several times as Green stood immobile on the cold tile floor, "frrr. . . . mmm. . . . . pppnnnishhhmmm. . . . ," comprised the only sounds Ron could muster.

Still hanging from the waist hook, Ron trembled in fright and anticipation as Green approached his vulnerable and shackled body. The trainer unhooked the waist lock and the trainee fell to the floor, his spent body secured now only by the leather wrist restraints that extended by chains from opposite walls of the silent room. On his knees and with his arms pulled tightly to his sides, Ron was a portrait of exhaustion and depletion against the sterile white and black tiles of the punishment room's cold floor. When Green finally released his hands, Ron collapsed like a stricken parakeet falling from its perch. He gave in to the cool comfort of the tile and wept.

"I told you that you would beg for pain and then thank me for it," Green began as he scooped the disheveled attorney from the floor and carried him out of the punishment chamber, "and you are halfway there. You have thanked me for punishment and now you will learn to beg me for pain." Even in his semi-conscious delirium, Ron resisted the notion but trembled in terror that Green would do everything possible to make his threat come true.

He was carried in the big man's arms like an over-tired child into a quiet room several steps from the main corridor. When he was dropped onto the cruel hard floor, Ron recovered enough to recognize the face of his partner of the other morning, the man who had been punished for failing to loosen his rectal muscles during Ron's attempts at "insertion ritual" practice. Joining him was his Green; the four men checked each other visually. Both Ron and the tall black-haired trainee had obviously just experienced similar situations and both their Greens glared at them with menacing looks that penetrated directly to both men's souls. The other Green spoke first.

"You will be offered either pleasure or pain," he began, "and you will choose pain." He hesitated so his words could take effect. "You cannot receive any pleasure without pain," he continued, "and you both are familiar with the ecstasy of pleasure. When you are offered a choice, you will choose pain." He let his words sink in. Ron's Green took up the conversation.

"Different superiors will offer you the choice today and you will always choose pain."

He paused and allowed his incomprehensible directions to permeate the men's formerly logical brains. Then he continued. "Your codes are as follows: you," he barked at the black-haired trainee, "are blue, then purple. You," he pointed at Ron, "are red, then purple."

The confused men sought to understand their directions. Colors? Ron mused.

"Repeat," the first Green commanded as he pointed at the black-haired man.

"Blue, then purple!" he responded like a dog salivating at the sound of a bell. Then the finger gestured at Ron. "You!" the voice commanded.

"Red, then. . . then. . . ," Ron stammered, confused by the combination of torture and orders, "red," he repeated, "then blue. . . ?"

The intense pain grabbed his already-abused genitals and sent him to the floor contorting and squirming in agony. Screaming in his affliction, Ron reached beyond human endurance into his adrenalin-pumped reserves and shouted, "PURPLE!!" and he perceived that the pain began to subside. Both Greens smirked both at his contortions and his compliance.

"Thank me for your punishment," Green ordered as his finger hovered above the jewels on his bracelet.

Through gritted teeth Ron spit out, "Thank-you-for-my-punishment."

The agony in his groin gripped him again. He rolled along the tile floor and thrashed his legs wildly about while his hands clutched his agonized genitals in an unsuccessful attempt to rip the offending netting off his body. Screaming wildly and without shame, Ron felt his throat tighten with the grip of the Green's strong fingers around his rasping voice.

As the pain slowly subsided, Green warned again, "Thank me politely for the punishment."

As Green lifted him by his throat from the cold tile floor, Ron rasped the simple five-word response, "Thank you for my punishment." Green opened his fist and allowed Ron to crash back to the tile floor.

"Again," Green ordered.

"Thank you for my punishment," Ron responded, trying to keep the sarcasm out of his rasping voice.

"Politely!" Green commanded once again.

"Thank you for my punishment," Ron offered meekly. There was no escape from his personal hell and he knew it.

"That's much better," Green said soothingly, "and I expect that tone every time. Let's move on to the next step." He let his voice trail off and allowed the trainees' minds to imagine every frightening possibility.

"The next event is the beginning of Level Four," the first Green finished, "and it is known as insertion." The very word sent a cataclysmic shiver down Ron's trembling spine.

The men were ushered from the waiting room, their penile rings were hooked together by a short chain, and they were led on a jog through a maze of hallways and corridors that seemed identical in color, direction, and length. Even though Ron's limited military background insisted he attempt to identify his location, the fast pace and need to concentrate on the man in front to avoid any shortening of the connecting chain attached firmly behind his testicles precluded any ability to recall the directions he traveled and the turns the group made. Finding themselves halted by a massive double doorway, Ron and his partner were instructed to wait for the door's self-opening mechanism to grant them access. With this final warning, the two Greens left and ran in tandem down a side corridor.

Ron and his partner were left unattended in the corridor and enjoyed the first unsupervised moment the two had experienced since their arrival at the facility. Unsure of what was allowed and still exhausted from the morning's punishing trials, Ron was reluctant to engage the taller man in conversation. Rather than risk further punishment, the two men stood in absolute silence and waited. Their training had accomplished its goal. The men were submissive and obedient. They neither strayed from their assigned spot outside the huge doors nor engaged in any prohibited discussion.

Without warning, the double doors began to spread apart and the two were ushered firmly into the sterile white room by gilded Golds. Pointing to two empty chair-like devices at the end of the line, Ron and his partner took seats similar to the thirty-eight other trainees from their arrival group. The barren and antiseptic room was arranged with white leather-looking dentist-style modernistic chairs in a circle around the outer edge of the room. In the center of the circle was a single white chair on a rotating platform. Golds filled the room and busied themselves with adjustments, levers, and knobs on the wall controls. Ron counted at least ten of them.

When the last corrections and modifications were completed, the Golds moved to the center of the circle. Ron stole a furtive glance around the room and concentrated on the faces of the partially trained thirty-nine men. He was sure from their looks and posture that all had been subjected to the same rigors that Ron had recently experienced. Each face bore an apprehensive expression and each body tensed slightly in anticipation of the beginning of the next training level. This was the inauguration of Level Four and the rituals of the final Level Five loomed in everyone's near future.

The lights of the laboratory dimmed and the Golds in the center of the circle stood reverently still. Taking their cue from the Gold leaders that something eventful was about to occur, the trainees strained to observe the goings-on from their awkward and partially laid-back positions on the sterile white recliners. Ron wasn't sure if he saw or heard it first, but the forbidding swish of the Mistress' robes preceded her entry into the chamber. She stood on the center platform with the single chair as the turntable raised slightly and began its slow revolutions. Each trainee could easily see her now and she faced each in turn with her pronouncements for the session.

"Now we begin Level Four. You have been trained competently to reach this point. Because Level Five involves insertion, Level Four is designed to introduce each trainee fully and personally to the process."

Ron was not sure he looked forward to this individual attention.

She continued, "Every man needs his own, individually designed insert. Without a proper fit, insertion will be painful. Proper fitting must be done carefully and under strict supervision. That is the purpose of this laboratory." She paused for her frightening words to sink into the trainees' ears.

Ron tried to take in her omnious words, but his concentration was interrupted when he saw the Golds begin to move toward the wall panels. Once they arrived at their electronic wall plates, they manipulated switches that caused great metal clamps to first extend and then lower to imprison each trainee flatly against his white leather chair. Chair bottoms suddenly dropped off and each trainee was supported only by his chest clamp that attached him to the back of the chair supported only by the blocks that secured each foot. Ron likened his position to sitting in empty air. The coldness under his backside was an unwelcome harbinger of the afternoon's activities.

His thoughts were interrupted by the Mistress's voice.

"Today you will witness a special event as we promote a White to the level of Gold. This man has provided me with dutiful and competent service for a very long time. The process of promotion strips man of his last pretenses and arrogance. Only the most perfectly trained of my graduates return to seek promotion and each must begin the process as a Green trainer. This man has showed me unwavering obedience. Bring him in. Engage the viewers."

The Golds manipulated more switches as a procession of Whites led their most recent graduate to his central position in the room. Standing beneath the raised platform, the man stood naked in the spotlight as the Mistress pressed a bracelet button that released his magnetically attached net bag. Tears of joy filled the man's eyes as the men in this former group cheered him on. They hoisted him onto the platform and he knelt at the Mistress' robe hem, lowered himself into a prone position, and waited for her beckoning. She bent low, spoke into his ear only, and lovingly patted his dark brown hair.

Ron noticed that the mirrored glass had been lighted so the Greens and Blues could witness at least this part of the promotion ceremony. With his clear view of his Green, Ron could see the man's anger and envy fill his face with fury and passion.

Lifting the prone man to his knees, the Mistress gently massaged her former White's hairy chest and patted his belly with her open hand. Reaching in to his bald pubis, she twisted his penile ring with an expert and practiced motion and released him from all his servile encumbrances. Clearly and loudly for all to hear, she asked the supplicant if this promotion and role was what he truly wanted. The man choked back tears to answer.

"I do with all my heart." He continued to kneel silently at her feet.

She bade him sit in the central chair on the raised platform, secured his clasps, and electrically removed the lower half of his chair. Except for his missing ring and netting, the man was positioned exactly like the forty trainees on the main floor. When she was sure he was comfortable and ready, the Mistress spoke.

"Golds, see to all of the trainees." They responded as if they had been electrically charged.

With a flurry of activity, the Golds darted from trainee to trainee and liberally lubricated their rectums in preparation for the ensuing activities. Reaching high inside Ron's spread cheeks, the Gold artfully and forcefully applied high-gloss pink cream to his canal and finished with a flourish by drawing a hard circle that

Ron could feel the impression of on his outer backside. Finally, he slapped the imprisoned man's buttocks with a stinging wallop that sent shock waves through Ron's seated form. Then the Gold moved along smartly to the next waiting man and repeated the process, ending with a resounding spank that echoed through the otherwise silent chamber.

"Good," she complimented their timely work when they were done. "Begin the insertion."

Ron felt the hum of motors before he actually heard them and his hips shifted nervously as much as the clamps would allow. Beneath his and every trainee's open and available backsides, plastic rods were slowly raised to rest dangerously on Ron's deep and pink opening. Golds rushed about, checking each rod to make sure it was properly tuned to each man's most personal location and finally stepped back to the control panel to push even more buttons and make yet other adjustments.

Agonizingly slowly, the tubing entered Ron's anus. Although it was painless, having his rectum violated in full view of the Mistress and all the Golds, Blues, Whites, and Greens was a disconcerting experience. Suddenly and without warning, the rods discharged their contents into Ron. A warm and powerful stream of liquid was driven up into him, filling him beyond all expectations. He inhaled with a force that surprised his nasal passages. The darkened room resounded with gasps of similarly engaged trainees. The former White on the raised platform gasped the loudest.

"Your insert is being formed as we speak," the Mistress instructed. "Please remain absolutely still. Your insert will become your best friend, and its fit must be perfect."

She paused as the warm liquid penetrated and clung to every canal and bend in Ron's lower being. He jealously watched the Mistress pat the former White on his belly and reassure him during the gel's hardening phase.

"Your major discomfort will be removal," she warned as the trainees closed their eyes and waited for yet another dreaded moment. "But first, relax and give in to the process."

Ron truly tried to relax, but his rectal muscles were desperate to expel the hardening gel.

He watched the center man's face contort with attempts at controlling his own sphincter and he envied the man when the Mistress gently rubbed his temples and soothed his aching legs. At long last, she inserted her own finger in the man's behind and pronounced him, "done." The Golds rushed to check their charges' progress.

Ron's Gold was ruthless in his inspection. Flinging his aching legs even farther apart, the Gold tapped the hardened gel roughly and Ron felt as if it would explode upward into his body. The Gold planted his feet on the floor beneath Ron's outstretched legs and grasped the outward bulbous end of the insert with a strong grip of a massive hand. He placed his other hand on Ron's belly for balance and tugged firmly, straight down, to remove the finished and hardened insert. Ron shrieked audibly from the pain. His ears tingled with the sounds of similar shrieks and bellows from likewise pained men. When the procedure was accomplished, the Golds returned only to oil the men's aching anuses with comforting salve. Another hose entered from beneath to wash away the remnants of the ritual and Ron was finally left alone to dry and heal.

The Mistress commanded the glass to darken and block the view of the Colors who stood in rapt attention and in envy at the ceremony that was about to be completed for the newest Gold.

The newly promoted man was the last to be removed. The Mistress stood at his upraised feet and invited a Gold to attempt the removal. The Golds argued and vied for position; each seemed to relish the opportunity to perform this duty. All trainees' eyes focused on the jockeying for position, the calling, the attention-getting methods the Golds were utilizing to gain the Mistress's nod. Finally, she picked one and the others hoisted him atop the platform.

He took her position between the now-contorting and twitching legs of the ready-to-explode new addition to their ranks. He smiled a frightening look of savagery into the man's fearful face. Planting his feet firmly and grasping both the end of the insert in one hand and the man's fully engorged member with the other, the powerful Gold yanked both straight down. He held the insert over his head in victory as the caged man screamed in agony at his violation. A great cheer rose from the ranks of the Golds gathered at the foot of the platform, and the Whites, Blues, and Greens behind the glass joined in the applause. The Mistress signaled for the removal of the clamps, the return of the chair bottoms, and the end of the session.

The centrally positioned man rose slowly and painfully to his feet. Staring at the trainees and superiors with a fear-inducing gaze, the Mistress opened a velvet box held by her personal Gold and presented the man with his new gold ring. Pulling him toward her by his naked penis, she drew his organ through the ring with ease, and then pushed each of his dangling testicles with great care through the opening. Pushing the shining metal back against his bald skin, she locked the band into place to yet another great cheer from the crowd of men. The newly ringed servant sunk to his knees in exultation.

Opening still another golden package, she waved his gold net bag aloft for the group's joyous approval and she bent to cover him completely in the brilliant gold netting. By now, the ecstatic groups of men were rooting and yelling their approval of his promotion. Clamping the magnetic netting to its new home, the Mistress called for the new Gold to stand alone in the center of the platform. He rose slowly and awkwardly, admiring his new color with unabashed pride. Raising his hands in naked victory and savoring the cheering of his accomplishment, the new Gold was asked to identify the sequence of colors he wished for his new level of pleasure and pain. Shouting his colors to his superior, he asked for what Ron thought was an incredible request.

"Please give me pain," he urged. And she obliged him.

When his own clamps began to unlock and feed back into the their underground home, Ron and the other trainees were ordered to rise by the Mistress.

And Ron knew exactly what was coming next. The dreaded question.

"Do you have a request?" the Gold teasingly asked. Through gritted teeth, but with a smile, Ron politely responded in a voice that he knew came from his throat but was unbelievable to his ears, "Please give me pain."

And the Gold extended his arm and offered Ron the opportunity to engage his own series of colors. Thirty-nine men and Ron reached out with unwavering hands and each touched his own special colors in the proper order. Then forty trainees and a single Gold fell in unison to the floor, writhing, clutching, and grasping at themselves in their self-induced torment. In the back of his tortured mind, Ron comforted himself with the knowledge that the pleasure would soon follow. The pain was good; Ron consoled himself, because it brought the pleasure. And the pleasure was indescribable.

Chapter Sixteen

As Ron and the other newly-fitted trainees were led back to their individual cubicles after the evening meal that gave them some comfort after their personal inserts had been ripped violently from their rectums, Debbie also returned from work to her bedroom, threw off the dark float dress and triumphantly fell back into the satin sheets while she waited for her Gold to bring the evening's pleasures. With her teal and black lace lingerie framed against the deep red silky sheets, Debbie was a provocative image of delight.

In his isolated cubicle, Ron lay naked and aching from his day's training, yet anticipated with both fear and inquisitiveness the nature of the night's procedures. Unannounced, several Golds marched into Ron's unprotected quarters while simultaneously a single gold-netted man begged permission to join Debbie in her happily decorated master suite. Ron's evening training, the introduction of Level Five, was ready to begin and Debbie positioned herself to both witness and participate in the man's next leg of the journey toward total sexual slavery.

On his knees at her bedside, the handsome young Gold waited patiently for Debbie to recognize his presence and invite him to speak. Busying herself with the joy of inspecting and caressing her newly discovered powers of the bracelet, Debbie barely glanced at the man in the submissive position at her side. Finally, she deigned to turn his way.

"Well," she began, "what's on the agenda for tonight?"

Gold was ready for the question. "First," he began, "we will join Ron in his final phase of training before he advances to

Level Five and completion. Then we will view some tapes that illustrate what the procedures of Level Five entail. Finally, we can practice, if you so desire." He knelt silently, waiting for her cue.

Debbie laid back and contemplated the plans he offered. She was torn between emotions of loving the process of training and the new excitement she felt of the discoveries she had made while she entertained a certain sadness that came with Gold's pronouncement that the training would eventually be completed. He sensed her mixed feelings but was ready to alleviate the sadness the dichotomy brought her by making the last days of his time with her both memorable and exhilarating. He rose to adjust the viewer, speakers, and lighting and the kneeling man narrated the scene that came into focus on the screen.

"Tonight Ron and the other trainees will witness their first insertion ritual," Gold began, "and they will come to know it as a very important and special time. In fact," he paused for her to collect herself among the sheets and pillows, "he will come to regard it as almost sacred. When Ron has learned how and performs those actions that will ultimately please you, you can choose to perform this ritual with him."

Debbie considered the prospect and wondered how she would be included in this "performance." Gold noticed her puzzled expression and continued.

"Ron will be trained to know that when you agree to insert him he has performed expertly for you. He will have fulfilled every intention of the training. You can express this in words, but our Blues have discovered that the insertion carries a more long lasting effect. Ron already enjoys the pain because he knows it will eventually bring the pleasure," Gold explained, "but when he is inserted for the first time, he will be overjoyed beyond the pleasure." Gold stopped and allowed his dramatic words to reach the depths of Debbie's brain. Finally he concluded his pronouncement. "Only then will he be fully trained."

Her brain was indeed working overtime. Now she understood for the first time why both Tony and Bob were so eager to receive pain earlier in the afternoon. Finally she could figure out why, when she asked them their favorite colors, they responded with the sequence that would bring them the pain rather than the pleasure. The only way she could truly show her co-workers that they pleased her would be to give them pain, and eventually, when they performed extremely well, she would have to participate in the insertion ritual with them too. But how would she know what constituted ultimate pleasing? Was the ritual only for spouses or for any partner? Adding to Debbie's confusion was knowing that no trained slave could perform regular sex with another woman due to the protective netting they wore. Their partners were the only ones who could release them, and Debbie continued to work out mentally, she wasn't so sure that simply having sex with any man besides Ron would give her "ultimate pleasure."

Gold interrupted her thoughts with a question. "I am here to make this very clear to you. We will watch a ritual, then we will view Ron's practice for real insertion. Perhaps you and I should discuss this if you have any inquiries or doubts."

He waited silently and patiently for her to form questions. Putting these thoughts into words was difficult for her and Debbie took her time to form appropriate sentences.

"First, I want to know," Debbie began cautiously, "if the ritual is expected to be performed daily?" Hidden behind her question was the often-raised idea of frequency, Gold realized, and rushed to straighten out the concept for her edification.

"No, it is not. In fact, the more often a man is inserted," he spoke from wise experience and Debbie recognized this factor in his words, "the less significance he and his partner will come to give the ritual. Actually, insertion occurs only very infrequently. You are the only person who can decide when this ritual is called for. He cannot ask for it. You must weigh and judge Ron's actions and determine that he has given you an ultimate expression of his caring and devotion. Nothing less than that can be rewarded." Gold stood silently waiting for the teal and black laced woman to offer him her next problem.

"I understand. Am I the only person who will ever insert Ron?" Her words were cautious and careful.

Gold was taken slightly aback by her boldness, but realized quickly by her insightful words that she must have come into contact with another former trainee and that initial incident probably happened today. It must have been the bracelet, he mused, but offered her a straightforward answer.

"No, it is not guaranteed. Ron can never have ordinary intercourse with another person unless you agree to it. However, he has been trained to please his superiors in every possible way. This is an attitude and skill that will enhance his career opportunities as well as his relationship with you. Don't you agree?"

Gold watched her chagrined expression and confirmed his earlier suspicion. He wondered which one she had come to know that day and hoped that her first meeting with a fully trained man satisfied her expectations.

"I agree fully," she breathed, a little too quickly, "and I accept your conclusion. I'd like to learn how to do this ritual. When do we start?"

Gold smiled the expression of accomplishment and contentment at having brought her to this point so quickly into their evening's learning experience. Now she could continue her personal excursion into the complexities and exhilarations of the ritual he loved so well and yearned for this night. He raised the television's volume and took his place next to his charge. Together they watched the trainees in Ron's class with their penile rings chained together gather along a hallway, their faces pressed tightly up to the glass windows, and their eyes peering down into the event that would forever change their lives, their relationships to each other, and their ways of coming to know the world.

Ron felt the warmth of his body against the coolness of the glass as his body was pressed firmly into an erect position of attention against its smooth hardness. The room inside and below his gaze was eerily dark and contained a two-level carpeted surface that exuded comfort and security.

He witnessed the Blues enter, each leading a Green by the hand, and guide the Greens into kneeling positions. The submissive men were forced to bear their weight on their knees on the raised level and they were instructed to support their torsos with their hands on the lower step. Their backsides were fully raised to the satisfaction of the Blues and the obedient Greens spread their legs, an act that invited intrusion. To Ron's surprise, the entire room became a revolving platform and the Greens began to spin slowly with the Blues who stood behind them. Ron saw his Green led in, positioned, and tenderly attended to by a Blue. The Greens' faces were serene and peaceful; they looked totally relaxed and happy. The Blues began the preparations.

Reaching into a large jar, each Blue gathered two large fingers of radiant green cream and worked the lubricant between the raised, spread cheeks of a supplicant Green. The recipient's eyes were closed and Ron could almost share his man's savoring of the comforting addition to his most private space. The Blue gathered some more of the lotion and covered the Green's anal canal with rich, soothing motions that circled, reached, and lathered every millimeter of his inside perimeter. With a flourish, Blue drew a small green circle inside the man's buttocks and lovingly patted, then swatted, the vulnerable area before stepping away. Ron could see both men's faces emit calm and joyful expressions.

When all the Blues were finished with their prescribed preparations and stood similarly positioned between their Greens' legs, a voice entered from hidden speakers.

"You are the finest of the Greens tonight. You have pleased me by your work and your competence. The ultimate pleasure is yours." The speaker lapsed into silence.

Ron saw tears fall from several supplicants' eyes and stain their cheeks; he could almost feel the gentle massaging of their bellies and members that was administered to them by their Blues for their personal comfort. Then Ron witnessed the most surprising act of all. Each Blue reached into a green velvet bag and withdrew a bright green elongated device which, in a flash of recognition, Ron realized must be the "insert" that had been formed individually for each man just as Ron's had been constructed that very afternoon. The length of the device frightened him and his own rectum twitched in involuntary sympathy.

The Blues liberally coated the devices with additional cream as they stood between their man's outstretched and raised legs once again. Ron stared only at his Green now to watch this one man's reaction to the painful intrusion of his person that was certainly about to happen. Instinctively, Ron's hands moved down and behind himself to protect his own rectum from such violation. All he could hear was the deep breathing of the kneeling men in the darkened room and all he could see was their serene looks of contentment that bordered on ecstasy.

His mind was cluttered with confusing emotions and his brain began to reel as the Blue nestled the tip of the heinously long insert against Green's richly lubricated and exposed rectum and elicited a great and astounding cry of delight from Ron's trainer. Green continued shrieking with glee and begged the Blue to complete the process. He implored him for the penetration; he urged the man on. Equal wails and pleading from the other Greens filled the room with a clamor of excitement that rose in both pitch and intensity as the Blues teased their men with slight intrusions, then mercilessly pulled it away.

Ron's Green began thrusting his hips backward and forward in an effort to bring the goading device well into himself. Blue repositioned it slightly and forced Green to alter his direction of movement and thrusts. Green began screaming in anticipation and was nearly jumping out of his assigned area to achieve the full insertion. Other Greens followed and soon the room was ablaze with the incredible sight of eight pleading Greens thrusting, parrying, and tossing themselves to bring about the culminating experience. Begging now, Ron clearly heard his Green urge his Blue to have mercy on his exhausted body and finish the job.

"Now, now, NOW!" the man howled, and Ron felt with unbelieving thoughts his own member begin its fateful flight upward within its pink netting. He pressed even more tightly against the glass. He crushed himself more firmly against the glass that was now streaked with his own perspiration and noticed similar adjustments being made by his fellow trainees. The entire row of viewers was deeply entranced by the spectacle and each of the pink netted men was fighting his personal urge to rub against the view screen lest he himself explode.

Green was now ablaze with passion. His glistening oiled skin was mixed with his effusive perspiration and the glowing man was wild with excitement and fervor. As he attempted to rise in his fury into a standing position, Blue placed an authoritative hand on the back of his neck and pushed him indelicately back to his former position. Leaping with his buttocks wide now, the Green was lunging backward toward the tickling insert. With each lunge, the Blue pressed it home just a little deeper, and then pulled back, an action that served only to urge the potential receiver onward. Green pursued the insert with all his energy, talent, and developed muscles, and when he was convinced the man had no more strength to offer, Blue allowed him one last attempt at a deep lunge, then pushed the insert into him to its final destination for the evening.

The great Green fell with a thud, his head and hands dangling over the edge on which his knees had now collapsed, and cried soft tears of thanks and joy. To his utter amazement, Ron discovered that he had participated in the spectacle and had become so excited with Green's insertion that he ejaculated all over the glass wall against which his naked body was firmly pressed. In a horrified glance to his side, he could not help but realize that every other trainee had come the full circle with him. No Green came to rebuke him or the other trainees. Spent and exhausted from watching the ritual, Ron slumped against the glass and gave in to its support.

In her satin bed, Debbie was barely under control. Silently observing his superior, the Gold in her bedroom had noticed her excitement and helped her along in her pursuit of climax. When Green was inserted and Ron spent on the glass, Debbie was in the heat of passion and lust for the orgasm she knew was only moments away. Gold knelt quietly and entered her femininity with his great tanned hand and worked his expert fingers to increase her arousal to almost unbearable levels. When the two recognized the urgency of her situation, he replaced his own hand with hers and taught her how to enhance her own experience. Debbie came in a shriek of agony combined with glee and she fell back into her pillows, spent and exhausted, as she sobbed the tears of joy that matched Ron's own.

"This is one form of insertion," Gold intoned as the weeping woman composed herself. "This is the joy so ultimate that you can bring to Ron that he will come to strive for it. And this was only one method. Shortly, when you are composed, we will observe how the Whites give the gift of insertion to the deserving Blues."

He noticed Debbie's tired but eager eyes and continued. "Later we will share the experience of the Golds' inserting the Whites. Finally, if you are still interested, we shall witness the insertion of the Golds. Only the Mistress can insert the Golds."

Taking it all in with great gulps, Debbie shook her head up and down several times to indicate to the smiling Gold her extreme interest in learning more about insertion. She would need this knowledge, she recognized even in her spent state, to share the ultimate experience with Ron. Later, she figured, she would invite Tony and Bob to share this with her. But they would have to really please her, she vowed, before she would ever consent to give them this much joy.

Chapter Seventeen

Friday evening and Saturday morning merged into one for both Debbie and her training partner.

The schooling persisted on the television through the other Color's insertions and Debbie noticed that each group of men was smaller in number than the previous, but what they lacked in numbers they made up for in intensity and creativity.

The insertion of Blues swept her away with the incredibly unique positions that the Whites ordered for the Blue recipients. She watched with rapt attention as the Blues were locked into wrist cuffs and were hung from the ceiling with their legs spread wide by a rod attached to their ankle leggings that served to spread the eager men out completely. The Whites challenged their Blues to lift themselves up by their own arm strength and come down expertly upon their specially designed inserts. Only the strongest of the Colors could continue such tremendous exertion and still focus on direction.

The finale took place when their inserts were driven home by the intensely accurate Whites and it became a popping up and down frenzy of screaming, wild, and ecstatic men, each of whom was enthralled to be in his personal height of passion. Debbie noticed that several of the Blues ejaculated simultaneously with the completion of insertion, an activity that her Gold informed her could be timed and accomplished only by very highly skilled participants. It was a competence that the Greens were urgently trying to master. Taking in all the new information and creative skills she witnessed with a voracious appetite for novelty and expertise, Debbie's attention never wavered from the screen.

During the next segment in the ongoing drama, the Golds led in the Whites who were selected to be presented the gift that particular night. Gold advised her that White insertion was as close to perfection as possible because these men were almost ready to graduate to the Gold rank. She saw the newest twist on positioning, as the Whites became the antithesis of the Blues as they were hung from the ceiling by their spread-apart ankles with their arms locked firmly onto handgrips that were attached to the wall in front of them. The men could raise themselves up only by powerful exertion of their muscular arms.

After administering the white cream to their excited and twitching backsides, the Golds stood behind the Whites and touched their personal inserts just upon their rectums. This simple action sent the highly-trained Whites into fits of frenzy and stimulated them to begin pumping their bodies as far upward as they could manage, then relax themselves downward until they gathered the strength necessary to raise their straining bodies up again. When a White missed his mark and the insert's tip eluded his unseeing buttocks, the Gold playfully pulled him by his member in an upward direction to encourage his accuracy. The Whites strained with every lunge upward and the Golds smiled with each teasing they applied to their men. As the begging and shrieking rose to a unified crescendo, the Golds waited for their man's final surge upward and rammed the insert home.

Fabulous cries of thanks and delight filled the room. Debbie felt that she could not handle yet another climax that was certainly upon her, yet Gold ushered her expertly into the ecstasy of personal pleasure once again. As the Whites were lowered and fell from their restraints in exhaustion and thankfulness, they rolled over to hug the feet of their inserters. Debbie rolled toward her Gold and stroked his handsome face.

Enough, she silently implored him and his equally silent answer indicated that one more event would complete their journey and bring her to know the true glory of insertion that he himself had come to know. With that knowledge, he assured the dissipated woman, her life would never be the same again. He massaged her exposed breasts and kissed her lower fuzzy lips while he knelt on the floor between her dangling legs. She felt the rising passion begin and felt helpless to restrain her innermost emotions. Gently and rhythmically thrusting her hips against Gold's expert mouth, she focused her eyes once again on the television for the final ritual of the insertion of the Golds. He was right, she later came to realize, her life would never be the same again. It would be much better.

Only the Mistress could insert the Golds. Debbie was informed when she asked about the very small number of Golds for insertion this night that it took a supremely high level of expert work to satisfy the Mistress and qualify for her personal insertion. He had been inserted by her on twenty separate occasions, he related, and each one was a more unique and fulfilling experience than the prior one. In fact, he continued, when he was informed by her summons to attend the insertion, his excitement rose instantaneously and continued its threat to peak even before he entered the room. No sexual experience had ever filled him with so much joy or passion, he shared with the totally absorbed listener, that on each occasion when he learned he was going to be included that night, he insisted on at least one or two doses of pain in the late afternoon to douse the flame that burned in his lust for the ritual.

The Mistress had a special touch, he confided for the first time in another, and he had never met her equal. The great man's heavy head was lodged in her caressing arms and he was close to sobbing at the poignant memory he evoked. Having been with Debbie these past several days and nights, he missed the potential for insertion by the Mistress.

Debbie swore to herself that she would reward the man for his gifts to her and Ron by becoming the most creative inserter he could imagine and then she would insert him with a special touch that could approximate, if it could not duplicate, that of his beloved Mistress. And she watched the spectacle in awe as she planned how she would compensate her special trainer.

The spectacle of the insertion of the Golds constituted a milestone event for Debbie and Ron's future sexual relationship. Debbie learned skill, technique, and demand for obedience and that the three levels had to be expertly mixed with tenderness and true caring. The Mistress, for all her high standards of obedience and rules of compliance, truly loved her Golds and wanted every insertion to bring each man to his fullest peak of pleasure. For all the hard work, dedication, obedience, and trust each man gave her, she repaid every special Gold with singular attention and personal fulfillment. But obedience was first and foremost in her expectations from her men. Too exhausted even to sleep, Debbie concentrated on the unfolding events with passionate interest.

The line of Golds was short. Only two men qualified for the ritual that evening and only that pair would reap the deserved sleep of the totally fulfilled. Gold explained to Debbie that sleeping with the insert earned the men unqualified admiration in the morning baths from envious comrades who were allowed to witness only the beginning of the ritual but were forced to endure the entirety of the extraction. The process of extraction, Gold continued, was an enviable event because the Mistress came personally to the bath to supervise each man's self-removal of the insert, his cleaning of the device, and their mutual wrapping of it in gold velvet until its next scheduled insertion. Finally, Gold completed, the Mistress applied the soothing salve herself after each man's personal cleansing. As the other Golds stood helplessly and watched, the Mistress tended to each chosen man's needs and saw to his comfort. The process was available to all who worked hard and qualified; however, only the select few were elected to receive its joys.

The two Golds selected for that evening could barely contain their enthusiasm as they entered the darkened room. Seated on a raised chair at the opposite end of the long room, the Mistress faced the expectant entrants with a formidable stare. They marched to a position directly in front of her elevated seat and knelt without command on the lower floor at her feet. She regarded them with pride and tenderness and the two men returned her favorable look with the faces that exemplified the personification of the deep bond that existed between them and her.

She spoke to them lovingly and in subdued tones, inquiring if either man had a preference for her method that evening. Neither man spoke, and the Mistress smiled. They would leave it up to her because she had never, and would never, they firmly believed; disappoint them in the insertion ritual. Debbie's Gold, his head resting on her outstretched arm, started when he witnessed the unfolding machinery that constituted his two comrades' ritual for that evening. He moaned softly in longing for the process that he termed, in his envious narration, the "swing."

Debbie watched attentively as four sets of cuffs were lowered from the ceiling on golden wire tethers that sparkled in the rising spotlights. Their entry into the otherwise silent room, save for the heavy breaths gasped by the kneeling Golds, went unnoticed by the supplicant men but were regarded with earnest excitement by those watching from behind the glass that separated the inner sanctuary from the frenzied delirium building in the corridor. The non-recipient Golds were reduced to vicarious enjoyment of this special spectacle. The Gold kneeling forlornly beside Debbie sighed audibly when he recognized the contraption of the swing. Debbie gripped his handsome head between her arms and held him to her breast in comfort.

Silently the Mistress rose and pointed toward the men to fall backward and remain supine at her feet. She slipped the cuffs around both sets of waiting wrists and ankles and rested herself once again upon the raised chair. At the touch of a button on the chair's armrest, the tethers tightened and their cargo began their upward journey. Shaking with excitement, two men were hoisted to a height several feet off the floor by their manacled wrists and ankles. Their hips sagged and their heads were thrust back as their passion grew. With freedom of movement of their legs and arms, the two hanging Golds eagerly spread and closed their legs as well as their arms, and their flexing motions set their bodies into a rhythmic swaying from side to side. Aha! Debbie realized, that's why it's called a "swing."

When the Mistress had seen enough of their oiled bodies rocking gently side-to-side, she stood. Standing atop the raised platform, the Mistress' waist was approximately even with the men's hips and their backward gazes prevented their realizing her close proximity to their positions. Without warning, she grabbed their gold netting with calm authority and a firm tug, changed the direction of their swings to a front- to-back movement. Using these convenient handles, the Mistress accomplished two deeds: she completely regulated their direction and efforts in swinging, and she completed her superiority over their absolutely helpless conditions.

"Are you ready?" she asked the Gold swinging to her left as she poised, ready to apply the lubricating cream.

He fairly screamed in urgency, "Yes! Now! Please, please, PLEASE!" His voice was throaty and raspy as his fever burned.

With a smile, she grabbed his netted handle once again and brought him to a painful but eagerly anticipated stop. He flexed his legs outward and tensed every muscle in his lower body to open himself to her reach as she brought several fingers' of shining gold lubricant to his entry passage.

"Relax," she said softly, as she massaged his belly and buttocks in an attempt to soften his supreme muscular constriction and allow her fingers to enter his body with the cream and complete the preparation.

The Gold felt her inability to penetrate him and he spread his legs even wider than Debbie thought possible for a man. Every muscle struggled and his head was driven back by sheer neck force. She watched the ripples flex and ebb and she saw the veins on his clear skin stand out. The Mistress appeared displeased.

"Relax!" she ordered and the Gold began to cry in sheer frustration.

His excitement had overtaken his ability to control his own body and he was unable to meet her demand to open himself to her. She repeated her command once again, this time adding the warning, ". . . or I will withhold the insertion. . ."

The great Gold screamed in fright and terror. His comrades on the viewing ledge were overcome by his abhorrent situation. Gold murmured to Debbie, "I don't think this has ever happened before. . . ." when the Mistress reached out suddenly and with an open palm slapped the struggling man intensely upon his gold netting and its delicate contents. The immensity of the blow reduced him to a semi- conscious sobbing and screaming hulk from which the robed woman turned away in disgust.

She considered the onlookers on the ledge and called clearly and without anger to them as well as to the unhearing Gold, "I demand absolute obedience. I expect more from a Gold. He will not receive insertion tonight."

And the great Gold howled in fury and frustration. The shocked spectators watched him as her personal Gold entered and lowered the appalled man to the floor, unshackled his cuffs, and forced him to kneel at her side and suffer the greatest indignity of all: forced observation of another's achievement and ultimately, the other's insertion. The punished man pleaded and begged, but she was oblivious to his supplicating behavior. He called for her reconsideration and she ignored his voice as well as his wreaked body. He lowered his head to the floor in absolute supplication yet she turned to the next recipient and quietly asked him as she rubbed his loins, "Are you ready?"

Her ministrations to the sole recipient that evening were as tender as her ignorance of the imploring Gold on the floor was merciless. She lubricated the man deeply and with great care. The neglected Gold, restricted to his position, began rubbing his own backside in sorrowful replication of her attention to his raised counterpart. When she unsheathed the gold velvet bag to reveal the recipient's personal insert, the suffering Gold at her feet reached the height of delirium and became almost uncontrollable in his rage and craving.

As the Mistress took hold of the swinging man's handle and thrust his screaming form with great force into a faster rocking motion, she teased his swinging anus with the insert's tip. At this point, the kneeling man was beside himself with grief and shame and he attempted to rise from his position and lunge for his own unopened gold velvet bag that rested near her feet. She turned quickly toward his moving figure and pressed a single jewel on her great bracelet. His gold netting dropped to the floor and the now denuded Gold sank back in despair and utter inability to comprehend the astonishing event. Staring at his naked hairless penis and testicles, he howled in torment at her ruthless reduction of his rank. He grabbed for the netting and attempted to replace it on his naked genitals, but the magnetism had been terminated electronically in her ultimate rejection of his pitiable behavior. Without addressing the suffering man's agony, she continued her process of insertion of the deserving Gold.

As the Gold swung rapidly toward her, she inserted the device bit by bit, but always removed it as he swung away. The Gold spread and closed his legs while working his arms up and down to increase the force of his swing toward her and his personal delight. When she shifted slightly to the side, he felt the insert's touch upon his thigh and tried to correct his direction on the next swing. He could not see the poor wretched Gold on the floor as the almost-crazed man attempted to beat the golden netting back onto his limp and useless member. In his passion and anticipation, he was oblivious to the pain his agonized colleague endured in front of all the onlookers and under the Mistress' feet.

As the man's swings became greater and greater, the onlookers cheered noisily behind the darkened glass, and when she was ready for full insertion, she ordered the complete blackening of the glass so the culmination of the pleasure would be shared privately, only by the Mistress and her favored Gold. Although they could not see his ultimate rapture, the observing Whites, Blues, Greens, and trainees heard his howl of delight as she carefully yet firmly brought the insertion home with authority and force. Ejaculating simultaneously with her insertion, the Gold sagged spent and swinging slightly in his tethers. She turned with a quiet fury to the now-disgraced former Gold who lay bedraggled and exhausted on the lower floor.

"You have acted pitifully," she began in admonition, "and I am disgusted by the sight of you. You have embarrassed yourself and your training. Let the others see you now."

And she relit the glass. In a gasp of horror, the onlookers saw a dichotomous scene. The swinging Gold lay back in his harness in total euphoria while the punished former leader wriggled and writhed on the floor in naked degradation. She picked up his useless golden netting and ripped it apart as he cried desperate pleas for her reconsideration.

"You need re-training," she spoke calmly as the observers looked on in horror and shock. "Until you provide me clear example of successful re-training, I will consider you apart from the group. You have no rank. Blues will design your program and it will be administered. I am done here." She exited with deliberate speed as the onlookers stood frozen with fear.

The Gold lying on the floor next to Debbie sobbed in compassion for his colleague but maintained that the man's poor management of the situation was his own fault and may have been a result of his too-rapid rise in the ranks and his personal character flaws. Amazed at the incredible scene she had just witnessed, Debbie and her Gold observed the caretakers enter and unharness the swinging, exhausted Gold and literally step over the recently declared non-existent former member of their ranks. With deliberate tenderness, they unfastened their friend and led him back to his quarters for much needed rest. The man on the floor was left utterly alone and cried wrenching sobs of humility and pain. Left with no identity, he had nowhere to go and no one with whom to share his pain. Slowly and painfully he arose, walked to the exit and to his quarters with only the program to be devised for his retraining looming in his future.

Debbie exhaled what had been her tightly held breath. Her Gold stood and shook his head from side to side in perplexity from the incredible events that had just unfolded before their eyes.

"I have never seen anything like this. . . ." he began, but Debbie shushed him with a manicured finger to her lips.

"Tell me what I can do to make you feel better," she offered with sincerity. He was touched by her caring and desire to help.

He responded meekly, "The swing. But you don't have one." And his voice trailed off.

Debbie turned away from his sorrowful form and he left her spacious master suite. In the morning, she knew, she would call the carpenter and would set this man's well deserved pleasure right.

Chapter Eighteen

Although it was well after ten o'clock in the morning, Debbie was in no condition to answer the incessantly-ringing phone. That Saturday she slept late due to her extensive hours in the company of her Gold, the television, and the spectacular show they had watched. Tony's voice on the other end of the line served to bring her back to reality and recognize that his urgent request for her return to the office and participate in the solution of the Tomlin contract was simply an inconvenient but necessary evil in the career path she had chosen. The company president had little sympathy for Saturdays spent lying in bed when contracts needed work and clarification. Debbie estimated she could arrive at noon and Tony agreed to relay the message to her co-workers.

Showering in record time, Debbie was eager to dress in the outfit that was gift wrapped and waiting for her on the freshly made bed. Opening the present with care and anticipation, Debbie hooked the leather open bra around her full breasts and arranged herself in the garment so her nipples were centered and free. The leather garter belt and black hose were exciting to feel so close to her white skin and the black leather g-string was alluring as the thong split her buttocks with carefully measured tension. Finding a dark silk chemise in the closet, she slipped into it and discovered black high heels adorned with a bright bow on the shoe shelf. Wriggling her feet into their comfortable new homes, Debbie was amazed at her excitement in the simple act of dressing. Applying some makeup to her tired but eager face, she tied her long hair in a simple ribbon and left for the office.

Tony and Bob had already arrived; in fact, Debbie assumed from the strewn papers and empty coffee cups that they had been there quite a while already. Dressed casually in honor of their expected day off, the two men delighted her with their complementary fragrances that were set off by combinations of their individual hormones and skin. Her office was virtually empty, according to the security guard, and the compliant officer agreed to alert her if anyone with business registered for her floor in the otherwise uninhabited building.

The two men rose in greeting upon her entry and moved aside from their work on the wide conference table so she could sit between them. Their aromas filled her nostrils with pleasure and their servile behavior facilitated their work. As she dictated new passages and deleted old ones from the contract, Tony set to work at his computer and produced new documents in record time. Bob had complete knowledge of the data he and Terrence collected on Friday afternoon and by two o'clock, the trio had packed off the contract for the attorneys' signatures. In their jubilation at the finished product, Debbie announced that she would offer the men a treat in celebration. Apparently Tony and Bob had entertained appropriate means for Debbie to celebrate with them.

They had come to the office ready for work as well as for pleasure. Each man had carried in a gym bag of toys and devices designed for Debbie's use with and on them. They suggested she reconsider her afternoon schedule, especially with Ron away "on business," and the pair offered her a diversion from what they believed was her otherwise empty home. She agreed to listen to their proposal and sat back in the office's large leather chair to consider their petition. Finally deciding that entertainment from Tony and Bob would provide her useful practice for Ron's return, she surveyed the situation and announced her decision by ordering Tony to turn on the stereo and find a soothing station for their listening delight. He complied with wide-grinned satisfaction and the two men waited for the invisibly leather-clad businesswoman to dictate the game of the day.

Full of delight at their completion of the contract and excited about the afternoon's potential, Debbie informed the co-workers that she would consider awarding them the conclusive definition of their pleasing her, that is, the ritual of insertion. The men drew in a sharp collective breath when they realized the high stakes she countered to their offer to her. Insertion would change the nature of their plans, and the two men, who had been comrades in collusion, metamorphosed into rivals for her attention and pleasure.

Tony was the speedier of the two in removing his outer clothes and revealed an oiled torso that glistened in the sunlight that pierced the open vertical blinds on his superior's picture window. Not to be outdone simply by speed, Bob exposed his well-oiled frame and launched into a posing routine that exhibited every part of his tanned and remarkable body. The two men vied for her gaze and competed for her good graces. After she had seen enough to ignite the fires that had burned and consumed her last night, Debbie waved a hand to dismiss their further efforts.

"I want something different," she began, "something unique. For me to award you the ultimate pleasure seems to call for an ultimate expression on your parts. What ideas do you have?" She sat quietly and patiently, fiddled with her bracelet, and allowed the men to consider her request.

Tony suggested the men each arrange a "welcome" scenario for her and she could reward the better of the two. Bob disagreed and proposed a session in which Debbie could reward or punish their actions in a meaningful way and offered his leather crop for her instrument of approval or disapproval. Tony termed the idea "overdone," and suggested they venture from the office and entertain their competition at another location. Debbie was finally intrigued with an idea and suggested they return to her home because she had carpentry work to arrange for and this way they could accomplish both tasks at once. The men agreed, dressed again in their silken running shorts, and Debbie drove them to the hardware store and then to her house with due haste.

Their noisy entry alerted Gold and he spied their arrival from the secrecy of the kitchen. Recognizing two of his former graduates, Gold was pleased with Debbie's choices and he recognized that she would have numerous opportunities for her own training with them. Much to Gold's surprise, they brought tools and packages upstairs with them.

Debbie closed and locked her bedroom door and the men set to work fulfilling her description and specifications to the letter. Their naked work left them sweating as their already oiled bodies gleamed more than usual as a result of their exertion. When the Gold heard the hammering, sawing, nailing, and related work finally cease, he was confident Debbie would unlock her door for his collaboration in her clandestine efforts. To his surprise, the men exited briefly only to return with rags and buckets to clean up their mess. Finally, Debbie ushered the two into her inner sanctum once again and firmly locked the door behind them. Gold stood alone in the hallway and was left to wonder about the scenario that unfolded behind that locked door. His training insisted he wait obedient and silent for her potential beckon.

Inside the large master suite, Debbie stood in front of the two naked men and whipped the leather crop noisily through the air. Hearing its familiar sound, the co-workers breathed even more deeply in their mutually rising excitement. When he could stand the pressure no longer, Bob turned and knelt and exposed his eager backside to his superior's readying stroke. She obliged him once and Tony fell excitedly to his knees. Eager to keep the men in competition, Debbie stroked Tony very lightly once on his olive skin. Not feeling the expected sting of the whip, Tony turned his head to plead with sorrowful eyes for her full attention.

Debbie ignored his pleading and reached into his gym bag and extracted a well-fitted leather harness. Instructing him to put it on and latch it securely, the submissive secretary drove his arms in the holes and belted the garment around his chest. Reaching for the dangling leather leash, Debbie informed the frightened man that he would now take on the role of her favorite pet and she led him by the vest's leather rein in canine imitation. He assumed the role completely for her, barking and heeling upon her command. She whipped him when he misbehaved and rubbed his belly when he pleased her.

Offering him a walk outdoors, Debbie opened the sliding glass panels that led to the wrap-around deck that decorated their second-story master suite. The secretary was electrified with her orders and commands and he strived to fill her every tug and pull on his leather leash. Ordering him to "stay," she brought him a bowl of water from her white-tiled bathroom and set it on the deck floor under his face.

"Drink," she commanded.

The six-foot man rested on all fours and lapped up the water from the bowl. His face glistened with the slobbered liquid and remnants that drooled down his chest toward the clear netting that housed his organs of delight. She watched his efforts to clean his belly with his tongue and, in a further effort to delight her, he rubbed his backside on the door frame as if to satisfy an itch. She turned her attention to Bob as Tony continued his role-playing and drinking on her screened deck.

"And what would I have you do, my pet?" Debbie asked rhetorically as the shorter but heavier man trembled in a mixture of fear and delight.

She moved the whip toward his glistening net bag and touched him playfully on his readying member.

"Do not allow it to rise," she commanded authoritatively and the distraught man beat furiously on his member to urge it to retreat from its unintended direction.

In spite of his efforts and punishment, the organ did not heed his command and continued upward in apparent defiance of his repeated efforts. He looked sheepishly at the woman's looming presence and shrugged his broad shoulders in embarrassment. She did not return his pleading gaze with a glance of understanding; rather, her countenance was one of such intensity that the husky man recoiled both inwardly and outwardly. She offered him a solution.

"I can assist you in your efforts," she began and raised her whip high over her right shoulder.

His understanding of her intentions was clear and he stared at her jeweled bracelet wrapped around the wrist whose hand was poised and ready. Obediently, he gripped his wrists behind his back and spread his legs as he stood waiting the relief she offered. Debbie struck him quickly, once on the upper inside of his right thigh and once on his left. He winced from the swing, but did not shift his position or cry out. His training held. Alarmingly, his clear net pouch continued filling with its enlarging contents. His face reddening from humiliation at his inability to control his desires, Bob readied himself for her next, closer blow. She did not disappoint him.

The whip sang out and the shock of its impact brought the contracting officer to his knees. Soundlessly he gripped his net bag and held its aching parcel in a useless effort to force the pain to subside. Bending almost in half to reach his abused sensitive organs, Bob's head graced the floor as he pulled himself into a small ball in an effort to shield himself from yet another blow. She ordered him to stand and inspected her effort and its result.

With a smile Debbie said, "I'm glad I could help."

Bob politely answered her, "Thank you for your assistance."

The Gold still stood silently outside the locked bedroom door and eavesdropped on the tantalizing conversation. He heard the sing and crack of the whip and the concomitant dropping of the big man to his knees onto the carpeted floor. He smiled when he heard Bob's polite thanks to her. His only regret was that he could not witness the drama unfolding among his three pupils, although he complimented himself on the success of his training with them. The next voice he overheard belonged to Debbie.

"Pull yourself together because I want you and Tony to perform together for me," she ordered and Gold listened as the suffering man sought solace from his wound but stepped dutifully out onto the balcony to retrieve the secretary who was still lapping at his water dish as she had ordered.

Wincing with each step, Bob grabbed the younger man's head full of hair and lifted his face from its drinking. He wiped the spatter from his cheeks, neck, lips, and chest with his own hands and took the man's leash to lead his crawling figure back into the bedroom. Jerking him by his leash to a full stop, Bob stood and Tony crawled directly in front of the now-seated woman. Picking through the contents of the contractor's gym bag, Debbie pulled out a series of leather straps, held them over her head, and tossed them to the standing man. Bob dressed in the costume without her direct order and she surveyed the occupants of her master suite.

"I'm hungry," she began, "and I think we should go out to eat." The two men looked at each other in horror before bringing their attention back to the seated woman. "Yes, let's eat. I'm in the mood for Italian. You may dress in your silk shorts and a T-shirt. I'll drive."

The men dived for their gym bags and pulled out silky soccer shorts and white T-shirts and struggled to draw them over their leather outfits. Debbie wiggled a finger at Tony and he approached her. She pulled his shorts down to his knees and attached a leather g-string to his waist and split his buttocks with a firm pull. He could barely stand straight from the tightening of the strap. Nodding, she indicated he could now pull up the shorts. Beckoning Bob, she disrobed him in like fashion and fixed his leather strapping to the same degree of tautness. He moaned audibly when he bent to retrieve his lowered shorts and was barely able to lift them to his waist. The men added sockless sneakers and the trio was ready.

Flinging the bedroom door open quickly, Debbie reached for the eavesdropping Gold she knew was loitering outside the room. Grabbing his massive arm in her small white hand, she ordered him to obtain his leather straps and she affixed the tension on his garment without mercy. The two former trainees stared in open-mouthed wonder at the sight of their former trainer embarrassed at his being discovered and then chastised by having to wear his straps in equal discomfort to their own and covered only by the tight flimsy shorts and t-shirt. Three members of the foursome climbed gingerly while one strode defiantly down the stairs and into Debbie's car.

The restaurant, a casual Italian eatery, was located a few minutes' drive from Debbie and Ron's home. The foursome emerged from the convertible with care and Debbie sent Gold in to inquire about seating. After a short wait, the group was placed at a secluded table where Debbie sat between two of her men in a position where she could reach the third with ease. Dinner began very quietly.

At the waiter's request, Debbie indicated that Tony should order a selection for the entire party. His ethnic heritage enabled him to make curious and educated choices and the waiter indicated he would bring the dinner with the intention for the group to share the varied appetizers and entrees he ordered. As the group sipped red wine, Debbie casually reached into Tony's shorts, squeezed his sack with a firm grip, and thanked the wincing secretary for his help and expertise. Her gratitude literally brought tears of joy and pain to her secretary's shining black eyes. When Bob refilled her wine glass, Debbie offered him equal thanks and the two co-workers sat sobbing and sipping their drinks while Debbie turned her attention to Gold.

"I think you should slice the bread," she half-ordered, half-requested and the great man picked up the serrated knife provided for the job. "Put butter on mine," she again requested, and when he complied and offered her the adorned slab, she took it with her braceleted hand and suggested, "Please butter your most interesting part." The group sat stunned.

Obediently, Gold put two fingers into the butter and withdrew a great chunk of the yellowish substance. Standing only very slightly, he rose from the chair and carefully entered the fingers into his silky waistband, continued down, and rubbed the butter on, under, and around the private space that was split by the tight leather strapping she had placed between his cheeks. When the job was completed, he excused himself to the men's room and returned quickly with sparkling hands and moist backside that decorated his shorts that covered the deed. The co-workers marveled at his skill and tact. Debbie smiled.

Throughout the dinner, Debbie led the animated conversation, interspersing comments and remarks with careful orders for her men to submit.

By dinner's end, Tony had applied olive oil under the front of his leather g-string and Bob's pouch and contents were coated with the creamy white pasta sauce. Their shorts glistened with the liquid additions to their private parts and by the time the group finished eating, the men were well-lubricated in front and behind. Debbie paid the check and the foursome quietly exited the restaurant amid stares of incredulity and jealousy from the other diners, not a few of whom had witnessed one or more of the strange happenings at their table. She spoke to them in the parking lot.

"Be careful not to get that stuff on my car," she admonished, "or you will pay for it when we return to the house." They listened intently to her warning and carefully entered her convertible.

She drove the group home as the men tried diligently to stand partially while seat belted in. Each placed a hand under his behind so as not to soil the leather of her open-roofed car. Once home, they carefully inspected their places and wiped up their telltale stains with clean hands.

In the bedroom, she ordered their shorts, shirts, and shoes to be removed and scrutinized each of their bodies individually under glaring lights. Satisfied they had fulfilled their orders in the restaurant, she suggested they clean each other up in the hot tub that extended from the bathroom onto the deck. Stripping off their leather the men jumped in, each eager to scrub the offending substances from the others' bodies. Debbie interrupted their struggle.

"Let's be orderly so I can be sure you are all clean," she remarked. "Let's put Gold in charge. Who would you like to wash first?"

Without a word, Gold grabbed Tony by his tight net bag and scrubbed both the contents and his anal area until they shined clean under Debbie's careful gaze. After he was approved, Gold tackled Bob and polished his most private regions with stern and powerful strokes.

When he was likewise approved, Debbie pointed at Gold and added, "Now I want the two of you to wash him."

The two men pounced on their former superior and soaped his darkest regions with vigor and care. They presented their finished charge to the observing woman for approval and smiled broadly when she nodded at their efforts.

"I believe you should complete the job," she directed to Gold and offered him the men's hoses and bags.

He reached for them eagerly and forced the surprised men into submissive positions to accept their internal cleansing. In

reprisal for their intensity during his own washing, Gold filled
their bags with hot soapy water and drove the contents into their
rectums with deliberate force and speed. His two former disciples
screamed at the heat of the entry of the solution and continued
their whining and moaning throughout Gold's completion of the
procedure. Not once, much to Debbie's surprise and Gold's pride,
did they move from their prescribed positions. Gold had the men
bend in half to ease his insertion of the plug and he used a careful
thumb push to secure the devices. Standing partially erect, Tony
and Bob struggled to respond to Debbie's orders that they face
her and when she saw their anguished faces, she smiled in victory.
Wearing only their glistening net bags and full rectums, the two
uncomfortable men sought approval from their superior to release
the plugs and expel the contents. She toyed with them in their
discomfort.

"Not just yet, guys, I think we have something else to take
care of," she replied off-handedly to their imploring gazes. "I
believe Gold has missed his turn."

With that quick comment, she produced Gold's cleansing
bag and hose and offered them to his reluctant hands.

"Wash yourself," she commanded, "and do a very good
job. We'll watch."

She sat on the edge of the hot tub as the former trainees
stared in awe as the great man filled the bag with soapy solution.
Debbie reached for his bag and poured the unused contents into
the tub.

"No," she corrected his efforts, "I believe it should be
warmer, like Bob and Tony's. Here, let me ready it for you."

She took the bag and filled it under the open tap with
steaming water and added a few drops of scented soap. Slipping
the hose and ring into place, she fondled the filled bag as Gold
watched her hands with eyes that reflected his inner trepidation.
Tony and Bob smiled through their mounting discomfort at
Gold's caution and Debbie's teasing. She swung the bag around
by the hose, barely missing the great Gold's head with her swings.
Finally resting the bag on her lap, she stroked it as if it were his
heavy head she sought to caress.

"All right, it's time," she announced and handed the bag and its contents to the trembling man. "Do it."

There could be no arguing with an order given in that tone. Gold positioned himself against the tub's edge and spread his muscular legs in the swirling waters of the hot tub. Debbie reached in and fondled his gold pouch as she reflected on the upcoming events.

"No," she interrupted his efforts once again, "I think you should move outside. Come on, boys, let's go." She strode through the glass doors and awaited their emergence outside.

The submerged trio dutifully waded to the glass wall that separated the interior portion of the spa from the outside. Slipping under the glass, the men reappeared in the tub on the deck while Debbie reclined on the lounge chair overlooking their immersed level. She nodded at Gold to begin and he repositioned himself against the outer edge of the tub. Spreading himself wide, he inserted the hose deeply into his anal passage and tossed the filled bag over his left shoulder. The bag dangled in front of his chest and he took a deep breath, planted his feet firmly, leveraged his balance, and removed his hands from the wall. Slapping them together around the bag of liquid, Gold forced its hot, soapy contents into himself at tremendous speed. His legs sagged involuntarily as the torrid solution entered its new home. He gasped and grabbed wildly for the tub's edge. Pressing his face into the cool fiberglass of the pool, he grunted rhythmically in an effort to bear the discomfort of the water. With superhuman effort, he removed the hose and inserted his own plug without losing much cleansing solution. Debbie admired his efforts; Tony and Bob stood amazed and in awe of his skill.

Now three filled rectums stood before her scrutiny and implored her silently for permission to expel their contents.

Debbie counted agonizingly silently to ten and asked, "Who wants to go first?"

Even in their discomfort, the three men considered the alternatives offered by the reclining woman. Would being first indicate leadership or eagerness? Would raising one's hand show her that the man was strong or weak? Would she respect or be disgusted by eagerness to respond? The men struggled with the implications of her simple question. Sheepishly, Bob brought his hand halfway up.

"You first, Bob?" she inquired with a smile. "Go inside," she directed innocently with a pointing finger, "and use the bathroom. Come back and clean yourself up. Then it will be. . ." she paused for effect and carefully watched their faces, "Tony's turn. Go now, do it, and return to me."

Bob half-ran, half-jogged toward the glass partition and ducked under it to enter the bathroom. A few minutes later he returned and positioned his posterior over one of the swirling jets. Relaxing his aching anus in the comforting rush of water, Bob rested on his elbows to observe his counterpart's trip for expulsion. As Tony stood, they saw his agonized face and debated betting on whether he could hold his contents without his plug. She considered his reaction to her removing the stopper, but allowed the poor secretary to relieve himself in private. Gold, she thought, would be a better candidate to benefit from her assistance.

Tony returned and assumed a position similar to Bob's and the two men eased their aching rectums while waiting for Gold to undergo the same procedure they had just completed. Raising himself on two powerful arms, Gold stood and started for the partition when Debbie called, "Just a minute. Let's show these two just how good you are."

Gold froze in mid-stride to discover what her words held in store for him. She raised herself from the lounge chair and walked to the side of the tub next to his erect body. Kneeling, she reached her bared arm into the water and inserted her fingers between his buttocks in search of the plug. Finding her goal, she twisted it without pulling it out, and noticed his fearful expression at her actions.

She challenged his training directly and without mercy. "If I remove this, can you hold yourself? I would be impressed if your muscle control were that great. Do you want to try?"

Gold swallowed hard and the two onlookers tensed for what they guessed would be an ultimate display of Gold's ability or his dismal and humiliating inability to fulfill her command. If he failed the test, he realized he would not receive the promised insertion later that evening. This punishment, especially in front of two former trainees, would be more than he could bear. But Gold was unsure of his ability to perform as she directed. He had simply never done this before.

Forcing his mind to dispel all worries and unenviable possibilities, Gold closed his eyes and concentrated on his rectal muscles. He flexed his buttocks several times and Debbie felt the contractions around her partially inserted hand. He exercised his internal muscles and moved slowly up and down in the pool. When he was ready, he nodded at his superior and she grasped the plug firmly between manicured fingers.

"Ready?" she inquired. He barely nodded.

She tugged unyieldingly and the knob released. Feeling a small rush of contents, Debbie was determined not to remove her hand from his most private space. Because she respected him for his assistance to her, she inserted her thumb into the hole and stopped the flow until Gold was able to control his muscles and retard further expulsion. When she was certain he was in control of his flexing sphincter, she released her hand and allowed the man to walk with dignity into the bathroom for his personal expulsion. Tony and Bob had not seen the underwater drama and could only assume that Gold had been in total control. They gasped as they realized the Gold was perfectly trained and they stared in admiration at his egress and waited in silence for his return. Debbie smirked at their naive acceptance of his prowess and exited the balcony for the bedroom.

Once inside, she first ordered the dripping duo to remain in the tub and await their Gold as she uncovered the device built by Tony and Bob that morning and pulled the tethers slightly so the wrist and ankle cuffs were raised somewhat off the floor. When she was sure that Gold had returned in triumph to the little group, she stood just beside the hot tub and addressed the trio.

"You have all pleased me tonight," she began, "but Gold has outdone you two," as she pointed at Tony and Bob. Your pleasure tonight will be to ready Gold for insertion." The three men stared at her and Gold's lower jaw involuntarily dropped.

"Out!" she called, "out of the pool! Inside with the three of you! Now!" The men scrambled to obey as she whipped their fleeing backsides with the leather crop she had so recently learned to master. Tony led the pack and was followed by Bob. Gold brought up the rear. Each man's buttocks gleamed a shiny red from the heat of the tub's jets and from her incessant whipping of their struggling backsides.

Once inside, Gold froze when he saw both the device constructed by his former trainees and his female superior posing authoritatively beside it in her leather lingerie and black stockings. Overcome with appreciation, he knelt on the floor in gratefulness for Debbie's caring and consideration. Most of all, he was impressed by her recognizing his burning desire for insertion, especially in this manner. Fondling the dangling cuffs, Gold wept tears of joy mixed with anticipation. Debbie handed the jar of lubricant to Tony and pointed at the two men and then toward Gold. Needing no further instruction, the graduates shackled Gold into the cuffs and cranked him to a hanging position approximately four feet from the floor. Gold allowed his buttocks to sag and he dangled joyfully in the swing. Stepping between his outstretched legs, Debbie felt his darkest district with her soft hand and massaged his cleansed tract. She stepped back and allowed both Tony and Bob to enter his spread legs to begin the lubrication of insertion process. Gold dropped his head back at their touch, closed his eyes, and relaxed in his personal rapture.

The two men alternated applying the gold cream to his eager rectum as Gold flexed his arm and leg muscles to begin the swinging motion. Tony reached deeply into the man with two fingers of brilliant cream and Bob added a similar portion. The duo liberally spread the soothing lotion inside the shackled man, and then Bob drew half the final circle while Tony completed the figure. She allowed them both to slap the backside that swung before them and inform its owner that the process had truly begun. Debbie stepped to the swinging man's side and by gripping his gold netting securely in one hand, brought him back to the reality of his impending reward. She took a giant step to her right and pulled the man along by his netted handle. Releasing him suddenly, she affected the first arc of his swing. He began yelling in delight.

He needed little other help to encourage his swing. Yelping with pleasure combined with freedom, Gold continued his flexing until he attained a full semicircle of motion. Opening his gold velvet bag, Debbie withdrew the device and offered it to the men who were eager to lubricate it for the journey's end. Debbie arranged herself at his opening and the end of one arc, and touched his willing anus with the sparkling golden device. He shrieked in glee when he felt the familiar touch of his personally designed insert.

He swung harder now, eager for the completion, yet Debbie toyed with him. She touched him on the inside of his thigh, an act that caused Gold to readjust his swing to meet her outstretched hand. She touched him again and inserted the device a short distance, then extracted it when he swung back. He swung even harder in an effort to force her into final placement. Debbie teased and cajoled the straining man and watched his gold netting fill with its engorging contents. She touched him with the device in one hand and elicited screeches of delight while she massaged his genitals with the other hand during the arc of each of his crescent-shaped swings. It was at this point that Tony, Bob, and Debbie recognized that Gold could not hold on much longer. In his fit of passion, he had come to the final stage of the process. She owed it to him to give him the definitive and irrevocable pleasure. Tony and Bob stood rapt in awe at the process. They had never been this close before to a receiving Gold. It was a reverent procedure.

When he undertook a great, final swing, Debbie grasped the insert with two firm hands and prepared to consummate the great man with his chosen crown. Grunting with exertion, Gold made a desperate plea with outstretched legs and Debbie drove the insert to its home. He howled with delight, spurted in simultaneous ejaculation, and ceased his pumping motions.

His exhausted body hung in mid-air and relaxed in the assisted suspension. The tears he cried were of gratitude and joy. Tony and Bob stood immobile in respect. Debbie pulled back her covers and lay in her leather underwear upon the satin sheets.

When she was comfortable, she extended her bare braceleted arm and fondled the jewels that adorned the black leather. Silently she pushed two quick series of buttons, and the onlookers gasped in pain, succumbed to positions of writhing and contorting on the carpeted floor. Debbie lay back in her plush sheets and watched their agony with anticipation of their offering polite thanks for her infliction of their pain. Then she would consider offering them some pleasure for their assistance in her efforts on behalf of her Gold.

Chapter Nineteen

On Sunday morning, all the trainees in the facility slept late. Their trainers did not come to greet them at their usual early hour and when they finally did arrive, they carried with them a certain air of humor and fun that had been sorely lacking the previous day. After the removal of his mask of pleasure, Ron opened his eyes to his beaming Green who insisted that morning routine would be much more enjoyable than his most recent and quite memorable experience. Ron rose cautiously, but Green took him by the hand and fairly dragged him at a jogging pace into the great bath. After using the joint facility to relieve himself, Ron stepped gingerly into the warm waters of the large pool. He was unsure what to expect; however, he realized quickly that Green's demeanor had altered remarkably. He stood with mixed emotions among the other trainees in the waters.

"Today is the beginning of the intense process of graduation," Green informed the surprised group who listened with rapt attention. "We must determine that you can perform all necessary functions with appropriate attitude and competence before we can certify you as ready for the final testing. Today's skill evaluation begins with stage one bathing. You will bathe each other and we will observe your dexterity and creativity. For your final test for evaluation, you will bathe your trainer and he will either pass or fail your efforts. Passing enables you to move to the next level. Failure requires further re-training. Grades will be cumulative."

He stood silently and waited for the usual reaction of bewilderment by the overwhelmed trainees. He was not disappointed by this group's startled reactions.

Green reached out suddenly and grabbed both Ron and his partner's arms and led the two men to the neck cushions along the wall. Out of the corner of his eye, Ron saw others pair off into groups and wade to the pool's edges. As the other Greens lowered their trainees' heads, Green pushed Ron's head onto the cushion and the tall black-haired man locked Ron's upper brace into place. Helpless and immobile, Ron stood immersed in the great pool and was horrified to discover he was at the mercy of the man who had been trained so well to seek the pleasure that he would easily endure all pain. His obedience was classic for this facility and Ron was frightened.

He felt his ankles being strapped into the floor braces and pulled up and away from his body as the warm water lapped over his chest and bald pubic area as he bobbed up and down in the wavy bath. Ron tried to relax and breathe deeply as his partner soaped him all over and brushed his sweaty body in all directions. He felt the man lift Ron's exhausted member and scrub the sensitive skin underneath. The application of the depilatory cream to his hairless skin made him feel cold and exposed, but he bore it with quiet dignity and calm, even breathing. As his partner moved up his chest and toward his face, Ron fought the urge to constrict his muscles in an effort to resist his painstaking and thorough job of bathing him.

His comrade reached Ron's face for the application of the soap and cream. He rubbed Ron's skin affectionately and carefully as he probed all crevices and nooks of Ron's skin. After washing him almost a little too tenderly and caressingly for Ron's liking, he coated his cheeks, upper lip, and chin with the inoffensive depilatory cream before moving back down toward his spread and fastened legs. Ron could smell the fragrance of the soap, but he was unable to anticipate the intensity with which his partner began polishing the sensitive area between his lower cheeks. As the black-haired trainee reached down into Ron's darkest region, he spread the shackled man's cheeks wide with one hand and secured his brush into place with the other. When he felt the brush against his anus, Ron squirmed in an attempt to resist the man's sadistic efforts. Noticing with a sort of pleasure his charge's discomfort, his partner became more ferocious in his efforts and depth. Ron's backside ached and felt raw. He was being pushed beyond his limit of pain and involuntary tears sprang to his eyes. Oblivious to Ron's pain, his partner scrubbed the anal region harder and deeper, eventually adding even more soap and raising significant but submerged lather.

Green noticed the entire series of events. He was not pleased with the trainee's relishing Ron's displeasure and pain. Remembering his infrequent but loving outside encounters with former trainees, Green shook his head sadly and slowly from side to side. He allowed the man to continue as he evaluated Ron's endurance. Finally, Green could allow no more and stepped in and grabbed the man's netted handle, an act that startled him enough that he dropped his brush and moved quickly away from Ron's exposed backside. Green sent the fretting man into punishment and waited for his agony to conclude before chastising him for causing deliberate and unnecessary pain to a fellow trainee.

"When you are in the world again," Green admonished, "you will be thrilled to see a fellow trainee. You will want to hug and kiss him because he recognizes what you are--perfectly trained. The behavior you just illustrated is totally unacceptable and shows that you have no appreciation of the training."

Green paused while the castigated man recovered from both punishments, the physical insult to his genitals and the oral admonition.

"Now, apologize to this man by kneeling and kissing the area you so abused." The massive Green folded his arms across his chest and waited for the trainee's compliance with his direct order.

The man dropped silently to his knees in the water as all unshackled heads swiveled toward him to witness what infraction had occurred and how it would be punished. As much shocked as pained by his punishment, Ron's partner began an incomprehensible sputtering of excuses and defenses as the entranced multitude listened in surprise and excitement. In an environment in he was neither invited nor tolerated to speak, the man's ramblings were an incredible but inappropriate action that ignited the group's interest and consternation.

Not daring to speak, the men in the pool were silent as they awaited the result of his unfortunate tirade. The black-haired man appeared to refuse to respond to a direct order and could not bring himself to press his lips against Ron's mistreated backside.

Ron, however, was not interested in this man's plight or his reluctance to follow this particular order. Having had about enough of his sadistic and masochistic follies as any man should have to bear, Ron wished that Green not punish the offender; rather, he decided that he would accomplish the deed himself when his turn came at bathing practice and evaluation. Where he had been extremely angry, when he recognized his own need and impending opportunity to retaliate against the big man's violations, Ron became calm. His breathing slowed and his anger diminished. Green stared at the raving and kneeling trainee man in disbelief, but when he turned his gaze toward Ron and recognized Ron's intensity, it seemed that a silent understanding between trainer and shackled trainee was reached. Therefore, Green amazed the mass of men with his unusual pronouncement when the lunatic finally ceased his blabbing.

"I will not punish you further," he announced calmly to the now-uncomprehending crowd. "However, I believe that your turn to experience punishment for this action will definitely come." Under his breath he added, "And very soon."

Green turned silently back to Ron and completed the washing himself. This morning, however, he did not complete the internal cleansing that Ron had almost come to expect and enjoy. In spite of the relief and the opportunity to find his vengeance, Ron was surprised to learn that he actually missed the cleansing of his inner self. Maybe, he thought to himself, I'll take care of it myself when the party's over. Yes, he decided, he would do it himself rather than experience the pain of missing what had become pleasurable for him.

At the signal given by an unseen Gold, the men were shifted and those on the receiving end became the givers. Ron, now a bather rather than immersed within the great pool of lavender soap, assumed an upright position and watched quietly as Green placed the overbearing partner in his neck restraint for Ron's bathing practice.

Smiling broadly, Green handed Ron the tray of tools of his new trade and ordered with a single word, "Begin."

Ron began in earnest with a rapid display of learned talents. He raised a heavy lather of soapy lavender suds and covered the man's bobbing body with foam. Using two strong arms in a sweeping motion, he managed to cover the entire lower half of his partner's body with a creamy, bubbly layer. His talents were showcased as he soaped his charge with violent and complete strokes, his powerful arms encompassing the man's entire body with fragrant lavender suds. Beginning at the man's lower legs, Ron cleansed every square inch of his top side, working the lather into every corner and crevice presenting themselves. He threw himself into his work, extinguished from his ears the sounds of the other trainees' efforts, and generated a rhythmic and steady pace. Popping and snapping of bubbles rang in the background as Ron worked the man's legs in a massaging motion that drew admiring glances from his own and the others' Greens.

Moving his intense attention toward the man's genital area, Ron added even more soap and fairly attacked the man's denuded and bald pubic area with fervent hands. Spreading the trainee's legs wider apart, Ron reached into the sensitive region and extended the ringed penis away from its testicles and soaped in a rhythmic motion that heightened the man's developing exhilaration. Confident that he had accomplished his secondary task of arousing his charge, Ron watched the man's penis engorge and begin to stand straight. Laughing quietly under his breath, he gazed at the product of his handiwork and imagined the punishment for disobedience this man would receive from the now-frowning Green. Acting in a fashion that bespoke his obliviousness to the man's desperate attempts to will his organ down, Ron continued toward the chest, underarms, and neck, all the while raising bubbles and fragrance that drove his man more and more to the heights of excitement. He worked with a passion and zeal that astounded his Green, but Ron had lost himself in his work and drove onward to completion.

Rinsing the trainee by pushing on his midsection and dousing him under the warm bath water, Ron opened the tube of depilatory and worked the inoffensive cream onto the man's face. Then he waded with determination toward the exposed, bald genitals, and squeezed a liberal handful of the stuff, worked it into a warm lotion, and lubricated the gleaming area with fervor and zest. Ensuring that no portion of skin was left empty, Ron massaged the cream into every fold of the trainee's skin and between the straining man's legs. Watching his reaction with one eye and his Green's with another, Ron smirked at the two men's reactions to his application methods.

Thrilled that his impassioned bathing had brought the great Green to arousal, Ron recognized an opportunity to exert his new-found authority and repay both of the men for their insensitive baths today as well as from a few days earlier. His trainee's legs thrashed in ever-increasing arcs of excitement as his penis filled with forbidden agitation. The poor man's arms reached in vain to quiet his anxious maleness and caused a rippling of the waters as he fought against the restraints. His hips moved up and down as his pelvis thrust against Ron's talented and malicious efforts. The trainee's face, hidden behind the padded neck brace, tensed against the impending explosion that he was powerless to prevent.

The Green stood transfixed and engorging as he watched the unfolding drama. The trainee's aching penis was ready to burst, yet Ron, cognizant of the impending eruption, worked more diligently to bring about the dreaded outcome and certain punishment for the deserving former-abuser. Anticipating that the Green would also be forced to the punishment rooms, Ron proceeded to increase his fervor and put on the best show possible. He forced his lips into a thin, straight line, and fought his own urge at rising excitement. Knowing and approving Ron's reasons and methods, Green stood apart from yet confirmed Ron's actions. He would not interrupt the events, but he would reward Ron's efforts generously. The Green never realized that he was as much an object of Ron's efforts as was the trainee who laid immobile under Ron's torrid hands.

The trainee's legs began to tense in obvious anticipation of the discharge that such potent physical pleasure would certainly bring forth. The black-haired man's thrusting became as acute as the silence in the great pool as the other Greens enjoyed the performance that unfolded before their eyes. As they kept part of their attention fixed on their own trainees, they fixated on the power struggle that Ron was bringing to an imminent conclusion.

Knowing that only the most trained and obedient among them could withhold audible ejaculation, they gathered in small groups to predict both the trainee's level of accomplishment and his Green's probable punishment. At the same time, they shook their heads in awe of Ron's dexterity. Green began to notice his own rapidly rising member and was torn between his obedience and his excitement at the incredible bathing experience that was playing itself out in front of him. He did not notice nor was he able to imagine in the height of his personal ecstasy the secreted Gold eye that evaluated Green's own performance as well as the performance levels of his trainees.

Ron suddenly seized the trainee's bursting member in his soaped hands and began to rub the depilatory even more intently into the skin of the man's organ. He creamed up and down, up and down, and made a small ring with his fingers through which the engorged organ could pass. The trainee groaned as his penis passed through Ron's fingers and thrust back again. Ron smiled at the man's distress. He continued his rhythmic motion in silence and brought the trainee closer and closer to finishing; yet, as the man approached culmination, Ron refused to allow the conclusion and reached under him and dipped a creamy finger into his darkest region, the violation of which gave the man cause to shudder and clear his mind and himself only a little bit. Once he was relaxed and his penis slightly softer, Ron began his fervent stroking anew. The torture he inflicted on the trainee was noticed and appreciated by all the smiling Greens in the great pool.

The trainee was literally beside himself as he thrashed within the confines of his restraints in the warm and sudsy water in which he was imprisoned. Deliriously gleeful, yet frightened to his inner core, the black-haired trainee unloosened a moan that barely reached the ears of the attendant Greens in the pool. To a man, they smiled at his inexperience and his neophyte level of audible enjoyment. Anticipating the dreaded outcome, both Ron and his Green stepped back and awaited the man's self-defilement and disobedience. Ron stood silent and watched. The Green, however, became more involved in the spectacle and finally reached down toward his own green net bag. He was horrified at the rigid and vertical organ that greeted his silent touch.

Ron did not have to wait long for the finale. Untouched by Ron's hands, the trainee moaned and groaned in both sexual exhilaration and shame.

Lying on his back in the warm water, the trainee was unable to control himself after Ron's generous yet malevolent abuse, and the organ took on a life of its own as it first danced, then exploded for all to see. As the now-spent trainee cried deep tears of a joy mixed with horrified contrition, Ron gripped the man's now-collapsed organ with one hand, the padded neck brace with the other, and flipped the spent man unceremoniously over onto his stomach as the water lapped at his aching muscles.

Keeping an eye on the Green who watched the scene from a distance, Ron stepped in immediately to complete the abuse he had begun with his former torturer. Taking a new palm full of lavender scented soap, he raised a great lather and soaped the black-haired man's anal area and buttocks. Placing his knee into the man's midsection, he forced the manacled man's legs down, and then spread them farther apart with an assured violence that opened the big man's cheeks and exposed his darkest inner area. Choosing the depilatory with great care, he creamed the trainee's hairy region, and rubbed the man's worn penis as the cream did its work.

Finally, when the area was ready to be denuded, Ron felt another engorgement of the man's organ that began to stand within his firm grasp. He smiled and noticed that his Green also stood transfixed in awe. As he stood watching the two men within the dance of degradation that Ron was inflicting on the other trainee, the Green did not notice his own excitement continue to rise in the great pool. However, his arising penis and engorging green net bag did not go unnoticed by the Greens whose job it was to demand strict and severe obedience from all in their midst, even from a fellow Green.

As Ron cleaned the man's outer backside of the depilatory and noticed its gleaming naked wetness, he reached onto the tray for the pink lubricating cream that was required prior to the insertion of the internal cleansing hose, the pleasure that Ron had been denied during his earlier bathing experience. Grasping two great fingers of shiny pink lotion, he plunged his hand into the anus that squirmed in reflex to the intrusive pressure. A soft moan escaped the tired lips of the abused trainee as the Green enjoyed the scene in growing excitement.

Still oblivious to his own excitement, Green's net bag filled even more fully and his hips began a gentle forward and backward swaying motion. The other Greens stood and watched in horror and bemusement. Ron lubricated the trainee's now-clean anal area with deep, thrusting motions and continued massaging his ever-rising penis with gentle stroking. The man began to realize with horror that he was in the hands of a master who would bring him to double orgasm within the pool and in front of the others. Determined to subdue his own excitement and avoid further punishment, he fought back with the only weapon available and closed his rectal muscles to the fingers probing deep inside.

Ron, feeling the attempted exclusion, took immediate action and withdrew his pink-creamed fingers and raised his open hand above the backside of the struggling and determined trainee. With force drawn from his inner self as well as from the memories of his former abuse at the hands of this trainee, Ron slapped the toiling cheeks with a crack that resounded throughout the great pool area. His discipline brought about an immediate cessation of the man's resisting efforts and reduced him to a child-like whimpering that bespoke his realization that the punishment would be re-administered as long as he continued to struggle against Ron's superior talent. He forced himself to relax his muscles and Ron drew two more fingers of pink cream and inserted them with authority into the now-docile man's flaccid rectum. The black-haired trainee offered a quiet moan and a short gasp that enabled Ron to realize he had taken full control of the bathing routine.

Ron continued to cream the region until he was sure it was full of bright pinkness and noticed at the same time that his other hand was beginning to become filled with the man's now-engorged member. He released one of the trainee's hands and silently instructed him to masturbate his own penis as Ron pulled the retractable hose needed for the internal and final cleansing.

As he turned to take hold of the hose, he noticed his swaying Green, holding and stroking his own engorged green net bag, and smirked at the unintended yet exciting result of his display. Taking the hose solidly in both hands, with one motion Ron kicked the trainee's legs apart, spread his cheeks, and drove the hose deeply into the pink cavity before him.

Without waiting for the gasping trainee to catch his breath or his balance, Ron released the valve full force and propelled the warm liquid deep into the now-berserk trainee. The man struggled for a moment at the encroachment of the liquid into his most private cavity, but fearing more chastisement, succumbed to the process that he knew would overtake him shortly.

The Green, noticing the man's immediate acquiescence, became more excited and his motions took on pronounced and immediate urgency. Ron noticed the Green's rhythm increase and inwardy smiled as he anticipated finally discovering through Green's disobedience exactly what Level Three punishment entailed.

With the trainee's rectum full of cleansing liquid, Ron inserted the plug into his anus, grabbed the engorged penis, and flipped the uncomprehending trainee over onto his back and then into a standing position. Continuing his massaging and pulling, he started to draw the man from the pool and toward his cubicle for the unplugging and final hosing. Only then would he return to bathe his trainer Green for the final evaluation. Full of himself and his accomplishment, he surprised himself by also grabbing the great Green's fully suffused net bag and dragging him at the same time from the great pool. His work was not yet done.

Taking the two sheepish men from the pool and from completing their morning routines, Ron noticed the respectful glances he was receiving from the other Greens who were witnessing this extraordinary series of events. The trainee and the Green, now aware of their own unsatisfactory performances, both began to cry silent tears of shame and embarrassment. At the same time, they recognized that Ron was in charge of this episode and dreaded yet were excited by the impending next phase of their punishment. As Ron instructed the trainee whose bowels were bursting from the cleansing lotion to continue his masturbation of his bald penis, he bent the Green in half with strong arms and kicked his legs apart. Standing silently with the two men on the edge of the great pool, he grabbed a handful of nearby green cream and drove it into the Green's anus with a force that sent the big man crashing to the pool deck in a heap. The Green, his breath knocked out of him and sensing his own defeat, struggled upward, but without success, and managed to return himself only to a kneeling position.

With the Green kneeling doggy-style, Ron drew out an unused hose and rammed it into the gleaming green anus. Turning the dial to "hot," Ron released the valve and filled another of his former-tormenters with hot, soapy cleansing liquid. Listening for the concomitant shriek and receiving it, Ron finally withdrew the hose and inserted the plug into the rectum lubricated with the squishy green cream. Satisfied that the men were bursting in both their bowels as well as in their organs, he grabbed each man's most personal part and led the struggling duo defiantly from the great pool and into the small cubicle that was his home.

The men struggled and cried from shame. Reaching upward with a well-positioned hand, Ron's well-placed slaps brought them to submission. He struck their backsides repeatedly in their march to the cubicle and the trainee and the Green each withstood four degrading blows before they submitted to Ron's direction. Their cheeks red-welted from his spanks, the men followed his pulling and were led into the cubicle. He shut the door, faced the men, and instructed them verbally.

"I'm not ready to release your plugs," he began ominously. "First, you will come to realize what I have in store for you."

The men cowered in fright and anticipation as Ron reached for and grasped the nearby leather-fringed crop and whipped it noisily through the air. He brought the feathered tip close to the humiliated trainee's glistening and enlarged penis and ordered him to continue his self-stroking while he watched Ron's administration of Green's punishment. Ron relished his new role as wielder of discipline. He took delight in administering punishment, and he devised a plan to repay the Green for his enjoyment of Ron's former distress during earlier days in training. Ron decided to play with him, like a tomcat with a frenzied mouse.

"You may not have an erection until you are ordered to do so," Ron mockingly intoned to the subdued and mortified trainer.

He watched Green's horror-stricken eyes as they darted from the masturbating trainee to the leather crop that was whisked closer and closer to his own private area.

"Would you like me to help you bring it down?" Ron inquired with mock caring and assistance.

The great Green stood silent, his penis standing well in front of his shining and dripping body, his anus straining at the well-driven plug that held the contents of his bowels. Unable to bring words to this situation, the Green struggled to force himself to gaze silently at the floor. Ron reached out with the crop and brought it to rest on the green net bag with urgent force. The Green dropped to his knees in pain. Walking behind the fallen man, Ron administered the crop to the glistening buttocks that knelt before him and brought a single red welt to rise.

"Would you like a matched pair?" he asked coyly.

Knowing he was defeated, the Green nodded.

"Speak!" Ron barked, as he swished the crop again against the other cheek and drew out another red welt.

"Yesssss!" the Green offered in a tone of defiance and submission.

"Politely!" Ron shouted and swung, as the Green fell completely to his knees and grasped his ever-readying member in an effort to forestall the inevitable climax he feared.

"Yes!" the Green replied with immediate submission as his years of training automatically took over. "But please," he cried, "remove the plug. I can't keep it any longer! Please!"

Ron took two fingers and grasped the plug, twisted it, and plunged it deeper into the contorted man. His actions drew an unearthly groan from the man's throat and forced him into a prone position on the floor.

"Up!" Ron barked, as he lifted the great Green back onto his knees. "Stand!" he ordered, as he pulled the fully extended member straight up. With a yelp, the Green complied.

"And you, you who could not obey the command to be tender where you had been abusive," Ron continued as he glanced toward the still masturbating trainee, "are going to help him. Kneel," he commanded, and the subservient and tumescent trainee fell to the carpeted floor with a thud.

Ron deftly retracted the green net bag and exposed Green's immense penis that was well on its way to discharge. "Take him in your mouth and bring him home," Ron ordered, and forced the kneeling trainee to grasp the huge member between his lips while continuing his own masturbation during the encounter. Ron stepped back and watched the scene unfold.

In his enjoyment and fear, the Green began to use his own hands to produce a thrusting motion with his hips and bring his full member in and out of the trainee's mouth. The trainee was stroking and massaging himself as the two men approached simultaneous climax. Their groaning came both from sexual excitement and physical pain as their plugs continued to hold in the cleansing liquid. Ron sat on the upholstered chair and gazed in satisfaction at what he had just accomplished. The well-trained men were fully involved in their ordered mutual caressing and fondling of themselves and each other and performed an esthetically appealing dyad of arousing delight. Ron administered occasional whippings to their reddening backsides to encourage the men toward fulfillment.

Ron sensed that their times were approaching quickly and he stood to perform his final function. As the groaning increased and the thrusting took on heated passion, he reached in simultaneously with both hands and twisted the plugs to loosen. The horrified men, too involved in their excitement and too well trained to resist, felt their bowels discharge at the very moment they came to joint orgasm. They came from all ends, all over each other and themselves, and onto the carpet of the cubicle.

Spent and exhausted from humiliation and sexual excitement, the men fell onto each other and cradled each other in horror and exhaustion in their powerful arms. "Say thank you to each other," Ron commanded.

The great Green, his body full of discharge and now-foul cleansing liquid, took the trainee's head in his hands and kissed his forehead first, then his cheek, and finally his lips. The trainee, too spent to consider any rebuttal this time, returned the kisses to his Green's perspiring face. The men fondled each other briefly and as their hands moved toward stroking of each other, Ron turned to leave the tiny room.

Over his shoulder he called out directions, "Clean it up. Then report to the punishment room. When you're done there, we'll have that bath." He walked silently from the cubicle toward the great bath and received the admiring and inquisitive glances of the Greens and their trainees as well as the astonished yet invisible stare of the Mistress's personal Gold.

Chapter Twenty

Green performed the function of cleaning the cubicle mindlessly as if this action would be his last performance as a Green in the facility to which he had dedicated so great a portion of his life. Prolonging his cleaning efforts assuaged his mind into believing that he could remain within the protective shell of the now-sparkling cubicle forever. Knowing that he had been disobedient was enough to cause the big man grief; however, realizing he had consummated mutual and unapproved orgasm with a trainee brought him more than shame. It brought him a long-forgotten feeling of absolute terror. In addition, he was haunted by the knowledge that he had done this sinful deed within the probing gaze of an overseeing Gold. By now, the Mistress, as well as the rest of the Colors, had been informed.

His anguish intensified as he scrubbed and hosed down the tiny cubicle, work, he had often described as too debasing for his station as a Green. In his horror and sadness, he disinfected the room as he had done countless times during his novice period. He cleaned it more than it needed cleaning as he believed this act of contrition would atone for his misdeed. After the fourth rinsing, a voice came over the speaker.

"Report to punishment Level Three," it stated unceremoniously and without direct address. Green knew that the call was for him as he recognized that the rarely utilized punishment Level Three would shortly be initiated.

He lifted his great body and straightened both his net bag and his armband. At least he could look proper, he thought, even if his actions had been absolutely fractious and insubordinate. As he left the cubicle through the hall door and stared straight ahead as he marched toward the inevitable, he felt the bodies of his compatriots fall into place alongside and behind him and he realized their function was both to ensure he reached the destination as well as to observe this seldom-visited cell. Parading with his shoulders straight, his head high, and his eyes resolutely forward, the great Green proceeded through the maze of multiple hallways toward the doors marked clearly and unmistakably with a black "3." The retinue halted with the humiliated Green deposited directly in front of the giant door. As his fellow Greens stood in silent awe, the shamed man waited for the doors to divide and then trod directly and alone into the hallway that led to the punishment room.

In silence, the Greens arranged themselves in front of the darkened windows that overlooked the transgressor's position and pressed their faces to the glass. Behind them the Blues and Whites assumed similar positions on the remaining open glass spaces. Their anticipating eyes searched the darkened expanse for clues of what Level Three would involve this infrequent time and their hot breath produced ringed steam vents on its opaque surface. Their perspiration of excitement and anticipation left rings of their bodies' outlines as the Colors eagerly yet fearfully awaited the Mistress's entry and the beginning of the real punishment.

The lights within the glassed-in room slowly rose and revealed a barren tiled room replete with chained ankle cuffs, steel-bar wrist locks, hanging chains and nettings, and various instruments of which the Whites, Blues, and Greens had no direct knowledge or experience. The torture-chamber atmosphere filled their hearts with suspicion and fear, yet an occasional penis responded with excitement to the event they would soon vicariously experience. With no Golds to castigate them for their prohibited sexual response to their terror, the Colors were free from fear of punishment to take full part in witnessing this phenomenon.

A side door slid silently open and the dazed and shocked Green entered with long, but hardly steady strides. The completely naked man surprised the observers and they struggled to watch his face as he recognized that his net bag and ring of distinction had been taken from him. Facing his unseen observers, the Green lifted his head and with great strength, looked at the mirrored glass on each side and above him as if to look each of his fellows in the eye. He stood proud yet not defiant in the center of this chamber of horror. Expecting and ready to take his punishment, the Green trembled only slightly as he positioned himself dutifully for whatever would follow.

The swishing of the side door could not tempt him to look at the parade of Golds who entered the stark white room. His careful ears told him that the Mistress walked between the front two Golds, yet he would not turn his head to determine how many had accompanied her to this place. The fact that she was there, he realized, bespoke that the severity of the impending punishment might surpass any he had seen take place in this place. He waited silently, standing at naked attention, as she came to stand directly in front of his sweating and trembling position. She spoke quietly, yet the microphone propelled her words into the ears of the entire assembly who stood in rapt attention just outside the glass partition.

"You have engaged in an affair with a trainee." She allowed her straightforward accusation sink into his torrid ears.

Her words were brief and contained no judgment or emotion, yet they pierced directly into his aching heart. He had disappointed her and she would never allow him to achieve the higher ranks, or ever to receive insertion directly from her again. His anguish penetrated his soul and tears fell from his burning eyes. Incredibly, she took quiet steps toward him and wiped his cascading tears with her bare hand. Her touch was wonderfully cool to his burning skin. Fighting his urge to allow her to give him more comfort, the Green stood immobile as she backed off and continued.

"Your punishment will be educational so you may proceed along the path with new-found meaning." Again she stood in perfect silence and allowed the stricken man to absorb her terse words.

In his state of anxiety and grief, he could not process her indictment. Proceed? Meaning?

She continued relentlessly, "No slave, especially a trainer, may engage in sex or achieve orgasm without his trainer's direct approval. I am your trainer. I did not approve. What you have not successfully learned is that you do not own your sexual organs or experiences any more. You have not come to know that I am the only person who can grant you this permission while you are banded with my color. You obviously do not know your place or your restrictions. This is what you must be taught. And this is what you will learn." She stepped back and the Golds, as a group, approached the totally naked Green.

From all directions they labored on the Green's body, shackling his wrists, ankles, head, torso, and legs in manacles that were chained to various parts of the walls and ceiling. Their noiseless work was interrupted only by the clink of chain or the snap of metal locks. Once within his bonds, the Green succumbed to his terror of impending punishment and became anxious only for the process finally to begin. He deserved this lesson, he knew, yet he dreaded waiting for its order to be given.

The Golds retreated to the room's outer edges A nod from the Mistress caused the machinery controlled by her personal Gold who stood at the wall panel to be set in motion. The shackled Green felt the chains retract and begin pulling at his body in multiple directions. His legs went up as his head proceeded down. His wrists and ankles were drawn toward the four corners of the white-tiled room as the leather band around his torso tightened and steadied him directly in the center of space. No part of his body touched the floor, walls, or ceiling; rather, he was suspended upside down, spread-eagled, and vulnerable to any punishment the Mistress was ready to command.

His eyes teared involuntarily and his penis quivered before depositing unwanted but unstoppable droplets indicative of his agony and fear as he was reduced to the status of a shackled, caged animal in terrible fear and horror. In his inverted position, the warm drops of urine flowed cold down his stomach and chest before resting on his bare chin. His flowing tears stained the immaculate white floor. His recently cleansed bowels urged him to eliminate the remnants of his most recent filling, yet he exerted the remnants of sheer forceful willpower to contain them and prevent what would be his final degradation in front of the Colors and the Mistress.

The Golds came forward and surrounded him in silence as the Mistress slowly entered their protective circle. His defenseless position was dangled in full view of the entourage who stood both within and outside the dreadful room. He was helpless and exposed, powerless to prevent their punishment, and more frightened than he had ever been in his life. She patted his trembling belly and grasped his penis in a warm and soft hand. She held the limp organ out unceremoniously for all to see.

"This is no longer his," she stated matter-of-factly. "It is now mine. His punishment is to lose this organ until I believe he is ready to wear it once again."

The Colors on the observation platform gasped and pressed their perspiring bodies even closer to the glass that separated them from this ultimate horror. Their own maleness crushed even closer to the window as the astounded group fought their rising dread.

She pulled even harder on the dangling man's flaccid and naked member until he was forced to moan aloud. Visible shudders of pain coursed throughout his suspended body. The audience gasped in a collective intake of breath at the horrific sight they were witnessing.

Gripping his organ harder and with a yanking motion, she pulled his body taut by this sexual extremity, then pressed the tip closed so no unwanted expulsion could occur. Green's eyes cried rivers of tears from pain and humiliation as well as from the fear that her ominous words caused to echo throughout his shocked brain.

She ran two fingers under his hairless testicles and gripped the entire package of the Green's sexual manhood in a vise-like clutch that betrayed the strength that had been disguised by her outer soft femininity. Having no green net bag to encumber his organs or intensify his punishment, the Mistress rotated her handful to personally inflict incredible pain on the shuddering and shaking man. He cried out great bellows of rage, anguish, and dread as much at her physical actions as at her frightening words. He had never expected that she could bring him to such a point of nothingness.

After what seemed an eternity to both the prisoner and the observers, she released her package and sent quivers of apprehension through the assembled Colors on the observation platform. No one, not even the Golds, had ever before seen her personally administer such torture to any Color, not for any infraction that had merited Level Three. A sigh of relief escaped from the lips of the observers when they saw the man's mangled testicles bounce freely between his legs once again. His limp penis hung straight toward the floor, pointed toward the inverted Green's chest, and lay reddened from mishandling along his bald skin. With a beckoning finger, she motioned a Gold forward and instructed him to bring the Green's head up so he might hear her words without encumbrance. The Gold bent down, grasped two hands of the man's hair, and lifted the shrieking man's face toward the Mistress.

"While you have no organs, you are a non-person within the facility. Only I can restore your manhood and I will do so when you have learned your lesson and pleased me. During the time you are emasculated, you may speak to no one, interact with no one, and approach no one. You will serve me alone for as long as I consider you untrained." Her words cut his heart and his tears coursed unabated to the floor.

Her merciless punishment continued, "When you are fully trained to my specifications, I will return your masculinity to you. The time is now. Bring me the tools."

Golds scurried about when they heard her brief order while the men on the observation platform crammed their collective manhood even more tightly against the slick glass. They longed to bring their hands to their own net bags for reassurance and comfort in sympathy for the Green's plight. No one had ever seen the Mistress so quietly outraged or so vehement in her punishment. Her sentence of emasculation was tantamount to castration and her administration of it sent shivers of cold fear through the congregation witnessing the passing of judgment and execution of sentence.

Her personal Gold handed her a large green velvet bag. Another moved to the control panel on the wall, made some adjustments, and the manacles holding the inverted Green's legs stretched him farther apart. The torso belt was released and the poor man was suspended from his spread out ankles with his hands chained securely to the floor as his only balance. Then she ordered the floor locks opened and his hands swung freely only inches from the gleaming white floor. She ordered a nearby Gold to kneel and on his outstretched arms she placed the green velvet bag. Ordering another Gold to open it, she reached in and extracted a series of black leather straps, a small chain, and a lock.

The Colors shook in their reaction to the shock of the blackness of the leather. Black, she had instructed them individually when she took them one at a time into the Green training program, was the highest source of embarrassment for a trainer. It indicated his failure and humiliation for the duration of his wearing any black garment. They had only heard of the black leather in quiet and contraband discussions among Golds and a Head White. Seeing it now brought murmurs of disbelief from their sweaty lips.

She threw the leather above her head and held onto only one corner. The device elongated as the men tried to determine in their fear and shock in what manner this unknown device was utilized. Whipping it about, the Mistress brought an exciting but horrifying crack to the ears of the men straining to figure out the purpose of what she held in her hand. She threw it once again, only this time her direction had purpose and she brought it to rest with a great thud between the legs directly on the exposed genital area of the dangling Green in the center of the punishment room. Without instruction, the personal Gold rushed in, pulled the leather harness down with force, and belted the howling and shrieking man into its confines. Its tightness threatened to crush his organs, Green felt, and he screamed with intensity as her attendant fastened the locks into place.

The black leather strapping was designed to fit securely across the man's genital area, between his legs, and up across his buttocks. A wide leather belt was locked firmly around his belly, beneath his navel, and across the hairless skin. The back strap was drawn tightly and connected with yet another lock to the belt, yet the front dangled free. The Gold stepped back and the Mistress strode in to make the final adjustment. When Green thought he could take no more, he learned his body could and would endure the full severity of the Mistress's wrath.

She had him raised upward by his ankle chains until his eyes were even with hers. As he dangled in shame and pain from the ceiling of the punishment room, she stared directly into his unseeing eyes and pulled the loose leather strap tightly down across his scrotum, testicles, and penis and secured it to the front latch of the bikini height black leather belt. As she locked the instrument into place, the distraught Green wailed sounds that seemed inhuman to the assembled ears. When she ascertained he had reached his limit, she nodded to her personal Gold at the wall panel and had the bedraggled man lowered to the floor.

Green landed with a thud as the leg grips were loosened. The Golds removed their equipment and exited silently from the chamber that sealed the Green's sentencing and punishment. The glass partitions were darkened and the Colors remained pressed tightly against the glass, waiting for their impending instructions and warnings that always followed Level Three. Her voice rang quietly throughout the observation post as she intoned their part of Green's sentence.

"You will not speak to or respond to this Black for the duration of his punishment," she began. "If you see him attending me, you will not acknowledge his presence. Interrupting this punishment is not in either your or his best interests. You are dismissed to return to your rooms to contemplate the meaning of this sentence."

The group of Whites, Blues, and Greens removed their sticky bodies from the dark glass wall and to a man each grasped his sexual organs in tender palms as if to insure that they were still attached to their bodies. Silently they filed each to his own cubicle in fear of similar punishment to themselves as well as in horror at the punishment this former member of their party had endured. Colors, an intensely loyal group, experienced this man's removal as a death and they grieved for their lost member.

Within the darkened room the Black rolled on the cold floor, grabbed for his leather-encased genitals and found none. His screaming and crying continued as he fought to endure the pain of the too-tight leather and the knowledge that his emasculation was a result of his own disobedience and weakness. He vowed in his pain and disgrace to become absolutely obedient and he swore he would endure all pain and humiliation the Mistress would certainly inflict on his practically-castrated body. She told him to kneel and he struggled in his agony to bring his body to an upright position. With extreme effort, he rose to his knees.

"You shall learn true obedience," she spat in his direction. "I will return your organs to you when you are fully trained." She turned to leave and called behind her, "You may crawl."

Black strained to fall forward onto his hands without jostling the black leather belt that imprisoned his organs, yet the sheer movement of his legs brought intense pain to that sensitive region. With each step, Black felt the pressure against his invisible penis and testicles and he could not imagine how he would manage to either stand or sit. He need not have worried, because the Mistress would allow neither action for the duration of his punishment.

"Heel!" she directed at the recalcitrant crawling man behind her feet. "Come, or I will be forced to administer a more direct order." Her shrill voice spoke with the intensity of her outrage.

The Black sped up, moaning with each step, and crawled alongside her quietly clicking heels. The unlikely pair proceeded up empty hallways and down yet other ones, turned multiple corners, as she quickened and slowed the pace to grant him just enough rest to enable him to complete the journey. She came to a stop at the silver doors that indicated her private quarters and she keyed the combination into the lock. The doors flew silently apart and the Mistress and her exhausted Black entered her lavish quarters. The thick white carpet eased his aching hands and knees as the crawling Black stopped just inside the entrance. With the Mistress's command to halt, the bedraggled man lifted his depleted head for his next order. It was swift in coming.

"Rest," she commanded as the spent man fell to the white carpet in sheer uselessness and nothingness. "You will need your strength if you are to complete your obedience training." He fell immediately asleep on the brilliant white carpet and never saw the Mistress change into her silk chemise or climb into her great bed for the evening.

In the morning, the disheveled Black was awakened rudely by the Mistress's high-heeled foot placed directly on the black leather bikini belt that housed his secreted maleness. His overwhelming sense of urgency to relieve himself overcame his disorientation and discomfort within his restricted belting. He gazed at his superior with beseeching eyes, and she returned a cold glance of indifference to his plight. Dirtying her plush white carpet was simply out of the question and Black scurried about searching for a place to empty his bursting bladder. Unconcerned with his predicament, she offered no solution as she turned to her morning schedules and papers. Calling her personal Gold over the speaker, she waited for his entry before directing any comment to her "pet."

"I hope you are housebroken," she threatened lightly, "or you will feel my full wrath." She returned her attention to her paperwork.

The personal Gold glanced only for a split second at the struggling Black who was crawling on all fours while searching for a place to empty himself. Turning to his Mistress and the paperwork, the Gold surprised himself at his ability to dissociate from his mind the Black's dilemma. Black, knowing that no help would come from his former comrade, scurried around the beautiful rooms in search of a means to evacuate his bursting insides. He slithered under the bed, combed behind the dressers, and nestled his eyes into the closet in search of a pan or dish into which he could find relief. Finally, his nose brought him to a flat sand-filled pan that reeked of chlorine only when he came into almost direct contact with it. This must be his place, he assumed, and in his dire need and emergency, he considered how he could direct his stream into it.

Pulling at the unyielding leather with two frantic hands, he discovered a small slit that approximated the height of his penis's tip. Kneeling over the pan in an effort to avoid ruining the white carpet, the Black rested on all fours across the sand-filled tray and tried to discharge his bladder. As the Mistress and her personal Gold continued their discussions oblivious to his distress, he found that his bladder had seized in fright and refused to empty. He strained, concentrated, and breathed deeply in vain as his restricted organ failed to respond to his urging. Imagining no discomfort or humiliation greater than what he was enduring at this moment, the Black cried in frustration and anger.

The giant tears fell silently from his eyes as his bladder finally responded and brought streams of hot liquid toward the sand beneath him. Craning his neck downward, he watched the entire process as if it were happening to someone else. Yet feeling the warm liquid turn cold on his skin instructed him that this man, urinating into a sand-filled box in the corner of this beautiful room, was truly himself. His tears were of the joy of relief and of the humility he now experienced. The Mistress watched the entire episode from the mirror above her head and smiled.

Having nowhere else to go, the empty Black crawled back and returned to her side and awaited her next command.

"Eat!" she commanded curtly as she pointed to a ceramic bowl on a silver tray on the floor.

He gazed toward the latest humiliation she had set out for him and noticed a large black bowl filled with granola-topped yogurt that had apparently been brought in while he relieved himself into the sand. He crawled with painful steps toward it, although his mind reeled from the concept of eating like an animal. Obey, he urged himself as he pressed his mouth toward the runny liquid. Eat, he forced into his brain, as he sucked the contents between his teeth and into his mouth. Swallow, he screamed to his throat as the runny mixture stuck on his tongue. Gagging silently, the degraded Black felt the stickiness of the yogurt decorate his nose, lips, and cheeks. Understanding the order in its entirety, he recognized that he could not use his hands to wipe his soiled face. He rubbed his nose onto his arm and understood with finality how the Mistress intended to teach him to obey.

"Come!" she directed to the Black as he stared at the now-empty bowl. "Here!" she ordered again as he reluctantly and slowly crawled back to her side. "Kneel," she continued as he approached her spiked slippers.

He complied by garnering all the strength he had left in his sore and aching muscles. Once he was straightened on both knees, she reached out toward his black leather belt. Barely containing his joy at being released from the horror of this affliction, the Black tried in vain to suppress the smile that threatened to break out on his soiled and sticky face. She touched the warm leather and as her soft and cool hand rested against his bald pubic skin, he shuddered with anticipation and joy. Grasping the front strap firmly between strong fingers, she lifted it directly upwards and tightened it to the next notch.

"It stretches," she commented to no one in particular and turned back to her paperwork as the formerly great Green screamed in anguish in his disappointment and pain. She let him howl until she tired of his inability to obey her command for quiet, then picked up a new black leather crop and stroked his backside until the red welts arose and the Black was no longer sure if he was screaming from anger, pain, or spanking. He carried his welted backside with him for the duration of his punishment as a reminder of the Mistress's rules, her demand for obedience, and his own transgressions of her direct orders.

Chapter Twenty One

Debbie lay back on the new satin sheets and awaited the alarm to ring that Sunday morning. As she stared at the clock and anticipated its call, she heard the soft treading of her Gold on the carpeted steps outside her bedroom. He entered silently and placed the silver tray before her. The aroma of the vanilla-flavored coffee brought excitement to her nostrils as she eagerly anticipated opening the wrapped box of special lingerie that presented itself from under Gold's massive arm. She sipped the heavenly coffee, munched at the scones, and gazed at the oiled and tanned muscles that rippled throughout his broad body.

Her Gold waited in silence for the satin-clad woman to acknowledge his presence and his gift. Standing cleansed, naked, oiled, and erect at the side of her bed, Gold controlled his breathing so as not to disturb her breakfast and awakening. Debbie smiled silently as her eyes wandered up and down his immense muscular structure and wavy hair.

She peeked at his golden net bag and wondered about the size and power of its secreted contents. Someday, she promised herself, she would find out just what he had hidden beneath the sparkling metallic sheath.

When she had drunk the coffee and enjoyed the scone, Debbie motioned for Gold to remove the tray from her satin-sheeted lap so she might better view his offering. Hurriedly the massive man took up the china and silver and placed it softly on the carpet outside her bedroom door. Returning with alacrity to his former place at her side, Gold lifted the wrapped package and offered it to his superior. She took it with white, milky arms and tenderly unleashed its contents. With wrappings and ribbons strewn on her bed, Debbie lifted out of the box a bright Christmas-red satin bra and open-crotched panties, garter belt and red hose, and an unusually high pair of red patent leather stiletto shoes. Throwing off her bedcovers, Debbie rose from between the sheets and casually allowed her red silk gown to fall open at the slit that started from her toes and rose to her tingling breasts. The Gold extended a warm hand to assist her, and she took it firmly within her braceleted wrist and drew it down to her warmest and most private region.

Gold knelt next to the bed yet did not remove his hand from her placement of it within her femininity. She took his empty hand and moved it firmly around his back and urged to him exhibit to her his skill and prowess.

"Use only this hand," she instructed, "and show me what you have been trained so well to do."

He needed no further urging. Gold closed his warm brown eyes and imagined the exciting snowy mountains and calming classical music he had once chosen so many years ago. The faint vanilla aroma permeated his nostrils with a message sent directly from his well-trained brain. Feeling warm despite his nakedness, Gold meditated himself into a calm and serene state in which he was comfortable, secure, and safe. His talented hands and experienced brain brought the rest to his nimble fingers. Clasping her clitoris gently yet firmly between his thumb and forefinger, Gold drew the tiny organ directly toward his body and sensitively implored the longhaired woman to relax back onto her sheets. Without stroking, he enabled the organ to engorge, stiffen, and stand ready.

Slowly he brought her to arousal as he moved multiple fingers around, up and down, and across her most susceptible area. She threw her head back as an almost audible moan began to emerge from her lips. Spreading her legs wide apart without his physical encouragement, Debbie thrust her hips up and down in rhythm with the tempo of his sensitive stroke. At times, she felt she could take no more; however, the Gold immediately ceased his efforts and allowed her to relax so she would not fulfill herself until she had experienced his full efforts.

During one such relaxation period, Debbie sat up slightly and urged his massive hand behind his back to clasp and join the other. Opening his deep eyes slightly, the Gold cast her an inquisitive look. Her throaty voice betrayed her excitement and arousal.

"No hands. Show me everything!" she almost screamed directly into his ear.

Gold closed his eyes once again and remembered his thrill and delirium at her hands during his ritual insertion the evening before. His entire body shuddered with response as he replayed the swinging and the service of the two trainees in accomplishing his ultimate pleasure. Moistening his lips with a succulent tongue, Gold leaned forward to bring his mouth to her pulsating and quivering lips. Turning his head only slightly sideways, Gold used his lubricated lips to spread her own most delicate area and inserted a ready tongue to taste the fruit of her excitement.

She moaned again, louder this time.

Debbie was beside herself with delight and fought her urge to spend herself at the rapid and torrid insertion and withdrawal of his magnificent tongue. Flicking and darting, the daring instrument caressed her inside with a delight she had never experienced. Ron! She thought with delight and rising excitement. Ron will be able to bring me here whenever I instruct him to do so. Debbie's anticipation served only to heighten her glee. Gold felt her inner organ tense, the very sign he had been so well trained to discover, and he knew she was well on her way.

He leaned in closer to her sweet-smelling region and used his now-dripping lips to spread her even farther apart. She moaned louder now and grabbed his sweating head within her perspiring hands to bring the expert's tool even more tightly into herself. Passionate in her desire to experience the most ardent and intense orgasm of her life, Debbie thrust her hips toward the mouth that brought her to the ultimate height of ecstasy. The Gold responded with intense lapping and, when he recognized the final signs, took the tortured organ within his teeth and chewed ever so gently along its ridge.

She screamed with delirium and ecstasy as she came to full completion as his teeth probed her and bit gently down. Wrapping her long white legs around his tanned and sweaty head and neck, Debbie thrust a final time and found the newest heights of sexual delight. Gripping him tautly, she spent herself over and over again and finally came to rest on her back on the satin sheets of her wide bed.

Soundlessly, the great Gold licked her sensitivity and warmed the cooling area with his smooth face. Recalling his training that demanded post-orgasm tenderness and insight, he cooled her down and allowed her to rest from her great physical exertion. Using his lubricated tongue to soothe her battered insides, he stroked the woman gently and caressed her as tenderly as he had been forceful just moments before. Debbie began to realize how right she had been to enroll Ron in the very same course that would bring to him--and to them--the wonders that this Gold had shown her.

"Bathe me," she mumbled from her supine position across the wide bed.

The Gold rose immediately to obey her command and strode to the remodeled bathroom to turn on the jets of the immense hot tub. He added a few drops of lavender oil and inhaled its welcome aroma with deep breaths. Recalling his experiences with the scented soap and the great baths, the Gold stood unmoving on the deep aqua tile of the master bath. Holding himself tightly in fond memory, the Gold allowed his well-trained mind to wander back to the first day he arrived at the training facility, an experience that was an unexpected gift from his fiancée, but absolutely and without question the finest present he had ever received in his life.

He dimly remembered the limousine ride, the initial shock of insertion, and the bus trip, but he recalled vividly the hanging ride into nowhere he took on his initial entry into the building. The blackness and void surrounded him; the tethers and flashing lights still felt like they pulled at and illuminated his sweaty form.

The first cleansing he experienced was stunning and incredibly seductive because it was that cleansing that finally drew him to service first as a trainee, then as a trainer, a programmer, a leader, and culminated in his promotion to Gold. Having been all the Colors, Gold's seasoning and training was beyond almost all others.

The novice cleansing flooded not only his bowels, but flowed almost directly into his brain. The deep lavender fragrance penetrated not only his nostrils, but his darkest regions as well with its delicious and delightful tingling. Gold always looked forward to the morning baths as he awaited the Green-administered immersion and purification. Feeling the warm oil enter deep into his entrails excited him in a way he could not easily express.

Eventually during his training, Gold became a master at administering and receiving the bath. Although Debbie could not have known his innermost secret, Gold concealed his admiration for Ron's skill in bathing his black-haired partner the previous evening. The video he and Debbie had witnessed bore testimony to the pleasures that Debbie would receive when Ron had completed his training and was returned to her as a full-fledged slave.

Even Ron's arousal of the Green had been awe-inspiring to the highly trained Gold. He had never expected a trainee to accept his training so fully that he could immerse himself so deeply into it that a trainer, especially a Green due for promotion, could become titillated by the event. Debbie had been so excited by Ron's expertise and the illicit spectacle between the trainee and the Green that she had come to want Gold's excitement that first morning after the scene had been played.

Standing amid the deep-toned aqua tiles, Gold reminisced about his first bathing in the great pool after his frightening yet stimulating entry into the facility. He recalled standing waist deep in the warm blue water and having his head forced into the plush padded neck brace. Ready to be outraged at the violation of his dignity, the young and inexperienced trainee that he once was forced himself to breathe deeply and endure the trespassing that was done to his body. He struggled somewhat against the application of the depilatory, yet he was fascinated by his hairless pubis and the smooth, baby-soft skin that lay underneath the golden curly locks.

When his Green lubricated his organs with lavender soap and stroked them repeatedly, lovingly, and tenderly, he was first disgusted; yet, within a short time, he came to enjoy the compassionate and delicate fondling. Once the Green had flipped the young man over and inserted pink cream into his dark and forbidding anus, the immature trainee instantaneously restricted his sphincter so as to deter the probing and insistent fingers. He stood in the center of the aqua bathroom, eyes shut, arms gripping himself tightly, and felt his gold netting begin to engorge.

With a sudden jerk and startle, the immobile Gold experienced both the memory and the actuality of the terrifying whipping that was administered to his buttocks that morning so long ago that seemed to be replaying itself in the aqua master bath suite. Flinging open his eyelids, Gold saw an angered Debbie inflicting repeated leather crop strokes to his tardy (?)rear cheeks. Having waited long enough for her command to be fulfilled, Debbie had arisen from her boudoir and come upon the daydreaming Gold who had not yet attended to her order.

The arrhythmic stroking of his backside brought the sheepish man in and out of the present. The spanks were dealt as Debbie saw fit; she had no need to be regular or give the disobedient man any forewarning. Rather, she struck him hard and then waited. When she was satisfied that he was quivering in anticipation, she waited a slight bit longer. When he relaxed visibly, Debbie struck again. The chagrined Gold endured this most demeaning punishment with dignity; however, the fact that it was the first punishment he had endured as an untrained beginner brought tears of shame to his wide-open eyes.

His mind darted between that first morning in the great pool and the humiliating repetition he was receiving in the aqua bathroom. That Green had spanked him long and hard, admonishing him never, ever to close himself to his superiors again. To drive that very point home, the Green had injected even more bright pink cream into the younger man's chastened orifice and then rammed the cleansing hose in as far as he could reach.

Surreptitiously changing the warm water temperature to a higher setting, the young sandy-haired man experienced an onrush of steaming liquid that buckled his knees, brought tears of pain to his eyes, and inflicted shame to his rectum. He endured the cleansing with howling and screaming, and learned that very morning that disobedience to one's superior was deadly wrong.

With his mind now returned to the aqua bathroom, the reproved Gold endured this scolding with significant memories. He abided each of Debbie's well-placed strokes with steely determination, yet he sensed a recollection of the process that brought him to love the process of cleansing so well.

After his initial lesson in obedience to a superior, the young trainee became fascinated with the art of lubricating his partner's secret orifice. Knowing that the lubricator eventually became the superior, the young man threw himself into the task of becoming the most proficient and skillful trainee of his group. Using the bright pink cream as a tool for advancement and power, the trainee alternated between using a probing finger, a scissor-like duo, or, especially with the most muscular men, the planting of his thumb on the lower bone and the thrusting of four spread fingers into the tiny, yet expandable orifice. He brought caterwauls of pain to some, and to others he brought excitement and glee. Soon he was able to recognize how the different ones would react, and he could ascertain before lubrication which method would bring either resistance or acquiescence.

After his promotion to the level of Green, he met one insolent recruit who bore the lubrication but never allowed himself to fully succumb to it. He had the impudent blond man brought before him and made sure that the video of the cleansing would be available to the man later that day so he might view it repeatedly and learn the humility that fully trained slaves must experience. First, he lathered the trainee's tanned body with the fragrant soap and then he stroked his willing penis until it stood of its own accord directly toward the ceiling of the room that decorated the great bath. The recently promoted Green then knelt in apparent supplication to the elongated member and took the organ in two great hands; his fingers cupped beneath the hairless testicles, and lifted the screaming trainee's hips directly out of the water.

He screamed into the petrified young man's face. "You are mine! You are mine!" the Green cried as the blond man wept and shrieked.

He jerked his handful of sensitive organs downward and flipped the padded neck brace so the anguished trainee faced completely downward. As he moved quickly behind the quaking man, he simultaneously drove his feet down and apart and slapped the tanned backside with the most forceful stroke he could muster. The almost-berserk trainee felt a great four-fingered hand ram pink cream into his bowels. The massive hand spanked the egotistical buttocks again and brought yelps of pain and suffering to his anguished mouth.

Without warning, the former Green inserted the hot hose into the man's resisting anus and released the bursting valve. The trainee sagged and panted, and tried to resist the inflowing waters. Plugging his charge, the former Green dragged the man by his blond hair into the cubicle for expulsion. Then he hauled the exhausted trainee back into the great pool.

He repeated the process all morning until the young man stood silently and willingly for the lubrication, insertion, and cleansing. The master filled the aching bowels and discharged them repeatedly. Showing no mercy to the exhausted trainee, the superior Green paraded him in and out of the baths, plugging his exploding insides and then releasing them after the forced march. After many cleansings and purifications, the dazed young man appeared to learn his lesson and he stood open-cheeked for the lotion, the cleansing, and finally dropped exhausted onto the red carpeted floor for the ultimate purification. By then, the former Green had established himself as the overlord of the baths and king of breaking brazen young recruits.

Debbie ceased her cracking of the leather whip behind the Gold's glistening buttocks. She had made her point, but she desired her bath. Putting a gleaming white hand on the Gold's sweating shoulder, Debbie spun the chastened man around and drove him to his knees. She bent to look directly into his burning eyes.

"You--will--bathe--me--NOW!" she commanded, and the Gold grasped the hem of her silk gown, rose slowly, and brought the garment over her head.

He stood in respect of her elegance and brought his tender lips to her milky skin. Kissing every inch of her warm shoulders, his mouth moved downward toward her breasts. Sucking slightly, he lifted each firm breast and nuzzled his face beneath it. Bringing his hairless and smooth face to her stomach, he kissed the skin and fell soundlessly to his knees to perform his talents on her thighs and legs. She stepped apart and allowed him entry to her inner thighs. His talented lips continued on their tour of her body and rested on her red-polished toes. Crawling behind her naked but straight body, the Gold began his upward spiral and licked and kissed the backs of her calves and thighs. Taking his nude face to her soft and warm cheeks, he pressed his mouth between her round backside and nuzzled his way in to her softness. He felt his maleness begin to answer the call that this orgasmic scenario could only demand.

He stood behind her and pressed his muscular body into her. She felt the hardness of his male member and she strained to flex against its gold net prison. Rubbing her cheeks up and down against his member, she excited the Gold to full erection. She spun, faced the electrified man, and reiterated her demand.

"You will bathe me now or suffer the consequences," she promised.

The Gold reached down and took the naked woman into his powerful arms. Striding purposefully into the swirling bathwater, he delivered her to what would become a very memorable morning.

Placing her head gently against the edge of the tub, Gold positioned her on her back, her legs spread wide apart. He took the tube of lavender soap and brought forth a great lather between his robust hands. Beginning with the feet he had just kissed in humility, the Gold cleansed every toe, her feet and ankles, and moved his strong motions up each of her outstretched legs. Reaching under her hips, he lifted the hairy lips from the water, kissed them gently, then poured the fragrance onto her and lathered them with his face in supplication. Gently dousing her lower body in the warm water, he soaped each breast and rubbed them with his hairless cheeks. Turning her over carefully, he again washed her toes, feet, ankles, and legs, then reached beneath and elevated her backside from the water. Reaching for his tray of utensils, the Gold automatically took the silver cream that was reserved for the Mistress and the spouses of the trainees, reached one finger into the squishy lotion, and withdrew a finger full to insert into her pristine anal cavity. He pushed his finger gently inside her darkness.

Debbie was stunned by the pleasure that the emollient brought to her suddenly sensitive posterior. Waves of undulating delight seized her insides and spasms of enchantment overtook her being. Her cleansed toes, feet, ankles, thighs, belly, breasts, and torso throbbed in rhythmic motion as she savored the lubrication that Gold offered.

The scrutinizing finger added even more special silverness to the frenzied woman's passion and investigated every possibility in her lower region. Gold was especially careful with gentleness and tenderness, for his overriding desire was to enable Debbie to remember this episode with as much pleasure and happiness as he recalled his first tender cleansing. She could understand and know Ron's pleasure, Gold thought, only when she had known it herself. He pushed the inquiring digit in and out while caressing her quivering body from above and beneath.

The delights that Debbie's anal massaging had brought to her consciousness were beyond any expectations she had formerly held. The experience seemed to continue forever as her internal muscles contracted and elongated with Gold's expert touch. He reached beneath her as she lay prone in the swirling water and raised her buttocks even higher from the pool. Her legs dangling now, Debbie felt her body give in fully to the Gold's massive arm. Her slackened and free legs swished together and apart in the jet stream of the hot tub as Gold applied ever so slightly more silver cream to her delicate darkness. Her braceleted hand was suspended from her raised shoulder and glistened in the glow of the overhead heat lamp in the aqua bathroom.

The delicious warmth of the swirling tub and gentle anal massage threatened to lull Debbie into a return to the exhausted state of sleep that overcame her last night as she watched the video of Ron's escapades in the great pool with his trainee and his Green. The excitement of Ron's acceptance of and enthusiasm for bathing others assured Debbie that the delirium she was currently in danger of losing herself to could be enjoyed by a simple command issued to her well-trained husband. She felt Gold's technique and hoped Ron would be similarly instructed. Quietly and softly, the welcome intrusion of Gold's finger ceased and Debbie was returned to the lavender-scented waters. She knelt on the pool's bottom and clung desperately to the tub's rim. Assuring himself that she was neither cold nor uncomfortable, Gold knelt at her side and awaited her command.

Finally, she turned and called in a throaty voice over her submerged shoulder, "I'll do you now."

Gold stood immobile, as he was totally astounded. If she were felt energized enough to perform the ritual cleansing on him, then it was possible that his presentation to her did not satisfy her ultimate urges and his skill and technique needed re-training and improvement. Incredulous at her suggestion yet expertly obedient, the big man stood, grasped the pool's edge, and spread his legs for her practice and learning. Standing ominously behind him, Debbie inspected the tubes, lotions, and tools on the golden tray adorning the pool's perimeter. She reached for the gold tube.

Pushing some glistening soap onto her fingers, Debbie considered all she had seen and felt regarding the bathing that both Ron and Gold had come to know and enjoy. She was determined to match and surpass any level of expertise that this Gold or even Ron had illustrated. Warming the lavender-scented gel in her soft hands, she brought what seemed like a plethora of bubbles to Gold's shining wet skin. Considering his position with his backside facing her and his legs spread-eagle along the edge of the pool, Debbie weighed her alternatives. And she was disappointed that he readied himself only for the cleansing. What was he thinking, she thought, when he took up that pose? That I wanted only to ram a tube into him? How insulting! Her mind raced and devised an ingenious plan to challenge the trained man's control once again.

Deftly reaching between the spread legs with a shimmering hand, Debbie took the golden net bag and pulled toward her as the stunned Gold stepped back into the pool's center in surprise and shock. His fully vertical body received the swirling waters as Debbie circled him. Toying with his questioning eyes, she refused to answer his innermost question and respond to his need to know what she wanted from him. Lunging with soapy hands at his male organs, she grinned as he winced from her feigned blows. He shut his warm brown eyes and allowed his body to experience the tantalizing attacks the surprisingly agile woman made. She was more than he expected, he thought, and she was more than he was sure he could handle.

Pulling his knees toward her, she sat the big man down in the center of the pool. Through closed eyes but open ears, he heard the clink of a lock that secured his penile ring to the golden chain that had been part of his tray of tools and lotions. His diligent ears and sensitive skin felt her alight from the pool and secure the other end of the chain around the base of the pedestal sink. His penis thus fastened, the Gold remained imprisoned within the hot tub of this aqua bathroom.

She set directly to work. Resting his head on an aqua towel on the pool's far edge, she pulled the length of chain to tautness and Gold's ring tugged at his sensitive and tingling organs. The gold net bag constricted slightly and he knew that she had figured out how to secure the two special golden loops to the lock. Any movement on his part, he recognized instantaneously, would inflict strangling, pinching, and choking of his maleness. Remaining absolutely still, the great Gold lay in awe of this woman's awareness and skill.

She lifted his toned and muscular legs one at a time and held them close to her naked skin as she bathed them delightfully with scented soap. Rubbing up and down and then in circles,

Debbie exercised proficiency at arousing his sensual delight beyond his wildest expectations. Relaxing and enjoying the bath, the Gold lost himself in hedonistic thought as his mind was torn between his expert training and his lustful serenity at this moment. Debbie watched his eyes close and the tense muscles of his face loosen as she smirked at the level of excitement she had brought to this master. He still had much to enjoy this Sunday morning, she vowed, as she set to work between his upper thighs.

Her small hands spread the massive legs wider to reveal fully the bald genital area that Gold himself had kept up with daily self-administered depilatories during his stay at Debbie's home during Ron's training. She admired his handiwork and began tickling his sensitive skin with her long polished fingernails. His delight was apparent and his gold net bag began to twitch as its contents, with a mind of its own, responded to her touch. Placing one hand deftly beneath his tense buttocks, she lifted his hips from the swirling water and exposed an elongated penis and two rock-hard testicles. The upward movement brought a slight constriction to the shackled net bag. Gold's eyes flew open.

"Don't move," she urged, "or you will know ultimate pain and simultaneous indescribable pleasure. It's up to you." The raven-haired woman laughed quietly at his face full of distress and fear. She lifted him inches higher.

Holding the open bottle of lavender soap directly above his trembling organs, she poured drops of the enticing liquid onto his pubis, scrotum, testicles, and eventually onto his penis. Spasms of joy and expectation greeted each drop as the Gold's maleness responded to every application. Replacing the golden bottle onto the poolside tray, she used her free hand to massage the contents into his denuded skin. His reaction was as immediate as it was intense and the shackled man's thigh muscles tightened visibly at each touch of her deft fingers. He threw back his head onto the soft aqua towel she had positioned under it for his comfort and his hands thrashed the empty water at his sides. He was losing control and his mind reeled.

Debbie used her strong nails to elicit even more sensation to this readying area. She touched and prodded his organs through his netting and watched in anticipation as his penis grew before her eyes. As it extended, she noticed the gold netting contract and she drew his upraised hips toward her, thus shortening his already tense gold chain. The secured loops and the unyielding penile ring were drawn tightly as she pulled the quaking man toward her scented vanilla skin. His mouth opened and a small inaudible moan escaped from his dry lips.

She had barely begun. Determined to illustrate to this expertly trained man her full capabilities, Debbie urged his tense legs apart and raised his hips fully out of the water. The tension to the caged organs increased along with the pleasure he knew from her darting and well-placed fingernails along his bald and soapy genital area. Holding his undulating hips securely in one hand, she walked between his dangling legs and stood at the base of the vertical penis and fully stretched net bag. Delighting in his dual discomfort, Debbie knelt in the swirling waters and brought her firm breasts to this excited member. Placing one breast on either side of the tortured penis, she rubbed against the bubbly soap that adorned him and felt the bag and its contents harden to an inspiring tightness.

Almost, she thought. But not yet.

Gold could barely maintain his control over his trained organs. Her skill and ingenuity had surprised and astounded his ability to exert by his own willpower a cessation of the hardening that threatened to explode in the aqua bath. Her up and down knee bends tormented his organs as she became a menace to his pride and dignity as well as to his governance of himself. He had never known another trainee's spouse to perform this well and he was overcome at his underestimation of this raven-haired peril.

She continued her assault by stretching the robust and muscular legs even farther apart and she succeeded in causing another more audible moan as his golden bag tensed dramatically. His hips were fully free of the water as she drew a palm full of golden cream from the poolside tray. The bent-over man's knees threatened his chest as she exposed the darkened area into which she immediately plunged four soft golden fingers. His scream of delight and pain resounded in the tiled bathroom and escaped to the master suite as the woman filled his cavity with lubricant. He yelped out of control as she twisted her wrist and brought the golden cream to every side of his canal and he tried to bounce away from the determined application she was dedicated to delivering. His cries of anguish mixed with ecstasy bellowed from his gaping mouth as he could no longer command his own body or its reactions to her extreme and wonderful bathing of the great man in the swirling waters.

Abandoning his training and expertise, the great Gold flailed and thrashed in the pool as she added more golden cream to his rectum. She drew a final circle on his shaking cheeks with one hand and exercised his uncompromising and unyielding penis with the other. Using a carefully devised up and down motion, she worked his member while applying yet more gold cream in and out of his open bottom. The man was out of control as he bounced and jiggled within the exposed position she had confined him to and his spasms brought the ultimate pain of the choking and constricting gold netting in which he was eternally incarcerated.

She continued the agonizing persecution of the man who believed himself to be the master and illustrated without question her superiority and skill. His mind could not focus and his deep screams betrayed her talent as she brought him closer and closer to the final completion of ecstasy. Lifting his hips yet once more high above the water, she grabbed the rigid member from above and inserted a full hand below as the Gold ejaculated directly upwards more forcefully than he had ever accomplished before from within his netting. His juices exploded in mid-air and came to rest on his hairless pubic skin. Leaving the sputtering and exasperated Gold to his own self-cleaning, the raven-haired woman removed herself from the warm water and showered in the clear glass booth in the corner of the aqua bathroom.

Unsupported and spent, his body sagged into the jet stream of the hot tub and the Gold slowly regained his composure and his thoughts. Dazed but beginning to comprehend the events that had just occurred, the humiliated and chagrined Gold allowed his body to sink to the floor of the pool as he cried tears of joy and pain. He had never experienced such a total loss of self-control, yet his still-shackled penile ring was evidence of the reality of what he had just undergone. Feeling childlike in his impotence at self-control, he gazed at the showering woman and complimented silently her capability and control.

Stepping from the shower, Debbie reached for a plush aqua towel and dried her dripping form as the Gold gawked longingly at her. Feeling his stare, she reached for the golden chain and unlocked it from the sink's base. Holding it securely within her hands, she tugged at it and dragged the spent and sputtering man from his comfortable watery lair. As he stood netted and naked before her, she allowed him to drip as she continued her toweling of herself. Satisfied she was dry, she led the chagrined man by his firmly attached chain into the bedroom area and latched him securely to the massive bedpost.

"Call Tony and Bob," she called as she left to dress herself in the red lingerie. "Have them report to me here immediately. I have wonderful plans for today."

The red-faced Gold obeyed her command, dialed the two graduates and ordered them to report to the woman's bedroom. Excitement overtook them and they hurried to pack their bags and arrive without delay to her beckon and call. The Gold stood at attention and awaited the instructions that his superior was sure to bring to him shortly. She reappeared as a red-clad vision in the open-cupped bra and crotchless panties.

Standing just out of his reach, she threw her red hose and garter belt onto the floor and ordered him to kneel. From his knees, he heard her instruct him to fasten her belt onto her body and draw each of her seamed stockings into place. Crawling gingerly toward her, he felt the chain extend and then tighten, and the loops of his golden netting, secured by lock to his penile ring, began to constrict. He still could not reach her polished toes. Taking another crawling step, the chain left the carpet and his bag tensed yet again. With tears in his eyes, he reached for her toes. Still out of reach, she beckoned him closer and with great determination, he complied. The chain was almost absolutely extended and the net bag threatened to strangle his spent organ. She smiled as tears sprang to his eyes and he crawled yet one more step toward her tapping and anxious toes.

Lifting her right foot, she awaited his fulfilling her order as the penitent man began to place the glimmering stocking on her delicate foot. Raising himself to greater heights, he brought the stocking to her thigh. Reaching for her left toes, the shackled Gold flailed at the elusive foot. With great effort, he crawled one step closer and paused out of reflex to allow the genital pain to subside. Finally applying the second stocking and drawing it despite his torture to her thigh, she smiled. Her lips opened and she spoke.

"Now the garter belt," she ordered the humiliated Gold.

He backed up to reach the delicate satin garment with his two tanned hands and struggled to reach her milky white waist. Pulling one leg painfully up, he attempted to straddle the offending chain and bring some relief to his aching testicles and penis. Succeeding in raising a massive leg above the golden chain, the Gold brought the chain within his cheeks and moved yet another step closer to his awaiting superior. He reached out with the garter belt, placed it gently around her waist, and secured it with its silver clasp. Hooking the front garters, the exhausted man could not contort himself to reach the two that hung freely behind her milky thighs. Stretching himself completely out and enduring waves of netted anguish, the great Gold's fingers could not reach to fasten the elusive garters.

Without warning, Tony and Bob entered the massive bedroom and surveyed the scene. Marching briskly toward their superior, Tony reached to fasten the garter on her left leg, and Bob completed the one on her right. The disobedient Gold knelt in contrition at his own failure and at the two graduates' success.

"I will not insert you tonight," she admonished the humble Gold. "But I will bring that pleasure to the two of you," she mentioned casually to the astonished secretary and contractor.

Delighted at the prospect of their evening's insertion at her hands, they fell to their knees at her feet. The defeated Gold, in utter exasperation, fell back into a sitting position on the carpet and the fully extended chain that split his abused buttocks was driven directly into his tortured genital area. He sat sobbing and screaming at the two pains he had been given: the physical pain of the chain and the almost bodily aching he felt at her denial of his insertion. As the thankful trainees knelt silently at Debbie's feet and waited for her next command, the humiliated Gold sat upon his chain and felt the shivers of denial course throughout his mortified body.

Chapter Twenty Two

When Ron's mask was removed the next morning, he awoke to the face of a new Green trainer and his immediate thoughts ran to questions and fears about the men he had brought to a new level of degradation during the previous day's training sessions. Having heard rumors among the Greens at the Mistress-less dinner regarding the Green's Level Three fate, Ron was torn between his love of his newly-found authority in forcing others to submit to his control and the uncertainty he felt about the pain, humiliation, and demotion he had brought to his former trainer. Awakening this special trainee slowly, the new Green assuaged Ron's consternation with a strange mixture of an outwardly strict demeanor and an underlying level of deep respect.

This Green embodied the facility's ideal male figure with his strong forehead, wavy hair, rigid posture, and well-toned musculature. Stroking Ron's troubled forehead with a cool, calm hand, the Green brought the slumbering man to full consciousness before leading him by the hand to the morning bathing. Ron's bladder was full but it no longer pained him as it had done earlier in his training. Control over this organ was an added and pleasant addition to the qualifications he had achieved through the training program.

Stepping hand-in-hand with his trainer into the harshly lighted pool area, Ron squinted his brown eyes shut from the glare and allowed the trainer to lead him along the tiled floor to his morning relief pool. The trainee quickly noticed that the great pool was virtually empty and the only sounds his ears could discern were those created by his own bladder's release and his Green's soft, controlled breathing.

Glancing warily around the great room, Ron found no evidence of others nor did he locate any telltale signs of routine bathing. Gone were the pink cream tubes, missing were the lavender soap containers, and absent were the body brushes. The absolutely still waters of the great pool shone a brilliant blue against the shocking white tile of the adjacent deck. His eyes rested on the solid Green who posed stiffly on the cool white ceramic floor. Ron's eyes asked a silent question to which the unyielding Green supplied no answer except for a casual glance that darted from the squatting trainee to the sedate and serene pristine waters of his morning bath.

Ron's brain screamed conflicting messages to his already-responding body. As he scurried to disturb the quiet waters and enter for the cleansing he so anticipated and longed for, Ron's mind urged his restraint from the unknown fate this new Green might provide. Questioning whether the vacant arena housed pleasure or pain for this too-eager trainee on this unusual daybreak, Ron's senses entreated him to consider whether this scenario would provide blissful comfort or abhorrent pain. His eagerness to be responsive and obtain his coveted internal massage and cleansing overcame his good sense of foreboding regarding this otherwise innocuous trainer who loomed ominously in the foreground. Ron entered the pool.

Ron stepped gracefully and completely into the silent pool as a rush of warm water lapped at his belly and chest. He stood in the comforting waters and waited for his trainer's entry. Unmoving, the tall Green surveyed his morning's charge. Recalling his uncommon interchange directly with the Mistress last evening, the Green stood silent and reflected on their conversation and her apparent as well as her hidden messages before he joined his trainee for the morning session.

Having been summoned to the sparkling silver doors well after the dinner and exercise hours, the Green experienced an urgent discomfort at the thought of the strange beckoning. Usually when the Mistress desired communication, she delivered her message to her personal Gold, who brought the request directly to the Head Green, who in turn delivered it to the trainer. Yet this time she had called him directly on his cubicle's speaker and ordered him to report personally to her private offices. Making haste to deliver himself at her behest, the Green ran full speed to her closed doors, collected himself outside her sanctuary, and composed his racing heart. He knocked once on the lustrous silver door.

An immediate opening of the double portals responded to his entreaty. The Mistress sat immobile and serene in a massive white upholstered chair. He entered with a single step and waited for her request or desire for his presence. He felt his heart begin to race anew and his moist palms and perspiring chest divulged his nervousness. Yet his training held and he stood at attention while awaiting her words. For what seemed an eternity, he stood in silence just inside the great silver doors of her private abode. Concentrating simply on breathing, the Green inhaled and exhaled with precision as he stood silent before the massive chair in which she perched and from which she examined her flustered Green trainer.

Finally, she spoke.

Coincident with her uttering her first word, the Green trainer spotted an awful sight entering the arena from behind the massive furniture in which the Mistress rested. Resisting his growing need to discover the identity of the black leather-clad crawler, the trainer froze his gaze upon the Mistress's moving mouth and struggled to concentrate on her every word. He had difficulty maintaining his composure as his eyes darted first to the creature crawling around her feet and then back to the woman's instructive lips. The enormity of the horror that brutish man brought to his trained senses astounded him and threatened and stunned his expert control.

This creature was a soiled mass of dirt and grime. Cowering under the Mistress's occasional gaze and her ever-present black leather crop, the man took painful creeping steps toward her chair, yet scurried away when she half-raised the whip. Striking him indiscriminately and without warning for no apparent cause, the Mistress succeeded in confusing the pitiful beast into a groveling and fearful animal who could not determine what she expected from him or in what manner he should conduct himself. The Mistress noticed the Green's darting eyes and called his attention back to the matter at hand.

"Until yesterday, this mess was a Green." She let her words sink in.

The Green gasped but stared at the shaggy creature at her feet still uncomprehending his purpose in the matter.

"He received Level Three," she continued as those four words took their desired effect and the rigid Green looked smartly away from the inhuman shell the man had become. "The trainee who helped put him here must yet be trained and I wish you to become that man's personal trainer. He may require more assistance and education than usual."

The Green smiled inwardly as he relished the ultimate challenge she offered him and the obvious confidence she had in his abilities. If he could become that trainer who broke the man who had destroyed the Green, he would certainly be considered during the next phase of promotions. The Mistress saw the glint of greed in his eye and welcomed his enthusiasm.

"First of all, you must prove your talent and capabilities to me personally by removing this filthy creature and bringing him through retraining," she ordered in a calm voice. "And it will be accomplished today."

The Green swallowed hard. Today? He was to retrain this degraded Green in one day? What had the Blues come up with this time for retraining? Using great discretion based on ultimate trust of his superior, he kept his skeptical questions unspoken as the crawling former Green came to painful rest at her feet which rested upon the virgin white carpet of her offices. With saddened eyes, the Black looked up at his Mistress for permission to move from his position of intense pain that was inflicted by the recently tightened black leather penitentiary by which she effectively removed his maleness and brought him to the lowest depths imaginable. She denied him even this small comfort. New tears rolled down his stained face and streaked the grime that covered his bristled skin.

The Green stood silent as the Mistress called for the Head Blue to illustrate the retraining procedures. Apparently waiting silently in an adjoining room, the Head Blue entered noiselessly and stood beside her great chair until recognized by her glance. Glancing benignly in the recent arrival's direction, the Mistress nodded once and the proud Head Blue spoke.

"Ultimate degradation must be followed by tender retraining." His words were cold and professional. "This Black will receive his final degradation tonight and in the morning; then he will be offered education to enable his return to the Colors. You, a comrade Green, will perform both the humiliation and the assistance for satisfactory retraining." The Green's heart rose and sank when it took in the enormity of his task.

"Take this person by his leash and illustrate to him and all the Colors that he has reached the debased nadir of humanity. Offer him to all the Colors and urge them to punish him for his prurient behavior that disgraced you all. Remind him that no one from your ranks can consider such behavior as possible or desirable. Bring him to his knees, and then bring him lower than that. When you have accomplished this phase of the punishment, I will outline your methods for release of his bonds." His ensuing silence punctuated the severity of his program.

As silently as he had arrived, he exited as the Mistress again nodded to him and allowed his departure.

Green expelled the deep breath that he had been holding unconsciously during the Blue's awful speech. The Mistress asked no more of the trainer, so he grasped the offered leather leash that dangled from the mangy man's neck collar and led him directly between the opened silver doors, down the identical long hallways, through the myriad turns and avenues, and finally into his own private green cubicle as his mind reeled and raced to evaluate and design the torture he had been commanded to administer to this disheveled and unkempt baggage that strained at his bondage. During their promenade, the Green had to snap the leash to command the crawling Black to hurry his pace and the messy package responded quickly to follow at his leader's heel. The creature's response had been quick, Green noted.

Once inside the trainer's personal cubicle's four green walls, the leashed being grasped the leather lead within his teeth and tugged gingerly at the strap as he pointed with his head toward the square of red carpet in the center of the floor. With greater and greater urgency, the poor creature illustrated his overwhelming need by whining and yelping as he indicated with a perspiring face that his bowels were bursting with uncleansed neglect. The Green reacted first with disgust and then with mild derision for his plight. Failure to cleanse oneself or to have oneself cleansed marked a man as adulterated and defiled among the Colors.

This horrid potential occurrence was overwhelming to the trainer and the Green let the creature know his contempt. With painstaking slowness, the Green released the red square and the grateful Black hopped upon it and lowered his buttocks into the orifice. Spreading his legs as wide as the leather constriction would allow, the Black cried tears of relief as his rectal muscles released and forced their unwelcome contents into its proper place. Once his unpleasant deed was accomplished, the Black sought the refreshing cleansing hose, yet the Green coldly turned his back upon the dripping and suffering man. Caught in the contorted position from which his leather harness provided no means of escape, the Black fought back tears as he silently and repeatedly jutted his hairy chin toward the hose's home in appeal for its cleansing power.

Green considered the situation within his cubicle and resisted the overwhelming urge to seek immediate personal egress. Following the Mistress's commands, he stood above the frozen being and planted a firm foot in the center of his tensed and painful black leather girdle. Pressing with only part of his weight, the Green forced the Black's cheeks deeper into the hole that had once been the red carpet square and brought a cry of anguish from the empty man's hoarse throat.

Reaching with a muscular arm toward the cleansing hose, the Green secured the nozzle and with a concomitant flick of his fingers, shifted the dial to "cold." Aiming the nozzle directly at the humiliated Black's dripping anus, he opened the valve full force and drove icy water into his deepest region. The shock of the temperature threw the man into rigid spasms, yet the Green continued the powerful stream until the Black's utter willpower relaxed his rectal spasms and allowed the cleansing waters to penetrate his impure orifice. His fingers searching for something to grip in order to withstand the torture, the Black's arms flailed wildly on the floor next to his sunken hips. By releasing his hands from their position of support, his hips and buttocks sagged deeper into the hole and the constraining black leather pouch did its diabolical work.

Through the eons of the torture leveled at his backside, the Black uttered not one word. Sensing that the creature had performed well enough to exhibit partial retraining, the Green shut off the offending stream and ordered the man to his knees. Their conversation was as brief as it was frightening.

"Up," Green commanded. "We're ready to go."

The uncomprehending Black tussled with his awkward position, the excruciating leather harness, and the sheer force of gravity that imprisoned him in the hole in the center of the carpet within this green cubicle that reminded him so much of his own. Shifting his weight to his right and then to his left, he tried to remove his tightly wedged buttocks from their jail. With every thrust, his girdle offered contractions and constrictions that overwhelmed him with soreness. Taking a huge breath, the trapped man laid two hands upon the deep green carpet at his sides, kicked with both feet, and thrust with his powerful hands in a final effort to liberate himself from his plight. Finally reaching the safety of intact flooring, the anguished Black wailed cries of grief and distress at his physical and mental anguish. Clambering to his knees, he breathed deeper and deeper in a valiant attempt to overcome this abuse and pain.

Tapping his foot in boredom at the man's tardiness, Green awaited the leashed creature's completion of his command. In frustration at the seeming eternity he took to ready himself, the Green grabbed the Black's leash and jerked his neck collar with a powerful and well-directed tug. The force of the leash's pull threw the man into a crawling position and only his muscular arms prevented his falling completely prone at Green's feet.

"Come," he commanded and the seemingly uncaring Green and his charge exited the cubicle.

Following the Mistress's orders once again, the Green offered the surprised Colors opportunities to perform their will upon the distressed but accepting Black. Strolling from the cubicle corridor to the exercise rooms, the pair visited a wandering White who eagerly took up the challenge. Yanking the leash from Green's hand, the White led the beast into the gym and into the hands of the congregated Colors who were completing their evening's workout.

The well-oiled White bodies responded especially avidly to the entrant's position. Gathering their bodies around the crawling Black, the Whites taunted and teased him as the poor man allowed their lascivious discussion and withstood it without response. Making his way through his comrades' position and striding into their circle, the Head White inspected the Black without emotion before ordering his team to leave the exercise area. The Black trembled and shook visibly with fear at the prospect of being left alone with the Head White who had assumed his distinguished position through expert control and flawless training. His legendary status overawed the bedraggled creature who was forced to open himself to this exceptional example of perfect regimentation.

The Head White held out his braceleted arm and waved it directly in front of the Black's runny nose. His ensuing words brought more fear and anxiety to the humbled man's ears and led directly to his heavy heart.

"You are without a net and cannot be given either pain or pleasure." The man paused so the enormity of the Black's humbling could be brought once again to his thoughts. Seeing tears form in the Black's red eyes, the Head White recognized his words had the desired effect. He continued without mercy.

"What you have not yet learned is that there is more than pain and pleasure. I control you in every way." The Black whimpered as the Head White smiled through gritted teeth.

Without another word, the Head White withdrew a small black device from the pouch that he wore at his side. Although the Black could not view it directly from his prone position, the Green who had led him to the gym caught a clear vision of the miniature insert. Enormously shocked to discover that the miniature was as black in color as the man's leather harness, the Green drew in a sharp breath and considered the purpose of such an unusual apparatus. Wasting no time, the Head White stepped between the crawling Black's legs, kicked them wide apart, and drove the replica into his now impure and hairy hole. As the dry region shrieked in agony at the unlubricated penetration and his powerful arms could exert no more assistance, the horrified Black's chest slumped to the floor as the White's powerful arms pressed the intruder home.

Even the Green winced in sympathy, yet his expert training proved solid once more. As the Head White pulled the spent man's head up by his stringy hair, the Green felt his net bag twitch in surprising excitement. Knowing that reaching for his crotch would alert the White to his plight, the agitated Green pressed one foot then the other into the brilliant white carpeting in an effort to relieve his personal indignity. He heard the White as he spoke into the man's passionate face.

"Now you will know why you were inadequate to the task of becoming a perfectly trained Color. I will stimulate the offender inside you and you will prove that only the expertly trained can endure it with silence. Any sound you utter will prove to me and the others that you are not of the same caliber that the Whites must exhibit." The Black mumbled a groan of fright and anticipation and the eavesdropping Green's net bag began to fill. White pressed two jewels simultaneously on his wristband.

Black's reaction overwhelmed and astounded the aroused Green, although White surveyed the man's response with an educated and dispassionate eye. Instantly after the buttons were depressed, the Black's legs thrashed outward and then upward, similar to those of a bucking bronco. His girdling pain momentarily forgotten, the inserted supplicant wriggled and writhed in an apparent effort to dislodge the well-planted stick. Although no sound exited from his lips, the Black's terror and terrible soreness were evidenced by his wildly rising hips and the great physical tossing of his legs. In sheer terror, the Black reached for his anal orifice and the offending device with both hands, yet the White took his own well-oiled hand and grasped the man's black leather emasculator and yanked it powerfully forward. Black fell immediately back into his crawling position, yet no voice offered complaint about the agony he felt.

Pressing two more buttons, the White ended the spasms of grief he had inflicted on the now-prone man. Hearing nothing except his gasping attempts to establish shallow and even breathing, the now-satisfied White stepped between the Black's outstretched legs, kicked them mercilessly apart once again and reached in for the wide handle of the agonizing encroacher. Without warning or preparation, he took the insert's wide base and wrenched it free, threw it onto the floor near the exhausted Black's head, and soundlessly exited the gym.

In his surprise and shock, the Green stood and observed the results of the control mechanism whose existence and function he had just learned. Recalling the threat to his organs that his own net bag posed for the erection he had allowed himself during the punishment administered to the Black, Green inspected himself. Observing that the bag was full and the contents rigid and stiff, the Green turned toward the corner wall where he had been leaning and pushed himself and his most private parts into the edge in an effort to bring himself immediate yet excruciating relief. Through his personal pain, he congratulated his training and testified to his expert control.

Then the newly assigned trainer turned toward the noiseless lump that lay still on the gym floor. Grasping the leather leash, he tugged at the collar and the soundless Black followed, a little more slowly this time, at his heel. The pair exited the gym and the Green turned their patrol toward the infrequently-visited red doors behind which were housed the female Golds, Whites, Blues, and Greens who led the sessions for the women trainees and judged the "welcomes" that the male trainees devised. Stopping at the massive double portals, the Green knocked once on the heavy surface and was received by a stunning Gold to whom he handed the man's leather leash. She pulled the creature inside, denied entry to the Green, and the heavy red doors shut tightly together.

Green waited by the double red doors for what seemed like a millennium until the massive portals re-opened and the same Gold offered him back the leashed creature. Not daring to look either the Gold or the humiliated man in their faces, the Green simply trod once again toward his home. He urged the creature inside and allowed him to lay in the middle of the floor for rest while the Green readied himself for bed. At this late hour, very little discussion seemed likely and the Green anticipated a difficult day tomorrow with the forced retraining of this Black to likely occupy most of his morning. Yet he wondered silently about the punishments that the Black had received at the hands of the women and his own member twitched and jerked violently with excitement as he contemplated what they had done to the creature. His thoughts were interrupted by Black's almost inaudible cough.

Turning his attention to the man's prone position, the Green offered a quizzical glance that offered just a little solace mixed with apparent disgust at the sight he witnessed on the floor of his formerly immaculate private room. The plaintive face of the Black seemed to request some consolation or comfort; however, the Green was reluctant to offer him any in fear of the Mistress's warning and her ultimate wrath. Yet the pitiful visage facing him required Green to at least acknowledge the plight of the distressed creature and he casually offered him a satin pillow for his bearded, dirty, and tear-streaked face.

Grasping the offering with fervor, the Black pressed the comforting softness against his agonized genital area, even though he knew that the black leather obstruction prevented his feeling any comfort from it. Pushing the pillow harder and harder into his leather harness, the Black pumped his hips firmly against it, then pulled his buttocks backward, and thrust them forward again. The uncomprehending Green witnessed the man's absurd display, yet its passion and zeal astounded him.

What had happened to him in there, he wondered?

It would be several days before he finally got his answer. Reaching up to lower the retracted comforting mask over his head and face, Green brought the nighttime rest he so craved closer to his consumed body. Securing the device around his head, he clipped the neck pins into place and savored the sweet vanilla aroma that filled his nostrils. As the classical violin concerto that he had chosen circled his brain, the scenes of warm sandy beaches filled his tired eyes. Laying his weary head upon his remaining satin pillow, Green spread his body out in the middle of the large bed and allowed his legs to separate so that he could enjoy fully his evening's pleasure. Slowly, the green net bag began to undulate around his genitals and soon it was providing him the ultimate ecstasy of delight. As the pace and intensity of the music, scenery, and massaging of his netting increased, the Green gave himself completely to his well-earned reward and yielded to the heavenly pleasures that the Mistress allowed him this evening.

The center of the room held an entirely different story. Panting and sweating, the thrashing Black labored without success to relieve the intense sexual arousal the women trainers had brought to him only minutes earlier. After Green had delivered him to his last punishment, the Head Gold handed the leashed man over to the Blues who had incessantly inflicted stimulating and passionate enticements to his girded organs. They rubbed up against his perspiring skin and licked, kissed, and chewed on his aching cheeks. Tickling his penis tip with an instrument poked through the small slit provided for his personal relief, the Blues drove the poor man berserk with purposeful titillation. Unable to control his hampered genitalia, the writhing Black's pain increased with every centimeter his organ engorged. As soon as he was stimulated into erection, the pain produced by his girdle forced his errant organ back down. Pressing agonizingly against the black leather harness, the stiff and rigid penis itself provided Black's ultimate degradation.

He had learned his lesson well. He was allowed no erection or orgasm without permission. There would be no one and no thing that would bring him to that level of disobedience again. Yet his brain vowed another solemn promise as the humiliated former-Green swore that he would one day bring to his trainee the full personal knowledge of what absolute obedience really meant.

His continued pressuring of his fully engorged member along with his heaving hip motion brought the distressed organ to its final but empty culmination. Ejaculating within the harness, Black's agony accompanied his relief. As he reflected on the Mistress's face of anger and instruction during his level three period with her, Black wept tears of frustration and sadness as he finally understood the power she wielded and the obedience she demanded. And he vowed always to obey.

As Ron stood silently in the great pool, the Green's wandering mind moved quickly back to the task he had been assigned. The Mistress instructed him to provide special treatment and training for this inventive newcomer and the Blues had offered quiet suggestions during the morning meal. Allowing Ron to slumber through the usual session, Green awoke the pink-netted trainee after the morning routine had been accomplished. Having the solitary figure to himself, Green licked his full lips in anticipation of fulfilling the Mistress's command and securing for himself a firmer grip on the ladder toward the coveted Blue position.

Ron felt the Green's gaze even before he found himself the courage to meet it with his own. Apprehension welled up inside his suddenly cold body as he lowered his hands into the water for warmth. The Green turned to the obviously expectant and somewhat flustered trainee.

"I will bathe you now," the Green began dangerously. He moved toward the pool.

Ron felt the wavy waters collide as the big man entered the great pool with solid steps. As he strode toward the cowering trainee, Green pushed the water ahead of him and directly into Ron's dry chest. Taking his pink net bag with a well-directed hand, Green hauled the stunned attorney toward the pool's edge and unceremoniously shackled his neck into the plush padding of the brace. With the great arena's ceiling his only view, Ron's rested on his back in the water and allowed his legs to fall apart.

Green entered the opening his spread legs provided and began his attack on the manacled man's feet, thighs, and hips. Using powerful slapping strokes, he applied the lavender lotion and forced a great mound of bubbles to form on his glistening pubic skin. Moving diligently up toward the trainee's chest and arms, the well-trained Green scoured every inch of available epidermis with a well-directed hand brush. Ron winced silently with the determined trainer's strokes, yet he did not utter a single cry of resistance. After applying the daily depilatory to the rinsed trainee's face and pubic skin, the Green, forced to wait for the chemical to complete its action, found the pink net bag's contents and positioned his fingers beneath their round ends and lifted the floating man's body inches out of the pool.

To Ron's horror, he found himself first submerged, then lifted, and re-submerged in the warm bath by a powerful vise-like grip upon his netted genitals. Too overwhelmed with physical agony to utter a cry of distress, Ron gritted his teeth for the power struggle he suddenly realized was taking place with this determined trainer. The great hand lifted and lowered, raised and extended, as the lathered trainee fought his rising panic through sheer determination. His body, imprisoned at the neck by the locked brace and at his most private organs by the unyielding hand, generated rolling waves throughout the immense and otherwise silent pool. Although his brain screamed, his lips were empty.

Using a dry towel, Green stropped the depilatory from Ron's pubic skin with violent strokes that threatened to send the near-delirious man into spasms of anguish. Taking the bag once again in his hand, the Green flipped Ron's body and his neck brace in one smooth motion. With no view except that of the naked pool deck immediately in front of his burning eyes, Ron focused on an empty chair in the distance as he awaited the Green's next step in his own personal torture.

The intense lathering was repeated, this time on Ron's posterior skin. His outstretched legs, although well planted on the pool's blue floor, were no match for the savage kick extended by the trainer's well-aimed foot. Without warning, Ron felt his legs buckle and was forced to his knees as the neck brace held his immobile head firmly. His tingling skin felt the closeness of the Green's body to his own and he feared yet insanely desired the purifying cleansing that would constitute the next phase of this unique bath.

The trainer's look shifted momentarily to the electronic sound that indicated the opening of the arena's double doors. Having lost himself within the rhythmic motions of the lathering, up to this point Green had managed to block out all distractions and thoughts within the silence of the pool's lapping waters. The intruding noise of the entering assembly awoke him from his intensity and brought to his motions a renewed vigor. Under the watchful gaze of the Mistress, her personal Gold, the Gold assembly, and the rest of the Colors, Green positioned the now-bathed trainee in perfect form for his internal cleansing. The Mistress seated herself in the empty chair while the entourage stood at attention in a semi-circle adjacent to her station.

As the entirety of the procession entered Ron's peripheral view, his hands gripped the pool's edge with tightened, frightened fingers. The muscles in his upper arms ached in protest against their firm grasp while his buckled knees shrieked with agony at the awkwardness of their tension and the load they were forced to bear. Ron was spread-eagled and locked into the most humiliating position imaginable in front of the entire professional population of the training facility and he was fully open and powerless to prevent his ultimate and imminent degradation at the hands of this determined trainer.

So this was his punishment, he thought, for bringing a Green to his knees.

Simultaneously, the toiling trainer entertained a fleeting thought of revenge, a thought similar to the dozens of like ideas entertained by the retinue stretched out on the pool's edge in front of the immersed duo. Ron took in a deep breath and awaited the Green's first move. He vowed he would not cry out and he would not beg for mercy.

Glancing upwards as high as the neck brace allowed, Ron caught a glimpse of the Mistress's stare at his own position. Her steely-eyed view drove his humbled eyes downward. He heard the slapping of the Green's hands positioned directly behind his fully exposed anus. Feeling his posterior cheeks spread agonizingly apart from the diligent trainer, Ron's facial muscles reacted with reflex-like response. As Ron grimaced, the Greens on the deck smiled inwardly and filed that move into their retinue of bathing techniques.

The scene from the front belied the extreme violations that were occurring from behind. Ron's grimaces, scowls, and frowns indicated only that he was uncomfortable and stressed. Had the party of on-lookers stepped in back of the struggling pair, the scenario would have unfolded differently.

Ron's experience with this vengeful trainer under the approving gaze of the entire faculty of Colors was one that would remain forever in the recesses of his mind and would be brought to the forefront whenever anyone would enter Ron's anus for similar purpose in the future. For the duration of the cleansing, this trainer brought to Ron's entrails the frenzy of joy interspersed with foreboding and horror; he threw the man into spasms of delight yet took it away with consequent agony; he brought the trainee to almost complete and utter fulfillment before stripping away his dignity and preventing his completion within moments of Ron's impending explosion. The trainee learned that this trainer was a master and he was no match for the Green's skill. Yet he vowed to learn while he was being subjected to this torture; however, the Green's complete control over the situation allowed Ron no room, time, or thoughts for intellectual memory.

Ron's seasoning this morning was entirely physical. Thought was extinguished from his struggling brain and was replaced only by sheer willpower enabling him to withstand the trainer's overwhelming efforts. Having struggled successfully with the frenzied trainer thus far, Ron felt him spread his cheeks wide. Then the trainer belted them by attaching a clamp to the inside of each cheek at Ron's hairless crack and then clipping them together with an inflexible belting across the bent-over man's belly. He tightened the belt until Ron was fully exposed and both of Green's hands were free.

Suddenly, Ron felt his neck brace unclamp as his head was dragged upwards by a strong handful of his own hair. He was pushed and prodded from behind to the center of the pool and climbed onto a small platform that positioned him in direct view of the room's spectators. His almost-naked body glistening wet from the lathering, Ron's skin gleamed in the spotlight as the room lights dimmed. He felt his cheeks spread wide by the clamps and watched Green climb up behind him as all eyes focused on the performers at center stage.

"I will own you. . . today!" Ron heard the Green whisper threateningly into his ear as he felt the man's unseen and unlubricated finger enter his dry orifice with force. Ron winced from the shock.

"Try me. . . ." Ron whispered, but he knew the trainer heard his challenge.

The trainer reached beneath the naked trainee's spread legs and grasped his pink netting. Jerking the package down and toward himself, the trainer managed the truculent man easily to his knees. The entourage on the deck approved with nodding heads. Ron's spread cheeks ached and he feared for his anus, this Green's potential, and the challenge to which he had just stupidly given himself.

Although Ron's face pointed directly toward the Mistress and her Colors, his backside felt both the hot lights focused on it as well as the point of the cleansing hose as it was pressed against his expandable hole. Almost looking forward to the purifying feel that the cleansing brought, Ron was torn between this degrading position and his relishing of the process. The tip of the hose was pressed slightly into his dry hole and brought an involuntary tear to his dark eyes. He felt the heavy arm of the trainer upon his backside as he forced the hose home.

Ron's entire body sagged as he felt the force of unlubricated entry into his most private space. The dryness of his cavity fought valiantly against the hose's equally dry sides. He heard himself gasp deeply and he just managed to stifle a moan that threatened to escape unbidden from his parched lips. He did not see the entourage on the deck nod in approval of the Green's technique.

Turning the dial full force, Green unleashed the hose's contents, a powerful stream that mixed with the pink lubricating cream and entered every inch of Ron's insides, coated his cavity, and greased his entrails. Knowing the trainee's shock by the incredulous look of astonishment on his suddenly raised head, the group on the deck smiled openly. The Green had performed well and the trainee was only one step from being broken. The Head Blue glanced toward the personal Gold and the two nodded in agreement as the Gold wrote a few notes on his clipboard.

His ability to control his reactions almost completely extinguished, Ron no longer felt his arms or legs, belly or back; rather, his only feeling was contained entirely between his buttocks. Feeling horribly full and having forgotten his almost-mastered technique of holding his contents until unplugging, Ron panicked at the first tug the Green gave to remove the empty hose. If he were to expel his contents in front of this great group as he stood in the spotlight in the center of the pool, Ron would be unable to face any of them or Debbie again with any shred of dignity when the training was completed. His thought of Debbie brought another series of tears cascading down his sweaty face as he longed to be returned to her and perform for her all the techniques and habits she had sent him here to learn.

The achingly full rectum went into a spasm as the Green suddenly and maliciously yanked the hose completely from the trainee's orifice. In horror and embarrassment, his inability to hold himself tightly, Ron screamed aloud in the silent pool arena. His curdling yell reverberated among the walls and off the water as the satisfied group of spectators silently praised the Green's knowledge that personal humiliation would grieve the trainee more than any group display would engender. The personal Gold took more notes on his pad.

As he stood on the platform in the spotlight in the center of the pool, the successful trainer took the sobbing trainee's shoulders and spun the degraded man around to face his gallery. With unclean pink cream staining his legs with telltale bright neon patches, the humiliated lawyer felt totally humbled before this expertly trained group. Feeling the offensive pink mass reach his feet and run through his toes, Ron's horror increased. Not yet satisfied that the man had learned his lesson, the Green bent the trainee's head down and exposed his open buttocks more clearly to the onlookers. Pressing Ron's belly in expert fashion, Green forced even more of the contents to spill. Ron had no control over his sphincter as the stuff exited with speed.

A voice cut through the trainee's tears of shame within the silence of the great pool.

"Stand and face me," the Mistress commanded.

Ron's unhearing ears were jerked back into comprehending reality as his head was lifted once again by a handful of his own hair and his body was swung once again into position facing the assembled group. He stared ahead at the Mistress's position and felt his eyes tearing volumes and his pink discharge continuing down his legs. She spoke again.

"I have never failed to break a trainee." Ron recalled those words from his entry ride into the facility. He winced at her accuracy.

"Green, come to me."

The Green literally jumped from the platform and raced through the waters to answer his Mistress's beckon. Under the approving glances of the Colors, the Mistress disengaged the green net bag that bound him and unlocked his magnetic ring.

As the uncomprehending former-Green stood horrified and absolutely naked in front of his comrades, the Mistress opened a blue velvet pouch offered to her by her personal Gold. She extracted a blue ring as the naked man sobbed tears of joy and fell to his knees in thanks. She ordered him lifted up, straightened, and she personally fit him with his new color. Locking the band into place, she asked him if this was what he truly wanted.

"Yes," he managed, "with all my heart."

"Then so it will be," she agreed, as she fastened the blue netting to his locked ring. "I have a special task for you and you alone. You will devise the insertion ritual for this group of trainees. I am pleased with your work."

Finished, she arose from her chair and led the procession from the great pool. Blue was given hugs and congratulations from his comrades for his job well done. Finally, the great pool was empty.

It was empty except for Ron who still stood in the center of the pool on the now-darkened platform, the pink goo running from him in uncontrollable spasms of discharge. The new Blue cast him a glance of disdain and called almost quietly to the bedraggled and forgotten trainee, "Go clean up. Your wife is watching."

And the proud Blue marched from the pool toward his new level and larger personal quarters as Ron stood on the platform, dripped pink discharge, and screamed in horror as he realized just what Debbie had just witnessed.

Chapter Twenty Three

Late that Sunday evening, Debbie lay smirking yet exhausted between the satin sheets as she reminisced about both the day's full activities and the evening's recently-experienced events. Her almost-numb brain reminded her that her afternoon's delights were sleeping peacefully within their satisfied bodies on the carpet at the hem of her hand-made dust ruffle and she relished in their deep steady breathing as she contemplated the possibilities for tomorrow with which she could outdo today's triumphs and innovations. Sipping her Amaretto and cream, Debbie enjoyed a dream-like trance in which she fantasized that her video recorder was replaying her day of frolic, romping, and cavorting with her graduates and her Gold.

With the long, manicured fingers of one hand, Debbie grasped the blue stem of the elongated wineglass and stroked the icy glass with the moist palm of the other hand. Rattling the remnants of the ice cubes and enjoying their clinking noises against the delicate crystal, she pressed her legs tightly against each other in an effort to suppress the growing sensation of pleasure that was rising within her excited body. Touching the wineglass first to her left nipple and then to her right, she delighted in their rising enthusiasm and relished their tight, pointed positions as she again scrutinized the spent bodies on the thick carpet beneath her feet.

God, this was good, she thought, and stroked her red silken teddy as she provoked herself to an even higher pitch with the wineglass against her perspiring skin. The cool edge of the glass against her neck brought the exhausted but satisfied woman almost to self-induced climax. Her thighs pressed one against the other in an almost rhythmic convolution that threatened to intensify even beyond what she believed possible. Without warning, her inner self exploded as her thighs pressed dutifully inward. Stifling a cry of delight, Debbie moved the icy glass's long stem against the snapped crotch of her silken teddy and brought herself again and again to complete fulfillment. She sat motionless as she enjoyed the waves of ecstasy that rolled through her thighs and up toward her most personal space.

As she came again and again in silence on the great bed, Debbie watched the three sleeping forms surrounding her bed on the carpet at her feet. This had been a most unusual Sunday.

When Tony had learned of the impending insertion that evening, he rushed in to suggest that Debbie make the day wonderfully special and accomplish with the three men delights she had not yet considered or imagined. Excited at the thought of new fantasies coming to life, Debbie agreed quickly and demanded the three men bring her their gym bags of treasures and devices for her inspection and use. Dutifully, Tony and Bob offered their bags to their superior, but the shackled Gold was unable to reach his secreted satchel without the former trainees' intervention with the red-satin clad woman. Upon realizing the Gold's dilemma, Debbie planted a spiked red heel frighteningly close to his gold-netted private parts, bent her perfumed body down toward his quivering delight, and used her long, manicured fingers to unshackle the poor man's penis from its chained prison. The humbled man continued to sit upon his golden chain as he considered the best means possible to honor her request in a timely fashion.

Agonizingly slowly, the great Gold rose to his knees and began a measured crawl toward the closet and his gym tote. Each crawling step brought reminders directly into his brain of how the cunning woman had gained the upper hand during his bath, secured his golden loops, and chained him amazingly accurately to prevent his completion of her every ordered task. This woman was a master, he finally recognized, and he may just have met his match. He took yet another painful creeping step forward as the three sets of spectators' eyes followed his every move. Debbie interrupted his thoughts.

"I like you like this," she began ominously as his heart leapt literally into his dry mouth. "Whatever we do today," she continued, "you three will be chained."

Tony gasped and smiled before inquiring, "What will you do with us?"

Debbie quickly considered her options to display her male threesome as Gold continued his tormented and arduous trek toward his satchel. She drew her forehead into a puzzled frown as she imagined the various locations in which she could show off her prizes. She gazed first toward Bob, then toward Tony, before finally settling her stare on the creeping backside of the anguished Gold. Watching his tanned and perfect buttocks twitch first to the left and then to the right as he continued on his slow hike across the carpet to the closet, Debbie felt her inner self flush and threaten to tantalize her sexuality with no direct touch between them. Noticing his tensed gluteus muscles as they quivered and relaxed first to lift and then lower his well-toned legs, Debbie flashed on a most interesting afternoon's locale. She moved into action.

"Strip," she ordered the two clothed men. "Let's see what kind of goodies you've got in those bags."

Tony and Bob jumped into simultaneous action as they ripped t-shirts from their backs and silken running shorts from their lower bodies. Exposing their near-nudity, the two former trainees reached for their shoelaces to remove their running shoes and socks.

"No, No!" Debbie insisted. "Leave your shoes on. You'll need them later when we get there." Her incomplete sentence tantalized the nearly nude graduates.

She turned and gazed toward the crawling Gold who was now returning to their central location, his gym bag dangling by its straps from his glistening white teeth.

"I want that bag, now!" she barked, and the tortured Gold forced his aching legs to carry him even faster to his superior. Tony and Bob stepped back and away from the bed to allow the bedraggled man entry to their conversation.

"Up!" she insisted simply and the Gold breathed in deeply, lifted his massive frame, and faced her as he rose to full attention. As the two co-workers stood in awe and amazement at Gold's Herculean effort and his well-controlled success, Debbie smirked silently at her own power over this man and his total obedience to her every command. When Ron returned, she thought in delight, he was going to be this good.

She tore into the three men's bags and dumped their contents onto her wide bed. "Explain each one of these things to me," she instructed no one in particular, and Gold rose once again to the challenge to offer her clarification in the use of each device and toy their bags contained.

"First," he began, "these are the various lotions and creams. I believe you know how to use them." He held out the tubes and bottles as he stood silent and waited for her confirmation.

She nodded and mentioned, "Yes, they're familiar to me." Sorting carefully through the clutter, she lifted a small gold-dyed clear plastic strap, she asked, "And this? How do I use this on you?"

Her intensity precluded her noticing the other two men's reactions to her lifting that particular item from the mass of devices, bottles, and tubes adorning her bedspread. Gasping almost audibly, Tony and Bob shuddered at her intuition that allowed her to recognize that this unique device was the one that would bring her absolute and final control over each of them. If she chose that simple malleable soft plastic strapping, she would learn immediately what it meant to own her trained men totally.

Debbie held the golden-tinged plastic in one hand as she searched with her free hand among the remaining devices for the two absolutely clear colored straps that belonged to Tony and Bob. Quickly locating the desired items, Debbie lifted the three harmless-looking plastic items aloft as Gold explained their purposes.

"These are simple but very effective handlers for your pleasure," he began. "By strapping us into them, you gain quick and easy control of us and our every move." He waited as she absorbed the information. After an appropriate pause, he continued. "Would you like me to demonstrate them to you?"

As quickly as Debbie jerked her head up and down in agreement, Tony and Bob stiffened in anticipation and apprehension. Both excited and fearful, the two stood immobile as Gold received a clear belt released from Debbie's intense grip. Turning toward the secretary, Gold motioned the man's legs apart and Tony jumped to comply. Spreading his legs uncomfortably wide apart, he presented an odd picture of a naked, netted, and muscular man adorned only in running shoes and white socks who stood patiently and submissively before his administrative and sexual superior and her Gold.

"Do it now," she urged and Gold stepped toward the trembling secretary.

"It's very simple to attach," he instructed as he placed the almost invisible cup at the base of Tony's clear netting and surrounded his penis and testicles by crushing them inside it. "First you enter his netting into the cup and then," he paused as he grasped the flat plastic ends, "you simply pull it into place."

As Gold lifted the wide strap directly upward, it spread itself neatly between Tony's tanned cheeks, a motion that caused the silent secretary to wince in apparent pain. Stealing a glance at the contracting officer who stood motionless while witnessing this awkward scene, Gold noticed both his reaction of empathy for his comrade's distress and the inevitable filling of his clear netting with excitement. Good, Gold thought. Both were appropriate reactions.

"How do I lock it into place?" Debbie asked, her voice bringing Gold quickly back to his position of instruction at the foot of the bed in the peach and teal bedroom.

He was satisfied with her question and her apparent knowledge that this device was only as good as it was secure. Grabbing two thin clear straps by their dangling hooks, he lifted them across Tony's struggling buttocks and inserted the hooks directly into the holes positioned the edges of the almost invisible cup of control.

"Like so," he remarked as he presented her with the secured secretary. "You tighten the tension by shortening the straps with the hooks. Let me show you," he commented benignly as he grasped the hooks, removed them from their homes, and drove the sliding locks backward to stunt their length. Debbie was amazed at the technology that was apparently stolen from the world of women's bra straps. "Hook them by grasping firmly," he taught as he positioned her fingers under his own, "and pull tightly." The unlikely pair accomplished the hooking of the gasping secretary on whom the short cup gathered his most private organs into a squashed heap of unseen constriction.

Debbie stepped back to witness Tony's predicament. She twirled a finger in the air as the staggering secretary spun round for her viewing pleasure. Inserting a long manicured finger into the buttock's straps, Debbie measured their tension. Reaching between his outstretched legs, she clutched the wide strap that split his cheeks and tugged slightly to ascertain its effectiveness. As a total package, Tony was completely dependent on her for every important bodily function. He could neither pee or be cleansed without her unlocking his hooks and his every step would remind him of her complete control. She pulled, twisted, tensed, and touched each of the straps on his new garment and was ready to pronounce her satisfaction when Gold interrupted her dreamy thoughts.

"And this is the leash," her Gold announced quickly.

Debbie riveted her eyes on the short and simple links to view the somewhat ordinary chain he held in his massive hand.

"Show me what this does," she breathed in a throaty voice as Gold moved to attach this latest feature to the now-anguished secretary. He secured the two locks on one end of the leash to the hooks inserted into Tony's cup and he allowed the leash to dangle free between his outstretched and quivering legs.

"That end is yours alone," Gold intoned with reverence and passion as he stepped away from the tanned body of the capable secretary.

Debbie needed no further urging. Grasping the single circle that swung from the dangling end of the chain, she placed a long finger within it and pulled it upward toward the perspiring man's naked pubis. He stared at her encircled finger and traced every move with alarmed eyes. As she lifted her hand and snaked the chain upward, his eyes darted and danced as he strived to predict to what extent she would threaten him during this initial learning period. As her bent finger swept enticingly upward, the chain began to strain and became more and more rigid. Any further movement, she noted from the apprehensive secretary's telltale eyes, would tell her exactly what that chain was designed for and capable of doing. She pulled slightly up with her encircled finger as Tony's eyes were redirected with firm self-control toward the slowly circling overhead fan. As he found a focal point and concentrated on his breathing, Debbie pulled firmly, unyieldingly, and directly upward.

His reaction was as immediate as it was fulfilling to her. First lifting himself up in an attempt to slacken the chain, Tony attempted but could not succeed at remaining silent. Crying out in physical reaction to her direction of his chain, she realized that her operation of the leash would cause him immediate further constriction of the too-tight and unyielding plastic pouch by shortening the attached straps containing the hooks. Simply, she recognized that pulling his leash tightened his straps forced him to redirect himself in a manner exactly in line with her desire of the moment in order to bring himself relief. Once ensconced within the transparent cup, the man was absolutely in her control for both bodily functions and physical direction. She smiled as she toyed with the circle that adorned her finger.

"Do him, too," she ordered the Gold who proceeded immediately to dress the contracting officer in his own neutral crystalline cup and straps. Hooking him tightly within its confines, he dropped the leash between Bob's outstretched legs and allowed Debbie to take it in her hand. Now wearing the two metal rings of her personal slaves, she again gave her Gold a simple order.

"I'll do yours," she commanded. He stepped back immediately after offering her his golden unclouded cup. "Hold these two by their leashes," she said as she offered him the rings of the tethers already in her grasp. "I'll want you to run these two through their paces and show me the tricks."

Gold was again amazed and impressed with her incredible intuition. She knew, he marveled, somehow she knew there were skills involved that could further enhance her enjoyment with these devices. She had a special sense, he guessed, as this extraordinary woman posed yet another challenge for his proud training. As he stood on the plush peach carpet alongside her bed and spread his recovering legs wide beneath his shoulders, she took hold of his formerly tortured genitals and stroked them lovingly in her silken hand.

"Thank you again," she cooed in his ear alone. "Because you have brought me pleasure one more time, I will bring you some, too."

Uncomprehending her appreciation of his instruction, he stood and waited for his cup to be applied and locked into painful place. Her red stocking rubbed softly against his well-toned leg as she soothed his aching muscles with comforting strokes. Bending her whole body next to his bald genital area, she rubbed her red silk on his surprisingly excited skin. Taking the cup gingerly in her milky white hands, she placed it gently against his hardening body and secured the buttocks strap to the hooks. Fastening the hooks into their homes, Debbie took care to loosen their tension and provide the grimacing Gold with astonishing comfort. Locking the reins into place, Debbie took the golden ring upon her finger and rose up to meet his wondering eyes. She breathed a personal message into his ear.

"If you please me, I won't punish you," she promised. "But if you are bad, then there's no telling what I might do to you. It's up to you." Debbie pulled her erect body away from his sweet-smelling skin as Gold felt his plastic cup fill further with his own sensual pleasure and he swore an oath at the inconceivable enjoyment this enticing woman brought into his life.

"Wear these," she ordered the three flexibly strapped men as she tossed each his silken running shorts and cut off t-shirts. "Get dressed now," she commanded. "We're going out."

The three struggled to slip their shackled bodies into their briefs as Debbie moved in to adjust their leashes against their clothing. Tensing each man's leash just enough to allow their rings to dangle from the front of their waistbands, Debbie inspected her charges and led them down the stairs, into her car, and off for an afternoon's pleasure that they would not soon forget. With the top down and the sun shining brightly on their tanned and oiled skin, Debbie sped her male threesome down the driveway, into the street, and through town on their way to the highway.

The open expressway air delightfully breezed through the flying hair of the foursome as Debbie made excellent time in the light weekend traffic. With the radio blasting Top 40 hits in their unhearing ears, the group made their way to the selected exit ramp, slowed for the impending curve, and swooped in one fluid motion toward Debbie's favorite location for tension relaxation, that is, the largest mall in her suburban area. As the invisibly shackled group made their way through the parked cars toward the main entrance, Debbie cast a watchful eye on her charges and led them on a quick scurry through the massive front doors.

Once inside, the group could easily have faded into the mass of customers who were patronizing the shopping center. Tanned and athletic male bodies accompanied thin women in their quests for perfect clothing and accessories for themselves and their homes. Debbie and her group melted silently into the throng as they made their way toward the most elegant anchor store for what Debbie often referred to as "power buying." Drifting from display to display, and from boutique to designer department, Debbie and her company lifted, touched, handled, and criticized all the merchandise within their reach. Ushering the assembly toward the lingerie department, Debbie grasped Tony's ever-present metallic ring and pulled the startled secretary to a complete and sudden stop. His eyes glistening with unwanted tears, Tony stood immobile as his companions came to rest immediately behind his position.

"Can I help you?" a soft female voice inquired.

Debbie looked the saleswoman up and down, nodded, and responded. "I'm looking for something special. Very special," she said as she gazed along the racks replete with soft satin teddies, long sensual gowns, and silken bedclothes.

The saleswoman finally took in the unlikely sight of her customer's male entourage and breathed in long, hard, and silently. Her years of experience in women's fine lingerie had brought her various customers with rather interesting needs and requirements, she thought, and this group would certainly qualify as "interesting." Nodding with excruciatingly complete understanding, the saleswoman indicated her comprehension of Debbie's unique demands.

"I'm Elissa," she offered. "Please follow me," she whispered and indicated for the foursome to accompany her toward the rear of the department.

The group marched quietly and without complaint toward the back wall and the sign indicating "fitting rooms." However the saleswoman accomplished a quick right turn into the corner, opened a nondescript door with a key braceleted to her wrist, and indicated that the group should enter behind her. Once inside, she shut the door with a firm hand and motioned Debbie and her men to be seated.

This particular fitting room was obviously used only for special purposes, Debbie mused, as the three men took in their surroundings with artful eyes and surreptitious glances. Decorated in soft and not unpleasant shades of pink, the rather expansive suite contained two walls of mirrors, four raised platforms, and several cushioned chairs. The remaining two walls were decorated with hooks for hanging items under consideration and the raised platforms, Debbie guessed correctly, were for potential buyers to view their considered items.

Breaking the silence, the saleswoman asked to no one in particular, "What do you require?" Six male eyes turned toward Debbie, not daring to speak until she gave them clear permission. Taking a deep breath and choosing her words carefully, she answered the patiently waiting woman.

"These three are entertaining me tonight," she offered with authority and without embarrassment. "They require suitable attire for my pleasure. What do you have that will help them perform for me this evening?" Debbie sat still, her hands folded in her lap, and waited for the saleswoman either to faint on the floor or satisfy her specific request. She was not disappointed.

"I think I have the very things you'll need," Elissa began with only a moment's hesitation. "Let me check the floor and the items we keep. . . behind the counter," she lied and Debbie caught her implied but unstated meaning. As she turned to exit the dressing room, she turned toward Debbie and mentioned with envy, "You're very lucky. I'll be right back." With no further words necessary between the two women who shared a single thought, she exited to inspect the lingerie available for this unique and enviable purchase.

The deafening silence in the luxurious, private fitting room threatened to overwhelm Tony and Bob's ability to secrete their growing excitement. The nimble secretary felt his plastic cup fill with his heightening happiness and his efforts at willing the independent organ down met with utter failure. The silent contracting officer noticed his own silken shorts straining as his personal pleasure increased and his efforts in preventing its expansion met with similar frustration. The two sheepish co-workers glanced furtively at each other and shared their mutual concern. When Elissa returned, they both worried, their secrets would be completely out in the open.

Gold sat immobile as ordered in the plush pink striped chair that was situated next to his superior. His golden strapping was comfortably warm against his hairless skin as he waited eagerly for Elissa's return. He considered Debbie's daring and her amazing and uncanny abilities to astound him again and again and wondered if Ron would be up to her insistent challenges and demands. As he perused Ron's chances of being trained successfully enough to satisfy his wife's apparently insatiable desires and her unique strategies to attain them, the locked dressing room door opened and Elissa breezed in carrying scores of brightly colored fine lingerie. The saleswoman wasted no time in hanging her wares upon the padded hooks around the room.

Debbie sat up to scrutinize the garments that Elissa had selected. Her keen eye missed no outfit and her reddening skin betrayed her personal satisfaction at Elissa's variety of selection. She knew this store to be classy; however, until now she had no idea just how varied and intriguing their collection had become. Almost too flustered to speak, Debbie managed a simple and straightforward direction.

"Check them out, boys," she ordered, "and try them on. I'll choose when I see what fits." Her authoritarian direction left no room for argument or question.

The three men rose and meandered around the large fitting room as Debbie inspected their choices. Realizing that her bracelet allowed her to approve or deny their choices with suddenness and finality, the men were at first reluctant to select their garments. Elissa viewed the scene with silent but utter amazement and coveted Debbie's demeanor, her entourage, and her evening that lay ahead. Both women's deepest and most personal regions began to twitch violently and invisibly as they relinquished themselves to their growing delight.

Walking slowly from the black teddy toward the purple garter belt and matching bra, Tony grazed each garment and enjoyed its silken delight against his perspiring touch. Bob's choice was torn between the red bodysuit and the teal blue and black lace pushup bra and its matching crotchless panties. Gold stood mesmerized by the jade green teddy with the Velcro crotch. Each man was transfixed by the glorious assortment of garments that Elissa had provided him and each anxiously anticipated the entertainment he could provide his Mistress with each costume.

As the men felt, touched, and stroked each glorious piece of finery, Debbie met Elissa's wandering and wondering eyes with a stare that invited conversation. Although her years of experience in this special department had afforded Elissa a kind of special understanding that indicated the best course was often one of silence, her interest was piqued by this atypical and novel display of male obedience and genuine intent to please this woman who sat, apparently unaffected, in front of her. Her judgment in this case was simply cast aside and she whispered the pertinent question.

"How did you get three of them?" the diminutive saleswoman inquired.

Debbie smiled as the three men, trained to respect her private conversations, continued their search for the perfect attire, oblivious to the saleswoman's question. Choosing her words carefully, Debbie responded simply but directly.

"They're mine. I can get as many of them as I want. I sent my husband to this training facility."

Elissa pounced on the singular information. "The facility! I've heard of it. I'm thinking of sending my husband there shortly.

Do you like it? Is it everything they say it is?" Her words tumbled out in a torrent of emotions mixed with naked curiosity. Debbie smiled, nodded, and turned her attention toward Bob as he reached out for the red bodysuit.

Extending her braceleted wrist, she turned toward Elissa and said quietly, "Here. Watch this."

Pressing a series of colored jewels on her wristband, Debbie gave Bob the simple and direct order that denied his apparent choice. The effect was electric. As the contracting officer dropped first to his knees and then into a ball on the floor and groped his plastic encased organs to alleviate the horror that Debbie had inflicted upon them, Elissa gasped and took in the scene with growing excitement. The saleswoman's skin began to tingle between her tightly pressed thighs and a glow of perspiration dotted her forehead. Bob's expertly muffled shrieks filled the pink room and the thrashing man's body was the sole motion among the five inhabitants. Standing perfectly still, her Gold and her secretary awaited the punishment's end and the rendering of judgment on their own choices.

Pressing another jewel, Debbie ended Bob's pain. Bringing his anguished body up to a kneeling position, he turned toward his superior and spoke the five words that caused Elissa to startle in her seat.

"Thank you for my punishment," he offered, and Debbie flicked her hand to indicate his dismissal and freedom to make another choice.

Elissa sat mesmerized by the performance and leaned forward toward her customer, lest her words be negated by possibly being heard by anyone else.

"That was great!" she breathed.

Debbie nodded and then approved both Gold and Tony's selections. The three men were ordered to strip and try on the fine lingerie Debbie had permitted them to select. Elissa sat spellbound in her comfortable upholstered chair as Debbie smirked at what would certainly be an interesting reaction by the saleswoman when she discovered the rather peculiar and erotic undergarments worn by her charges. Again, she was not disappointed.

Undressing his perfect form quickly and decisively, Gold stood nude with his golden plastic strapping firmly attached in full view of his comrades, his superior, and the startled saleswoman. Unable to resist physical expression of her delight and surprise, Elissa stared at his wonderful form in open-mouthed wonder. Shifting her gaze rapidly from Debbie's smirking face to Gold's delicious presentation, Elissa finally rested an inquiring stare at the seated customer facing her.

"May I?" the enraptured saleswoman queried.

"Be my guest," Debbie agreed as she sat captivated by the woman's excited yet polite request.

Elissa stood, braced herself with a deep intake of breath, and approached the glistening and naked body that was fully erect before her. Reaching out with a quivering hand, she stroked Gold's massive arms and his rippling back. Gaining more courage with every caress, she moved her soft white hand toward his slowly heaving stomach, reached down toward his tight buttocks, and dropped to her knees to pat and rub his well-toned legs. The entire scene was titillating to the observers and both Tony and Bob lost their battle of wills to force down their now-excited maleness. Gold stood impassive and unresponsive as the electrified and enthusiastic saleswoman turned to Debbie for yet another permission.

Reaching for Gold's now-dangling chain, she asked, "Would it be all right with you if I. . ."

Debbie interrupted her impassioned plea with a simple nod. Her chest rising and dropping with almost delirious breaths, Elissa pinched the golden ring tightly between two fingers and raised the chain almost to the point of tautness. Gold followed her every move with careful eyes and sucked in a clear, sharp breath in anticipation of her next move. Settling the golden ring around her red-manicured index finger, Elissa brought the circle to her lips, kissed its cool metallic gleam, and delighted in the sputtering Gold's immediate reaction to her sudden movement. His entire musculature now straining in resistance to her action, Gold mumbled in pain and excitement at the novice's persistent and well-executed move. Although she caused him intense pain, he appreciated her warm lips upon his metallic leash.

With a sudden relaxation, Elissa let go of the threatening device and allowed Gold's strapping to lengthen and relax. His eyes brimming with tears, he responded as his training insisted.

"Thank you for my pain," he intoned as Elissa's breaths quickened noticeably.

Turning to the beaming customer in the upholstered pink chair, Elissa thanked her benefactor for the simple delight she had just experienced. "I'm going to sign him up today," she breathed, as she gathered Gold's selection of lingerie and dressed him for Debbie's inspection. She placed the jade green teddy at his feet and drew one leg at a time into the appropriate holes. Raising the silken garment slowly yet urgently up his perspiring form, she coaxed the lingerie up his gleaming body toward his golden straps. Lifting with both arms, the saleswoman gathered the satiny fabric and secured his private parts tightly into its surprisingly cool fit. Taking the black straps carefully in each hand, she persuaded his rippling arms into each and drew the lace bra cups toward his gleaming chest. Her final move was one of both authority and cajoling as she adjusted the stretched fabric to smooth it over every inch of his perfect body. Before allowing him to turn and face his superior for approval, the saleswoman scrutinized his appearance by patting his buttocks with a surprisingly firm hand, correcting the folds in his solidly filled crotch, and encouraging him to stand even straighter for Debbie's perusal. Finally satisfied, she turned his form toward the seated woman and presented her charge for consent.

Watching her trained Gold perform adequately for this woman's expert touch, Debbie forced her face into a neutral visage for an inspection that was already causing her thighs to tighten and her crotch to moisten. Prior to granting any expression of approval or disdain, Debbie opened her oversized purse and withdrew her brown leather whip, much to the delight of the saleswoman and the apprehension of her three charges. Whistling the leather stick through the otherwise quiet air of the private fitting room, Debbie gathered the attention of her rapt foursome, stood up quietly, and moved silently toward the saleswoman and her prize.

"I approve of the color," Debbie began ominously, "but I'm not sure about the closure. Demonstrate it for me," she commanded the twosome on the raised platform.

"Yes ma'am," Elissa responded immediately as she reached between the Gold's stationary legs. "Allow me," she continued as she reached out toward her client and received the leather crop in her now-excited hand.

Showing signs of great enjoyment in her work, Elissa grasped the offered crop and delivered a well-placed blow to Gold's unmoving right leg. Before the man could react and illustrate his excellent conditioning or training, Elissa conveyed an immediate second stroke to his non-reactive left thigh. The great man winced silently and spread his legs wider. Still unsatisfied, Elissa brought the instrument of instruction soundly to his plastic cup and watched in wonder as the startled man succumbed to her demand. Eager to respond and end her inflictions, Gold jumped his legs apart, bent his knees, and offered her his bald, encased pubic area by thrusting his hips forcefully forward.

Illustrating a talent both for lingerie fitting and administration of pain, Elissa tore the Velcro open and lifted the front for Debbie's delight. Grasping his encased genitals solidly in her deceptively feminine hand, Elissa commented, "This garment provides you great freedom as well as opportunity. May I wrap it up for you?"

Debbie nodded eagerly and requested the item be gift-wrapped. Urging Gold to remove her purchase, she required him to stand naked save for his golden plastic as she turned her attention to the two co-workers who stood gaping at the display they had just witnessed. Ordering them likewise to strip, Elissa repeated the scene for her own as well as for Debbie's satisfaction, and calculated mentally the commission on her sales. No amount of money, she thought, could pay for this delightful Sunday afternoon.

Before allowing the men to dress and continue on their shopping odyssey, Debbie had one more request of the nearly orgasmic saleswoman. "Bring me a long piece of bright ribbon," she asked mysteriously. Elissa exited the locked room first to fulfill Debbie's unusual request and after returning with the ribbon she exited again to wrap and total the purchases.

As the customers awaited the return of their purchases, Debbie ordered the naked men to stand in front of her, their hips touching one another, and their legs spread comfortably apart. Reaching out with her milky hand, Debbie seized all three rings that dangled between the men's legs and drew them up in front of her face. Slipping the bright green ribbon through the three rings, Debbie tied their leashes together in a massive knot and then drew the dangling ribbon ends into a bow. Allowing the bound-together men to re-dress, although clumsily, in their shorts and t-shirts, Debbie positioned the bow so it hung lazily from the central Gold's shorts and swung carelessly in front of his cupped genitals. Viewing their dilemma in dressing with a smirk, she paid the returning saleswoman for the lingerie and exited the private fitting area by drawing the green bow casually behind her as she stepped briskly into the bright lights of the store once again.

Tony, Bob, and Gold struggled to match her every step. Trying to out-guess their leader's next direction, the three men posed an odd dance of pain behind her quickly moving form. Every wrong step cost one or another a dose of carefully-inflicted pain, and the threesome grappled and tussled with one another in a valiant but vain attempt to imitate Debbie's turns and straightaway. Giving no thought whatsoever to their plight, the intent woman led the group through the store and into the mall, up one corridor and down another, and came to rest at the entrance of her carefully selected shop.

The men stood gallant but silent as they considered her preference. Realizing that this woman never ceased to amaze him, she gained Gold's respect one more time. Tony took in a great gasp of air when he realized her intention, and Bob let out a sigh of delight when he considered their next escapade. Dragging her three tied recruits behind her, Debbie spoke to the awaiting salesman.

"Do you have a private room?" she inquired.

The photographer viewed the entourage and nodded. "Please follow me," he encouraged her as she drew the green bow hastily once again toward a locked door.

"In!" she commanded, and Tony, Bob, and Gold struggled to obey.

The photographer was silent, in awe of the scene that was unfolding in front of his unbelieving eyes. Securing the door solidly behind him, he gaped in wonder as Debbie ordered the men to strip down to their plastic strapping and stand naked in front of the agitated worker. Sensing his own maleness beginning to engorge in excitement at the spectacle she had produced, he offered lamely, "My name is Craig. How may I help you?" He felt himself push against his own zipper and he fought the urge to grab his own genitals and endorse their journey.

Witnessing his rising excitement, Debbie played the scene to its fullest. "These are mine," she said with a sweep of her hand toward the bound trio of naked men. "I wish to record them on film for my own entertainment." She saw his pants strain with their contents.

"Of course," he replied a little too calmly, she thought. "Does the lady wish to specify scenery?"

Debbie answered in an even-cooler fashion, "No," she commented, "I require you to be creative with that." Her demanding tone was not lost on his torrid ears. "As for poses," she continued, "I have certain ideas in mind."

Craig shifted nervously on his feet and then sprang quickly into action. Drawing the sandy beach background into place, he loaded his camera and busied himself with his equipment. Trying not to stare at the unclothed but firmly strapped men in his private studio, he presented an odd image of a man struggling with both his professionalism and his personal rising excitement. When he looked up from his intricate work with his camera and lights, he stood in rapt amazement at what she had done.

Debbie had drawn Tony to his knees in front of the standing contracting officer and placed the former's mouth directly in front of Bob's ensconced genitals. Taking his two hooks firmly, one in each hand; Debbie unshackled the standing man and exposed his cupped penis and testicles. Clutching his cup in absolute mastery over his helplessness tempered with his strict obedience, she tore the plastic from his crotch and exposed him fully to the photographer's relentless stare. Blushing with immeasurable embarrassment, Bob stood motionless as Debbie took a handful of Tony's black hair and guided his head firmly into place at Bob's netted penis.

Speaking directly to the photographer, Debbie instructed him to take a series of photos that illustrated Tony's skill at bringing his partner to erection and then to complete fulfillment. She ordered pictures of Bob's rising maleness and others of his facial reactions. In addition, she mandated several close-ups of Tony's technique and then bid Craig to use his professional judgment and shoot any other photos that would entertain the woman that evening. The startled photographer nodded and drew his thighs tightly together to combat his rising excitement.

Sitting gracefully on the captain's chair provided for her comfort, Debbie reached into her purse and withdrew the leather crop once again. Handing the item to Gold's outstretched hand, she told him simply, "Encourage them. I believe you know how."

The ever-obedient Gold took the brown leather and stood behind the motionless pair. With Tony's eyes riveted to the netted penis before him, and Bob's eyes focused on the wall over Tony's lowered head, Gold provided an unseen threat that could lash out at any moment and bring the pair instantaneous whippings. As the photographer leaned into his camera's eye and waited for the action to begin, Gold brought the whip solidly across Bob's backside and forced the yelping man to thrust his hips toward the secretary's now-open mouth. Reaching with a long arm behind the kneeling secretary, Gold stroked Tony's cheeks firmly and the younger man moved brilliantly into action.

Grasping Bob's netted member in both hands, Tony drew the organ between his lips. Once he established a solid grip on the tender maleness, Tony reached behind his quarry's hips, grasped his cheeks tenderly but firmly in his hands, and pulled and pushed the thrusting man's body in and out of his salivating mouth. With each forward thrust, Gold stroked Bob's buttocks firmly with a room-filling crack, and Bob was forced to propel himself harder and harder into the eager lips of the kneeling secretary. Sensing the impending explosion, Gold sought to slow down the scenario.

He whipped Tony's hands until the exasperated man dropped them to the floor. Positioned on all fours now, Tony's backside was fully exposed to Gold's delight. Offering the crop slowly and landing each blow with a sharp snapping and popping,

Gold encouraged the young man to become more inventive with his lips, tongue, and teeth. Moving deftly from one man's backside to the others', Gold produced a rhythmic and fluid dance that filled the camera with unbridled passion and scintillating exposures.

Debbie witnessed the provocative events with cool but rising passion. Feeling her female urges welling up under her short, tight skirt, she spread her legs and reached toward her femininity to satisfy her upcoming delight. As Tony slobbered over Bob's thrusting penis, and as Gold continued his whipping of the men into a height of passion and sensuality, Debbie thrust a milk white finger between her legs to gratify and fulfill her personal pleasure.

Noticing the agitated woman's desire, Gold momentarily ceased his whipping and dropped to his knees in front of her outstretched legs. Using only his face to struggle into her most private region, his head disappeared under her clothing and only her face revealed his success at reaching his goal. Maximizing all his talents and training, Gold stroked the dancing pair of men in random fashion as he fulfilled Debbie's needs and desires with his dancing tongue.

The contracting officer gasped audibly and began whimpering in fright as he felt himself ready to explode with every talented tonguing Tony could offer. Gold grunted and groaned as he taxed his coordination, training, and strength to continue the flogging with his arm as he simultaneously brought his superior to completion with his face. Debbie groaned as she thrust her seated hips toward Gold's manipulative mouth and helped bring about her own realization of ecstasy. Tony's basic animal urges overcame his chagrin and the young secretary threw himself totally into his efforts.

With a great roar, the foursome erupted as one. As Bob fell to his knees in gratitude and joy, Tony's mouth dropped with him. His buttocks raised almost directly upward, the secretary withdrew his face from Bob's clear netting and the two men fell literally one on top of the other in their mutual exhaustion onto the floor. Debbie's orgasm came in waves and Gold ushered her into ultimate and repeated explosion with his well-trained lips, tongue, and teeth. Craig bent over his camera in reverence and admiration and clicked continually upon the darting camera shutter's release. These would be, he knew, works of art.

Rising slowly to her feet as she adjusted her skirt, Debbie took the crop from Gold's sweating hands and replaced it in her purse. She bade Tony and Bob to dress themselves and then ordered them to dress the exhausted Gold. As the men completed their tasks, Debbie paid the photographer and ordered him to deliver the finished prints to her home that evening. Without a thought of disagreement, Craig nodded, took her address, and rushed out of the studio toward the darkroom with his many rolls of exposed film.

Adjusting their plastic strappings one final time that late afternoon, Debbie drove the men to her home and laid them naked on the floor to rest.

She reclined in her evening's attire on her wide bed and watched their rhythmic breathing. Her red silken teddy now clinging to the perspiration on her excited body, she called to her Gold to awaken him from his gentle slumber.

"Wake them and send them home," she urged. "It's time to check on Ron."

Chapter Twenty Four

In the quiet of her private chamber, the Mistress conferred with her personal Gold to consider the three items on her agenda that morning. First, she had to consider whether to unshackle her retrained Black and free him from his black binds or to dismiss him from the facility. An unpleasant choice, she thought, as her eyes wandered to the next item on her schedule. Second, she recalled, was that her newest Blue was to demonstrate his concept for the first insertion of the group of trainees that was readying itself to graduate. Good, she judged, he was quick in offering a new design. He might just have the makings of a fine Blue, she happily wondered. Finally, she noticed that that same group of trainees was scheduled this very busy morning to undergo its definitive training in assisting women to achieve their sexual fulfillment and pleasure. The importance of this particular experience was paramount and the Mistress smiled inwardly as her eyes perused the daily calendar. Each of these tasks, she noted, was both an important and an extremely valuable lesson for each targeted individual or group to master.

Her personal Gold's gleaming form stood rigidly by her side as the Mistress organized the day's activities to enable her to visit each site. Recognizing that her presence was required to either release the Black and restore him to the service of his trainee or banish him from further training, the Mistress scheduled that liberation as her first priority. Working with the newly-appointed Blue in his model first-insertion seemed an appropriate second task. She considered scheduling the novices' training to begin prior to the Blue's introduction of his effort, thereby allowing their training to continue while the Blue demonstrated his ideas using as examples the designated Colors her Gold had chosen. Smiling at her ability to juggle scheduling problems and allow herself to participate in each, the seated and robed woman prioritized each event for her Gold to arrange.

Obedient to the ultimate degree, the Gold received the initialed list and knelt for permission to exit her chambers. The Mistress reached out with her soft hand and encircled his netted genitals with a tiny squeeze of appreciation. He encouraged a response from his most private organ and, in doing so, her hand recognized her definitive and total control over his entity. Recognizing his dance of delight within her palm, the Mistress brought her full grip upward and encouraged the supplicant assistant to rise.

"Black!" she barked toward the recesses of her chamber, "Attend me. It is time for you to go."

From the farthest corner of her massive quarters, the recently returned Black crawled in the direction of her enormous desk. His disheveled appearance appalled the sleek and manicured Gold and the man's disgust registered all over his beardless face. Looking toward his Mistress for permission to address the creeping mongrel, the Gold received a curt nod and he spoke to his former colleague.

"Bring your leash to me," he began ominously, as the bedraggled and spent creature collected himself for yet another arduous journey. "Come!" His voice was an order that might have been given to any pet or errant child for rebuke.

The Black fought against his hot tears that coursed down his bearded cheeks and landed with a salty taste in his slobbering mouth. Creeping painfully toward the Gold's well-oiled body, the chastened former-trainer fought to flip the dangling end of his leash toward the man's outstretched hand. After the personal Gold lifted the thick black leather strap and jerked the defeated trainer toward the doorway, the Gold wrenched the rein and sent the unfortunate victim sprawling into the hallway.

Striding with giant steps, the Gold inflicted his fury upon the man's tortured body and dragged him, kicking, squirming, and yelping, toward the great pool. As the great electronic doors parted to welcome them to the bathing chamber, the sobbing Black tried to gather his muddled thoughts clearly into his head. He could take no more, he decided, and he silently begged the Mistress to grant him clemency or release him from his home at the facility. But his actions, he reflected, had been beyond forgiveness and her supreme authority forced her to punish him in this manner. Accepting both her superiority and her decision, he forced his agonized body into the sweet-smelling room for whatever fate lay ahead for him.

His tearful eyes were astounded at the sight that awaited him. The entire cadre of Colors was amassed around the great pool and the awesome sight sent shivers of fear through his unusually cold body. The contradiction of sweat and frigid fear permeated his soul as the Gold led him deeper and deeper into the chamber. Harnessing the very last ounce of his courage and strength, the Black achieved a sort of rhythmic gait that was derived from his almost-forgotten pride at having achieved the rank of Green.

Gold pulled the creeping man to a sudden halt by sending waves of pain through his harnessed genitals. The emasculated former-trainer knelt on his raw and aching hands and knees for what he feared was the ultimate punishment: banishment from the Colors. Fearing the worst and expecting ritual expulsion, the bedraggled Black cried a flood of tears accompanied by wails of sadness and sorrow. He neither heard nor saw the Mistress enter through the secreted doorway behind the viewing area. His only thoughts were with his own pitiful situation.

Managing to see that the corps of Golds was approaching his position with purposeful steps, the petrified Black responded banefully to his terror. Without warning, his frightened bladder emptied within his black harness and the telltale residue of discharge and odor wafted around his supplicant position. The Golds responded with immediate disdain. Grasping his belted harness forcefully, the highest level of the Colors lifted the suffering and anguished perpetrator to an upright position. Screaming in pain, the former-Green's squashed testicles and penis persecuted his body as the Golds held him vertically and allowed his legs to dangle mercilessly several inches from the floor. As they carried the creature to a position directly in front of the seated Mistress, the abused and suffering penitent shrieked unashamed and unabashed in his ultimate distress. The Mistress spoke slowly.

"I believe you have been punished and re-trained," she began. "Are you ready for your release?"

His unhearing ears were filled with his own wailing voice as it filled the great chamber with a cacophony of calamity. Unable to hear her offer of solace and reinstatement, the anguished former trainer dangled in the firm grip of the Golds and shrieked pitifully and hopelessly before the entire cadre. She listened for a few moments and flipped her hand toward the nearest Gold.

"Get his attention," she directed to her obedient servant.

Taking his muscular hand and directing it firmly and forcefully into the thick black leather that surrounded the agonized man's genitals, the Gold sent shock waves of incredible pain into his most sensitive area. Too stunned now even to scream, the dangling servant utilized his final ounce of strength and fortitude and gazed pitifully, but silently, at his Mistress.

"I asked you a question," she spoke in his direction, "and I would like a reply. Are you ready for release?" She waited for his reply.

Any inability on his part to respond might indicate that he was beyond reinstatement and she would have to exercise the necessary finality of expulsion. Too bad, she thought, he had great promise. She sat silently and waited for his response.

His tortured genitals aching beyond belief, the former Green's body shook with horror as he felt his entire body beginning to engage in unpreventable panic. Release? Did his ears hear or did his mind? Was she releasing him from his bonds or from the corps? Did it matter anymore? Gathering his voice, the astounded man replied.

"Yes," he muttered. "Please. Help me." His voice trailed off.

She asked yet another question. "Do you recognize your

transgression? Do you understand what you have done?" She waited again for the suffering man to gather his words.

The dangling man squirmed in the Golds' tense grip. "Yes." Each word came painfully. "Yes, what I did was unforgivable. I am so sorry. . ." His words were lost in a new rush of tears.

"Stand him down," she ordered the Golds as they immediately released their prisoner into a fallen lump of fetid and putrid humanity on the cold tile floor. "Rise," she instructed the body that lay curled at her feet.

To the utter amazement of the Colors, the former Green brought himself finally to his knees in a series of agonized motions. Bringing his bearded face as erect as he could manage, he faced the Mistress with a sort of empty courage and false bravado. Expending every ounce of his capability, he lifted one foot, planted it firmly onto the tile floor, and hoisted himself to a bent-over but standing position. Admiring his tenacity, the Mistress wagged a finger and commanded him to walk toward her.

Stumbling forward in less-than-perfect response, the prisoner stood shakily before his Mistress as she reached out to unlock his girdle. Detaching first one strap and then the other, the codpiece fell harmlessly toward the tiled floor and the penitent creature emitted a huge, heartfelt sigh of relief. She spun him around with another finger and detached the binding leather straps from between his buttocks. As the putrid garment released its death grip on his body, the naked man sobbed tears of freedom and gratitude for her clemency. Facing her once again, he fell to his knees in supplication and thanks.

"Thank you for my punishment," he spoke clearly and directly to his Mistress.

"Your lesson has been a warning to the entire cadre," she intoned solemnly, "and now you must be cleansed. When you are done, I will reinstate you to the Colors." As soon as she uttered the final syllable, the Golds dragged the stunned man toward the great pool and began his ritual cleansing.

Every member of the corps participated in his bathing as the Greens lathered their comrade's body with sweet lavender soap and brought the bubbles to a great crescendo. The Blues saw to his depilatory and ensured that no telltale bristles protruded from his physique. When the Head White flipped the trainer into a prone position, the corps of Whites took turns filling his rectum with soothing cleansing liquid, marching him toward the room for expulsion, and parading him back to the great pool for re-cleansing. Each insertion of unlubricated cleansing lotion brought him pain mixed with pleasure and the nearly overcome man offered neither resistance nor remark toward their zealous efforts. Deciding that he was finally clean, the Head White nodded toward the Head Gold and the cadre of Golds lifted Green unceremoniously from the great pool.

Dropping him onto the padded bars, the Golds spread the Green's legs mercilessly wide to enable their lubrication of his darkest area. Having forgotten the ultimate experience of Gold lubrication, the Green relished their probing and investigating fingers as they drove the Green cream higher and higher into his rectum. Forcing himself to relax and enjoy their investigation of his inner self, the Green savored each intrusion into his anal canal. When he felt the Gold finally draw his circle and slap his buttocks, the Green stood from his abased position and once again faced his Mistress.

"Come," she commanded and wagged yet another finger at his responding form. "It is time."

She bade him kneel in front of her with his backside elevated and his legs spread wide. Opening a green velvet pouch, she took out his personal insert and touched its smooth form against his quivering anus. Pushing the insert millimeters into his expansive hole, she brought about great waves of delight from the excited man's buttocks. He reached his backside toward her gift and thrust his hips in rhythm toward its pointed end. Forcing himself further and further back toward the insert's position, the Green threw himself into his acceptance of the ultimate gift as the Mistress forced home his private pleasure. He wailed with delight and ecstasy as the welcome intruder worked itself home. She ordered him to stand and exhibit his insertion for the entire corps.

His renewed tears this time were tears of bliss as the woman extracted yet another memory from the velvet bag and showed him his Green metallic ring. Dangling the instrument of obedience between two beautifully manicured fingers, she offered him the return of his manhood and respectability. Stepping even closer to her seated form, the Green thrust his naked pubis toward her in silent acceptance of her gift. Fondling his denuded skin with her soft hands, she massaged his genitals in a manner that did not threaten his engorgement; rather, she offered him solace and comfort for the tribulations she had been forced to visit upon him. Accepting his blame for his own misdeeds, the Green offered himself wholly and without reservation to his Mistress once again.

She slipped his testicles and penis through the warm ring. Pushing it firmly to his abdominal skin, she twisted the device and locked it securely into place. Sneaking a look at his remembered green netting, he watched her fix the housing to the ring and elongate the net over his genitals. He smiled broadly in his joy at the return of both his possessions and his manhood and he knelt at the Mistress's feet as he was overcome by her generosity and forgiveness.

"What can I do for you now?" she inquired and sat back for the inevitable reply.

Filled in both his rectum and his soul, he replied in earnest. "Please give me pain," he spoke loudly and clearly.

She indulged him by pressing a coded series of jewels on her bracelet. The entire corps watched him fall to the floor and writhe in agonizing distress as he suffered silently between her feet on the cold tile of the great chamber. The sweetness of the moment brought tears to the eyes of the Colors as they witnessed his re-entry into their midst. When the Mistress brought his pain to an end, he rose, thanked her again for her infliction upon his body, and turned to face his comrades. Raising his arms in victory, the Green ran toward his colleagues and shrieked the cry of fervor and happiness as they embraced him and welcomed him back into their fold.

The joyous party broke up as the Mistress exited the great chamber and the Golds indicated to the entire body that it was time to begin the morning procedures for the trainees. As each color exited in its own separate direction, the reinstalled Green headed directly for Ron's room with a fervor that bespoke the potential for a foreboding morning for the peacefully sleeping lawyer who was idly dreaming inside his mask of delight on the wide bed in his tiny cubicle.

As he entered the darkened chamber, the Green found the sleeping trainee enjoying his rest. With the mask drawn firmly over his semi- conscious head and face, the trainee's obvious sensual arousal was plain for Green to see. Reaching over the sleeping form to disengage the images and sounds that the mask was affording the trainee, Green unlocked its hinges and freed Ron from his peaceful rest and welcomed him to his morning routine.

The startled trainee awoke in shock from his slumber and found his full pink netting being gripped tightly in the fist of his returned trainer. Holding the trainee's netted organ in a position perpendicular to the supine man's body, the Green smiled without meaning and sent a cold shiver of fright down the spine of the helpless trainee.

"Oh, God," Ron mumbled, as Green lifted him from the bed by virtue of the handle ensconced in his massive hand.

"I'm ba-aack," Green half-sang to the disconsolate trainee. "And I remember what you did to me. Let me tell you about my punishment." Green's foreboding manner threatened the hapless trainee.

With careful analysis and chronology, Green revealed what Level Three punishment entailed as he continued to drag Ron around the cubicle by virtue of the organ on which the Green maintained a firm and provocative grip. He described the tortures of losing his ring, of the hell of the black leather, and of the agony, misery, and torment he endured at the hands of the Mistress and the Colors. With each detail so fresh in his mind, the Green drove himself into a greater and greater frenzy as he enumerated each degradation and described each painful episode. When he detailed the events leading up to his imprisonment with the female trainers, Green suddenly stopped his rendition.

"Those women trainers, you know, are even more demanding that we are," Green informed the stricken trainee.

"You'll find out for yourself pretty soon, I guess," he warned as Ron's stomach suddenly felt queasy and he longed for his daily trip to the communal bath.

He chanced a question of his trainer. "What training will I receive today?" he queried.

Throwing a glance over his shoulder toward the body of the man whose penis he was leading dutifully toward the baths, Green apprised the struggling trainee, "Today isn't for you. It's for your wife."

With that intriguing but incomprehensible statement, Green dragged Ron toward the great chamber where Green had so recently found his release and renewal. Laughing inwardly, the massive trainer spun the hapless lawyer in a circle and grabbed his most private organ once again to bring him to a complete stop. Enjoying this morning to the fullest, Green taunted his charge.

"You get women today. Women! You've gotten too good with men, and the ladies are much more challenging, don't you think?" His voice was a challenge, a threat, and Ron's ears burned with passion when he considered this new twist.

But first, Ron considered what the big man meant by this comparison. He risked another question. "I like women. I know what to do with them. How are they going to teach me about women?"

Green responded with a roar of laughter. "You don't know a thing!" he barked at the startled trainee. "You are about to learn more than you ever dreamed possible. Your training has only just begun," he concluded with another burst of uncontrolled snickering.

Although the trainer's demeanor frightened the nude attorney, Ron also found himself quite excited by the day's possibilities. After all, he mused, he was being trained to serve Debbie totally and expertly and this training must be designed with her in mind. Women! The thought struck a responsive chord deep within his soul. He considered the potential for this activity and wondered how Debbie would take this news. Never unfaithful to his wife, Ron agonized over today's impending encounters with other women. How would he explain this to her?

Ron would later learn that he needn't have worried. After Debbie had her Gold dismiss the exhausted secretary and contracting officer, she and her well-trained expert viewed video footage of what Ron's training would involve. She watched other trainees manipulate women until the women's bodies ached from on-going orgasm, and she witnessed the men's training in techniques that seemed to arouse the women with barely a physical touch. Handcuffed trainees were schooled in efforts to stimulate their captors into frenzy and passion using only their mouths, yet they were consistently punished when they failed to treat the women with the utmost reverence and courtesy. Bringing a woman to orgasm was not the goal of the training, Debbie learned; rather, the men were instructed in variety, originality, creativity, and, above all, gentleness. Debbie and her Gold beheld the trainees' activities with silence interspersed only with Gold's infrequent demonstrations of those positions and techniques Debbie did not understand or could not properly experience from the video presentation.

Pausing the video, Debbie faced the Gold who was kneeling at the ready on the peach carpet next to her bed. "Tell me," the dark-haired woman began, "what can I expect from Ron?"

Gold's face took on a calm and serene posture as he outlined what Ron and the other trainees would master. "He will be able to bring you the greatest joy imaginable," the sandy-haired supplicant informed her. "His techniques will be honed and perfected with repeated direction and schooling. His hands will become secondary and he will master methods and strategies that will enliven your lives together. Most important of all," Gold intoned with passion, "his experiences with other women will intensify and magnify his times with you."

Debbie frowned and played her finger against the satin sheets when she heard Gold's final statement. Not sure that she wanted Ron involved with other women, she reacted with quiet displeasure to the possibility. She thought about Tony and Bob and her diversions with them as well as about other potential slaves she would likely meet in the workplace and elsewhere. Unable to reconcile those enticing thoughts with her vexation at

Gold's message, she struggled with her conundrum in silence on the wide bed.

Recognizing her dilemma, Gold offered the sullen woman some comfort. "By working with and serving other women, Ron will learn secrets and techniques to bring home to you. Don't consider his pleasures with others as rejection of his love for you. Instead, remember where he is and why he is doing this."

Debbie tried as hard as she could to imagine Ron's total commitment to her as evidenced by his wholehearted participation in the training. She recalled his obvious disdain and horror when he first arrived at the facility and she recollected his growing attraction and talents in learning how to become totally obedient. Wanting with her whole soul to believe that Gold was right, Debbie lifted the video recorder's remote control and reactivated the machine.

Trainees were being moved rapidly from one woman to the next as they were forced to bring each woman to a higher level of passion and excitement. Focusing on their hands cuffed securely behind their backs, Debbie lay amazed at the undulating and writhing female bodies that lay before her. Gold described the trainees' task.

"Talented trainees must be able to arouse their intended with virtually no notice. You might want Ron to excite you while you are cooking dinner. You may order him to show up at your office and bring you to fulfillment as you take phone calls or work with other contracting officers. Perhaps you will command him to strip his clothes in a more public place and then bring you ultimate satisfaction. With no warning, he will have to be ready immediately and perform without delay. This training enforces that behavior." Gold waited silently as Debbie fumbled with the remote control.

"You mean," she asked, "I should encourage Ron--and all the trained men I meet--to perform for me without notice? That I ought to simply command them to accomplish their mission and then ignore them? Will Ron be trained that way?"

Smiling, Gold answered her passionate question with a nod. "Of course," he replied evenly as he felt his rising excitement at what the next few days might entail. "You should order every slave to meet your every whim and desire, no matter how capricious they might be." He waited for his words to sink in. Then he added, "Trainees find that very stimulating."

Debbie felt her own female passion overcome her former distress regarding Ron's obligations and responsibilities to those women who he would meet in his daily life. With her thighs twitching and her inner self offering moisture to her most delicate area, Debbie felt her excitement build and threaten to overcome her demeanor of outward calm. Sensing that this woman was readying herself in anticipation of the delights that tomorrow might bring, Gold climbed upon the satiny bed, placed his massive hands behind his back, and knelt as low as he could manage to bring the now-thrashing woman to fulfillment.

His expertly trained mouth found her targets of delight in ways Debbie had never experienced. Endangered with impending orgasm, her raven hair flying all over her pillows, she thrust rhythmically with Gold's darting and daring tongue, teeth, and lips. Her lower lips were on fire as she felt herself lose control of her convulsing and writhing torso. Reaching upward with her last ounce of strength, Debbie grasped the headboard with two silken hands and raised her back completely off the sheets as Gold performed masterfully for her personal pleasure. Shrieking in ecstasy and delight, the delirious woman felt Gold's mouth enter into her as no organ had ever reached before. He would not allow the woman to spend herself; rather, he delighted her with excitement and ravished her with titillation. Straining to maintain his balance, he found the secret organs of her supreme euphoria and brought her time and again just to the point of orgasm. Relinquishing his oral grip, he allowed the shaken woman to relax before he once again managed her artfully to the point of rapture. She lost all track of time and space as she gave herself fully to the moment.

Screaming a song of exhilaration, Debbie forced her agonized but delirious body up and down in tempo with Gold's agitation within her secret self. She had no thoughts of Ron, the facility, or the impending meetings that the next few days might bring; instead, Debbie's total concentration was focused on her own fuzzy lips and their unlikely contents. In her frenzy, she could not see Gold's face as he recognized that her arms were giving out and her back muscles might be straining and that he must give her release before she hurt herself. Probing gently with agile teeth, lips, and tongue, the expert managed her howling and wailing sexuality to explosion.

Screaming with never-before experienced delight and exhaustion, Debbie fell flat onto her satin sheets with a soft plop. The captivated Gold enjoyed bringing her to final pleasure and began his professional massage to cool her torrid skin. Bringing fragrant balms and salves to her aching arms, the Gold worked the solutions into her soft skin in an effort to reduce any muscle strains or aches she might develop overnight.

When he was satisfied that the woman was soundly asleep, the proud Gold switched the video recorder on again and watched intently as the trainees exhibited new techniques and learned novel approaches. Fast-forwarding to the final scenes of the experiences, Gold hit the "play" button in time to watch again his own graduation from training as he brought five consecutive women to the heights of orgasm and massaged each to sleep. He watched the Mistress congratulate him once more time and reward him with his golden ring and netting. The episode concluded with his first ritual insertion as a Gold. Shutting off the television and the video recorder, Gold found himself crying tears of satisfaction and pride as he recalled the many women he had served during this past year.

Ron would learn that pleasure, Gold realized, as Debbie would surely give that pleasure to other graduates. And, Gold thought with amusement, she would probably begin that very exercise shortly, perhaps in the next few days.

Chapter Twenty Five

Debbie awoke Monday morning completely refreshed from a restful sleep. In fact, she thought as she stretched her long arms wide over her dark hair that decorated her satin pillow, she couldn't recall an evening in which she had so unconditionally and perfectly fallen so deeply to sleep and then felt so invigorated the next morning. The sweet smell of aromatic coffee filled her nostrils as her always-servile Gold brought her the morning meal. Taking the proffered silver tray into her warm hands and resting it solidly across her lap, Debbie sipped the sweet vanilla coffee and munched on the absolutely delicious muffins that her Gold served.

"Stand alongside," she directed her awaiting servant as he vaulted to obey her command. When he offered himself in position, Debbie took his full net bag into her palm and squeezed gently upon its delightful contents. "I appreciate your efforts last night," she cooed as Gold beamed with pride and accomplishment, "and I anticipate your performing for me again this evening."

Gold smiled as his mind raced to plan the evening's entertainment. "Your morning gift is ready," he mentioned as he brought forth a brightly beribboned package from its secreted position on the floor by his feet.

Taking the gift eagerly in two outstretched hands, Debbie tore open the bow and revealed the provocative contents. The purple tissue paper disguised a lovely magenta demi bra and silky open-crotched panties. Enclosed also were purple-tinted hose and a matching lacy garter belt. Her spent femininity began its uncanny call for more.

"First you will wash me," she ordered, "and then you will dress me. I expect that this will be a most unusual day and I want to be ready." She munched another scone and refilled her china cup as she ate in a delicious silence, broken only by the rapid breathing of her bedside servant.

Finishing her breakfast, Debbie wagged a finger to inform Gold that it was time to remove the tray, then rose from the sheets and stood upon the carpet directly next to his well-oiled form. Without her needing to express her order aloud, he slipped the narrow shoulder straps of her silk teddy down each arm and released her upper body from its restriction. As he kissed her firm breasts in morning greeting, he proceeded to slide the silk lingerie down, managing to expose fully her milky-white torso, and finally, her firm stomach and buttocks. Caressing her skin tenderly, the massive man knelt silently on the carpet by her bare feet to supplicate himself in front of her. Bending low as if to pat his quivering backside, Debbie jolted the Gold back to reality with a firm swat across his startled cheeks.

Suddenly his eyes shot up to look into his superior's face and Gold heard her warn, "I've got to get to work. Get moving."

He propelled himself into action and followed her toward the aqua-tiled bathroom. Her bathing was required to be complete yet quick and the expertly trained figure lathered, rinsed, and massaged his superior with cool professional technique. After having shaved her legs and rubbed lotion into the sensitive skin, Gold helped her stand. When she withdrew from the bath, he patted her lovingly with a fluffy aqua towel, applied cologne to her naked skin, and began dressing the woman with the utmost care and humility. Cupping her erect breasts within the soft fabric of the purple bra, he adjusted her so that her nipples extended provocatively just above the bra's low lace edge. Squatting deeply while holding the silken panties near the floor, he allowed her to step quickly into the garment and once it was in place, he spread the open crotch to allow her fuzzy region the utmost exposure.

Opening the richly hued garter belt, he encouraged Debbie to step to its center and with massive arms, he encircled her waist with the frilly enclosure. He knelt in adoration at her feet and awaited delivery of her pointed toes so he could wrap her legs in the magenta hose. As he endeavored to extend the stocking up toward her thigh, she rested her foot upon his golden netting and pressed firmly, then even harder as Gold attempted to hook the stocking into its fasteners. Debbie duplicated the pressure on his golden netting while he completed the second leg, only this time, she added a force that brought a small gasp from the kneeling man's throat. Smiling at his discomfort, Debbie stood in front of the mirror and considered her alluring purple form.

Somehow, she guessed, this outfit was chosen with great care and with the knowledge and assurance that she was ready to demand absolute obedience and performance from any graduate she might meet today. Purple just made her feel like that, she giggled inwardly, and recalled Ron's purple sequins from several nights prior. Perhaps there was more to the choice than she first realized, Debbie thought, and her tight thighs increased their pressure on one another as she considered other choices she might make.

Oddly enough, she was really looking forward to going to work today. The huge office building loomed ominously as she drove her convertible into the parking garage. Having chosen a short-sleeved outfit for her nefarious purposes this gorgeous sunny morning, Debbie wore her bracelet proudly exposed as she secretly sought potential candidates for her personal pleasure. It wasn't long before she gained the attention of two men in the building. Yet she toyed with both of them and refused to allow them to serve her until she was ready to take them into the protection of her private office. Maybe someday, she mused, she would be less reluctant to make a public display. But not today, not yet, she thought as her mind enjoyed the fantasy.

Tony noticed her unusual demeanor quickly. Assuming she had new plans, he wasted no time in helping her re-arrange her day. "You have an open morning," he lied as he scurried to cancel two appointments. "There are three calls, two are from engineering. One is from the shipper's company and the VP over there wants to talk with you. He said he could be in the building by ten."

She marveled once again at her secretary's proficiency and capability in ordering and re-ordering her day. Wondering briefly how well the agile secretary had slept that night after his laborious and interesting Sunday afternoon, she pushed the intruding but exciting thought firmly from her consciousness and ordered him to call her the moment the shipper's executive arrived.

"I'll be in engineering," she called as she marched toward the elevators and disappeared behind their automatic doors.

The ride was a short one, only two floors, and Debbie smiled at the car's only other passenger. He smiled back at her greeting and attempted to make light conversation. "Are you from contracting?" he began and sputtered a choking sound as she extended her right hand in salutation. Riveting his eyes on her jeweled bracelet, the official fell to his knees and kissed her wrist's adornment.

"Up," she commanded as the elevator arrived at the floor and the doors flew open. "Be in my office in thirty minutes. And don't be one second late," she demanded as she stepped smartly from the elevator and walked briskly into the engineering wing. That was one, she calculated mentally as she strode from the now-silent car.

Striding purposefully toward an outside office, Debbie waltzed past the representatives of the heavily male-dominated department and swung her arm with pleasure and sly cajoling as she proceeded without comment toward her destination. Flinging open the door of the project engineer's private office, she entered without knocking and faced the chiseled visage of the department's supervisor. God, he was good-looking she thought, as she took the offered seat and handed the chief her file. He reached for the papers clumsily and knocked the contents onto his plain brown carpet. As he bent to retrieve them, his arm brushed his coffee cup again and the remaining liquid spilled forth onto the papers.

"Damn," he muttered as he reached for a button on his intercom. "We've got a mess in here, Thomas, and I need some help." Scant seconds later, two large men entered and began assisting their supervisor in organizing the soiled papers. Turning to Debbie, the project engineer apologized. "I'm sorry," he began and added, "I'll take care of these. Thomas can bring them to your office later this morning after they're copied and gone over. Do you mind?"

Debbie shook her head from side to side as Thomas and his partner studied the soiled mass of documents and drawings. Glancing up from his position on the floor gathering papers at her purple hose, Thomas inquired in a blasé voice, "Where are you?"

"Down two floors," she replied, and thought she caught the glimmer of recognition in his shining eyes. "Can you be there in an hour?" His manner of answering would be more important than his answer, she reflected as she perched on the edge of her chair and waited.

"Yes ma'am," he caught himself responding more to her bracelet than to her face. "I'm sorry," he sputtered, "but. . . umm. . . I can be there. Yes. In an hour. Exactly." She delighted in his discomfort, rose, and paced from the confines of the office in which the three men were desperately sorting saturated papers while attempting to organize the disaster into something meaningful.

Retracing her previous path toward the elevators, Debbie mumbled almost inaudibly but in a contented fashion, "That's two." As she pressed the button for her floor and the doors shut silently, Debbie pressed her reddening face against the cool metal wall to regain her composure so she could collect her thoughts and maximize the two appointments she had just made for what would become a most unusual morning. It was with an eager and renewed step that she sped toward her corner office and awaited her first selection. She busied herself with necessary paperwork and edited two proposals before Tony stuck his bronzed head into her office.

"Do you have an appointment that I don't know about?" queried the somewhat perturbed secretary. "There's a guy here from upstairs, from the exec suite, I think. Name's Reynolds. Do you want to see him?" Tony's agitated face spoke volumes to his unperturbed boss.

Debbie looked over her glasses at her secretary's face and she recognized with delight an expression of mild annoyance cross his features. Good, she thought, let him recognize that he's not the only one available here. Let him try a little harder to gain my favor.

Responding aloud, she offered, "Yes, I'm expecting him. Send him in." At her commanding tone, the flustered secretary retreated from view and was replaced in the doorway by her first conquest, the passenger Debbie had met only minutes earlier on the elevator. She glanced at her watch and murmured to herself, "Good. He's right on time."

Reynolds stood absolutely still just inside the doorway. Teasing him by refusing to look up from her stack of paperwork, Debbie toyed with him until the confounded executive coughed slightly in an effort to gain her attention.

Raising her head only slightly and not really meeting his penetrating gaze, Debbie remarked absent-mindedly in his direction, "Shut the door but don't lock it. My secretary will take care of things out there."

She sat peacefully in her huge leather chair and continued her intentional neglect of the agitated visitor to her private space. The befuddled man shifted his weight nervously from foot to foot and initiated a sort of rocking motion that Debbie viewed from her peripheral vision with mild amusement. The silence in the sunny room threatened to deafen the uncomfortable intruder. At last, Debbie recognized his presence.

"Over here," she barked in his general direction while pointing at the carpet by her feet with a wagging manicured finger.

The shocked visitor leapt to obey her command. Planted nervously before her, the executive presented a faint aroma of pleasing cologne mixed with well-earned sweat and Debbie's nostrils filled with an excitement that was soon directed toward her tightening thighs. As she laid the stack of papers she had been reading carefully down on the desk, and her sensations heightened as she considered her requirements of this particular slave. Finally, she decided.

"Strip," she ordered monosyllabically, as the electrified official tore open his knotted tie, shirt buttons, and belt and deposited them carelessly on the carpet behind his rigid position. Gripping each of his slip-on shoes with one hand, he ripped them off his feet and dived into the removal of his long socks. Standing in front of this woman of authority, the chagrined executive worked his fingers clumsily around the button and zipper of his richly hued suit pants.

"Let me help you," Debbie cooed. "Here!" she mandated as she grabbed his most personal organ through the suit pants and dragged the sputtering figure closer to her seated form.

Yanking the remaining offending button, Debbie opened his reluctant waistband and drew the zipper toggle agonizingly slowly in a downward direction. When the zipper reached its fully open position, she spread the loosened garment wide and allowed the slacks to fall unencumbered to the floor. As the now-nude executive stepped out of his last remaining article of clothing, Debbie took her leather crop from her desk drawer and proceeded to position the naked executive by grasping his clear sparkling netting and its contents and jerking him to a central location in her office.

She sat on the nearby-upholstered chair and viewed his body carefully up and down. Spinning a long finger, she ordered him to turn so she might take in every perspective and profile he offered for her pleasure. When she was satisfied that he was in excellent shape and of provocative aroma, Debbie required him to bend over and allow her eyes to view and her fingers to enter his darkest and most tender region. Quickly bending low and exposing himself fully to her, the obedient executive spread his cheeks wide so she could view his tender ingress fully.

Her crop did most of Debbie's work. The unlubricated entry screamed with agony as the bulbous end of the whip infiltrated the man's posterior cheeks. His obedient muffled cries drove her to press the intruding object further and with determination. Satisfied that the instrument had been driven home, Debbie urged the delirious newcomer to spin around once again, only this time she indicated her request not with a waggling finger but with a sharp tug on the remnant of the brown leather whip that protruded from the struggling man's anal orifice.

Her action drove the perspiring corporate officer to near distraction and he spun wildly round and round in the center of the sun-filled corner office. Reaching out and grabbing his glistening net bag and its trembling contents with a solid grasp, Debbie propelled his gyrating form to a sudden halt. The frantic man attempted to collect his thoughts and regain control over his torrid body. Debbie chuckled quietly as his efforts at self-mastery ended in failure. The poor man was losing it, she realized, as her liquid thighs melted from their sensual ecstasy.

He tried to speak to her but the words came out jumbled. "I haven't had any. . . you see there aren't many women. . . this is wonderful. . . upstairs I don't think there are any. . . Oh, God," he ended his brief soliloquy. She watched his penis continue to engorge and strain the twinkling netting that housed it. He stared at his own excited organ as if it belonged to someone else and was no longer attached to his groin. "Oh my God," he moaned, and Debbie recognized the imminent explosion that was threatening this slave's coherence and clarity. She laughed again, a little louder this time. The aroused slave stared at her incredible reaction to his plight.

"Don't you dare," she threatened, "or I will punish you severely." The horrified man's face contorted in a grimace of self-loathing.

"Help me," he cried. "Give me pain. Please." His pleading touched her heart.

Debbie offered him her bracelet and she watched him encode the two colors that would satisfy his particular need. With a yelp of terror, he fell directly at her feet and writhed in horror and self-flagellation; the stricken man attacked his own genitals with pounding blows to ward off the self-inflicted agony he had induced. Rolling around the plain brown carpet on her office floor, the upstairs executive thrashed wildly and came to rest in his contortions between her legs encased in their purple silk. She pressed a "discontinue" button and his twirling and whirling ceased.

The exhausted officer brought his heavy head and tearful face to meet Debbie's serious gaze and offered politely, "Thank you for my pain." Debbie chuckled once again and the embarrassed officer hanged his head in remorse.

"Have you been very well-trained?" she asked the kneeling penitent who remained between her spread legs.

He wasn't sure exactly what she meant, but her tone was definitely serious. This woman exhilarated and frightened him simultaneously in long-remembered pleasure and the executive felt two compelling needs: one to answer her immediately and the other to thank her properly for the enjoyment she was giving him. He spoke nervously, "I am. Trained. . . well. What can I do to please you?"

Debbie frowned and responded, "I want you to surprise me." She added to his consternation, "I have had the best. Let's see how you compare." With that, she sat back and waited for the well-educated supplicant to perform his best for her. She did not have to wait very long.

Falling doggie style onto his hands and knees and exposing the leather crop that continued to protrude from his anus, the trained slave projected his face and head beneath her short skirt and drove his shoulders forward until he rested his lips against her fuzzy warmth. Tilting his entire body slightly to the side, he managed her lips open with his own and inserted his teeth to locate her most sensitive organ. Taking the impatient woman carefully between his jaws, he gently massaged her internally until the woman moaned with delight. Pulling herself toward his kneeling form, Debbie slumped back in the comfortable chair as the executive opened her wider and pushed aside the remaining confines of her panties and drove his darting tongue deep inside. Her throaty voice betrayed her outward calm as he exercised her femininity firmly but tenderly and brought her to a level of complete delight.

"I've had a Gold," she breathed heavily in no particular direction. "You must be able to do better than this," she challenged his straining backside. The mortified graduate withdrew his head from the confines of her skirt and Debbie witnessed tears fall from his dark eyes, down his face, and toward the corners of his frowning lips. Suddenly, the executive's tearful eyes glowed as he came upon an incredible idea that would certainly delight this challenging woman. He turned completely around and projected the leather crop toward her most exciting region.

Shifting, thrusting, and re-aligning himself, the kneeling officer attempted to invade her crotchless purple panties with the soft fringe of the whip that she had moments before driven into his unlubricated backside. He pushed so deeply that his thighs thudded against the upholstered chair and he was prevented from reaching his goal. Picking up one leg and placing his knee on the chair cushion, the well-conditioned slave contorted himself almost against gravity in search of her delicateness. Using his powerfully developed arms in a grotesque sort of pushup, he pressed the jutting crop deeper under her skirt and toward its home.

In an effort to assist his gallant attempts, Debbie took his hanging sparkling netting in two soft hands and manipulated him into the highest expression of utter delight and delirium. His grunting with every thrust was now accompanied by intermittent moans of exultation that quickly accelerated into shrieks of joy. As Debbie exploited his genitals with expert control, the trained slave thrust himself even harder and managed to increase his own pleasure remarkably. She felt his rising excitement within her two hands as she fondled his rock-hard testicles and massaged his elongated and engorged penis until it was ready to erupt.

"Ahh. . ." he cried loudly from his unlikely position. "NO!" he wailed, as his impending orgasm could no longer be delayed. To his horror, he spent himself forward and the intensity of his orgasm splattered his sweaty chest with his own juices.

Recognizing his inability to please her, Debbie reached up and took the long brown handle firmly between her soft hands and lifted the offender from her lap and dropped him casually upon the plain brown carpet on her office floor. He landed with a thud and remained spent in a heap in front of her.

Raising herself in anger from her comfortable chair, Debbie stepped over his ragged body, returned to her desk chair, and proceeded to continue her review of the papers requiring her attention. Her thoughts were interrupted by frequent moans and sighs from the form squashed against itself on her floor and she tolerated his interruptions as a necessary result of his misplayed strategy. She frowned when he cleared his throat as rose to his knees and required more of her already-involved attention.

He found it very difficult to speak. "I. . . don't know what. . . happened," he began apologetically.

"I require no explanation," Debbie interrupted. "And I don't want to hear one. Get dressed," she spat. "And get out."

The humiliated officer crawled across the floor to gather his heedlessly strewn suit, shirt, tie, socks, and shoes. He rose on painful legs to face his superior before leaving. He stood rigidly at attention until she finally deigned to glance in his direction.

"I'll take this!" she directed and reached out to grasp her wonderful leather crop and to replace it in the long top drawer of her huge glass-topped desk.

Still holding his clothes, the mortified executive allowed his angered superior to take hold of the feathered end of the most delightful intruder into his darkest space. In her outrage, Debbie wrenched the leather instrument mercilessly from his unlubricated anus and sent the exhausted man into yet another fit of delirium. Screaming, the agonized failure greeted the withdrawal of her personal leather whip from its temporary resting place inside his rectum.

Using every ounce of his remaining strength to address the woman he had so recently failed, the corporate executive spoke. "I. . ." he began.

"I don't want to hear it!" she screamed into his face. "Out!" she sputtered as Tony came flying into the sunny office to ascertain for himself what had caused his boss such consternation that she would raise her voice. "Get him out of here!" Debbie commanded to her secretary as the latter grasped the frightened executive's colorless netting and pulled him directly from the confines of her office. The man's sputtering face revealed all that Tony needed to know. Whatever he had done, Tony surmised, his superior did not like it at all.

Tony returned to Debbie's comfortable office after disposing of his chore in the suite's restroom and faced his seething employer while awaiting her recognition of his proximity.

Continuing to ignore her favorite co-worker, Debbie astounded her secretary with her deliberate expression of antagonism and bitterness. Finally, she spoke to him, although he was pained to realize that her words were without warmth and were directions that could have been spoken to virtually any employee.

"Thomas from engineering will be here soon. Show him in." She returned her gaze to her work. For the second time that day, Debbie had made an appointment without Tony's knowledge, and he was dismayed that she had shut him out of her plans so completely.

Disheartened, he offered meekly and disconsolately, "I'll let you know when he gets here." He turned, exited her office, and sat down at his desk with a plop on his vinyl chair to await the arrival of her next visitor.

He had better do a classier job than the one who just left here, Tony silently demanded of her next guest. She deserves more than this, and so do I, he added for his own comfort. I can do better than these guys, the secretary mused as he challenged her next appointment to provide her suitable excitement as well as fulfillment. Or I'll teach him how myself, Tony promised. His dejected head held in his hands, Tony sank deeper and deeper into self-pity interspersed with envy as he considered his own shortcomings that had prompted his boss to seek alternative selections.

The discouraged secretary never heard the approaching engineer tread softly toward Debbie's closed door. Tony's melancholy demeanor was snapped back into reality when he heard the doorknob rattle within Thomas's firm grip.

"Just a minute!" the secretary demanded of the new arrival. "You can't go in there," he warned the tall and athletic entrant.

"I've got the re-worked contract," Thomas offered cagily to the ornery secretary. "And besides, man, you looked busy with your thoughts."

Tony scowled and pressed a red button on his telephone. The response was less than immediate. When the light glowed, he spoke into the intercom.

"Your next appointment is here," he offered in a matter-of-fact voice. "Shall I show the gentleman in?" Tony's voice reeked with a sarcasm that was not lost on the waiting man.

"No. Thank you," a quiet voice responded without emotion. "Just send him in." Tony's heart was crushed with her obvious rejection of his inclusion. Then Debbie added for his comfort, "I'll call you if I need you."

If. If she needs me. Tears welled in Tony's forlorn eyes. "Go on in," he spoke unnecessarily to the engineer who was proceeding in anyway without his approval. The rejected secretary felt his netting close tightly against his bald pubic skin as resisted the increasing urge to rub himself hard and bring his rebuffed organ some satisfaction.

Thomas's entry into Debbie's private quarters was greeted with silence and no recognition that he was waiting for her attention. His long muscular arm held out the re-printed contract but Debbie's lack of attention to his offering left the man standing ignored and rebuffed in the doorway. Standing in absolute silence, Thomas waited his superior's gaze.

She kept him waiting for what seemed to Thomas like hours. What the technician could not have imagined were the scenes that were simultaneously playing themselves out under both Debbie and Tony's desks. Denied satisfaction by the inept executive, Debbie attempted to mollify herself as the rejected Tony grasped his own shiny netting through his wool slacks and worked its contents in anger. The two unlikely masturbating employees continued their efforts for some time. Debbie was the first to cease.

She extended her braceleted hand to accept Thomas's papers. His jaw fell from his face, as he considered close up the jeweled leather strap that held within its power his ultimate pleasure and his pain. The engineer was so overcome with anticipation that he fell awkwardly to his knees upon the plain brown carpet of her sunny office. Debbie heard the rather disruptive noise and turned her stare to his position.

"Drop your pants," she invoked without ceremony, "and crawl to my feet. I wish to inspect you before I allow you to attempt to satisfy me." Her voice was replete with derision and her tone was as frightening as it was challenging. Thomas obeyed without thinking as he unbuttoned and unzipped his slacks and allowed them to glide gracefully around his knees. His clear net bag shone brightly in the morning sun that entered through the large picture window behind the seated woman. As the kneeling engineer crawled toward his superior, his steps entangled his suit pants and they were pulled farther and farther from his body. When he reached her feet, the pants were firmly enmeshed around his ankles and he knelt fully exposed for her inspection.

"Let's see," she began casually as she took his most personal and sensitive netting in her milky white hand. "Hmmm. . . you're not very big." She lifted his penis and testicles firmly upward and drew a silent wince from the big man's chagrined face. "I hope you're larger when you're full," she warned with a facial expression that sent fear directly into the deepest regions of his excited soul. "If this is the best you have," she continued mercilessly, "I may just not be interested. Show me your best!" she concluded.

The gauntlet had been thrown down. Silently, the engineer began an immediate and frenetic massaging of his entire genital area with his two massive hands in a valiant attempt to raise himself up for her approval. Frightened inside, Thomas worried that his extended self would not meet her demands; after all, he thought, she must be very well experienced to parade that bracelet so brazenly around the office like that. He had never before met a woman who was so calculated and sure of herself that she would order an unknown such as himself to serve her so suddenly. He wondered how she knew about him. Maybe, he wanted to believe, his expert training and varied experiences were transparent to a woman like this.

He continued his kneading and massaging and managed to bring himself to a fullness that extended vertically away from his naked skin. Proud of both his efforts and his success, Thomas withdrew his hands and planted them firmly on his own buttocks as he awaited the woman's glance in his direction. He wanted her to be as proud of him as he was becoming of himself. Although she did not look directly at his face, Debbie could feel the sense of exalted superiority that emanated from this boastful slave who knelt fully engorged at her feet. This one needs a lesson, she thought, and resolved to give him one that he would not soon forget.

"Oh," she remarked casually several minutes after his standing penis danced silently for her pleasure, "you're ready. Let's see," she continued as she probed his glistening netting with a careful investigative hand.

Her long red fingernails scraped just slightly and not by accident against his rock-hard penile skin. That unforeseen move drew a sharp intake of breath through the kneeling man's nostrils as Debbie continued her scrutinizing of his most personal area. When her manicured nail entered his penile slit ever so slightly, he shuddered in heightened arousal. As the edge of her leather bracelet glanced intentionally along the trembling skin of his saluting member, Thomas's hips began a slight forward and backing rocking motion. He recognized with embarrassment that his aroused condition threatened to explode and disgrace him before this extraordinarily talented and exceptional superior. Thomas shook in reaction to the fearsome thought that challenged his very being. This woman might be superior to his abilities as she was obviously more extraordinary than any Mistress he had ever served before.

"You'll do," she threw down at his formerly cocky ego. Stand for me," she ordered the agitated slave who fairly jumped into an erect position next to her oversized leather chair.

She cupped her left hand in the air at her own nose-high level and the semi-nude engineer raised himself upon his toes to place his shiny netting quickly within her soft palm. She took him and massaged his fragile penis and testicles as Thomas moaned and sputtered from the glorious touch upon his hot and throbbing skin. Suddenly, she released him from her grip.

Her command was as simple as it was devious. "Higher," she enjoined him.

Still sitting in the comfort of her leather desk chair, Debbie raised her cupped hand well above her own head and waited for the trained slave to place himself as quickly as possible within her open palm. Thomas stared at the insidious height of her raised arm and allowed his eyes to dart around the sunny office in search of possible ladders or benches he might use to fulfill her demand. The conference table was too far away, he recognized immediately, and the upholstered chair was too large and clumsy to move as quickly as he needed. His choices remained between the wood and leather chairs used by guests to sit across from the woman at her desk, or. . . the desk! Thomas was appalled by his own lack of perception. Raising one mighty and naked leg onto the glass top of Debbie's polished desk, Thomas attempted to raise himself fully directly in front of the seated woman.

But the distance was too high. His powerful leg could not by itself lift his well-endowed body fully onto the desk and Thomas was literally stuck with one foot balancing most of his weight on the plain brown carpet while the other was bent upon the immense desk. He was fully exposed and entirely vulnerable with his most private genitals dangling precariously in a direct line with Debbie's other, closed hand, the hand that wore the leather and jeweled bracelet. Thomas's throat began a moan that increased with his rising horror.

The seated woman recognized his plight and relished his distress. As her left hand remained waiting to be filled with Thomas's contents, Debbie's right hand reached out for the errant genitals and took their net housing uncompromisingly in a firm grip. Thomas's face betrayed his inner turmoil as his features grimaced in recognition of his own failure and Debbie's complete mastery of his helpless situation. Totally exposed, accessible, and defenseless in front of his female superior, Thomas's body began to tremble in fright and in anticipation of her next move. He did not have to wait long as the seated woman's next move brought their encounter to a complete and inarguable resolution.

With a tug, Debbie took the netted genitals and yanked them closer to her own seated position, a move that caused Thomas to lose his already-precarious balance and fall backward toward the desk. His back landed solidly upon the glass top as his powerful left leg kept him from falling completely onto the floor. His disobedient right leg would not yield from its elevated position and forced the exasperated engineer to plummet with his hips thrust directly toward Debbie's face. With his spread-open crotch balanced unstably directly before her eyes and easily within her reach, Debbie examined him up close and considered his shaky and unsteady position with eager interest.

Now she had a direct view not only of the unmoving man's netted genitals, but also of his darker and more private orifice. With one hand, Debbie spread his cheeks wider with the edge of a manila folder that had held the re-printed contracts he had so recently delivered to her, and with the other she rolled the new contracts into a tight and secure cylinder against her own tense leg. Thomas had neither opportunity nor angle to view the goings-on, but his ears informed his brain that something insidious might imminently penetrate his unlubricated entry. He gritted his shining white teeth in anticipation and apprehension. She brought the tightly coiled contracts closer to his quivering hole.

Thomas's spread-open cheeks had a mind of their own as they attempted to preclude Debbie's efforts at injecting the cylinder of contracts into this very delicate area. Horrified that he had been betrayed by his own reluctant buttocks, Thomas willed every muscle in his lower body to relax and permit his superior access to his inner self. Throwing his head backward and flat onto her desk, Thomas attempted to calm his growing apprehension. Instead, he felt his own netted contents engorge of their own free will.

She could not help but notice the growing sack that began standing directly in front of her eyes. As the engineer's penis stood more and more vertical, Debbie rolled the cylinder tighter and tighter. When she was sure he was fully engorged and almost ready to explode, she took the erect organ in her soft hand and manipulated the engineer almost to the danger point of explosion. Feeling the throbbing and thrusting of the organs within her hand coming to their most exciting point, Debbie took the cylinder of contracts and inserted it directly, firmly, and without mercy into his dry anus. Thomas's screams of pain were mixed with ecstasy as he ejaculated simultaneously with the insertion.

Debbie reached down to grasp the dragging leg of his suit pants and pulled the disorderly garment over his soiled abdomen and net bag. "Get up," she ordered the spent man and Thomas rose from his awkward position to manage himself onto two feet and stand directly next to her leather chair. She smirked when she saw the cylinder of contracts shoved firmly into and extending from his naked lower body. Playing with him once more, Debbie continued.

"The outside paper of the contracts is blank. Remove the set of papers and press them out flat. I will sign them now."

Leaving the astounded and half-naked man with the anally protruding papers to his own devices, Debbie turned her attention to the other contracts she needed to peruse on her desk. Soundlessly, Thomas stepped into his dark suit pants and drew them up toward his hips. Holding the waistband with his large left hand, Thomas reached toward his rectum with his right, clutched the tense roll of contracts with his left, and pulled the intruding cylinder free. Unwrapping the roll, he disposed of the blank outside sheet and, after buttoning and zipping his pants, tried to flatten the series of papers into a careful and neat pile.

Casually, Debbie glanced in his direction and noticed that he was fully put together after his ordeal. She reached for a fountain pen, uncapped it, and waited for her slave to offer her the final paper to sign. With a flourish, she authorized the contract and turned back toward her work.

"That's all," she announced to the obedient slave who stood silently at her right hand.

Thomas began to speak, thought better of it, and exited the sunny office past the startled and masturbating secretary whose actions under his own desk escaped the notice of neither the flustered engineer who strode by him with renewed excitement nor of the seated woman at the over-sized desk in the office from which that engineer had so recently learned about superiority in a new and different way.

"Tony, I need you," the voice called over the intercom. "Immediately!" she barked as the almost-orgasmic secretary rose quickly from his desk and ran into her sun-filled office. She ordered him to attention directly next to her leather chair and had him raise his arms above and behind his head She opened the waistband and dropped his pants unceremoniously into a pile around his ankles. His naked lower body disclosed his complete and full engorgement at his own hands.

"I did not give you permission," Debbie admonished the swaying and thrusting secretary who was ready to burst from his self-induced excitement. Tony's eyes were beginning to fill with embarrassment and chagrin for his disobedience and impropriety. Without warning, his eyes overflowed.

"I couldn't stand it!" he screamed both to himself and to Debbie. "How could you prefer those. . . those. . . creatures. . . to me?" The corners of Debbie's mouth rose slowly upward as she recognized his jealousy mixed with pride. "Look at me! Look!" the twitching secretary called to his superior as he moved his fully erect member in a dance intended for her delight.

"I have many needs," Debbie intoned slowly and carefully. "When I need you, I will have you. When I don't, you are uninteresting to me. And my needs are fully my own."

With that admonishment, Debbie extended her long right arm, fondled her leather bracelet, and just when Tony's eruption overtook his ability to control himself, she pressed two buttons that reduced the cocky secretary to a pile of writhing and screaming humanity that whirled unceremoniously on the plain brown carpet of her sunny office. She turned quietly back toward her paperwork and considered the contracts carefully that other engineers and other contracting specialists had worked on to get ready for her approval.

Chapter Twenty Six

Ron rested exhausted and panting in a state of shock that was mixed with uncontrollable wondrous passion as he leaned up against the wall of the unusual laboratory. Feeling the hook attached to his penile ring strain from his every movement due to the chain that connected him to his coupling along the room's outside perimeter, Ron grimaced at the wave of pressure that his restricting net bag brought, yet he relished in the pleasure that this day had brought. Awash with contradictory emotions, he marveled that his training with the female Colors had been remarkable; however, he was still so overcome with intensity, wonder, and amazement at his day's activities that he was exhilarated with the required time for reflection that the Mistress had ordered the Golds to schedule for the exhausted trainees, and especially for Ron. Having believed himself to be an adequate and slightly inventive sexual partner, Ron had been overwhelmed with the immensity of what he really did not know about making love to women.

The trained attorney recalled with rising excitement the amazing display of sexual delight he had just learned to administer to the female partners to whom his Green had assigned him. Still chained to the wall, Ron's aching body believed that all he needed was a rest and time to consider and adjust to what he had just learned. Flattening his buttocks against the cool wall, he allowed his overflowing mind to reflect on his experiences and to replay the afternoon in his head.

The pink-netted trainees had been ordered to report to the curious lab immediately after the mid-day meal. Immediately after eating, the Blues had gathered the trainees in a long line and secured a hook to each man's penile ring. After the Blues connected the hooks one to the next by running a metal chain from each hook under each man's genitals and through his buttocks' crack, the Greens ran the shackled group single-file down the massive corridors, through several electronic doorways, and eventually into the wing of the facility that housed this particular chamber. Each man struggled to keep up with the jogging backside of his leader. Lagging behind assured both the man and his followers immediate constriction and pain. The pressure on the trainees to conform increased as they ran and turned down hallways and completed quick exits through other corridors. Panting, the weary thirty-nine trainees and Ron entered the mammoth doorway at a fast jog and witnessed an incredible scene.

The well-lighted room was filled with forty narrow, raised gurneys on each of which rested a completely naked female body. Almost surreal in its singularity, the women reposed fully exposed to Ron's and thirty-nine other pairs of eager eyes. Adding to the mystery of the unexplained exposure was the fact that every woman was prevented from witnessing the men's entry because a screen that hung from the ceiling and shrouded the periphery of the chamber came to rest securely upon each supine woman's neck. The women could neither see the trainees nor could their faces be known to the mystified pink-netted neophytes. Their headlessness was as uncanny as it was provocative, and Ron felt his deepest emotions stir within his almost-naked torso.

Hungrily, Ron eyed every vulnerable body lying totally oblivious to either his entry or his lustful gaze. Almost perfect in their feminine composure, the women's long arms ended in soft hands from which extended perfectly manicured nails; their smooth and silky legs culminated with lovely soft feet; and their elongated torsos each sported an immaculate and hairless pubic area. Their well-oiled breasts seemed to glisten in the well-directed overhead lighting, while the soft up and down movement of their chests gave the awkward presentation an almost-unearthly demeanor. The focus of his and every other trainee's careful stares had been broken only by the unseen voice on the speaker.

"This will comprise the most serious phase of your training," the Mistress's voice spoke clearly and tersely to the bewildered trainees and their serious-minded Green trainers. "Experience with expertly-trained women will enable you to discover realms of delight that you have only dreamed of and imagined. Listen carefully to your Greens and comprehend. Your spouses and lovers have paid dearly for this training and I expect that every single one of you will become masterful and proficient at bringing a woman to the full sensual heights she deserves. This, ultimately, is your most important purpose. Learn well."

The voice grew silent as the Greens stepped forward, each to his man, to begin the most important and crucial training, and one that Ron found himself surprisingly eager to master. He stared at his Green's moving lips and attempted to concentrate on his rapidly delivered directions. But his mind could barely take in what the imposing man ordered in rapid succession. He heard various verbs: fondle, manipulate, caress, hold, flex. He listened to strong admonitions: don't grab, don't pull, don't twist, don't bend. He watched the Green exhibit impressive soft caressing of the female body that lay closest to his position.

Green required Ron to imitate every move and stroke the trainer applied to the woman's body. Beginning with her feet, Green had described the sensations and rationale behind his actions.

"You begin by offering yourself in supplication to your superior," he intoned almost religiously. "You can wash her feet, rub them, massage them with creams, or simply kiss them to show her without words how debased you are in relationship to her." Ron absorbed every syllable with increasing fervor.

Green then stroked the woman's long smooth legs and massaged her calf muscles with two strong hands. He required Ron to mirror every movement, and the willing trainee complied with earnest effort. When the trainer's manipulations reached the woman's thighs, he carefully turned her legs outward and kneaded the interior well-toned muscles with care and serious energy. The sight of her spread hairless lips filled Ron's thoughts with wonder and his pink net bag with rapidly anticipating excitement.

The well-conditioned trainer's hands moved softly up toward the woman's relaxed arms and continued their journey toward her supple abdomen and shoulders. Ron thought the Green had been impressive in not yet stroking her most sensual areas. Green's perceptive words interrupted Ron's thoughts.

"Never, never dive into the sex organs prematurely!" he warned. "Women are especially stimulated in other ways. It is your responsibility to find those ways and to maximize them. Only the inexperienced consider sexual organs as a woman's primary delight. This is the initial critical lesson." His massaging hands continued their assault on the reposing woman's rapidly exciting posture.

Standing in the empty and softly-lighted chamber, Ron struggled to recall the particular events that ensued after the first demonstration of Green's extraordinary display of talent. The trainer's earlier warning was true: Ron really did not know how to make love to a woman. The trainer's hands illustrated impressive methods of touching and arousal; he concentrated on seemingly unimportant areas of the woman's body and brought her long legs to a peak of excitement. Ron viewed Green's tongue, fingers, teeth, lips, and arms apply unbelievably electrifying stimulation to the unseeing woman's readying personal parts. With a flourish, the Green stroked her sensitive abdominal skin with his hairless face and once again accomplished a rising crescendo of orgasmic delight for the accepting female to whom he had been assigned.

Thirty-nine trainees and Ron took in every motion, every stroke, and every response with alert and inquiring eyes. The pink-netted men stood immobile as their superiors illustrated the ultimate arousal of women insightfully and carefully for their personal edification and expertise. With a flourish, each Green finally brought each woman to the height of frenzy as evidenced by the women's raising of their hips from the tables, thrusting of their pelvises toward the unseen stimulators, and silent but urgent undulation of their entire bodies in a rhythmic display of sensual excitement. In silence, forty recruits applauded their trainers' skill and deftness in their masterful performances with the exhausted and spent women.

Then, Green announced, it was Ron's turn.

Each trainee, along with his Green, was required to move to another woman's body among the remaining thirty-nine. Ron approached his trainer with an inquisitive stare as if to ask permission to begin. With a simple nod, the Green acquiesced to his request and Ron, along with thirty-nine other neophyte trainees, began his attempt to arouse the woman whose inert and recently spent body lay beneath his willing fingertips. As he proceeded with his retinue of actions, and as he waited patiently for the woman's reactions to his efforts, the novice concentrated his efforts with an increasing passion and a heightening sense of self-stimulation.

Ron treated the woman's body as if it were a temple. He supplicated himself at her feet to induce an initial posture of servility by rotating and massaging each polished toe. Raising her foot and resting it upon his chest, Ron's nimble fingers soothed her disciplined muscles completely. Her calves received equally humble caressing and her thighs turned liquid under his gentle but carefully directed manipulation. Although his arms, hands, and face sweated from the intensity of his work, he continued his strokes included her arms and hands, her shoulders and chest, and her abdomen and belly. Ron's stimulation produced the desired effect as the woman appeared eager to complete the journey on which he propelled her supine form.

Gently, he tilted her long legs outward and exposed the inner sanctum of her most excitable area. As her hairless lips spread and revealed her succulent femininity, Ron gasped audibly as he viewed this woman's fully engorged darkest secrets. "Oh," he stumbled for words, "she's ready."

"Don't allow her to complete until she has received every effort you can manage," the Green warned. "You must cool her down before proceeding."

Ron threw him another quizzical look. "How?" was simple question.

The Green responded with two massive hands that pulled Ron's arms away from the woman's tensing body. "Be creative," he advised. "Stop stimulating her this way and try something else. What ideas do you have?"

Recognizing for the first time the need to consider only the woman's needs and not his own, the trainee attempted to calm the eager woman before assisting her in completing her journey. Ron's brain quickly considered his options and the young attorney chose to position his own hairless face on her soft white belly. Petting her abdominal skin with his velvety face, the trainee redirected the woman's thoughts away from her rising tension and brought her farther away from sexual completion. The Green nodded a silent approval. An unseen White made additional notes on a rapidly filling chart.

The prize pupil looked closely and witnessed the woman's soft secret area return to its supple composed state before he continued his arousing motions. Lifting his trained body completely up onto the raised bed, Ron spread his legs across her form and straddled the resting woman. Using his netted member to rub her neck and his testicles to dance on her breasts, the agile attorney managed to increase the woman's pleasure dramatically. The Green nodded one more time. Another series of notes was written into Ron's chart by an observant White.

Crawling downward, Ron continued his penile dance on her urgently tensing body, and eventually crawled down far enough to bring his own lips in line with hers. Their lips met and Ron danced his tongue and teeth in and out of her spread labia. Another Green nod greeted his effort; another White wrote notes on a chart.

The trainee then allowed his bagged genitalia first to bounce softly and then forced them harder upon the straining woman's hairless region. His soft teasing brought great convolutions of response, with her hips and pelvis rising and falling on the raised bed. Her hands grasped wildly for the sides of the platform for balance and she raised her thrusting hips higher and higher from the satin covers to greet Ron's every thrust.

When the two performers' efforts culminated in a mutual explosion, Ron found himself writhing in pain atop the naked woman with his pink net bag pinching his just-erupted penis with unyielding cruelty. Her irate legs threw him off her exhausted and spent body and he landed with an unpleasant thud upon the brightly carpeted floor. His horrified eyes could only implore his Green for explanation. His Green stared down at the inexperienced trainee with a gaze of scorn.

"Never, never allow yourself to come until after your woman has achieved every possible delight and has then been cooled down by you." Ron drank in his words of admonition. "Your job is to serve your superior, not yourself," the Green completed with uncompromising severity. Until then, Ron had never known how selfish he had become in lovemaking. At last he recognized Debbie's needs and vowed silently to fulfill every one of them before he considered his own.

The chagrined trainee rose to a kneeling position and spoke politely toward his trainer. "Thank you for my punishment," Ron uttered simply and rose to complete his assignment and bring his spent woman to suitable comfort after her consuming experience. His tired and aching muscles were dismissed from his mind as Ron's singular passion turned toward this woman and her needs. Each trainee had to learn that one's own discomfort must be discounted, as only his superior's requirements were important. Ron had learned that valuable lesson.

Satisfied that Ron had achieved a first level of learning about the proper methods of satisfying a woman, Green grasped the hook attached to Ron's penile ring and re-attached him to the short chain that hung from a wall hook. As other trainees completed their missions, they were likewise hooked to the outside wall by their diligent trainers. Some men appeared almost wildly out of control as they had achieved their woman's orgasm without first having spent their own pent-up excitement. These fully-erected trainees suffered in silence by pressing their erect maleness to the wall alongside the post-orgasmic apprentices who were also fastened securely to their posts. In a short time, every hook was taken and the trainees were finally removed from the wall and joined together, ring to ring. The cadre of trainees was marched out of the room through the massive electronic doors.

Once again, the struggling each member of the group fought to keep up with the others as they attempted to avoid the stinging pain that lagging behind or striding too far forward from the group incurred. The assembly ran up long corridors and down others. Jogging through yet another passageway, the harried company of perspiring and grunting trainees was brought to a sudden and painful halt as the Head Green first stopped the lead runner then motioned him through a small open door.

The elongated file of chained men performed a sharp left turn and entered the narrow room. Moving the column straight ahead toward the farthest wall, the Head Green suspended their movement and commanded each man to place his two feet directly on top of a small pink square on the floor. The band of runners diligently obeyed his command.

At the Head Green's signal, a heavy white screen was lowered to the floor and separated the lineup of trainees from their trainers on the other side of the narrow room. The heavy screen fell noiselessly down and completed its journey with a thud. Each man's trainer, standing invisibly opposite him across the solid curtain, then reached through the hip-high holes that had been stitched through the fabric. Yanking each trainee's pink net bag and its contents through the hole, the trainers propelled the men into the impenetrable divider and flattened them against its bulk. With a sudden jerking motion, the trainers drew the laces tightly that surrounded the holes and framed each man's genitals against the background of the drapery's stark whiteness. With their faces and bodies pressed securely against the shroud, the emasculated men were unable to either turn their heads or to view their comrades' discomfort on either side.

Their unseeing eyes and unhearing ears made them unaware of the Mistress's entry into the room's opposite side. The Greens knelt immediately beneath each trainee's pink netting with their heads bowed in humble adjuration to the Mistress's entrance. Her gaze was strictly for her trainers, and the Mistress greeted each man with a silent nod of affirmation. Ron's Green bent low in humility as the Mistress passed his station with a curt nod and a slight brush of her fingertips against his torrid skin.

After greeting her trainers, the Mistress viewed the gallery of genitalia that decorated the landscape in front of her. She walked from trainee to trainee and fondled each silent man's most personal organs with a firm and inquiring hand. Lifting high one set of genitals after another and inspecting them, the Mistress paused to consider each man's endowments. She checked each for size and capabilities as she mercilessly and repeatedly grabbed the pink netting of each uncomprehending subject. From their darkened positions of solitude, the trainees stood pressed tightly against the white curtain and endured the embarrassment of having their most private spaces invaded, viewed, and ultimately discarded.

After her journey down the line of dismembered genitals, the Mistress nodded to the Head Green who passed the permission to each kneeling trainer. Without a sound, the penitent trainers pressed a series of jewels on their bracelets and the forty pink net bags dropped silently to the floor. The jettisoned garments were swooped up by a Blue programmer who disposed of the nettings through a slot in the wall. The naked trainees neither felt nor experienced their loss of status.

Again the Mistress proceeded up the line of the now fully nude novices and re-examined more closely and more intimately every set of male apparatus that dangled from her side of the white screen. Taking one man's penis fully in her grasping palm, she pulled it inflexibly away from the divider and calculated mentally its potential. Moving to the next trainee, the Mistress cupped his testicles and bounced them sharply in her hand. Confronting the next man in her private gauntlet, she slapped his penis firmly from side to side and viewed its response to her urging. Yet another trainee suffered her open- palmed cuffing of his elongated member up and down to determine his elasticity. Still another was forced to endure her grabbing and circling of his penis in a wide arc that strained his legs' ability to hold him erect. In her wake remained a bedraggled train of stricken trainees who could not understand what harrowing series of events had befallen their naked and almost detached genitals.

Required to stand for a full hour for the duration of her agonizing personal inspection, the trainees' penile rings strained at their aching positions and from the genital abuse. The impenetrable curtain denied them any opportunity to witness the Mistress's actions or to deduce her purpose. Her torture of their bodies and minds was overwhelming in that no single trainee could predict when she would grasp his fully exposed organs or what she would do with them when she did finally take them. Standing naked and chained behind the imposing curtain, the forty men winced from shame and degradation as well as from fear of what lay ahead for their bodies within the mysterious grip that took them.

Her technique had been carefully honed, and the Greens hoped to attract her attention. Some Greens sought to extend their charge's genitalia in hopes that she would respond to their erect potential. Other Greens offered their trainee's personal organs to her by snapping their fingers against the man's hairless testicles and causing their bearer such fits of pain that the trainee behind the curtain was forced to sway without potential for success in any and every direction possible to try to avoid the painful snap against his tender testicles. The solid curtain held firm, and each swaying prisoner produced only a slight wagging of himself that often served only to attract the Mistress's ministrations of further and more intimate investigation. The Greens' scheme was brilliantly conceived and executed.

When the Mistress's attention was directed far down the line, Ron's Green sneaked his oiled hand up toward his trainee's swinging genitalia and surreptitiously stroked the man's member until he demonstrated a firmness and elongation that satisfied the kneeling trainer. Continuing his secretive moves, the trainer flicked the imprisoned man's testicles until he felt a hardness develop that assured the trainer that arousal had been instigated. Furthering his clandestine efforts, the Green slapped the engorging member with his palm and brought the horrified and tortured trainee to visible purplish pleasure. Satisfied that his was now the most erect trainee at the curtain, the Green knelt silently as the Mistress approached his position.

Giving no outward sign of either pleasure or displeasure, the Mistress took Ron's fully erect penis in her hand and lifted it up and with it brought the invisibly struggling trainee onto his toes. His penile ring straining at his chains, the confounded man felt himself lifted up and dragged side to side by an unseen grip upon his excited maleness. As the Mistress grasped his now-leaking handle and circled her arm in a great spiral, the agitated attorney fought to control his urges as he directed his aching body to follow her every movement. Unable to control his horror of this infliction upon his body, Ron's dry lips parted and a deep moan began to rise from his rasping throat. As his pain and humiliation rose, so did the unearthly voice that greeted each manipulation of himself that the unseen Mistress perpetrated upon him. As his distress overpowered his uncomprehending mind, Ron's voice roared his degradation. Screaming in agony and embarrassment, Ron shrieked wildly from his encumbered position and strained savagely at his fetters. As if he and his fellows were again on the conveyor belt in the blackness, his cries for relief went unheard. His pleas fell on no ears except those of his similarly imprisoned fellows.

As the single trainee screamed and struggled against his chained ring, his undulations spread in a wave down the line of attached trainees. Unable to control his animalistic responses to the horrifying torture his invisible genitalia were enduring, Ron contended valiantly against the Mistress's painful inspection, yet with each of his jerking motions or wrenching responses, Ron brought eruptions of pain to the entire membership of his class. Each man tensed immediately from the wave-like punishment and reacted physically to its intrusion upon his own body.

The entire corps of trainees bound in chains behind the massive white curtain screamed in unison from their own and from Ron's personal torture. As the one man bounced, weaved, and shrieked, the others followed suit from their resultant physical abuse. Their agony was no longer isolated as it transcended the individual and inflicted itself mercilessly and uncaringly upon the group.

Their sounds were inhuman and their voices betrayed their primal urge. Utterly unable to control or to stop the convolutions of agony that the Mistress's single actions with Ron had brought to the entire lineup, the trainees gave in to the absurdity as well as to their agony as they stood screaming and crying through the remaining indignities of the program. Their hips swayed their bodies, and their toes danced the crazed men up and down, as the pain would not abate.

The massive white curtain separating the wailing and undulating trainees from their Mistress and their trainers also prevented the shrieking cadre from inflicting their noises and agonies upon the silent group of Greens that was intent solely upon presenting their trainees' endowments to their Mistress. Unable to hear their cries or view their distress, the kneeling Greens remained silent as they awaited the Mistress's final choices. Unhearing of their torment, the Mistress gave Ron's organs a final, firm, and powerful smack that threatened to force the bellowing trainee to lose consciousness from shock and astonishment. Struggling against the pain, Ron placed his hands upon the white curtain for balance and tried with all his might to pull his agonized organs through the firmly-laced cutout to safety.

Ron's pulling motions grew ferocious and savage as the untamed trainee resorted to primitive responses in an effort to counteract the brutal and ruthless attack the unseen Mistress had made to his agonized genitalia. The chained trainees responded in kind and mimicked Ron's barbaric efforts at achieving personal safety. Soon forty sets of male genitals were dancing savagely against their housings as forty pair of legs and forty pair of arms pulled ferociously at their chained prisons.

Despite their frantic efforts, the shield held firm. Unbelieving of their predicament, its hopelessness, and in utter finality, the forty trainees renewed their crude efforts and planted their hands and feet even more firmly. In an unbelievable display of raw power and force, the forty trainees thrust their hips violently backward in a vain attempt to force their aching testicles through the tight hole. Not one hole opened an inch and not one lacing relaxed.

From the other side, the spectacle was as eerily silent as it was almost ironically unnoticed. The straining and thrusting hips of the horrified trainees caused only slight jerking movements in their dangling genitalia through their imprisonment within the great shield. Against their white backdrop, the purplish engorgement of their organs was actually enhanced by the minimal movements caused by their superhuman efforts on the other side.

The Mistress continued carelessly up and down the line as she took one set of organs into her hand and then another. She prodded each almost-berserk trainee until she felt his ultimate hardness and then dropped his organs unceremoniously, leaving them dangling against the white frame. Although their wrestling against their bonds was heartfelt and urgent, their successes were absolutely invalid. She had absolute and total control over every aspect of their bodies and their resultant erections in the midst of their ultimate pain and degradation pleased the robed woman who continued her ministrations through the safety of her closeted and silent partition.

The men's strength was dangerously expended and the forty trainees were in danger of utter exhaustion. Ignoring their plight, the Mistress continued in silence to handle roughly every set of maleness that greeted her stringent inspection. Using all ten of her carefully manicured fingernails, the Mistress raked the few remaining reluctant penises until they too stood straight. She tackled all eighty testicles until they achieved a satisfactory level of hardness. When she attained the response she desired of every organ on the line, the Mistress stepped back and spoke to her trainers.

"I am satisfied," she spoke calmly to the silent kneeling group that shrouded her from the machinations and wild gesticulations that were occurring behind the substantial and fixed screen. "Bring them all to completion," she added casually and the forty trainers spun wildly from their subservient positions to take each fully engorged member into their well-oiled hands.

Uncaring of their trainees' spent brains and abused genitals, the Greens slapped each trainee's member and proceeded to bring each man to the throes of wild orgasm. The trainees fought valiantly against this additional humiliation, but to a man each spurted forcefully, powerfully, and dynamically from deep inside his loins. In spite of each man's horror, he came to orgasm completely and pathetically easily. For most, it was the unique experience of ultimate pain interspersed with pleasure that constituted a further example of the Mistress's uncanny ability and total dominance over their most private possessions.

She was unwilling to allow the totally exhausted trainees any respite from their torture. Once again the robed woman marched from one set of shielded and empty genitals to another, inspected each intimately, and made her ultimate and conclusive judgment.

After her final scrutinizing of each man's physical attributes, the Mistress dismissed several Greens with a careless flick of her hand. Each discharged trainer frowned angrily at his termination from the group, unlaced his charge's genitals, pushed them mercilessly through the elongated hole so they became invisible, and marched hastily from the narrow room. No one witnessed each freed man's dropping unceremoniously onto the bare floor and no trainers' ears heard his whimpering cries or those of his fellows whose organs were strained beyond belief by the wrenching of the mutual chain caused by each rejected man's falling. The Mistress was finally left with two men fully exposed through the curtain. She walked up toward the high divider and grasped one man's most private parts in her left hand. She grasped Ron's with her right.

The two selected trainees winced with shock and astonishment with the idea of the further abuses they imagined would occur shortly on their almost-unfeeling bodies. They had just heard their comrades fall and they felt the unyielding tension of the chains upon their rings. Unable to turn their heads to the side to recognize that the pink nettings were gone, the two trainees believed that the straining chains would shortly bring waves of constriction to their netted members. Pressing themselves closer to the safety of the white divider, Ron and the other selected man tried to push their rings toward the almost-empty expanse and ease the imminent abuse they feared.

With their genitals firmly in the Mistress's grip, the two chosen candidates were unlaced from the front and unshackled from behind by unseeing hands that reached between their weary legs to unlock their harnesses. Now naked and freed, the two trainees were released from her firm grasp and dragged by their trainers in silence to yet another small cubicle. Ron was pushed down firmly upon an upholstered chair and his partner was forced into another. Only when the trainers exited and the two were quite alone did each man gaze down through his tears to inspect his tortured organs. And only then did Ron realize that his protective netting was gone.

They sat in a silence that was broken by the occasional whimpering of Ron's partner and Ron's own deep breaths. Trying desperately to take control of this unearthly situation, Ron breathed deeply and evenly and forced his mind to consider what new fate might befall his wracked body. The partner, wincing in sporadic pain, fear of pain, and memory of pain, suffered almost silently as the two men tried to steady themselves for their next trial.

The duo did not wait long.

Their small cubicle was quickly filled with the oiled and handsome bodies of two Golds, two Whites, two Blues, and their own personal Greens. The eight additions to the cramped quarters filled the men's minds with fright as the seated trainees fought against the horrified thoughts that permeated their brains without cessation. Without warning, Ron and his comrade were whisked from the comfort of their chairs and were ordered to run full out behind the pair of Golds and Whites and in front of the duo of Blues and Greens. Exhausted both mentally and physically, Ron screamed at his own brain to force his legs to carry him down the hallways and through the corridors. His thighs and calves were numb and his toes ached with every hastening step.

Together, the two selected trainees were led through an electronic door and were grasped on their arms and legs by the charging Colors that ran the distance with them. Their hands and feet were secured into cuffs and chains as the astounded trainees were each tossed carelessly into a small pool of bright blue water. One Gold, one White, one Blue, and their personal Green entered each pool and tightened the men's fetters so they were suspended tightly from their arms and legs and hung inches from the pool's warm water.

"You are very lucky," the Gold announced in a tone of envy mixed with pride. "The Mistress selected you to be evaluated for your group."

The White continued. "She has chosen you to represent your class." He paused and the tension in Ron's rigid body became more intense. "If you are successful, your entire group will be inserted tonight."

A Blue's voice spoke and filled Ron's ears with terror. "If you do not pass the final exam," he noted, "you will not receive insertion. But there's more." The tall Blue hesitated for a moment. "If you do not perform to her standards, your group will fail."

Ron's brain could not process the terrible position the Blue had just described. His spent member winced in pain as the unseen hands of the Colors forced his penis into a coupling that hung from the small room's ceiling and then tightened its tether. As the chain shortened, his organ was pulled directly away from his body. The weight of the world and of his class was upon his body as it hanged lifelessly from its shackles and drifted slowly from side to side.

His Green described Ron's predicament. "The Mistress selects two trainees to perform for her based solely on their genitals and their performance. Because we are all here to serve our superiors, the most important offering we can make is ourselves. She liked what she saw in yours." The Green paused.

As the tethers lowered and Ron sank into the mercy of the warm water, the Green added, "You will be her sex slaves this afternoon." Ron gasped in horror at his words. "She will run you through your paces and you will perform flawlessly." There was an uncloaked threat in his voice that Ron recognized from earlier when the Green had returned after his Level III punishment. His heart raced and his ears burned as the foursome of Colors cleansed his body inside and out without mercy and without cessation.

He heard a voice moan and make barbaric sounds that he did not recognize as his own. Frightened to his core, Ron fought the urge to flee from his restraints and recognized once again his inability to escape. Having been designed to give him both pleasure and pain, this bath was a combination of flagellation and lashing mixed with petting and stroking that drove the manacled man wild with anticipation of either pain or pleasure that was given without warning and without provocation.

The unknown voice continued a shrieking that echoed off the small room's walls and mixed with the horrified cries of the other who was receiving his alternating mistreatment and soothing at the hands of a representative of each of the Colors. Together they endured in the otherwise silent chamber as they were cleansed internally as well as externally, lathered, and rinsed.

The hands that propelled their bodies up and down in the warm water sought to remove every trace of perspiration and offense from their glistening skin.

Satisfied that their charges were clean, the four bathers lifted Ron's supine body from the pool and flipped the bewildered trainee naked and face down onto a narrow metal table. Lifting his unresisting hips and placing a bulk beneath his belly, the Colors exposed his pristine anus by spreading his knees wide apart. Forcing his hands down to rubber-covered handgrips, they unclamped the table's end and lowered the plate beneath his face. His backside elevated and his hands secured beneath his belly, the fully revealed trainee was unable to move any part of his body for fear of falling quickly to the tiled floor.

Ron shut his eyes in horror and held tightly onto the handlebars. He felt an intrusion in his loins as well as between his rear cheeks as two pairs of Colors invaded his sexuality. A warm rod entered his anus and was pushed up his rectum as another pair unlocked his pink penile collar and replaced it with another unseen band. While the entry into his anus was warm, the attachment to his shaft was painfully cold. He heard a voice.

"You are under irrevocable control," he heard as his body squirmed to escape from the finality of this insertion. "The Mistress and your wife now have achieved total ownership of you. There is no longer any escape."

"This ring is not removable," Ron heard the voice of his Green utter, "and if you try, it will become an extremely dangerous device. You can either succeed in achieving your life's dreams with it, or you can end your sexual experiences forever. There is no inbetween, but there is always a choice. It is always up to you."

Screaming now from fear and discomfort, Ron shrieked in horror at what had taken over his body. It was done; he could hope for no escape from the permanence of this predicament. Debbie and the Mistress could each demand total obedience from him. There was nothing he could do to prevent their insistence and his own fulfillment of their every desire. His agony filled the room, yet his hardening penis revealed his secret predilection for this potential activity.

As the Colors stepped back from his vulnerably positioned naked body, Ron was astounded as he recognized that the feeling deep within his groin was not that of pressure from his trainer's hand; rather, it was the weight of his own lust for his new role as Debbie's sex slave that enticed him and excited his sensual drive. His voice quieted as his muscles slackened in response to his new and profound discovery. When the Colors witnessed his transformation, they lifted him from his perch and stood the newest potential graduate on his feet in their midst.

Tears of joy ran down the recipient's face as he considered his metamorphosis of the past few weeks in the training facility. He abhorred the egotistical attorney that was bound and fettered and forced to enter the conveyor belt trip to a fantastic world. Rather, he considered the obedient servant that he was to be (consummate) (?) because he now knew how to bring to his superiors the heights of sexual pleasure and in doing so, to bring to himself the delights of strict compliance and submission. He calmed down visibly as the Colors prepared him for his imminent performance with the Mistress.

"She will choose one of you," the Gold announced to the two calmer, yet excited men. " She will take a final look and then she will select."

The two net-less men looked each other up and down in wary evaluation. "You enter through here," the White announced as he held back a curtain.

The Blue added, "Do your best. The futures of thirty eight others are riding on you."

Green added in a paternal fashion, "Remember what I taught you. And don't fail."

As Ron and the other chosen trainee left the small company to enter the Mistress's quarters, they heard the voice of the Gold add for their edification, "You better not fail. You won't like what happens to those who do."

With a lump of fear in his throat and a strange and wonderful fire burning in his belly, Ron marched toward the Mistress's final exam with his head, and his penis, held high.

Chapter Twenty Seven

Their nostrils were completely overwhelmed with the familiar sweet vanilla aroma as the two selected candidates puzzled their way through the darkened passageway leading to the Mistress's private chamber. Ron led the unlikely pair through the pitch-black winding corridor and he reached out with both hands in a desperate effort to feel the narrow hallway's walls and find their way. Treading carefully in utter silence and virtual blindness, the naked, banded offerings crept slowly toward their imminent final test.

Seemingly endless, the slender walkway shifted and turned before straightening out for short periods, only to twist and bend moments after it relaxed into comforting straightness. Just as Ron composed himself enough to proceed straight ahead for a few yards, the unforgiving floor plan forced him to reach out and examine the walls for new information and fresh direction. The utter silence and emptiness of their journey hung like murky shrouds of fog upon their tired but strangely invigorated shoulders. In confusion and utter desperation, yet with a confidence born of the recent removal of his pink net constrictor, Ron dared a simple statement.

"Ron," he uttered modestly.

A hushed voice responded to his unasked question. "Jonathan," was the eager yet terse reply.

The two new acquaintances joined hesitant hands in their single-file effort on their struggle toward the refuge of their conclusive trial that would be administered directly at the hands of the woman they both feared and respected more than any other. Their unspoken reluctance to proceed was coupled with shared intrigue and rising passion. The two men paced gingerly along the seemingly-endless twisting and winding path. The scent of vanilla grew stronger and Ron felt himself relax in spite of his nervousness.

A dim light finally emanated as a shrouded glow from a distant point straight ahead. Ron pointed out the journey's end to his silent companion by placing his warm hand on the other's tight belly and bringing the follower to a rapid halt.

"Ahead," he informed Jonathan. "A light. We're almost there." Ron felt his muscles constrict, his skin tighten, and his penis twitch in the rising panic that threatened to overtake his sensibilities.

The eager trainee responded. "I see it. Good luck." Jonathan's words rang hollow as they echoed between the walls of the narrow hallway.

Taking a dual deep breath, the two resumed their unsteady pace toward the faint glimmer that was partially obscured beyond the next bending and twisting section of the bizarre maze. As they approached the nebulous glimmer, the vanilla scent became overpowering and their nostrils and brains were enveloped completely within its sweet and relaxing fog. Now calm and assured, the duo arrived together at the draped portal that separated them from the cadre of trainees they had left behind. They were frightened to recognize the immensity of the situation that loomed mightily in their upcoming graduation and eventual freedom.

Afraid of the sight that would unveil itself as he stepped through the curtain and revealed the source of the brilliant luminous glow, Ron unconsciously slowed his pace and was practically run into by the other trainee. The pair of potential graduates stood immobile just in front of the entrance with their hips roughly touching one another's in a terrifying attempt to gain support from each other. Hands grasped and skin melding into one, the frightened and expectant twosome marched torpidly ahead.

The Mistress was ready for their entry, as she had been for so many others, and she languished atop her huge bed in the center of the room, perusing her plan for the evening's events. Choosing was always so difficult, she reflected, and disposing of the loser was often distasteful. She really did not care what happened to those who failed. But she always enjoyed the fruits of the handiwork of her Greens and tonight's group seemed enticing enough to cause her mild sensations of pleasure. She hoped this class was stronger and more inventive than the previous one as the most recent graduation division had failed miserably at the trials of endurance that every slave must pass to be fit to serve so many masters. The last one she experienced, she recalled, would do his own spouse very well, but he might not service a group with enough tenacity to bring pleasure to all. She had to mark him down for that and his reaction had been unpleasant, to say the least.

The amber light that glowed forebodingly atop her doorway indicated that the two had finally arrived from the final baths and their personal readying. Smiling inwardly, she shifted her glance back toward her newest brochures and pressed the single yellow button on her immense leather bracelet.

Behind Ron and Jonathan, an electronic door snapped shut. Their ears heard the sound but their brains refused to process it and the two well-oiled and glistening bodies stepped through the solid curtain. They walked gingerly yet with rising trepidation into the Mistress's private examination rooms.

Cowering in fright and surprise, the two men hugged each other tightly as they viewed their surroundings with mounting alarm. Ron checked the suite for exits and found none, while Jonathan's eyes searched the mammoth room and its perturbing decorations of delight. The Mistress eyed the pair with her peripheral vision as she continued to lounge and read upon her shiny satin sheets and consider her initial course of action. These two were scared to death, she laughed inwardly, and she vowed to toy with them until they were fully and absolutely spent at her pleasure. In turn, she surmised that they would offer her a fair example of her trainers' prowess and she could judge fairly and first-hand the Blues' newest developments, changes, and additions to their program for slave training.

In silence, the twosome continued to hug each other and dared not move from their initial entry point. Ron felt his penile hardness increase and he also felt the concomitant engorgement of Jonathan's member as the latter's body pressed more tightly against his own. The sight of the groveling and recoiling men, with their unfettered genitals in full readiness, amused the silent Mistress. She allowed her eyes to travel slowly up and down their clean and sturdy bodies as she considered which of the two she would play with this evening.

Rising from the comfortable bed, the enrobed Mistress approached the squirming men and without introduction, reached for and took their nude and erect organs. Her soft touch but firm grip informed the trainees that they had truly arrived and the prophetic words of the Colors in the bath began to ring true. They realized finally that they would become her sex slaves this night and their penile rings and warm inserts served as reminders that they were enslaved to her every desire.

Subordinating himself without thinking to the absolute dominance wielded by her touch and direction, Ron took small and skittering steps to follow her on the course she chose. Twisting his penis in her fingertips, she danced him in narrow circles and surveyed his sleek, perfumed, and readying body. With a flick of her hand, she discarded his erect and inspected genitals and released him, before turning her attention to his petrified partner. Revolving him also around the room, she probed his sexual posture and discarded his organs with equal disdain and disregard. Although his throat ached with terror and his belly tightened with fright, Ron was surprisingly anxious to begin once and for all whatever stratagems she had ordered that would befall him this night.

"You will both serve me for a time," she apprised as Ron's memory recognized her voice from the loudspeakers that decorated his daily training sessions. "Then I will choose the better of the two of you. The victor will stay with me this night." As she spun away, her long robes fell away from her almost perfect body, allowing the quivering trainees a split-second revelation of her sensual form.

With that pronouncement, the Mistress strode away, her back turned upon the dumbstruck trainees, and seated herself upon a spacious white chair that was positioned against the elongated room's far wall. The chamber was expansive and its bright white carpet overpowered Ron's eyes but vied with the great bed that intermittently grabbed his attention. Unable to focus his concentration in any one place, his eager but vigilant eyes darted around the suite. Jonathan stood rooted in amazement to his place on the brilliant white carpet and followed the Mistress's moves with wary eyes.

The pair of naked trainees watched their seated superior lift her index finger and waggle it toward herself as the two astounded novices wondered silently toward which man she beckoned. "Come here!" she commanded both or neither of them as Ron and Jonathan sprang from their stead. Almost in unison, two hairless pubes with fully erect organs sprinted without delay or thought to position themselves directly before her.

"I expect a better response than that," she angrily demanded. "You must learn that I mean what I say." Her tone scared the two trembling trainees and her long hand reached for her tyrannical jewelry.

As the Mistress fingered her leather bracelet, Ron and Jonathan each felt uncontrollable rising tension within his rectum as the two men's anal inserts were finally called into application. With each jewel stroked by the Mistress's racing fingers, Ron and Jonathan's backsides experienced the ever-increasing pain of swelling that threatened to explode within their deepest and darkest regions. Unable to control either their fear or their growing discomfort, the two horrified trainees fell down and flattened their backsides quickly and firmly onto the shocking white carpet as they attempted to dissuade the inserts from detonating within themselves. Ron pounded his rear cheeks firmly and frequently upon the floor's virgin whiteness in a dance of desperation, while Jonathan rubbed his backside back and forth on the same surface in a vain attempt at personal relief.

Watching the two perform such inane machinations, the Mistress was pleased that their cleansings had been so complete that they resulted in the pair's heightened ability to experience this novel sensation of inflation. She laughed inwardly as Ron's rectal pounding was interspersed with grimaces of his fear of possibly degrading himself upon her carpet and she applauded silently Jonathan's shifting to his knees, spreading his legs, and attempting to dislodge the offending intruder by thrusting his hips toward the carpet. She always enjoyed her trainees' reactions to new and different experiences and she had learned through the various histories of training classes that fresh and inventive positions, accoutrements, and demands truly separated the great slaves from the simply serviceable ones.

When the horrified men seemed finally at their collective wits' end, she fingered another jewel and the sensation slowly abated as their offended rectums returned to their normal quiescent state. Secretly, she was proud and pleased that the two punished trainees never once used their hands to reach for the offending instruments or attempted their removal. Wonderful, she thought, they have learned well that another will control even that area of their bodies. The Blues must be commended for their ingenious lessons.

"Don't move a muscle!" she commanded as the two groveling penitents remained absolutely still within their supplicant positions. "Don't forget that I allow and control every sensation you will experience. Obey my orders and your sensations will be pleasurable. Fail to obey, and you will see what other surprises I have ready for your. . . delight."

She allowed them to reflect in silence upon her warning and promise. Ron felt his backside finally calming down and Jonathan sensed the soothing contraction of the offending invader. Joyful to be freed from their immense discomfort, the two still petrified trainees stared open-mouthed at their Mistress and awaited her next command. This time he would respond without thinking and without delay, Ron promised himself. He did not want another dose of that frightening pain.

"You will show me total obedience," she interrupted their reverie, "and I will show you how affable it is to obey." Turning her face toward his partner who was still rigid on all fours, the Mistress issued a casual instruction in his direction. "Open yourself to me," she voiced and wagged another indicative finger at his perspiring face. Finally comprehending her meaning and her desire for his presence, Jonathan turned his crawling body and backed his rear quarters toward her seated form. Then the obedient man spread his powerful legs even wider to afford her a better view. Still, she was not satisfied.

"Up here," she demanded toward the supplicant's backside and the obedient slave lifted himself from his knees and rose onto his feet but kept his strong hands firmly on the pure carpet.

She examined his anal opening carefully and toyed with the protruding edge of the small insert that he had recently experienced at her instigation. Pushing the encroacher slightly deeper into him, she brought a delighted but terrified moan of response from the man's throat that emerged from his dry lips. Pulling the insert's bulbous end slightly out from its resting place, the Mistress caused the degraded trainee to shriek a bottomless cry of fear intermingled with apprehension as his bowels involuntarily spasmed at her flexing of the handle. Fearing that he would disgrace himself, his class, and reflect badly on his honored position at her feet, Jonathan fought with determination against every dreaded and impending rectal urge to expel himself that repeatedly thrust its insidious demands upon his straining sphincter. His raised backside and low arm position afforded him practically no control over this flexing muscle and his throbbing brain screamed against these violations.

In response to his predicament, the Mistress tugged even more fiercely upon his insert's handle and generated from Jonathan's throat wails of shame and humiliation that he expended in his Herculean effort to control this reluctant muscle.

Ron witnessed and felt as if he participated in the horrifying spectacle with a rising excitement that resulted in a further humiliating engorgement of the organ that protruded from his groin. As she twisted and flexed the malleable insert, Jonathan forced himself to follow her tugs and pulls with his suspended hips and backside in an effort to release the pressure that was threatening his bowel reflex and his ultimate degradation. Watching the poor man's gyrations, Ron recalled with horror his first day of training as he remembered the incident in which a trainee spilled himself before the Mistress's evaluating gaze. With rising inner horror, he conjectured as to what the Mistress might do to the poor man if he performed equally inauspiciously upon her brilliant white rug.

The kneeling attorney enjoyed her battle with the thrusting backside that catapulted in front of her in its levels of rising distress. Recognizing the ultimate nature of his plight, the Mistress reinforced her dominance over him by pulsing the insert rhythmically in and out, thereby forcing the almost-prostrate trainee to thrust his hips and buttocks back and forth according to the alternating frequency of her timing. As she increased the rapidity, his flexes grew in both tempo and intensity, as the poor man's readying penis seemed prepared beyond explosion.

Oh God, Ron thought, he's going to come on her rug.

To both men's utter surprise, and to Jonathan's absolute terror, with a mighty haul the Mistress snapped the insert free of its warm home as she simultaneously stood up, pressed the man's head firmly upon the white carpet, and forced his exposed backside straight up into the air. Ron was impressed with her sudden movements as his spinning brain deduced her ingenious plan. Hearing the nefarious gurgle of an abused rectum and its seemingly uncontrollable sphincter, Ron backed away from the revolting and offending trainee in a protective need to distance himself from the ghastly consequences he feared would shortly unfold.

"Don't you dare!" the now-standing woman seethed into the trembling man's ear. "You will obey me, now!"

Her words were as uncaring as they were demanding and she slapped his rigid rear cheeks with an open hand. The crack of her palm against his oiled skin reverberated menacingly throughout the massive room. Even in his distress and personal revulsion at his own inability to control himself completely, the sagging trainee gasped great lungs full of air and fought heroically against bodily urges that demanded immediate relief. She continued her outright spanking of his pulsing backside and achieved the addition of bright red welts to Jonathan's humiliation. To his utter amazement, Ron found that her frightening words overcame Jonathan's most basic and animalistic needs. Her carpet remained brilliantly white and the poor man at her feet cried tears of succor.

As Ron attempted to match the other man's breaths and gain control of his own heightened desires, he saw the Mistress's face turn agonizingly slowly in his own direction. His head shot down quickly in adjuration as his willful penis blasted up in an unwanted signal of his rising frenzy. The Mistress silently recognized the sign she had been expecting from this intractable trainee and turned her complete attention on his quivering form.

Ron beheld the challenge in her face as his body screamed for flight, but the panicking trainee's obedience overcame his sense and he stood his ground more in abject terror than from his learned sense of submission. His feet felt rooted to the white carpet and his numb legs were unresponsive to his brain's edict of escape. He never saw her inward glee as she considered the potential she had for her evening's fun with this particular novice. Her threat, although unvoiced, was real.

Bring down a Green, she apprised the trainee silently, and you will deal with me.

Two strides of her high-heeled shoes brought her face to face with the shuddering amateur. Smirking in delight of her absolute power that was evidenced in his quaking body, the Mistress took Ron's member in one taut grip and continued striding toward the far wall while dragging the struggling and stumbling man behind her. Jerking his penis to the side, she clipped a solid metal lock to his new penile band and slid the other end with its dangling chain through a ring attached to the post that stood unyielding by his side.

Continuing her vigilant and honed techniques, the Mistress quickly imprisoned Ron's genitals by shackling him in every direction to dangling manacles and into bonds secured to the floor. When she had completed her handiwork, Ron was positioned straight up, spread-eagled, and (absolutely immobile). With her trainee vulnerable now to her every whim, the Mistress began to persuade the stubborn man that he was under her absolute control in every way. This final lesson was designed to convince Ron that any resistance was futile and that obedience must become his lifelong direction. She taught her pupil his lesson very well.

Her lessons were directed toward him from every direction. Feathering his burning skin with the leather strips that dangled from the end of her immense personal leather whip, the Mistress flailed at his elongated body with just enough force to make him wince, yet she avoided causing him intense pain. Too soon, she calculated, just a little too soon. Turning her attention to his glistening buttocks, the Mistress stood behind the struggling prisoner and whipped slightly, then harder, and even harder still in an increasing series of detailed messages that landed upon and were addressed directly to his quivering backside.

Adding yet another tool from her arsenal of torture, the Mistress reached for her flat leather strap, doubled it over, grasped it uncompromisingly, and whacked him solidly on his reddening behind. As she continued her assault on her captive, she motioned silently for the now-recovered Jonathan to attend her ceremony. Scurrying quickly to her position, the unshackled trainee was commanded to kneel in front of the spread-eagled man. She ordered Jonathan to grasp Ron's hips and take the punished man's penis full in his mouth. Eager to oblige her every whim, the penitent trainee spread his lips and allowed the rigid penis to enter his moistening mouth.

As the Mistress flailed with the leather strap repeatedly at his chafing cheeks and alternated her delivery with firm smacks to the kneeling Jonathan's tight backside, Ron's hips thrust into the man's mouth with every one of her strokes as Jonathan's face fell forward to accept Ron's maleness at a tempo in accordance with every one of her blows. With each thrust, the one's penis plunged deeper and deeper between the other's salivating cheeks and Ron recognized in terror that his explosion was only moments away.

"No! NO!" he screamed over and over again as he tried to gather his last ounce of control in a useless effort to bring the offending member to a calmer state.

"No, indeed," the Mistress hissed into his burning ear. "Not until I am ready for you to finish. Bring it down, now!" she ordered into the ear of the frazzled prisoner whose torrid skin brushed intermittently against her own milky coolness.

Raising her spiked heel high, she planted the sole of her shoe directly onto Jonathan's genitals and sent the astounded man spinning backwards onto the white carpet. His penis finally free from its incomprehensible but wonderful stimulation, Ron thrashed wildly within the limits of his confines to prohibit his own expulsion before he was commanded or allowed by the Mistress to conclude. The Mistress retreated from the fray and inspected her trainees in their mutual plights. Good, she thought when she saw Jonathan's posture. He is waiting for another command. Then she turned her visage toward Ron.

The attorney buckled and tossed every extremity of his shackled body in all directions as his wild penis flung freely from his hips. As the man plunged himself in the limited directions she allowed him but with his own intense force, the Mistress admired his effort to beat his genitalia against himself and produce the necessary shock and pain that was needed to compose his errant erection. She appreciated his self-infliction of pain, allowed him to continue, and turned her attention to Jonathan's unmoving position even though he was still experiencing the resulting intensity of her recent kick.

This would be a tricky decision, she calculated, and proceeded to the final test.

Glancing at the time, she commanded Jonathan to unlock Ron's chains and, once freed, allowed the latter man to fall to the pristine white carpet with a thud. Ordering the kneeling man to massage the fallen one, the Mistress seated herself again on the comfortable white chair and awaited Ron's recovery. When Ron raised himself up to kneel in penitence before her, she knew that both men were ready for the finale.

"A good slave is creative," she uttered without mercy to the almost exhausted men. "You will each entertain me shortly and I will select the winner to stay with me this night. You have fifteen minutes to ready yourselves. I will summon you one at a time to perform for my amusement." She added almost unnecessarily, "Please remember, you will not like what happens to the one who fails."

She reached up with her jeweled arm and flicked her hand in careless dismissal of the two shocked trainees. As she fingered another series of jewels, a great door slid open and the kneeling men snapped their heads to view the familiar sight of the closet replete with costumes. Vying for her approval, they scurried simultaneously through the wide opening and sprinted inside. Soundlessly, the great door slid shut behind their naked and running forms.

Dashing crazily through the racks of costumes and leather toys, Jonathan grabbed wildly at brightly colored garments as well as at leather strappings. He stuffed glittering jewels into long skirts and leather harnesses into lace bedclothes that he managed to use awkwardly as a sack. With no apparent plan of action, the feral trainee collected numerous items of apparel and immense quantities of leather. His last "purchase" was that of a long, thin crop to use, Ron imagined, for the poor man's personal stimulation.

Approaching the collection as calmly as he could, Ron surveyed the assortment of remaining choices. Securing only one leather garment and one short, stubby, large-handled whip from the racks, Ron secreted himself in the second dressing room, shut the door, and proceeded to make himself ready for his upcoming performance. Within the safety of the locked portal, soft rock music playing over the speaker soothed Ron's aching muscles and the sweet vanilla aroma calmed his tortured brain. In fear for himself, his class, his graduation possibilities, and the consequences for those who failed, Ron mapped out his strategy.

The quiet and tranquilizing music was soon disturbed by a commanding voice that broke in through the intercom. Concomitant with his hearing her voice, Ron's closet darkened completely and his door locked solidly shut.

"I'll have you, now," the Mistress's voice directed, apparently to Ron's partner. In locked and blind silence, Ron's heart began to race. He heard Jonathan's door snap open and the first performer faced a dimly lit suite of rooms with the spotlighted seated Mistress seated. Stumbling in the darkness, Jonathan emerged from his cubicle and took small and reluctant steps toward her centrally elevated position.

Ron could see nothing of the spectacle that unfolded outside his tiny room but he could hear the grunts and groans that Jonathan offered in response to the Mistress's commands and directions. She had him perform agonizing calisthenics and pose in muscle wrenching positions as she considered the quality and intensity of his efforts on her behalf. Hearing the crack of leather against skin, Ron was unsure if the trainee received her sizzling blows or inflicted them upon his own body. He empathized with the man's efforts in thrusting and jerking, as he perceived the rhythm of Jonathan's performance. In the solitude of his dressing room, Ron alternated between states of abject horror and intense sensual arousal as his rising genitals betrayed his ascending fervor.

The intermittent and alternating wails and sighs of the tall trainee penetrated through Ron's blindness within his dressing room. Ron imagined the Mistress's long fingers toying with the dark and shining jewels on her bracelet and he could almost visualize Jonathan's degrading reactions resulting from the responses she demanded from him. Requiring him to exhibit every ounce of his training, the Mistress must have given him every pain imaginable before she allowed him even the slightest pleasure, Ron assumed. Her attention to him was considerable and Ron felt a twinge of insane envy at the duration of her regard and concern for the other man's performance. Feeling abandoned and alone within his tiny room, Ron grasped his own penis and worked it until it stood straight so he could feel better about his abandonment and enter his performance in full respect to his superior.

A single horrifying shriek resounded in the great chamber and filtered into Ron's cubicle. Hearing the Mistress's clear commands even above noise of the fray, from within the safety of his cubicle Ron deciphered her orders to remove the performer from her presence and he heard the ominous sounds of scurrying feet that obviously belonged to summoned members of the Colors. Visualizing without success what horror had befallen his comrade, Ron grew more agitated with every moment of the delay that kept him prisoner within the dressing room prior to his summons to perform. Soon his entire body shivered from the unknown even though he was not cold and the vibrating attorney stood unmoving with his organ at full attention while waiting for the Mistress's entreaty.

Seconds that seemed like hours passed and suddenly his door was unlocked electronically. Stepping through the portal, Ron's eyes teared up in their attempt to adjust to the scene that lay before him. The brilliant light that bathed the seated Mistress stood out in stark contrast to the room's dimmed vastness. With his outstretched arms feeling his way from the darkness of his tiny waiting room, Ron hastened to arrive to his Mistress's beckon. She spoke to him in a calm voice that did not betray either consternation or pleasure on her part.

"It is your turn," she ordered simply, sat back and waited, as the attorney sprang into action.

Running up to her elevated dais, he spread himself prone at her feet and lifted his lips slightly so as to grasp the tall heel of her black shoe in his eager teeth. Grunting and groaning, he managed her stiletto heel from her foot and lowered his face in total supplication to kiss and suck on her red-polished toes. His body spread totally open on the white carpet, Ron moved only his lips, teeth, and tongue on her foot to assure her of his admission of her absolute superiority over him. In a silent response, the Mistress smiled. His thorough re-training at the hands of her recently promoted Blue seemed adequate, she gathered from his dutiful actions. Now she was absolutely sure she had been correct in approving that new Blue's plan for these trainees' first ritual insertion tonight. That is, she checked herself, if either of these two passes.

As if in response to her unspoken challenge, Ron lifted himself up onto all fours and felt his genitals dance beneath his belly and sway of their own mind in response to each of his movements. He crawled away from her platform and turned his rear quarters toward her for viewing and inspection. Forcing his most private muscle to open for her probing and approval, Ron urged her without words to remove the small insert of control so he might adequately receive the ultimate pleasure later that night. His obedient sphincter pushed the tiny intruder in and out and his contraction of that same muscle brought to the device a slight and interesting twitching that did not go unnoticed by the observant Mistress.

Smiling again at his cocky attitude and the audacity of his request, the Mistress waited for Ron's lifting of himself just a little closer to her outstretched hand. Understanding her unspoken order once again, Ron raised his hips playfully toward her raised chair, positioned his anus almost directly in her lap, and flexed his tight sphincter to force the insert to dance for her pleasure. In appreciation of his efforts, the Mistress grasped the bulbous end of the device, twisted it directly away from its home, and lifted the insert with a flourish from his drying anus. The trainee felt and his superior witnessed the spasms that accompanied her firm withdrawal and as the one sat immobile, the other knelt on his hands stolidly awaiting either his demonstration of absolute control or his incompetence that would result in his immediate failure.

Happily, he did not disappoint his Mistress. Demanding that his sphincter stay still and steady, Ron fought against repeated flows of urgency from his bowels and brought his insides under his total control. Impressed with his work, she squirted clear cream into his now-aching hole and massaged the orifice with her milky hand to bring the hard-working trainee some small comfort. Satisfied that he was soothed, the Mistress casually pushed his unsteady hips from her lap and the trainee landed with a soft plop on the carpeted platform beneath her chair. In his pain and sudden degradation from her rapid dismissal of him after his great effort on her behalf, Ron rolled his body away from her platform and urged his weary legs to stand. Unbidden, he posed dramatically for her and exhibited his single selection from the costume closet. Having chosen a simple leather sconce to cover only his testicles but undergird his erect penis, Ron's member jutted firmly out of his groin and pointed directly toward the Mistress's robed body. His hairless pubic skin glistened from its covering of oil and he offered himself totally to her for her own personal delight as well as for her use.

Taking the gift of himself with one hand and his stubby whip with the other, the Mistress raised the small crop directly above his vulnerable and exposed organ in a threatening gesture. Sucking in a great gulp of air, Ron tensed for the upcoming blow. To his utter amazement, she lowered the whip and placed it directly into his sweaty hand. Closing her fingers around his in their mutual grip on the whips fat handle, the Mistress illustrated how Ron should deprecate his own organ for her pleasure.

His mind racing once again with confused thoughts of flight, Ron felt his own unfeeling arm rise well above his shoulder height and position the whip for self-flagellation. Spreading his legs wide and bending his knees in offering, Ron gasped, brought the whip down savagely on his own leather-supported penis, and screamed and groaned in abject terror at both the pain he experienced and the idea of what he had just done. His yelps and the level of his efforts brought a smirk of delight to the Mistress's face and she enjoyed his dedication as the beaten man first fell and then writhed and screamed under her feet on the glorious white carpet.

When she was certain that he had played out his shock and excitement, the Mistress ordered Ron into action once again.

"Stand!" she commanded and his weary legs fought to obey. "Bring him in," she called to an unseen body outside the massive room. To Ron she offered, "I think I have seen enough."

Two Golds entered in silence from the same portal through which Jonathan and Ron had so recently entered, and had the struggling former performer between their fierce grips. Tossing him like a child to the center of the room, the naked Jonathan stood next to the nude Ron as the Mistress considered her final selection.

The Golds stood in silence between the hushed trainees as the Mistress looked each man up and down. To scrutinize their bodies more closely, she alit from her chair, climbed down the two steps, and inspected the men by pulling, pushing, prodding, and poking every organ of their bodies and every fold of their skin. She lifted, squeezed, and discarded then she poked, tickled, and pinched. To their credit, the men stood unmoving in their total humiliation under the full intensity of her investigation.

Then she decided. As she grasped Jonathan's now-limp penis, Ron's voice wanted to scream "NO!" but his lips held steady in their defeat. The grasped man's face lit up in exultation as she spoke to his burning ears.

"This one," she said as she pulled his dangling member directly up toward her chest, "has failed."

Astounded, both Ron and Jonathan gasped at her teasing words. She added in a menacing voice, "You won't like what happens to the ones who fail."

The Golds burst into action when they heard her words and the two Colors took the dejected man's sagging organ from the Mistress's hand. Running around the room in a frenzy, the Golds led the screaming and shrieking reject along a humiliating path of ultimate penance. Forcing him to flatten his body against the white carpet directly under her raised heel, the Mistress squashed his exposed genitals with her stiletto heel and greeted his squawks and screeches of agony with an unhearing ear as she turned her attention to the victor.

"He will be a good slave," she intoned solemnly as they began to drag the writhing failure from the vast room, "but you will be a great one." Ron's ears burned and his face reddened at her praise. His penis also responded to her commendation.

"Out!" she barked to the Golds who responded with alacrity and hustled the sobbing trainee for the last time from the Mistress's presence. "See to it that he remembers what happens to those who fail."

When they heard the door bolt firmly behind the exiting Golds, Ron heard the Mistress's voice clearly above the cacophony of joy that resounded inside his brain. "Tonight will be unforgettable," she murmured for his ears alone. "Let's get started."

Chapter Twenty Eight

When the doorbell rang, Debbie looked up absently from her mail with the brochures that she had received that afternoon from the training facility and turned toward her dutiful Gold who was seated at her feet next to her lounge chair. As he arose to greet the newcomer, she marveled at his wondrous body and she stared intently at his now-limp organs that were still imprisoned in the Mistress's golden net protector.

As he approached the front door and asked politely for the caller's identity, she watched his dangling maleness bounce slightly with each step and she promised herself that she would find out how good he really was before his time with her was done. Continuing to peruse the full-color advertisements from the facility and wonder vividly about the advanced level courses that were available, Debbie sat comfortably in the living room and barely listened to the conversation between her servant and the woman's voice she overheard. Her Gold approached her lounger and waited in his reluctance to disturb her reading. He waited to be recognized.

"Yes?" she inquired vacantly after a suitable pause. "Who is it?"

The Gold spoke only as many words as were necessary. "Elissa. From the lingerie department."

From the surprised and intrigued expression on Debbie's upturned face, Gold deduced that admitting Elissa might be agreeable to his superior. The seated woman nodded in confirmation of his upraised eyebrow and, having received her permission, Gold spun about-face to return to the foyer and welcome the visitor properly. As he swung the door wide open and unlatched the clear glass storm door, Elissa gaped at her nude welcoming committee of one but collected herself quickly enough to walk inside with only a moment or two lost to her initial shocked reaction. Her arms were full of brightly wrapped packages but she bore her load easily as if the routine of delivering packages herself were an old habit. Gold led her to the living room and offered to relieve the saleswoman of her colorful burdens. Taking the offered parcels from her arms, Gold stood in his place and waited for his next command.

Reaching for the spread-open edges of her robe, Debbie half-heartedly pulled at the sides to cover her chocolate brown lingerie. This evening's outfit was so beautiful that even Debbie had gasped when she unwrapped it that morning. The deep brown silk was offset with even darker brown lace and the open-cupped bra felt especially cool and satiny against her white skin. Having her crotchless panties held open for her to step into was a dreamy way to dress and she vowed that Ron would assist her like that every morning in their future. The garter belt and matching hose were shiny and glittered in the soft lighting that Debbie had installed when she redecorated the large living room last year.

The robe certainly did not cover much, but it enabled Debbie to remain partially exposed yet remain comfortable upon the lounger. Eying the unexpected visitor up and down, Debbie was unsure if the saleswoman were more interested in Debbie's ensemble than she was in Gold's more simple and revealing attire. The easiest way to find out, Debbie figured, was to invite the woman in and discover her real purpose for visiting in this unannounced fashion.

Elissa spoke first and helped solve the mystery. "There were a few other items I thought you might like to see," she lied, but both Debbie and her Gold already knew that. "I found your address from your charge card and I brought these special items for your perusal."

Debbie eyed the woman intensely and then shifted her gaze to the naked Gold's armfuls of artfully decorated bundles. She did enjoy presents, Debbie acknowledged, and she wagged a finger once to her lingering supplicant. Elissa's eyes shifted nervously from the seated woman to the naked man whose pleasing aroma she could perceive easily from his short distance from her chair.

Offering one package to his superior, Gold held out a bright blue and deep pink bundle for Debbie's consideration. Delicately balancing the remainder of his load in his other immense arm, Gold remained perfectly attentive at Debbie's side as he assisted her in her efforts to unwrap the parcel. His position was awkward and unbalanced.

"Put them down," she ordered the almost-nude man and he dashed to unburden his full arms.

After placing the packages gingerly down upon the soft peach carpet, Gold turned his attentions and sped immediately back to his superior's side. Debbie reached carelessly up toward his standing form and grasped his dangling net bag in her right hand. Pulling firmly downward, she forced the sputtering man to kneel diligently at her side.

"The ribbon," she spoke tersely. "Open it."

Gold pounced upon the package and tore at the unyielding decoration with his hands and then with his teeth. As the last offending string broke, the kneeling man offered the parcel to his superior for her inspection. As he handed the package to her, the edge of the package caught Debbie's chocolate brown bra and nudged her soft exposed nipple. The force of the package edge nudged Debbie's robe slightly away from the closed position in which she had just arranged it. The offended superior looked sternly into the face of the suddenly chagrined Gold. Elissa sat across the room, transfixed by the unfolding spectacle.

The enslaved man dropped his head onto his chest in mortified silence. Having pledged to serve perfectly this woman and having just struck her with the package and displaced her clothing, the menial subordinate could offer no words of apology or explanation where none would be either welcome or accepted. Elissa forced herself to take deep, even breaths and try to regain control over her rapidly rising emotions. She felt her femininity moisten as her own lingerie felt stuck to her skin.

The tension between Debbie and her Gold rose to a silent and inaudible fever pitch. His twitching organ danced in the uneasiness of trepidation as the reclined woman began to straighten from her lounger even more. His face radiated a fearsome glow that bespoke his anxiety at her distress and her dangerously rising anger. Elissa noticed that his backside flexed involuntarily as the woman rose fully from her chair, her robe flowing openly about her well-kept body. Elissa began to twitch visibly but her voice stayed silent as she tensed for the intriguing climax of punishment for this man's obvious infraction.

She lifted his reddening face by his strong chin and forced the humiliated man to look directly into her expression of anger. Kicking his legs apart, she bent to take his filling netting in her free hand and jerked suddenly upwards to lift the penitent from his position. Agonized, Gold scurried up and stood trembling before his superior and her guest.

"What should I do to punish you?" she asked sarcastically but not rhetorically to the almost-whimpering servant.

"Pain," was his brief and unnecessary reply. "Give me pain."

Turning her head away from her suffering servant, Debbie asked the same question to her guest. "What would you have me do to this clumsy one?" Debbie's tone was both challenging and inviting. If she had guessed correctly, Elissa was as up to the challenge as she was eager to participate.

Although Debbie could hear the catch in her voice and her failure to respond immediately, she did admire the woman's tenacity and her confidence to respond at all. Elissa might provide her with an evening's entertainment, Debbie conjectured, as she continued to hold the embarrassed Gold's face in her solid grasp.

"Pain might be appropriate," Elissa began in earnest, "but have you considered other options that may be available to you?" Her words sank directly into Debbie's brain.

Interested in the woman's fascinating question, Debbie stared at the visitor for clarification. "Options? What did you have in mind?"

Elissa considered carefully before responding to her query. "Perhaps he could be punished in another fashion." She thought for a moment before continuing slowly and with a slight hesitation that was not unnoticed by Debbie and her gold. "Maybe what he needs is more. . . extensive. . . practice."

Debbie caught her idea immediately and loved it. "Yes!" she cried, as the Gold stood immobile while waiting for the two women to ascertain the nature of his punishment.

Fear of punishment was worse than pain, he had decided long ago. Better to get it over with because the pleasure always follows. Although she didn't realize it, Debbie had already punished her Gold more severely simply by forcing him to stand before another woman and wait for her decision than if she had quickly administered the delights of her jeweled bracelet to his firming organs.

"Yes," she repeated and added almost casually, "he needs practice. He needs more honing and more toning rather than simple punishment. But what kind?" she asked herself and answered. "Of course!" she cried in discovery. Pointing at Elissa, she revealed her plan to the astounded saleswoman and the silent and rigid Gold.

She gave them both clear directions. "Take her upstairs. Bathe her and dress her. Then you may return to me. Your punishment will be an evening of practice." The Gold seemed ready to respond, yet Debbie thought she caught the glimmer of sorrow in his handsome face. She continued in her decree. "You will serve her for a while and then I will evaluate your performance. If you seem to have learned your lesson, I may give you pleasure and perhaps I will even offer you insertion tonight. If you fail. . . well. . . I don't think you'll like what happens to those who fail." Her words struck his heart as he thrilled at the possibility of insertion and was repelled at the thought she might not value him that evening if his work were not able to pass her scrutiny.

Gold gulped audibly at her final words that continued to resound inside his head. He had heard a similar warning once before and he had come to know that it was absolutely true. He hadn't at all liked what he had seen happen to the ones who failed. His reflection took only moments before he whirled and knelt at the feet of the woman to whom he had just been given. The seated saleswoman reached down for his golden netting and grabbed it firmly in her deceptively feminine hand. Taking his soft member on an upward journey, Elissa forced the penitent to rise and led him as the two exited the living room, leaving Debbie to enjoy opening the wrapped offerings Elissa had just delivered for her examination.

Elissa climbed the stairs quickly and dragged the struggling Gold behind her. Sputtering with each step, the big man overshadowed the small woman; even though he stood one step lower than she. After she stepped aside at the top of the staircase and allowed him to precede her, he led the way for their entrance into the sparkling clean master bathroom that Gold had polished earlier that day. Elissa stepped behind the tall man and blocked the way between him and the door with her body. Her throaty voice betrayed her excitement.

"You're mine, now," she seethed at her slave, "and I intend to enjoy every moment of you." Her face radiated the excitement of the fully aroused.

She finished her instructions. "Bathe me," she ordered to his unsmiling face.

Responding from the depths of his expert training rather than from his heart, Gold knelt to supplicate himself before her. He grasped her shoe and lifted it slightly to remove it and then he performed his carefully practiced ministrations upon her body. Each piece of clothing fell silently to the aqua tile and soon the woman's readying body was naked and glowing under the heat light Debbie had installed during the remodeling. The waters filling hot tub swirled as mists of steam rose toward the ceiling and Elissa's dark brown nipples stood erect and pointed directly at the Gold's perspiring form. She stepped her legs apart willingly and waited for her servant to perform his functions.

Soon she was carried aloft in his colossal arms and the two stepped into the swirling waters of the bath. He lathered and soaped her with sweet lavender suds, then rinsed away every bubble from her skin. After resting her head on the large tub's edge on a thick folded aqua towel, the big man reached beneath her buttocks and lifted her hips level with the top of the water. Applying the sweet depilatory with great care, the Gold frothed it delicately with his face into her fuzzy feminine lips. Carefully lowering her tiny body beneath the lapping waves, he rinsed the remaining residue of hair and soap from her relaxed torso.

Ensuring that her head still rested comfortably, he flipped her cautiously onto her belly and walked around to step between her dangling legs. Placing his firm hand upon her now nude pubis, he again lifted her hips high and introduced his expert hand toward her tensing buttocks. Gingerly he patted and probed and indicated to the woman that he had a mission to perform in that special area. Using a great pearl of silver cream, the Gold brought one finger full to her anus and presented his gift to the now-thrusting woman. Inserting his warm and lubricated finger to her unyielding anus, the Gold was torn between forcing his hand into her body or massaging her respectfully as he waited for her reluctance to his intrusion to yield.

Combining his choices, the Gold pressed his dutiful finger of his right hand inward with only slight pressure and encouraged the woman to relax her muscles with a massaging left hand. She succumbed to his machinations and the bath proceeded with fascinating results.

The entry of his creamy finger electrified the diminutive woman's rectal area with exciting results. She suddenly thrashed her hips violently up and down as he fought to lubricate her orifice satisfactorily and completely. As her hips rose and thundered down in the wavy bath, his massaging fingers probed deeper and deeper inside to bring her the delights of pre-insertion that he had come to love so much. When she dropped her spread legs to gain balance and force herself into even greater convolutions, Gold fought to keep his right fingers firmly ensconced within her darkest hole. In her frenzy, she tilted off-balance, and his right hand which had sought to continue caressing her creamy anus instead plunged between her now-naked lips and firmly stroked the engorged organ that hid beneath her hairless lips.

Her explosion was as rapid as it was intense. Mortified that he had not been able to cool Elissa down before allowing her to culminate her experience, the Gold knelt quickly on the floor of the aqua hot tub and brought his well-trained mouth onto the organ that he had so recently abused. Within minutes, with his expert strategy, the spent women again rocked her hips in rhythm with his stroking and raised and lowered her pelvis in succulent tempo. She groaned with every lift and she sighed with every dropping of her lower body. Her hoarse, throaty voice performed as a barometer of her readiness and Gold listened intently for any changes in her audible signal. Downstairs, Debbie listened to Elissa's throaty cries as the woman seated upon the lounger continued her delightful conversation on the telephone. Silently, she grinned at the thought of the spectacle that was unfolding upstairs.

Pleased that he had been able to recover suitably from his initial accident, Gold brought the small woman to sexual heights she had not believed possible. He tantalized and teased her; he brought her to the cliffs of passion and allowed her to back down the mountain. When he was assured that her final climax had taken place in joy, he drained the water from the aqua tub and dressed her in the fine lingerie in one of the carefully wrapped boxes Debbie had obviously secreted upstairs. As she stood in warming in the glow of the heat lamp, Gold scrubbed and polished the aqua hot tub once again.

Her navy blue teddy with its Velcro crotch bound her anointed body with a clinging that complimented her petite figure. Finished with his chore, the Gold knelt at her feet and rubbed her legs to soothe the muscles that been worked so hard during her recent experience. He crawled submissively in front of her bare feet and performed the entirety of his work. She bent low over his stooped form and signaled her dismissal of him by lifting his limp netted organs toward her own body. Responding to her call, the Gold straightened and followed the demanding woman through the bedroom, down the carpeted stairs, and back into the living room.

During their absence, Debbie had been busy. Absolutely confident in her mastery over his services, Debbie had arranged a larger practice session in which to test her Gold. Seated before the entering pair were two additional women, and each had chosen to attire herself in one of the outfits of delight that Elissa had selected. The three seated women lounged carelessly on the soft and comfortable living room furniture. The sight that greeted the returning Gold and his recent superior was one of sheer satin enchantment.

Their clothing choices told Gold more about the three women than he could have learned from useless banter or prolonged conversation. The tall, thin blonde woman had selected a black split gown that bespoke her confidence and her desire to offer her intended slave a severe seasoning in sexual passion. Wearing only a sheer bra and similarly open panties, the short, brown-haired one was obviously provocative and could probably be strict as well as demanding. Debbie's selection from the pile of ripped-open wrappings revealed what Gold had already surmised. The silver bustier and open-crotched silver and gold lace bikini that replaced the rich chocolate brown informed his expert eye that she had engaged for the two of them an evening he would not soon be likely to forget.

The three seated women invited the newcomer in navy blue to join their discussion. Virtually ignoring Gold's entry, the foursome engaged in a lively conversation that ranged from their past sexual exploits to their present partners' shortcomings, endurance, and stamina. As the women lounged on the sofas and chairs, Gold kept an eye on his superior for her next requirement of him for herself or for her friends. He could only imagine what she had discussed with these two newcomers before she had invited them to share her willing servant.

He saw her finger waggle in his direction and the big man rushed to bow humbly at her side. Unable to dismiss the other women's stares at his naked and netted body, the great Gold fought the increasing urgency he felt to blush in front of these silken women. Yet he concentrated on Debbie's face and sought to please her, especially in front of her friends. Her first chore was to dress her slave in appropriate and arousing attire. Debbie intended to evidence to all assembled in her living room that she was firmly, absolutely, and totally in control of every aspect and profile of the massive Gold who was eager to fulfill her every wish.

"Bring me your tote bag," she ordered without ceremony and the Gold spun in haste, darted to the doorway, and ran upstairs to fulfill her command. For the short time he was gone from the room, the four women continued their comparisons of their sexual partners with the physique and capabilities of the absent Gold and hardly missed his presence at all.

The returning servant offered his bag to his superior and she had him unzip it and hold it open for her review. The clink of metal that reached his ears told him that her choice was finally made. As he lowered the bag as she extracted a series of long golden chains. Forcing him to kneel at her side, she dressed him in his gold leather collar, bracelets, and anklets, and clasped the ends of the chain to each of his appropriate hooks. Drawing the long chain tightly from his collar through his legs and snugly up to split his buttocks crack, Gold was soon trussed and gleaming in his newest ensemble. Golden chains dangled from his wrists to his ankles and stretched taught when Debbie had the big man raise his arms.

Clipping a short chain between his ankle cuffs, Debbie reduced the Gold's posture to taking short, cropped steps that kept him off-balance and unsure of his movements. One free end of chain fell loosely from his penile ring and Gold was filled with trepidation when he wondered as to its final purpose. The shackled man could take only very short shuffling steps and felt completely exposed and very vulnerable to these four women's plans this evening. There would be neither escape nor flight from whatever experiences they had in store for him tonight.

Finished with her dressing of him, Debbie turned away from his body in merciless ignorance of his plight. Rather, she spoke to the others. "Do we want drinks?" she inquired in a hospitable tone to her comrades on the couches. "Soft, hard, you name it. What will you have?"

Each woman responded directly to her, even though they each realized that the golden attendant would eventually be the server of their requests. Elissa spoke first. "I'm very thirsty," she glanced for a moment at the bowed and chained master who had so recently entertained her upstairs. "Make mine club soda and lemon."

The shorthaired one also responded with a brief inspection of her new butler. "White wine. And see if there's a twist," she added with intent and purpose. She perused the silent Gold with a careful eye. His mind told him to watch out for this translucently clad female.

The tall, leggy blonde tilted her head back and made her request in a singsong tone that danced around the room and curtsied in Gold's ready ears. "Amaretto and cream," she ordered and Debbie concurred with a similar request.

Finally, the small saleswoman spoke. "Scotch," she said simply. "I've had a long evening and it's early!" Laughing at her joke, the other women joined in the festive mood that had overtaken the lively and jocund group.

Gold looked to Debbie for permission to leave and she granted him egress with an offhand flick of her head. The sudden movement caused her long brown hair to swing gracefully from her neck and land languidly around her soft shoulders. The rapid shift of her hair around her silver lingerie filled the man's flaccid organs with yearning and delight. Standing as straight as the chains allowed, the Gold exited the room and he felt the women's eyes fix solidly on his well-toned and tanned backside that jumped and flexed with each awkward shuffle he was allowed to take within the confines of his golden chains. Resisting the urge to flinch at their unabashed inspection, Gold stumbled to the kitchen to fill their orders.

As he worked with difficulty from within his bonds, he overheard their bright voices talking in an animated fashion in tones that were just beyond his ears' grasp. Maintaining the strictness of his training, he avoided the urge to listen in when he recalled that their exchange was superior to his role and was therefore none of his business. His job, he reminded himself, was to service and serve. The silver tray was soon beautifully laden with drinks, napkins, and stirring sticks and Gold returned to his audience with short clinking steps taken with alacrity and care.

Debbie eventually noticed his entrance. "Service my friends individually," she commanded him as he balanced the silver tray between his manacled massive hands.

Nodding, the big butler knelt cautiously before each woman and proffered her selection to her. His golden metal gleamed from the light of the overhead recessed fixtures and the imprisoned Gold felt that his kneeling effort had dug the polished metal still deeper between his rear cheeks. The tight chain that held his feet close together forced him to spread his knees open before his female audience. Completing his serving with his superior's refreshment, Gold presented her drink and began to creep noisily away so as to allow the women to converse without any further of his interruptions. Debbie halted his withdrawal.

"Stay!" she ordered sharply. "Girls, can't we use him just a little bit before I allow him to depart?"

The blonde added quickly, "I sure can. My husband is in Canada for the rest of the week. Can I borrow him?" Her eyes darted longingly from Gold's bent form to Debbie's keen eyes.

"He belongs here and to me," Debbie added with a reassuring pat on Gold's netted organs, a pat so firm and convincing that he winced from her comforting guarantee. "But you can use him for a time while you're visiting," Debbie offered in exchange. The blonde woman smiled and leered at Gold.

Debbie continued. "He's a little rusty, or at least he was a short time ago." Gold was embarrassed as she described his earlier infractions. Her relentless voice continued. "Why don't we agree to share him, give him a little workout, and see what develops?"

She waited for the others' reactions to her unusual offer. Gold was humiliated at his earlier failure and was doubly chagrined with Debbie's revelation of it to her group. Her friends, though, were eager to forgive his errors and to use him, at least for the night. The women argued happily with one another for playtime with the big Gold.

Elissa broke into the bargaining with a counter-offer. "I don't think he's in top form, especially after his clumsy workout upstairs. Do you think he's capable of satisfying all four of us?" Her description of his bathing expertise was a challenge that struck out at Gold's dignity and her implied threat tested his training to keep silent and accede to all demands.

The clearly clad neighbor likewise offered little solace to the naked attendant. "He's not very big, is he?" she asked as she reached for his limp organs, pulled them stringently toward herself, and smirked as he winced from her inspection.

Gold was stung by her condemnation and disparagement of his endowment. Feeling his outrage rise, he resisted staring at her hand that was holding his limp member and instead turned his eyes toward his regal silver-clad superior and awaited only her command. When her mellow gaze met his silently outraged face, he felt his netting strain with its engorging contents. Debbie smiled and laughed both at his discrediting by her guests and at the offense he took from it.

"Serve us all well," she threatened, "and the gift will be yours tonight. But fail us, even one of us, and, remember what I said: 'You won't like what happens to the ones that fail.'"

He recalled her words vividly and remembered having heard them before. She was more right than she realized. He knew what they did to the failures, and he did not like it at all.

Amazingly, the women turned their attentions away from the kneeling and shackled servant and moved back to their earlier conversations as they sipped their drinks. Unsure of what to do next or when to begin, Gold continued to kneel penitently at Debbie's feet.

Raising her bare foot suddenly and planting it squarely and firmly in his engorged organs, she commanded, "Well, get on with it! Are you waiting for an invitation?" The women chuckled at his distress at her sharp words.

Taking on four women, especially when one was as cunning and clever as his assigned superior, was an awesome task for any slave, no matter how well he had been trained. Doing so while so expertly shackled constituted one of the most serious challenges Gold had ever faced. This particular woman, he considered once more, was an expert. Her authority and tone often frightened him and that very fright mixed with longing encompassed Debbie's most fearsome hold on the big man.

Gold commenced his assignment with no further instruction. Creeping on his long, chained belly toward the feet of the tall blonde, he licked his lips, swallowed, and began kissing her toes in supplication. Wrapping his shackled hands around her ankle, the servant began his efforts in earnest. His plan was to work his way up her lithe legs until he reached her fuzzy doors that would yield to his entry and later to his stimulation of her inner feminine self. As he proceeded on this tried and true course, he heard a disquieting sound, that is, the voices of the women in happy, cheerful, and complacent conversation that contained no recognition of his role, his function, or, worst of all, his presence.

His mind reeled from the indignity. Using every trick he learned in training and others he had gained from his several years of experience, Gold sought to arouse the blonde woman to ecstasy using his well-instructed mouth. To his horror and amazement, she continued her discussion and ignored his efforts and even his very proximity at her feet.

He was at her knees when she crossed her legs, virtually locking him out of her inner self. With fright in his eyes, he sought Debbie's reassuring gaze, yet his superior was herself involved in animated discussion and he dared not intrude on her private conversations. She ignored him in his distress and somewhat confidant Gold succumbed to the depths of increasing self-doubt.

Moving his chained form with noisy creeping steps toward the woman in the filmy attire, Gold mentally altered his plan. Resting his face on her soft knees, he sought her recognition of his entry into her space. To his utter dismay, this one also continued her obliviousness to his efforts and she rejected his attempts to bring her to delight by casually sipping her drink and resting the frothy glass on his perspiring face.

Again the slinking Gold sought Debbie's reassurances, but again was rebuffed as she continued her outward unawareness of his misery. In utter despair at his failure to properly service his superior's company, the sullen Gold slinked back from the seated group and rested on his haunches in the center of the peach carpet. Fighting (the exhortation his mind demanded to sob in acquiescence of his dereliction), (?) the expertly fettered Gold succumbed to his incompetence and knelt awkwardly and alone, far away from the group.

Debbie interrupted his pouting with her consternation. "I am deeply distressed with you," she threw at the hobbled penitent who knelt almost sobbing in the middle of the carpet. "Do you intend to continue to insult my guests?"

She stared directly at his horrified expression and waited for a response that he would never offer. Looking directly into his tearful eyes, Debbie was merciless in her demands.

"Here!" she ordered and pointed at the floor between the blonde woman's feet and her own. The dutiful Gold gathered his chains and crept dismally toward the spot she indicated. Reaching beneath the silver couch, Debbie pulled out her secreted leather whip and tantalized the Gold's buttocks with firm and lingering strokes. Elissa's eyes fixed on the instrument of instruction and Debbie returned her envious gaze with an offer the small woman readily accepted without reservation or hesitation.

"Would you like to direct this phase of his practice?" she coyly asked of the visiting saleswoman. Elissa's head bobbed up and down in avid response. Debbie reached over the perspiring servant and handed the respondent the leather crop.

Standing and positioning herself directly behind the kneeling man's backside, Elissa looked over his head and faced her new friends with a determined glare. Raising the whip well above her shoulder, she brought the instrument down in educated and well-placed blows upon the gleaming buttocks and golden chains that split the huge man's backside. The blonde woman reached forward and pushed his head down to her own feet as his backside was forced up and the servant's immediate response was to attempt to begin his stimulation of her again even as his rear cheeks were achieving red welts from the small woman's almost-expert blows. The scene was intense as Gold sucked, licked, and kissed the polished toes of his consort while he received shocking punishment from the heavy hand of the churning saleswoman.

Debbie was enthralled with the scenario her friends were performing for her with her slave this evening. As the remaining woman joined the fray, Debbie relished in watching her Gold perform for the audience that she had arranged. Grabbing his head by a great handful of his sandy hair, the newest member of the group forced the struggling man's mouth directly onto her hairy region and bade him open her and bring his expertise to her lower lips. Setting the crop down on the coffee table, Elissa joined the seated women and stole the active mouth from its temporary home as she ordered the servant to offer her similar delights.

The three guests took turns with him and commanded him without warning to shift among the objects of his attentions. The two nameless women alternated taking him by his netted organs, his full head of hair, and his dangling chain, and directed his efforts to their own femininity. Elissa was not shy in her potency to produce her own enchantment at Gold's expense. He projected an image of a delightful machine whose function was limited to these three women as his head was bobbed up and down among the women's laps and his tongue jumped from giving one delight to performing fully for the other.

Yet none of the trio was ready to climax. Debbie entered the unfolding drama by adding a firm and resounding smack to the man's raised backside with the open palm of her well-directed hand. The force of her blow pushed his head forward and the temporary object of his labor gasped in ecstasy at the forced intrusion of his lips, teeth, and mouth into her deepest region of sexuality. The remaining two women gasped at their friend's abrupt and dizzying climax with full lungs and envious stares.

Realizing instantaneously what type of stimulation the Gold needed to succeed in his efforts, Debbie reached between the man's shackled legs, took his netted penis and testicles, and raised his face suddenly upwards. Forcing her arm toward the next woman's position, Debbie forced the great Gold's face directly over her quivering crotch and dropped his head into its newest home. Allowing him to perform his function on this woman, Debbie approximated his endurance and his success before she once again smacked his delirious backside with a firm, hard, and severe stroke that sent his intended into spasms of joy.

She repeated the process for the visiting saleswoman's pleasure and smiled as her Gold performed satisfactorily for each of her guests. The spent women watched each other culminate in joy and happiness, then relaxed their heads against the soft couch's cushioned rests. Completing the odyssey, she had her Gold stand and massage the women's aching muscles before she ordered him to remove the tray of half-finished and now-forgotten drinks.

Within the confined steps his manacles allowed him to take, the Gold removed the used glasses and cleaned up the living room with soundless labor. He returned to her presence with a clean face, sparkling chains, and a rigid net bag that was completely filled with his almost-leaking member and rock-hard testicles. Debbie dismissed the overcome women, who happily wrapped themselves in their coats, thanked her for their use of her servant, and exited through the foyer to their homes and their evening's dreams.

Turning toward her quivering and trembling Gold, Debbie announced, "Upstairs with you," and the great man tussled within his trussing to report to her bedroom for the delights that only he could bring to his superior.

Gasping with the exertion required to direct his readying body to climb the carpeted stairs, his netted penis stood erect and away from his body as he trod the carpeted steps. His golden shackles produced the only sounds that pierced the quiet of Debbie's home.

Following him up the stairs with repeated hard spanks to his quaking backside, Debbie drew in great breaths in an effort to control her own rising excitement. Her clinking servant endured each stroke with rising agitation as he was as yet unsure if he had passed or failed the examination she had so recently given him. His distracted mind contemplated his evening's successes as well as his failures; he concentrated mainly on his incompetence and his need of Debbie's assistance in his final efforts for her friends. Chagrined and chained, the bulky man slithered toward the master suite and stood in the center of the peach carpeting at the foot of the massive bed ready for the ghastly punishment she was certain to inflict.

She considered his humbled form and relished in her superiority over his entire being. Taking his dangling chain in her soft white hand, Debbie dragged the stumbling servant to her bedside and hooked his leash firmly to the frame of her bed. Shackled, humbled, and dangerously erect, Gold awaited the pronouncement that would seal his night's future of pain or pleasure. His eyes filled with wild tears as she prolonged his torment with her silence. His stiffening penis was engorged beyond pleasure and his urgency threatened his expert self-control. This woman was wild, his mind screamed at his brain, and he feared his imminent reaction to the stimulation she had forced upon his willing body.

Debbie relaxed on the cool, chocolate brown satin sheets that Gold had put on her bed that morning. Sliding into a comfortable position, she absently stroked his leaking penis with her braceleted hand. His grimacing face told her he was absolutely ready yet she toyed once more with his dripping maleness. And then she threw down the gantlet. "You can come tonight only if you discard the netting," she challenged him. "I want you to perform your best inside me."

Horrified at his inability to fulfill her command, he sobbed great tears of mortification and helplessness. "No," he moaned. "But I have no permission." The tears fell hard and hot upon his chest.

"Are you willing to perform for me?" she teased the pulsating giant without letup.

"YES!" he screamed at her, "I WANT to. But I can't! I'm not allowed! Not without the Mistress's permission!" His voice rasped in his agony.

"Is that all?" she mocked him once again and was secretly glad that she had attended to her mail earlier that afternoon.

Pressing a series of jewels that his well-trained eyes had never before witnessed, Gold watched in horror mixed with joy when his golden netting dropped from his body and exposed his gigantic maleness in front of this unpredictable and remarkably shrewd woman. He had been right, he suddenly realized. He was no match for her. She was infinitely superior.

"I'll put it back when we're done," she eased his worried countenance. "Get on with it. Remember, you won't like what happens to those who fail."

Giving himself totally to this marvelous and unbelievable woman, Gold brought her over and over again to heights she could never have imagined before he finally allowed himself to fulfill inside her. He freed himself from his months of servitude, self-denial, and enforced prohibition. Screaming wildly and bellowing in ecstasy, the Gold timed his culmination perfectly with the last of Debbie's climaxes and their two exhausted bodies fell into dreamy sleep. That night, Debbie lay quietly and contentedly on her brown satin sheets while Gold dreamed the dreams of the totally fulfilled as he rested on the floor at her side on the peach carpet in the silent bedroom.

Chapter Twenty Nine

Circling her captive like a tigress sizing up her prey, the leather-clad Mistress approached Ron's trembling body as his evening of unequivocal and consummate slavery commenced. He felt absolutely naked without his net. For the first time Ron realized how much he had come to appreciate the covering and the protection that his pink netting had afforded him. As crazy as it sounded inside the gravely terrified trainee's head, his former almost transparent pink net covering had made him feel somewhat dressed. Right now he was embarrassed in his total nudity and he felt both shamed and disgraced as the Mistress continued her seductive assessment of his unclad body.

As he stood unclothed while she displayed him in the center of the immense white carpet, he forced his attention back to the rhythms of her petrifying dance when he realized that for the first time since he had arrived at the facility, he was totally alone. Free to use and abuse him at her discretion, she allowed him no weapons or strategies with which to cope with her overwhelming authority over him for fulfillment of her urgent personal desires. Ron's arid throat swallowed a dry gulp and he wobbled on unsteady feet as her alarming show continued.

"Are you hungry?" she suddenly cooed at the quaking attorney who stood rigid in rising alarm before her. His incredulous ears dismissed her polite yet seductive request as incomprehensible in this situation and she had to repeat it before he could find the words within himself to answer.

"Do you want something to eat?" she inquired again, more simply, and a little more kindly, Ron thought. Thinking about food made him realize his gnawing hunger and his head bobbed up and down as he indicated his response.

"Well, I know that a hungry slave is an unhappy one, so we'll call a car and grab a bite before we return to complete our evening," she declared to his impassioned ears. The Mistress pressed a single golden jewel on her leather bracelet as she wagged a single long finger in Ron's general direction. Responding with lively steps in spite of his humiliation and fear, Ron strode to her side and knelt at her feet. She smiled at his effort to please her.

"I don't think you ought to go out like that." She pointed at his bare body as she toyed with his limp, oscillating, and exposed organ. "Let's get you dressed," she added as she opened the costume closet for him once again. "Come with me."

Moving quickly through the multitudes of racks replete with costumes, the Mistress pulled him by his flaccid maleness and selected Ron's attire for their outing that evening. She held aloft her selections for the cringing and abashed trainee to wear. He allowed her to dress him as if he were a child and the Mistress's careful selections served to reinforce his feelings of immature dependency on her. Forcing the naked man to spread his legs wide apart, she placed a flat leather strap between his buttocks cheeks and lifted the front and back ends to encircle his trembling genitals. As she tied the front to the back at a bikini length well below his waist, he felt the firmness of the leather first cover and then totally obscure the dark entry to his aching anus. His sagging penis and testicles were forcibly shoved by his dresser into a tiny leather pouch that was tightly hooked into his leather harness. A tiny pair of flesh tone silken running shorts with Velcro side closures covered his dark habit diaper-style, and a short neutral tee shirt barely shrouded his chest. She allowed him open leather sandals that coordinated. He laughed inwardly at her touch of class, with his now-invisible girdle.

The final step in his accoutrements for the evening's escapade was the latching of a short metal chain into the firm leather belting. She arranged its secured position from the elastic waistband of his shorts by drawing the chain tightly through his legs and hanging the clear loop in front of his pouched genitals.

His speculation regarding the chain's function was short-lived because the Mistress gave him a quick and painful introduction to its function.

"Follow me," she ordered, and the barely dressed trainee bolted behind her immediately but with a slight reservation. She demonstrated the chain's purpose by striding quickly across the immaculate white carpet with her provocatively attired slave following directly behind her determined steps. As Ron half-skipped and half-jogged to keep up with her gait, she reached backward for the tiny chain and jerked its ringed end upward toward her. His genitals screamed from the brutal assault.

"You will remain two steps behind me, no more and no less," she directed to his burning ears as the doubled-over man's hands ran down his torso in their futile attempt to soothe his abused but invisible genitals. "When I turn and look, you will be exactly where I expect you to be." Her words were brutal and her expression without emotion. "When I reach back," she demonstrated with an open hand reaching behind her body, "I expect to find you right at my touch." Grabbing the leather cover of his recently abused organs, she squeezed firmly and further demonstrated her domination over his every movement. Ron shook his head rapidly up and down in total submission. Yes, he demanded of himself, exactly two steps. No more. No less.

She smirked at his quick reaction that bespoke his dependence on her orders and his recognition of her control. "Your second lesson for this evening," she continued, "is that you will perform exactly as I order." His bobbing head preceded her concluding her next demand. She scoffed at his rapid deferment to her wishes, an agreement he offered even before she had completed her sentence and before he could understand what she would specify. He was a good slave, she thought, and after tonight, he would become a great one.

"It doesn't matter what I order you to do," she continued. "You will perform it exactly and completely. Do you understand?" She waited impatiently for his answer to her somewhat rhetorical question and indicated her displeasure with his reticence by whipping the ever-present leather crop noisily through the air.

Ron recognized from the quickening sound of the airborne leather that he was supposed to answer her question at this time. "Yes," he replied simply. Then he added, "I understand."

"Good," the Mistress concluded her directions. "Let's get some dinner."

Her personal Gold entered silently on cue and stood in his place as he waited for the Mistress's directions. She tossed a golden silk shirt and matching running shorts in his direction, and the silent attendant dressed with neither question nor comment. The golden servant turned and led the duo through the pitch-black maze that marked the singular egress available from the vast chamber. Turning first left and then right, the small group walked up a passageway and down another before the chained trainee glimpsed a dim light ahead. Their path was confusing, awkward, and totally dark. Ron had no chance of recalling this route for any possible escape, and besides, he thought, why did he want to flee and where would he go? The group finally emerged into a darkened parking garage and Gold held open the door of an elongated white limousine so the Mistress and her slave could enter.

There was no light visible through the opaqueness of the darkened windows, but Ron felt the idling car move silently and slowly foward. Their trip was short; after only about ten minutes, the long vehicle was stopped, parked, and opened by the personal Gold for the passengers' exit. The Mistress took the proffered hand of her scantily clad golden servant and left Ron to struggle from the back seat within his leather grip of pain. She did not stop to allow his emergence; rather, she strode quickly through the parking garage toward the elevators as Ron galloped behind her and muttered to himself as if in reminder, "two steps, no more and no less."

The spandex and leather clad Mistress marched with determination toward an elevator and awaited her Gold's pressing the "up" button. When the car arrived, the threesome entered and Ron was chagrined to discover they were not alone in the compartment. Although he kept his eyes properly lowered, he was able to perceive an impeccably dressed woman and a man accompanying her whose casual attire seemed almost out of place next to the woman's regal finery. Further illicit and surreptitious inspection revealed what Ron feared most. Under the other man's clothing were the telltale signs of a studded leather collar, wrist manacles, and some sort of intriguing arrangement of chains.

What struck Ron foremost was the way the man kept his face turned away from the newcomers and toward his partner. In addition, he forced his eyes to stare intentionally and directly down at his own bare feet. The two masqueraded men rode in absolute silence as the elevator began a prolonged ascent toward his dinner, and something Ron feared even more, a nagging suspicion that there was something else that he had not quite expected. The Mistress's harsh comments interrupted both his worrisome thoughts and his growing fear.

"Kneel!" she ordered calmly yet inarguably firmly and Ron found his legs obeying her curt command even though he was humiliated in front of these unknown passengers. The Mistress grasped the clear ring of his dangling chain and pulled the trainee in pain toward her. "Two steps behind me," she reminded him as she grabbed his chin and pulled his face to a position in which she could stare acute waves of terror into his burning eyes. Yanking the chain upwards, she forced him to rise from his knees again and she turned her back in silence to his perspiring and shaking form.

The display was not wasted on the pair of onlookers. Without missing a beat, the well-dressed woman responded by directing her male companion to strip off his shorts and shirt while the elevator continued its interminable rise. Without question, delay, or even a moment's hesitation, he performed as she bid him and soon stood naked and carefully chained in the roomy car with its strange mixture of humanity. Ron could not keep himself from staring open-mouthed at his companion's nude and shackled form. With a great gulp of fear, Ron turned his head away from the other man's total degradation to spare his comrade further embarrassment but worried silently about his own fate this evening. The idea of dinner was dislodged quickly and forcibly from his reeling mind.

As the elevator car slowed, the Mistress once again reached back for the waistband of Ron's silk shorts and tugged fiercely. The Velcro closures gave way and she handed the now-useless garment to her attendant Gold. Ron's pale leather harness glimmered in the pallid lighting and his chain, now freed from its constriction, dangled dangerously between his legs. Not yet finished with her public display of her total domination of him, the Mistress flicked a long finger at her Gold and the big man lifted Ron's shirt from his now-quivering body. Totally naked except for his sandals and his leather girdle, Ron stood fully exposed behind his Mistress as the elevator car doors slid open.

The scene that greeted Ron's unbelieving eyes was a sight he had trouble digesting. Scores of well-dressed women sat at comfortable upholstered chairs and sipped drinks while almost-naked and leather-clad servants offered them hors-d'oeuvres from silver trays. Chained men danced on platforms while women sometimes watched but more often ignored their efforts. An assortment of whips, crops, and paddles were wielded by intent females to attract the attentions of their servants, and to occasionally correct their failure to respond quickly to the women's demands. Still standing in the doorway of the open elevator, Ron stared at the macabre scene that greeted his gawking eyes.

The sudden jerking of his chain pulled him forcefully back to reality. "Two steps," the Mistress shouted into his fervid ear and Ron was grabbed vigorously from his reverie back to the reality of the restaurant into which he awkwardly trod at a careful two-step distance behind his Mistress. He watched the room's occupants shift their gazes toward him and recognized the smirks and smiles that greeted his Mistress's arrival were accompanied by rapidly rising females who vacated chairs and offered them to Ron's dominator. Smiling at no one but apparently recognizing everyone, the Mistress chose a comfortable spot and lowered herself seductively into a big chair.

He didn't know where to go, what to do, or how to wait. Standing erect but humiliated next to his seated and somewhat amused Mistress, Ron decided to stare straight ahead until he was commanded to move. Standing still, he thought, was better than doing something wrong. With his eyes staring vacantly at the surreal scene around him, he never saw the Mistress level an open palm at his leather-covered genitals, but he felt the resulting shock waves course through his electrified brain. He knelt quickly at her side because he did not know what else to do.

"Get me a drink and a snack," she called in his direction but without really looking into his face. "Watch the others and follow. Hurry," she added unnecessarily, "I'm thirsty."

Allowing his eyes to meet those of the other humbled men in the restaurant, Ron discovered their curious commonality. Each man who was carrying a silver tray was allowed to walk; however, if the man had none, he crawled in ignominy across the carpeted floor toward what must be, Ron surmised, the kitchen. He followed their lead.

As his six-foot form crept behind a line of others with similar orders, Ron felt the sharp sting of leather across his buttocks. Lifting his head and looking over his shoulder, Ron felt yet another slap of punishment greet his reddening cheeks. Each woman that the line of humbled men passed added yet another spank or whipping to any man's backside that presented itself within her reach. Crawling through the gauntlet, Ron experienced shame and helplessness, but vowed to continue his trek to fulfill his Mistress's desires no matter how much mortification he was forced to endure. The colorless band around his penis that he would wear proudly for the rest of his life reminded him with every step that he was bound totally to his superior.

He endured the repeated affronts to his dignity and his backside as he traipsed the short distance to the low doors that would admit only crawling and creeping servants. Once inside, he was forced up by a worker and handed a silver tray that contained an assortment of drinks and a variety of snacks. The aromas that greeted him forced his hunger to increase and the gnawing feeling in his stomach spiraled and swelled until his mouth salivated from the smells. A fleeting thought of stealing a bite to eat crossed his mind, but when he witnessed another slave engage in that prohibited behavior, he gave up the idea entirely.

Ron had a clear view of the errant servant bring quickly taken from the line by an overseer and chained to a nearby wall at which time he received what Ron recalled as similar to level one punishment. The spoke lifted and struck the shrieking man before sliding back into its home beneath the floor only to rise once again and do its operator's bidding to the man's exposed genitals. The guard who administered the punishment walked away from the tortured offender and continued his work filling empty trays and emptying used ones. During Ron's short wait for his Mistress's refreshments, the unyielding spoke continued its upward journey, performed its punishment, and rotated down into its invisible home. The violator received continuous discipline and paid the penalty for his single errant action. Ron forced all thoughts of sneaking a snack firmly from his mind.

Returning to his Mistress with a full tray, he bent low to offer her the choices he had been assigned. Virtually ignoring her trainee, she took a glass and sipped at it slowly while Ron waited, bent over, for her next selection. He felt the muscles in his back strain in his rising discomfort. His arms turned leaden and his servile posture forced his biceps to scream in agony. He dared not stand straight up without her express permission. Without regard for his discomfort, she took a small sandwich from the tray and ate it casually while she chatted with her neighbor. Ron continued his half-bent position beside her comfortable chair.

He heard some of her words in conversation. "Oh, this one? No, not yet." Her words were meaningless to his ears. "I'll show you," she added and turned toward her slave with a casual glance.

"You!" she called as she reached out with her long leather whip and flailed the backside of a creeping servant who happened to be returning to the kitchen. "Attend me." The hulking, naked man raised himself up as his chains clinked noisily against each other with his awkward effort.

"Take his tray," she ordered the newcomer who readily grasped the silver from Ron's throbbing arms. "Step closer," she commanded Ron who jumped to a position immediately at her side. The Mistress reached between his legs for his dangling chain and pulled sideways as the sputtering trainee limped directly to the position she desired for him in front of her chair. She turned back to her conversation.

"First you unhook these," she instructed as she lifted the latches from Ron's leather harness. "Then the front drops down. It's all one piece," she added somewhat unnecessarily as the codpiece was freed from its constriction and dangled from its former home across Ron's genitals toward the floor. "Do you see?" she asked her intrigued comrade. "It's very accessible. This is one of my favorites." A small crowd gathered around his Mistress's demonstration of Ron's harness. She gave no thought to the man wearing the leather harness; rather she treated him as if he were invisible and served her purposes to no greater extent than would a department store mannequin.

Ron shuddered at the thought of his total exposure in front of these female strangers and his Mistress's virtual ignorance of his quandary. Raising his eyes above the seated women's heads, Ron tried to stare at some point, any point, to focus and breathe and attempt to regain his dwindling composure. He was failing miserably, he realized, and his debasement soared.

One of Ron's dominator's guests offered a polite, "May I?" and received quick and uninterested permission from Ron's Mistress. Feeling his organs taken in hand by a stranger, Ron trembled in shame and then shuddered as he felt his willful penis harden despite his maniacal efforts to bring the transgressor down. Not daring to look his handler in the eye, Ron continued staring at the restaurant's back wall. Concentrating on the nude dancers and the women who whipped errant backsides without provocation or warning, Ron's excitement grew as his penis defied his self-control and engorged without mercy.

"You may borrow him," he heard his Mistress offer off-handedly as he felt the handler's eagerness in her grip on his genitals. Ron looked down only to witness his controller take another sip of her cool drink and ignore his obvious and increasing trembling. Feeling abandoned to the unknown woman who still maintained a firm grip on his errant organ, Ron sighed silently and brought his eyes to rest on his new superior's face. She was pretty, Ron thought, and ordinarily he wouldn't have minded. . .

A sudden slap to his vertical organ forced his reeling mind back to this reality. "I gave you an order!" he heard her yell, "and I expect you to obey!" Humbled, Ron suffered her incessant whipping of his buttocks, a punishment he felt he truly deserved this time for his lack of concentration. His bright red cheeks stood as a marker of his insolence to her demand.

"Kneel," she ordered again, and Ron dropped quietly and quickly into the position she ordered with his backside confronting his new dominator and his face to the stage. "Watch what they do and learn well. You will dance for me shortly."

His ears filled with the sweet sounds of the alluring music and his eyes beheld the men on the platform who presented themselves for the women's entertainment. Their costumes were as immaculate as they were intricate and Ron marveled at their designers' talent. He watched the men masturbate themselves to erection and he witnessed their eventual entry into the audience for the female members to feel their individual hardness and extend their enormous lengths.

Returning to the stage, the dancers performed both individually and in groups and utilized many of the accoutrements and liveries Ron had seen in the costume closet at the training facility. They played with each other and actually seemed to enjoy it. Ron knelt staring and open-mouthed at the sensual display on the stage as he felt his uncontrollable organ again harden and elongate. He was ashamed of his response to the male dancers, but his rising sensual excitement threatened to overcome his personal chagrin.

Suddenly, he felt his head pushed down toward the floor and he allowed it to descend to his hands that were spread in front of his knees on the carpet. His ears heard portions of conversation and his skin felt various fingers rubbing his midsection as the Mistress offered her guests instructions as to the loosening and complete removal of Ron's leather girdle. His elevated backside shuddered involuntarily as he felt the secured strings first slacken and then his harness slipped from its roost. Feeling the garment drift downward, Ron pressed his cheeks tightly together lest it drop from his buttocks' crack and expose his defenseless anus to these strangers who sat behind and around him. A resounding crack of leather against skin stung his already volatile backside.

Without his superior's verbal direction, Ron recognized what had constituted his transgression and immediately relaxed his gluteus muscles so the thick leather strap could fall down and land between his feet. With no prodding from his dominator, the expertly trained man obediently spread his knees to allow her total entry to his well-cleansed private space. Without shame, Ron surprised himself and forced his anus open to the women's inspection, probing, and inquiry. What he did not see was his Mistress hand her neighbor the very same small insert of control that she had removed from his anus earlier that day. But he did feel a woman's fingers enter him and spread his red-welted cheeks wide.

The woman's insertion of him evidenced a less well-practiced hand than that of the Mistress who always performed ritual insertions with expertise. The suddenness of the procedure startled him and Ron's face fell completely to the floor; he was saved from rug burn only by his strategically-placed hands. Once his rectum was again filled with the frightening device of control, he raised himself up to a kneeling position and waited for the woman to make yet another demand of his naked and filled body.

"Stand up," she ordered, and the prone prisoner rose. Then she added to his horror, "Get up on stage."

He felt her smirking behind his back even without being able to see her taunting face. Yet his legs carried him obediently forward and his almost-numb feet climbed the stairs of the rostrum. Turning slowly, he faced the audience as a frightening cloak of quiet descended upon the suddenly transfixed gathering. They stared at Ron's firm penis, his amazingly hairless pubis, his stripped body, his oiled skin, and the feathers of leather that dangled from the bulbous end of the anal insert he once again sported. Searching for the comforting safety of his Mistress's face, Ron's ears heard the music start as his acquiescent body began to move spontaneously and rhythmically in a dance that was performed for all but was dedicated in his mind solely to his Mistress.

He shut his eyes in fear and allowed his body to react to the tempo that his ears took in and his feet felt as the bass speaker rumbled reverberations through the stage's floor. Throwing his self-respect and his final shred of diffidence out of his ravaged mind, Ron presented a vivid rendition of creative movement that transfixed the onlookers and overcame the remaining scraps of his reluctance. Dancing wildly and without restraint, Ron tantalized the crowd with his savage machinations and feral calisthenics before finally succumbing to physical fatigue and lowering his tortured body to the floor.

Resounding cheering greeted his ears as the group of leather-clad slaves applauded his efforts and his apparent success. Creeping in submissiveness silently from the stage, Ron returned to his Mistress's feet and she petted and soothed his torrid skin with a cool and soft hand. Sitting gingerly upon the leather feathers of his intruding insert, Ron laid his weary head into her gentle lap and received a calming petting that an over-tired child requires from his mother. He sobbed tears of joy mixed with exhaustion and he turned his tearful face toward his Mistress for affirmation. He was not prepared for the sudden jolt of agony that astounded his rectum.

"You were ordered to dance for me!" he heard an outraged voice cry. "How dare you dance for another?" He knew the Mistress's angry neighbor was waiting for a response, but his agonized brain and his offended anus could offer none. The internal thrusting of the insert threatened his control. It grew and retracted, then grew again. Pushing against his sphincter, the insert forced his overwrought muscle into spasms of contortion that intimidated the suffering slave into wailing tears of fear and horror. Unyielding in its torturing of his darkest hole, Ron felt his insides readying to offer his ultimate humiliation and spilling before the patrons of this eerie restaurant. In his total exhaustion, he knew that he could control himself no longer, that his sphincter would empty before this excited assembly, and he squatted in frightful readiness of his final degradation.

"No," he heard a familiar voice intone. "He is my slave and he performs solely for me."

The Mistress pressed a series of jewels and the thrusting insert silenced itself as Ron's tortured rectum slowly returned to a state of calm. When he regained control of his body, Ron knelt low and kissed the feet of his savior with the ardor and passion evidenced only by the recently reborn. She rose and led him by a handful of his own hair toward the elevator. The Mistress brought her happy slave home to the comforting bosom of the training facility in her white limousine and to the privacy of her quarters where the two unlikely conspirators spent the night in the unrestrained joy that his enslavement to this wonderful and caring woman happily engendered.

Chapter Thirty

Early the next morning, the trainees' masks were removed and each man was required to stand in an identical corner of his cubicle. Each cubicle housed a totally exhausted trainee who was then chained to the wall of his quarters from the clear penile ring that had replaced each one's pink training band. Every potential graduate had witnessed individually the edited video replay of Ron's evening as personal slave to the Mistress and every man stood transfixed from his attachment to the wall as he reflected upon the incomprehensible presentation. No sounds of their discomfort emerged from their lips; no complaints or wails of their agony permeated their rooms. Silent men stood affixed to the unyielding firmness of their imprisonment and attended to their comrade's endurance and stamina while serving their Mistress in her trial of their class through Ron's incredible performance. Today was graduation.

The hushed group was jolted into reality by the sudden and unexpected sliding open of their doors and walls. Leaving the thirty-nine shackled men totally exposed to each other and to the corps of Colors that marched intently toward their vulnerable positions, the stark openness of the trainees' quarters startled the riveted audience into reaction. With their short chains attached at one end to their penile bands, the thirty-nine stood at attention and virtually ignored the solid links of metal that ran between their legs and split their buttocks cheeks before coming to rest on the hip-high hook. Unmoving, the group attended the words delivered by the Head Gold.

"The Mistress has informed me that her slave performed well," he intoned as the group of thirty-nine broke into spontaneous and wild cheering. A glimmer of a smile greeted the stolid Gold's lips. "Your group will be inserted today."

The wild cheering rose again from deep inside the throats of the overjoyed audience. Gold smiled a little more. "Congratulations." He finished his delivery and strode silently from the excited group.

Within the silence of the anteroom of the Mistress's chambers, Ron stood similarly chained to his wall, but without the camaraderie or brotherhood of his fellows that was being enjoyed at that very moment by the thirty-nine members of his training class. His room's walls stood firm and did not allow his ears to hear any cheering or adulation. Alone with his thoughts and memories, Ron recalled the evening's events with a sort of longing in which he had finally come to actualize the heights of the joy of service to his superior. Only Ron endured the uncut footage of the evening's trials and only Ron, not the Golds, Whites, Blues, Greens, or the thirty-nine trainees, could report first-hand fully or completely about the nature or the bliss of the happiness he experienced at the hands of his Mistress.

Only the training is hard, Ron mused. Once trained, a man's service was enrapturing. Having an expert Mistress, he concluded, was the key to future pleasure. The only melancholy note, he thought, was that Debbie could never be as expert as his Mistress had been. Oh, well, the single chained man lamented, at least he had savored the experience once, and that was one more time than any other trainee in his class would ever enjoy. Unbeknownst to Ron, it was one more time than many of the Colors had survived either. He was soon to discover that the demeanor of the Colors would alter in his favor as some of the men he would soon face would hold him in awe because they had never received the Mistress's perfect attentions for a similar private session as had Ron.

Pressing his aching back and his welted backside against the wall's coolness, Ron stood in reverie and dreamed the daydreams of the totally satisfied. Even the entrance of his

Green into his private chamber could not dissuade him from his private thoughts. Silently unlocking the peaceful trainee's hooks, the Green stood in admiration of Ron's countenance of delight. As he took the man's limp penis in his hand, Green felt no response to his urging so he tugged gently at the spent man's organ to encourage him to walk to his final ceremony. Even with the gentle prodding, Ron did not budge from his spot against the soothing wall of his chamber. With an understanding born out of his own punishing night's experience at the Mistress's hands, Green tenderly massaged Ron's genitals until the dreaming trainee responded to his caresses.

Whispering, Green spoke kindly to his man. "It's time. Let's go. They're waiting for you."

An uncomprehending Ron gave no answer and responded only with his mechanical and leaden legs. Taking slow, careful, and measured steps, the rhapsodizing trainee ambled behind his trainer and never felt the lengthening or tensing of the chain that secured him securely to his trainer's own green ring. He was led down hallways and through corridors, yet his mind would not be able to recall either the duration or path of his journey. Ring to ring, the two men sauntered toward the waiting thirty-nine who stood ready for the return of their honored comrade.

As the two shackled returnees approached the exposed group, Green slowed his pace to allow his shaken follower to recover further from his provocative encounter with the Mistress. Agonizingly slowly, a glimmer of recognition crossed Ron's face. Walking the gauntlet through the thirty-nine trainees, Ron enjoyed back slaps, hugs, embraces, and cheers. As his mind slowly returned to reality, sensation was also restored to his physical body. Enduring each physical welcome in rising agony, Ron's eyes filled with tears of complete happiness that were intermixed with gripping pain. His arms throbbed and his legs were slow to respond to his mind's demand for motion. His denuded face bore the telltale chafing of the neophyte and his ailing rear cheeks were marked by the well placed and frequent stokes of the Mistress's firm hand. But worst of all his wounds was his stinging organ that draped limply between his legs.

Her demands upon his unnetted genitals had been merciless.

The mixture of pain, memory, and greetings from his fellows was unbearable. His tears would not abate. The Heads of the Colors recognized the same grimace that they had once borne in the mixed agony and joy of being chosen to offer service to the Mistress, and they joined to clasp Ron around his shaking shoulders in sympathy. The four seniors of the Colors who had once shared his ultimate experience led the suffering trainee from the crowd of well wishers and deposited him carefully into the comfort of the great pool for his very special and final morning cleansing.

In utter silence mixed with empathy, the four bathed and cleansed Ron with fervor and compassion. Lathering him for the last time, these four officials tenderly scrubbed and massaged his muscles and allowed his aches and pains to dissipate under their expert gentle touches. Lubricating him with delicate strokes, the Head White ensured that his internal cleansing would proceed smoothly and when he was plugged, the white-netted superior led the filled trainee slowly and carefully for expulsion before carefully and caressingly placing him upon his rack.

Ron neither heard him exit his tiny cubicle nor did he realize that every one of the thirty-nine remaining trainees was positioned similarly upon his own padded rack. His unhearing ears never heard the entry of his personal Green although his spread buttocks recognized the man's entry into Ron's innermost sanctuary. The only thing he really noticed was the aroma of the cream that Green was applying to his anal orifice. The shock of recognition of the memorable fragrance from his odyssey within the Mistress's sanctum snapped his reeling mind from its delirium.

"Oh, God!" he cried as Green continued his soothing massage of Ron's well-used anus and rectum. "That's wonderful. I remember this smell. From last night! Oh my God!" he ended his deluge with an outpouring words that tugged at the Green's tortured ears. With envy mired with admiration, Green could only imagine Ron's delight in his night of service with his Mistress.

Ron felt the man's fingers enter and probe his passageway with expert talent. Green recognized the man's utter joy in response to the lubrication so he applied the cream more carefully and with distinction. As Ron felt the rounded circles signifying the finale of the ceremony, he sobbed in realization that his training was near completion and his excursion in the facility was almost over. Sharing his joy mixed with sadness, Green patted the difficult trainee's backside with tender strokes and released the man from his position on the padded metal rack.

Forty lubricated trainees were led single file into the auditorium in which their ritual insertion would take place. The recently promoted Blue sat next to his Mistress to observe the results and potential success of his program for this ceremonial and solemn event. Each man was inspected one last time by his personal trainer before each Green escorted his potential graduate to the center of the room for the culminating episode of the training.

Blue had worked hard on the presentation of the insertion. Draping a heavy white curtain in a circle in the center of the room, he positioned raised pads on which the trainees would kneel around the curtain's perimeter. He watched carefully as each trainee climbed onto the pads and knelt silently with his face toward the curtain. Greens were instructed to place the men's heads into the circular cutouts in the massive divider. Once they were in place, the trainers laced the cutouts snugly around the trainees' necks. As their heads appeared separated from their oiled and lubricated bodies, the Mistress's voice on the speaker within the curtained circle instructed each man to grasp the low handlebars and to ready himself for her approach. Ron took the padded bars as he had been instructed and without further order spread his tired legs as wide as the platform allowed. He felt his backside rise dutifully for the Mistress's admission and he waited quietly for her firm but loving touch. Forty trainees' faces stared at one another within the silent and invisible central circle of the unmoving white curtain. The sequestered faces of the corps of Colors observed this ceremony from behind the glass walls where this training class once had stood. They were mesmerized by their first observance of an astounding spectacle of insertion.

The new Blue pointed out the gleaming buttocks of the Mistress's favored slave from the previous evening and she positioned herself directly behind Ron's raised and quivering cheeks. Although the elite trainee could not witness her taking steps toward him, he felt her electrifying touch upon his passionate gluteus muscles. Within the silence of the forty faces, Ron expelled a cry of delight that greeted her soft touch and echoed within the disconnected space the men's heads shared. As she moved her hand from his cheeks and closer toward his trembling anus, he continued his shrieking of happiness and began to rotate his hips in an eager circle. He thrilled at the touch of her fingers as she placed the clear netting upon his fully erect penis and drew it out fully to attach it firmly and forever to his clear ring of distinction.

The fraternity of trainees neither felt nor experienced Ron's rapture at the Mistress's tender touch but they perceived his zealous response and took it as their own. As the Mistress pressed the tip of Ron's new personally designed insert on its virgin journey, the thirty-nine brothers encouraged Ron with their shrieks and cries of support for his ceremony. Bellowing their backing for their comrade, the trainees hollered wildly as Ron's hips undulated and thrust in rhythm with the Mistress's teasing and tantalizing of his readied hole. Although they could not witness his body's gyrations, they were able to discern from Ron's face when he greeted the insert with solemn joy.

Gripping the handlebars more tightly with his passion and glee, Ron lunged his hips dutifully toward the Mistress's hand and offered himself to her fully. Unable to recognize anything or anyone except her expert tormenting of his backside, Ron screamed from the bottom of his throat to urge his superior to complete the job. Within the silence outside the circular curtain, the Mistress smiled as she watched his hips flail, his anus thrust, and his backside strain toward her readying hand. To the amazement of the entire corps of Colors, she drew out her personal marker from the depths of her robes and etched an indelible mark upon this special trainee's uplifted backside.

The trainers gasped at Ron's sudden stillness as the corps shuddered when they recognized what the Mistress had done. Many of the cadre had never before witnessed the Mistress's invitation for a graduate to consider entering the training to become one of their own. Entrance into the Colors was a sacred event and several witnesses cried tears of excitement as her marker disappeared once again into the confines of her flowing robes.

The chant inside the curtain grew louder and louder. "Now, now, NOW!" the men recited in a unique tempo in support of their companion. Cries of "Go for it," "Reach," and "Do it," were shared among the witnesses to Ron's intimate journey. His colleagues' cries enervated his efforts and Ron felt his hips rise frighteningly high from the small platform as his thrusts and lunges lifted him completely off the padded stage. Like a wild man, he attacked the teasing insert as he pounced upon his platform with increasing urgency.

The interior spectacle paralleled the rising excitement that was developing outside the circular divider. Outside the glass partitions, the Colors urged the trainee on and several men commented enviously about the unique length of time the Mistress was spending on this single recipient's insertion. In jealousy intermixed with admiration, the Golds, Whites, Blues, and Greens chanted in unison in support of this special trainee. Soon the crescendo built and cries of "Now!" comprised the single syllable of support for Ron and his insertion.

She heard every word and she continued with her Blue's plan until the entire group came together as one and the room resounded with a single voice. Smiling quietly at her new Blue, the Mistress nodded approval of his program's design and she lifted Ron's insert high above his aching anus for the final thrust. The neophyte responded to the removal of the tip from his lubricated orifice with horror mixed with rapidly rising emotions as he reached down for the remaining strength he could exhort from his aching arms and legs and threw himself straight up toward her elevated hand.

A sudden hush descended over the entire corps of Colors and the thirty-nine witnesses to the agony that spelled across Ron's face. No one had ever seen a recipient work so hard or expend such energy for insertion. No selected slave had ever exhibited such ardor and passion for his Mistress before this one. Murmurs of consternation mingled with concern rose from the ranks of the onlookers as Ron's hips were launched from their sanctuary.

In one singular motion, the Mistress's hand began its furious descent as Ron's tilted backside soared to meet it. With an astounding effort, the descending insert entered the man's rising backside perfectly and was driven deep into its home. He came with a never-before experienced passion in simultaneous timing with the placement of the insert and drew the spectacular admiration of those who were privileged to witness such a talented display of sensuality, timing, and puissance.

An unearthly gasp was emitted from Ron's throat and was followed by his gut-wrenching cries of rapture. The thirty-nine brothers he had dwelt with for so many weeks joined in his sobbing of exhaustion and completion as the inserted man's head was pulled back through the unlaced hole by his astonished but respectful trainer. A White, a Blue, and his Green pulled a shroud of blankets over the shuddering and trembling man's head and body and whisked him silently from the room. The Mistress stepped to the next man in line and readied herself for her ensuing insertion. A sharp pang of loneliness entered her otherwise solemn thoughts as she watched her favored slave ushered out by his trainer and the assigned Colors and readied for his long journey home.

In the privacy of her vast bedroom, Debbie lay upon the satin sheets of her wide bed and wriggled in excitement from the intensity of the scene she and her Gold had just witnessed. Jumping atop the bed and submitting himself at the feet of her supine form, Gold offered his fingers or his mouth to complete her rapidly rising passion. Reaching for her bracelet, Debbie pressed two jewels and offered the gallant Gold prolonged and severe pain. As she enjoyed her self-stimulation for the last time before her husband was returned to her side, she mumbled toward the Gold's thrashing body, "Ron's coming home. I don't need you anymore."

His rectum filled with the joy of his insert and his thoughts reeling from the experience of a lifetime, Ron was positioned on a moving sidewalk as his trainer steadied him for the ride to the waiting bus. Standing with the support of his accompanying Colors, Ron straightened, lifted the blanket from his head and wrapped its warm comfort around his almost naked body, and inspected his surroundings. He was riding behind a tall plate glass window that revealed the line of another set of incoming trainees who were dangling from ankle and wrist manacles within a darkened chamber. He recalled his earlier ride on that very conveyor.

Watching their journey in silence, Ron saw their agonized faces filled with horror and pain. He laughed inwardly as he recognized their first cleansings and he smirked at their careless expulsions. He saw their horrified faces grimace with shock and fear as the pitch-blackness of the chamber afforded them no safety or sanctuary from their impending imprisonment and training. They were lifted, turned upside down, and rotated back again. Their rectums filled and expelled, and their silent screaming filled his head with amusement. And they would be trained, Ron thought, because they should be. Being trained was better, he realized, and he also comprehended that he was going home.

Hands reached out to grasp his wrists when the moving walkway came to an end. Pulling him upwards, the unseen helpers raised him onto the platform that led directly to the bus and then to home. Retracing his steps down the aisle of the bus that led to his private cubicle, Ron entered the small quiet room and sat on the comfortable upholstered chair as he waited patiently for his next instructions. There would always be instructions, Ron thought, and he would complete every one of them. As his Green entered behind him, Ron grasped his trainer's hand.

"May I speak?" he inquired politely and the big man nodded in confirmation.

"Thank you," he offered simply, "....this has been the best...."

Green interrupted his comments. "I know. We all know. You don't have to say it." The two men sat holding hands in silence for a long time before the chambers were filled with inserted graduates and Ron felt the idling bus begin to roll on its journey home.

The video screen came to life and Ron recognized the Head Gold's face and voice. He received instructions regarding the gym bag of clothing and accoutrements that were delivered to him and now became Ron and his wife's personal possessions. He itemized its contents with his Green and he fingered each leather and plastic device with fond fingers. The two men discussed techniques and strategies as Ron's anus wiggled with recognition of his prized insert which he wore proudly within himself on this long journey home.

Before their settling down for the duration of the trip, the accompanying White and Blue joined the conversing men in Ron's cubicle. They offered their delight at Ron's success in the facility as they added their warnings and experiences to guide him in his new life. Explaining that they would return him personally to his wife, the three trained experts assured Ron they were confident that Debbie could manage to entertain him in a style that might parallel the exquisite delights he had recently experienced at the Mistress's hands. Unbelieving of their assurances, Ron imagined his wife's style and shooed from his mind any dreams or thoughts that she might excite him in the manner the Mistress had so recently accomplished with him. Having read Gold's astounding and graphic reports of his experiences at the hands of Ron's wife, the three men smirked silently and allowed the recent graduate to mire in what would be his short period of melancholy.

The sweet vanilla aroma wafted within Ron's cabin and the three experts and their newest graduate fell silently to sleep for the remaining hours of the ride home upon the comfortable cushions. The dark spot upon Ron's right cheek settled into his skin and became one with his body. Never to be removed, the mark inducted him into the ranks of those few who were born to their positions, just like the three who shared the sleep of the absolutely exhausted with their newest success.

Chapter Thirty One

Although Debbie slept late, Gold rose early to scurry throughout her home and prepare the house for Ron's imminent arrival and Gold's own bittersweet departure scheduled for later that afternoon. Glancing at the grandfather clock, Gold mentally surmised that the group of returnees now would be aboard the charter and rolling without cessation and with joy toward the individual limousines and the eventual delivery of the trained slaves to their respective homes. He also assumed that the group of four that contained his superior's satisfactorily trained graduate would be sleeping the peaceful dreams of the successful and satisfied as the massive bus continued its uninterrupted journey home. The experience was as new as it was old and another group of successfully trained slaves was on its way for delivery home.

As the big man worked his way through the home and scrubbed bathrooms, counter tops, and polished woodwork, he itemized his remaining requirements the Blues had indicated were necessary for a slave's homecoming. Checking off mentally those chores he had yet to accomplish, Gold prioritized his plan of action and decided to install the hardware first. When he completed the cleaning, he opened his prepared kit of metalwork and began the arduous but critical chore of implanting the hooks, clips, and rings that Debbie would certainly learn quickly to utilize in her daily routines. Taking the hardware silently from its secreted carton, Gold attached the implements carefully according to his prior well thought out plan. His search for wall studs was made significantly easier by the tools he carried in his Blue-designed satchel.

In the silent concentration of this quiet and peaceful work, Gold deposited the neutral-colored chains in various pre-determined drawers and other suitable hiding places and he automatically included the requisite locks, keys on rings, and hooks that would enable Debbie to fulfill every spontaneous or strategic desire with the least amount of her struggle or prior planning. Reviewing mentally Ron's predispositions from his videos, Gold was certain to provide his superior an assortment of leather ornaments of discipline in each hiding place. As he proceeded with his work, Gold checked off mentally yet another item from his agenda as he continued on his most careful chores.

The business of readying the woman's home for her returning graduate ensured the man's subjugation to his partner and it facilitated her ease of first establishing and then reinforcing the man's training. The first days home were the most critical, Gold recalled from the Blue's flawless studies, and his efforts on Debbie's behalf took on more than a functional capacity. Gold saw personally to every fitting, checked and re-checked the tightness of every hook and clip, and laid brightly decorated gifts of appropriately-selected lingerie and other essential accoutrements in specific locations that would expedite their discovery by the home's new Mistress. His mind raced through his plan of action as Gold strived to complete his work before his superior arose from her restless slumber.

Hardware, hooks, housekeeping, and hosiery. That simple alliterative litany comprised the song of readiness that the Blues had driven carefully into every Gold's memory. Checking off mentally another item on his list of duties, Gold visually surveyed the home and smiled at yet another one of his successes. Yet a lingering doubt crossed his frowning and troubled brow as he recognized that his own particularly outstanding training period with this alluring and elusive woman was coming silently and mercilessly to an end. Ordinarily these endings were routine and never bothered the superiorly trained Gold; however, this particular woman's expertise and talents had offered him a rarely recalled warmth and happiness that tugged at his surprisingly fragile emotions. This particular woman had been supreme, he thought, and he would miss the nearness, the intensity, and the frequency of her exquisite touch.

The custom-designed bus cruised along the highway as its silent passengers slept the peaceful rest that only the successful were allowed to enjoy as Gold stood in the immaculate foyer in contemplation and reflected on his own churning emotions. His reverie was shattered abruptly by the sounds of swishing of satin sheets upstairs that his well-trained ears perceived from his place in the large and immaculate foyer.

He glanced at the ticking grandfather clock in the entranceway and noticed that the hands were readying to strike ten. She hadn't slept that late in weeks, he smirked, as he scrambled to arrange her morning tray and assume his position at her bedside before she was totally awake.

The huge servant entered her bedroom for the last time with a tray of coffee and scones for her pleasure, and a twang of poignancy that tugged at his heart. Stretching her arms tightly and sensually above her head for his benefit, Debbie surveyed her entering underling as her face shone with the knowledge and assurance that her husband had been particularly noteworthy last night in his efforts on her behalf. Smugly, she sat up among the many pillows and began to toy for the last time with her naked attendant. He drank it all in and enjoyed her full attention as a telltale pang tugged silently at his impassioned heart.

"Today is it, isn't it?" she asked rhetorically as the subservient Gold nodded in affirmation of what they both already knew. "It's a little difficult for me," Debbie confessed to the somewhat startled man's burning ears. "I want Ron back with me, but frankly," she paused and Gold wasn't sure if it were for effect or if it signified her true feelings on the matter of the naked and netted man who stood at her bedside with full hands and rapidly beating pulse, "but I'm going to miss you. I wish I could have both of you." She smiled a little forlornly but she tried to mask her melancholy with a small grin for his benefit. Or was it for her own, Gold inquired silently.

"Come here," she ordered without harshness or malice in her soft voice.

The big man deposited the breakfast tray on the night table beside her bed and placed himself at full attention by her side. Watching her braceleted arm reach for his netted pouch, Gold winced involuntarily as her soft hand approached his rapidly engorging organ. Staring at his automatic response of excitement to her nearness to his sheathed genitals, Gold felt the rising passion threaten to overtake completely his well-disciplined self-control. Unsummoned by her voice, his penis shot up at her touch and pointed toward her as he felt his testicles shift nervously and expectantly within their netted home. His golden ring throbbed menacingly as his massiveness threatened the limited confines of the netting. Shifting his twitching body from side to side nervously while perched on two bare feet that stood immobile on the soft peach carpet, Gold began to wag his genitals in the dance of the novice that twitched a newcomer's obedient tail and marked a neophyte's inability to calm his errant organ from its insistent yet unrequested rise.

Debbie smiled broadly as she watched the rhythmic undulations of the big man's sexual organ. Realizing that he was responding to her as yet undelivered touch, Debbie smirked at his inability to force himself down. She relished in her power to bring him to full erection without touch and her inner self throbbed at her complete prowess over his most personal sensations.

Pointing her long finger at his rigid organ, her question to him was again rhetoric, "That's for me, isn't it?"

The mortified yet fully aroused servant nodded obediently as her soft fingers barely stroked his readying organs. His mind raced as she bounced his firm testicles in her white hand first softly and then harder and harder in an up and down dance, and his legs trembled when her polished fingernails raked up and down the increasing length of his well-extended golden netting. He stumbled for words.

"I. . . this is for you. . ." he agreed with her unnecessarily because the alluring woman silently recognized and delighted in his plight. In her caring and concern for his weeks of delightful service, she eased his worries by redirecting his thoughts. He knew what she had done to soothe him and he gulped down the knowledge that this expert Mistress had overpowered him once again.

"How much time?" was her single unfinished question but the massive Gold already knew and could finish the rest of her sentence. She was interested in her husband. In Ron's return.

"Soon," was his terse reply. For her elucidation he added, "About three hours." The Gold stood rigid but his organs swayed at her velvety touching of his fully engorged and wavering vital maleness.

Her hand moved down and caressed his inner thigh as his brain fought against its imminent explosion caused by his sensual excitement. Debbie had become a master at his stimulation, his trained brain concluded, and she readily recognized exactly what kind of touching of which particular organs would bring this now-shivering man to the most terrifying heights he had ever before experienced. The marvelously expressive hand pressed against the most tender part of his groin and the trained expert responded by spreading his legs wider than her soft slapping and massaging required. He was too ready, he lamented, but his torrid brain would not listen to her silent urges to retract his powerful legs.

Unrelenting in its inquiry, several fingers of her probing hand rested upon the recess of his exposed hole. Without her specific request or demand, Gold reached for his packed tote and unzipped his gym bag. Silently, he extracted his tube of personal golden cream. Recognizing his urgent yearning, Debbie accepted the proffered container and squeezed a large dollop of the sparkling cream onto her free palm. The Gold gasped as she reached for his tensing and tender orifice that he had cleansed especially thoroughly that morning.

He sprang into well practiced but always fascinating action. Rotating his body fully around, the naked man plunged both of his hands to the peach carpet and spread his muscular legs wide apart. As his darkest orifice opened fully to the reclining woman's touch, Debbie toyed with his quaking anal muscles and applied the cream only to the perimeter of his eager bowels. He groaned at her glorious touch and he thrust his hips farther backward to greet her palpating palm with respect and encourage her to complete the final entry into his now-spastic hole. The fervent movement was not lost on the calculating woman; however, she teased him even in his urgency by allowing only a single finger to enter a fraction of an inch into his shivering hole. The big man moaned in greedy anticipation.

Extending his legs even wider than Debbie could imagine comfortable, the Gold was able to press his hips somewhat closer to her satin sheets. Her unrestricted view of his most secret insides excited her innermost sensuality and the rising crescendo between her thighs threatened her own self-control. Their battle of wills had grown to frightening proportions.

"Please," he moaned in his agony of urgent expectation. Debbie's single finger entered him slightly deeper and Gold's mewling voice took on an urgency that further excited the woman's tensing thighs.

"God, oh God!" his quaking voice rose in sensual response to her probing gold-creamy finger.

Finally she drove her hand intensely into the front of the groin that controlled his thrusting hips and the entry brought spasms of delight to the vulnerable man's bowels. He constricted his sphincter around her hand for her delight and Debbie relished in her absolute and total control over every movement and every thought this Gold could entertain. She pressed the golden cream deeper into the bottomless orifice that he dutifully had made available to her touch. His bent-over body now resting entirely upon his massive hands, the Gold's hips rocketed up and down, back and forth, and left and right. Trying to keep up with his rising sensual excitement, Debbie squirted even more gold cream onto her palm and worked the unguent with immeasurable force into his churning hole. Forced to reach out with her free hand to steady his contorting hips, Debbie rested her extended fingers against his anxious skin and pressed firmly into his accelerating bowels. A second finger endangered his rectum as Debbie crushed her control farther into the big man's inner self.

He groaned loudly in appreciation and delight of her masterful plan. Even though he knew she would tantalize his expectant anus before she might consider allowing him to experience total delight, he gave in to the seductive woman's control over his satisfaction. Thrusting and lunging his burning body with frenzied abandon, Gold threw himself into receiving all of her adroit strategy. The increasing fullness that he perceived inside himself forced waves of terror mixed with frenzy into his disobedient body. Against his front, her steadying fingers increased their pressure on his sensitive groin and Gold responded to her insistence by enlarging his convolutions and propelling his agile hips into deeper and more forceful swings toward her hand.

She crowded a third finger inside. The golden cream spurted slightly from his overfilled cavity and washed over her inserted hand. Barely cognizant of the squishing sound that greeted her intruding fingers, Gold continued his barrage of gleeful acceptance of her domination over his every desire. As his hips rose and fell, his powerful hands pushed his body even closer to her welcome touch. His voice betrayed his wavering self-control and the great Gold began bellowing his approaching uncontrollable orgasm.

But Debbie was not ready for his coming so quickly.

It was too soon, she thought. Ron still needed two and half more hours and she would not allow the big man to receive his pleasure until just before Ron's arrival. Debbie required Ron to recognize her ability to tantalize a Gold and bring him to culmination at her specified timing for Ron's benefit. Then her husband would recognize the full capacity of her capabilities. She had seen her spouse's vacant face after his evening with the Mistress and she insisted to herself that he would come to know that his own wife would rival that expert woman's competence and dexterity in his own bedroom.

"Not yet," she cooed to the struggling Gold. "I'm not ready for you to climax."

His ears heard her words but his mind could not take them into his brain. "No. . ." he moaned and added a plea. "NOW!" was the insistent cry that emanated from his parched lips.

She added a fourth finger to antagonize both his errant backside and his disobedient brain. Her steadying hand felt the churning inside his groin and her four fingers filled his satiny rectum with golden cream and were followed by her insistent thrusts of urging. Knowing his time was fast approaching, Debbie shocked the poor man's reason by withdrawing her golden fingers as well as her steadying hand from his cavorting form and relaxing her body back onto her silken sheets.

He wailed a cry of terror and rage and spun to face his dominator as she offered him a taut smile that tore at the core of his soul. Dropping to his knees in supplication, he shouted, "Don't leave me here! Please allow me to finish. . ."

His pleas were greeted by her silent head shaking a negative response. Tearful now in his agony, he beseeched his superior with cries of anguish and distress. "Help me," he entreated her as she reached for the silver tray and began nibbling at the muffins he had baked fresh that morning. He supplicated himself completely on the carpet beneath her braceleted arm.

"Later," she replied briefly before sipping the scented coffee. "It's not time yet."

He screamed horrifying self-castigations at her denial of his completion and the massive man's hands moved toward his bursting and dripping penis in an appalling attempt to relieve his burden.

"I said NO!'" she spoke clearly, firmly, and directly into his torrid ear in a voice similar to that of a mother's disciplining an errant child. "I will allow you to finish when I am good and ready." Turning back to her breakfast, Debbie munched softly as she watched his kneeling and trembling form cower from her angry words.

As he blazed from the humiliation and the torment she had inflicted on his over-ready body, Gold admitted finally to himself her absolute regulation over his body and his soul. He removed his hands from attempting to assuage the organs within his netting and allowed his afflicted genitals to suffer silently at her denial. He was no match for her, he tearfully acknowledged, and he knew that he would immediately sign up for specialized training when his time with this incredible woman was done. His re-training would be swift and merciless, he knew, and the Blues would be forced to come to this same conclusion when they read his required report. He had failed to control himself with this expert woman, he lamented, and he knew what the Mistress would do to the ones who failed. And he also knew that he would not like it.

Debbie continued eating until the muffins and coffee had satisfied her appetite. Glancing down at the penitent Gold, Debbie demanded that he initiate her morning bath, then dress her, and offer his last advice for Ron's homecoming. In his pain, Gold complied with every one of her instructions.

His golden netting was sticky with his own errant leaking yet the massive man performed valiantly for his superior. Offering her a delightful bath of scented soaps, depilatories to smooth her legs, and powerful massage for her gleaming skin, Gold rendered every service to his overseer that she could either imagine or verbalize. After having dried her with the fluffy aqua towel and oiling her sensitive skin, he dressed her in glittering transparent lingerie that cupped her firm breasts yet exposed her dark nipples and allowed her lower lips full display. The long open robe supplied for Ron's homecoming flapped noiselessly against her soft skin and her open-toed slippers' high heels clicked dangerously against the aqua tiled floor.

She felt as ready as possible to greet her returning husband. Gold crawled backwards from her alluring display as his willful penis presented itself in full erection to her in recognition of her consummate authority over his every thought and desire. Still sporting the remnants of her application to his anus, his own golden orifice glittered in the overhead lighting and reminded him of her unique ability to overcome his well-developed self control.

When the shrill ringing of the bedside phone interrupted Gold's self-deprecating thoughts, Debbie strode from the bathroom, followed dutifully by her creeping servant, and listened to the voice that announced her husband's impending approach. After softly hanging up the receiver, Debbie waggled a manicured finger at her supplicant and bade him crawl to her position in the center of the aqua and peach bedroom. Obedient to the absolute end, Gold crept silently toward his newest Mistress and wept heartfelt tears of chagrin, of joy, of humility, and of pleading for her to allow him one final relief at her hands.

Touched by his entreaty, she mentally acquiesced and reached out for his leaking member. Straightening up from the command issued by her adamant eyes while remaining penitent on his knees, the Gold's fully erect, throbbing, and bursting penis greeted Debbie's gaze. Smiling, she reached out for his maleness and toyed momentarily with his agony before she pressed the unknown and unknowable series of jewels that allowed his golden netting to slide silently from its home and fall quietly to the peach carpet.

He knelt absolutely naked just under her outstretched hand. Throwing his tanned face fully backward with his neck straining at the effort, he moaned loudly when she touched his passionate penis and again when she encompassed his solid testicles. As she massaged his struggling member, he groaned with a fever he hadn't felt since his graduation night with the Mistress. Readying himself mentally for his final physical release, he shrieked in wild submission to her fondling as the careful woman palpated him to bursting but forced him again and again to retreat from his explosion with practiced strokes and firm insistence so that a chorus of "not yet" somehow permeated his tortured brain.

She allowed him no sympathy and showed him no compassion. Forcing him again and again to the breaking point and insisting he retreat, she brought him repeatedly to the point preceding orgasm before she demanded his backing away from personal culmination. He stood up in his passion and offered himself without reservation to this vixen that stood smiling in her bedroom and extracted from him every ounce of his strength and control. When she was ready, she took him without remorse.

Glancing at the bedside clock, Debbie calculated the minutes until Ron's return and listened for the sound of the limousine's entry into the driveway. Hearing the back door open and footsteps on the stairs, she lingered on the Gold's frighteningly ready penis for her husband's ingress to their bedroom. From the corner of her eye, she witnessed the white shirt and the blue one stride silently into her chamber and she pumped more furiously on the naked Gold's organ as the big man screamed without recognition of his place and his audience. As the green shirt joined the stunned assembly, she knew that Ron would be the next to step through the wide doorway and her performance would be exact and her timing would be perfect.

An absolutely naked and clear-netted man entered as Debbie's manicured fingers worked their magic on Gold's penis and testicles. His head thrown back and the shrieks rising from deep inside his throat, every muscle in Gold's body reacted to his long-awaited final orgasm at the mercy of his recognized superior. She took him right then.

Standing and spurting in his exuberance on the peach carpet in her bedroom, the Gold pumped his hips in fervent tempo to his own rhythm of ultimate explosion and the group of four returnees watched in silent horror for the disobedient Gold mixed with admiration for the woman's obvious expertise and remarkable proficiency. She took on a Gold and won, the Blue noticed as he calculated the big man's re-training program.

The horrified White and the Blue rushed to the spent and shivering man's side and escorted him gently but firmly from the room as the Green trainer hastened to clean up the remnants of the big man's explosion. When the Colors exited the chamber, Ron eyed Debbie from the distance of the doorway and stared open-mouthed at her carefully-clothed body before he fell to his knees in absolute supplication and growing glee at his delirious thoughts of what the rest of their lives would be like.

As she wagged a finger at his kneeling body, she glanced at her breakfast tray and noticed the as yet unread brochures about the facility's other programs for couples that encouraged trained men to be brought by their spouses and lovers for refinement and further training. And, oh yes, Debbie recalled, for her to master some additional and very interesting skills. Maybe for their anniversary, she conjectured, as Ron's creeping body continued its trek to his wife's position in the center of the peach carpet in their bedroom.

Also available from
Daedalus Publishing Company
www.daedaluspublishing.com

Nominated for the 2004 Stonewall Book Award!!!
Painfully Obvious
An Irreverent & Unauthorized Manual for Leather/SM
Robert Davolt's new anthology takes an unorthodox look at leather relationships, community, contests, business, tradition, history and leadership. Inside perspective and practical tips on "What To Wear," "Leather On The Cheap" and "Passing The Bar," are delivered with authoritative research and barbed humor. **$16.95**

10th Anniversary Edition, Lambda Literary-Award Nominated
Leatherfolk
Radical Sex, People, Politics, and Practice
Edited by Mark Thompson, this anthology has become a classic, must read book on human sexuality and identity. The diverse, contributors look at the history of the gay and lesbian underground, how radical sex practice relates to their spirituality, and what S/M means to them personally. **$17.00**

Spirit + Flesh
Fakir Musafar's Photo Book
After 50 years photographing Fakir Musafar's own body and the play of others, here is a deluxe retrospective collection of amazing images you'll find nowhere else... 296 oversize pages, three pounds worth! This book is a "must have" for all serious body modifiers, tattoo and piercing studios. **$49.50**

Urban Aboriginals
A Celebration of Leathersexuality – 20th Anniversary Edition
As relevant today as when it was written 20 years ago, author Geoff Mains takes an intimate view of the gay male leather community. Explore the spiritual, sexual, emotional, cultural and physiological aspects that make this "scene" one of the most prominent yet misunderstood subcultures in our society. **$15.95**

Carried Away
An s/M Romance
In david stein's first novel, steamy Leathersex is only the beginning when a cocky, jaded bottom and a once-burned Master come together for some no-strings bondage and S/M. Once the scene is over, a deeper hunger unexpectedly awakens, and they begin playing for much higher stakes. **$19.95**

Ties That Bind
The SM/Leather/Fetish Erotic Style
Issues, Commentaries and Advice
The early writings of well-known psychotherapist and respected member of the leather community Guy Baldwin have been compiled to create this SM classic. Second edition. **$16.95**

SlaveCraft
Roadmaps for Erotic Servitude Principles, Skills and Tools
Guy Baldwin, author of *Ties That Bind*, joins forces with a grateful slave to produce this gripping and personal account on the subject of consensual slavery. **$15.95**

The Master's Manual
A Handbook of Erotic Dominance
In this book, author Jack Rinella examines various aspects of erotic dominance, including S/M, safety, sex, erotic power, techniques and more. The author speaks in a clear, frank, and nonjudgmental way to anyone with an interest in the erotic Dominant/submissive dynamic. **$15.95**

The Compleat Slave
Creating and Living and Erotic Dominant/submissive Lifestyle
In this highly anticipated follow up to The Master's Manual, author Jack Rinella continues his in-depth exploration of Dominant/submissive relationships. **$15.95**

Learning the Ropes
A Basic Guide to Fun S/M Lovemaking
This book, by S/M expert Race Bannon, guides the reader through the basics of safe and fun S/M. Negative myths are dispelled and replaced with the truth about the kind of S/M erotic play that so many adults enjoy. **$12.95**

My Private Life
Real Experiences of a Dominant Woman
Within these pages, the author, Mistress Nan, allows the reader a brief glimpse into the true private life of an erotically dominant woman. Each scene is vividly detailed and reads like the finest erotica, but knowing that these scenes really occurred as written adds to the sexual excitement they elicit. Second Edition. **$16.95**

Consensual Sadomasochism
How to Talk About It and How to Do It Safely
Authors William A. Henkin, Ph. D. and Sybil Holiday, CCHT combine their extensive professional credentials with deep personal experience in this unique examination of erotic consensual sadomasochism. Second edition. **$17.95**

Chainmale: 3SM
A Unique View of Leather Culture
Author Don Bastian brings his experiences to print with this fast paced account of one man's experience with his own sexuality and eventual involvement in a loving and successful three-way kink relationship. **$13.95**

Leathersex
A Guide for the Curious Outsider and the Serious Player
Written by renowned S/M author Joseph Bean, this book gives guidance to one popular style of erotic play which the author calls 'leathersex'- sexuality that may include S/M, bondage, role playing, sensual physical stimulation and fetish, to name just a few. Second edition. **$16.95**

Leathersex Q&A
Questions About Leathersex and the Leather Lifestyle Answered
In this interesting and informative book, author Joseph Bean answers a wide variety of questions about leathersex sexuality. Each response is written with the sensitivity and insight only someone with a vast amount of experience in this style of sexuality could provide. **$16.95**

Beneath The Skins
The New Spirit and Politics of the Kink Community
This book by Ivo Dominguez, Jr. examines the many issues facing the modern leather/SM/fetish community. This special community is coming of age, and this book helps to pave the way for all who are a part of it. **$14.00**

Leather and Latex Care
How to Keep Your Leather and Latex Looking Great
This concise book by Kelly J. Thibault gives the reader all they need to know to keep their leather and latex items in top shape. While clothing is the focus of this book, tips are also given to those using leather and latex items in their erotic play. This book is a must for anyone investing in leather or latex. **$11.00**

Between The Cracks
The Daedalus Anthology of Kinky Verse
Editor Gavin Dillard has collected the most exotic of the erotic of the poetic pantheon, from the fetishes of Edna St. Vincent Millay to the howling of Ginsberg, lest any further clues be lost *between the cracks*. **$18.95**

The Leather Contest Guide
A Handbook for Promoters, Contestants, Judges and Titleholders
International Mr. Leather and Mr. National Leather Association contest winner Guy Baldwin is the author of this truly complete guide to the leather contest. Second Edition. **$14.95**

Ordering Information

Phone
323.666.2121

Email
 info@DaedalusPublishing.com

Mail
Daedalus Publishing Company,
2140 Hyperion Ave, Los Angeles, CA 90027

Payment
All major credit cards are accepted. Via *email or regular mail*, indicate type of card, card number, expiration date, name of cardholder as shown on card, and billing address of the cardholder. Also include the mailing address where you wish your order to be sent. Orders via regular mail may include payment by money order or check, but may be held until the check clears. Make checks or money orders payable to "Daedalus Publishing Company." *Do not send cash.*

Tax and shipping
California residents, add 8.25% sales tax to the total price of the books you are ordering. *All* orders should include a $4.25 shipping charge for the first book, plus $1.00 for each additional book added to the total of the order.

Over 21 Statement
Since many of our publications deal with sexuality issues, please include a signed statement that you are at least 21 years of age with any order. Also include such a statement with any email order.